Whispered Secrets Whispered Prayers

To my dear friends
Jo and David

Donna Mack

A novel by
Donna Mack

BLUE SKIRT WALTZ, THE (with permission)
Lyrics by MITCHELL PARISH Music by VACLAV BLAHA
© 1944 (Renewed) EMI MILLS, INC.
All Rights Controlled by EMI MILLS, INC. (Publishing) and ALFRED MUSIC (Print).
Acknowledgment is here made to the following literary publications in which some version
of parts of this novel originally appeared:
Alaska Literary Review,
and *Cirque.*
Missing Socks and Honeybees Press, paperback edition May 2013
Whispered Secrets Whispered Prayers
General Fiction, Prairie Fiction, North Dakota, Germans from Russia, Historical Fiction
ISBN:1-4826-8666-X
ISBN-13: 978-1-4826-8666-1

Dedication

To the memory of Barbara Bachmeier Kriedeman Mack and her twin Eva who we never got to know, as well as all the Germans from Russia who settled the great plains and prairies of the United States.

And to my granddaughters, Brooklyn and Madrid - Barbara's new generation of Macks.

Dear Reader

My husband speaks some German and his parents spoke a lot, so I was surprised when I learned his people were from Russia. As it turned out, they were Germans from Russia. As a Midwesterner myself I had never heard of them. Who were these people? I became intrigued.

My original research didn't tell me much, but over the years I learned more. It seems that many of these Germans from Russia (also known as "the other Germans", or "Ruzlanders") came to America stripped of everything but their sheep skin coats with its pockets full of sunflower seeds.

In Russia they clung to outdated German ways as best they could, never considering themselves Russian. In America they were a part of our heritage denied, forgotten, or unknown. *Whispered Secrets, Whispered Prayers* is the story of one such family. Now a bit about the novel.

Urs Wagnor, is a tenant farmer with a fierce love for the land that should be his. Instead, his fields belong to "Humpy" Chris, a calculating landlord deformed in body and soul, who begrudges men like Urs, scratching lives from the poor North Dakota soil.

Urs doesn't own his land any more than he owns the heart of his wife Margaret, who loves the God that sustains her, just as it sustained her German peasant ancestors who settled and struggled on the Russian steppes a century before. Now Margaret is pregnant again—and Urs wants a son.

With the simple words and sentiments these common people become unwittingly ensnared in a web of calamity and ruin. Set on the desolate North American wind-flattened prairie, the poor rocky land is itself a powerful character, as is the vast ever-changing sky, shifting with the narrative from dreamy solitude to churning conflict.. Only six year-old Annie, possesses the innocent powers of insight, imagination and compassion that might save them from themselves.

I am hoping you enjoy this fictionalized tale of one family of these late coming settlers to the American Prairies.   .

Sincerely,
Donna Mack

Stones in a pouch rub each other smooth
.....................anonymous

Prologue

Sofia stood at her window watching the woman and child approach the house. As they crossed the windswept farmyard the edge of the woman's long coat flapped like the dark wing of an injured bird. Beyond woman and child, the icy sleeved stalks of last year's sunflowers jutted from the flat North Dakota prairie. The March day was cold and bright. The sky a piercing blue. How like Mother Russia, the old woman mused wrapping herself in the black shawl. Now Sofia was Hebamme.

The old woman bent to turn the kerosene heater up a little and went to open the door. "Come in, come in." she nodded, as mother and daughter climbed the steps and entered the closed in porch. "You stay out here." she added to the girl. "This business is not for children."

Annie's cheeks grew hot. Stunned, she wilted to the floor, straight-out legs ending in brown high top shoes. The Hebamme opened the curtain to the hidden room off the porch and the two women disappeared inside.

The old Hebamme saw at once that Margaret was pregnant. She struck a match and lit the candles flanking the Virgin while whispering a few *Gelobet seist du Marias*. As she chanted Margaret focused on a mole dancing on the woman's upper lip.

"How are you feeling, Margaret?" she asked, slipping the fine silver chain from the nail where the golden drop of amber hung.

"I get sick with this one," Margaret answered. "I wasn't sick with any of the others. Not since Danny." The scent of candle wax blended with dried herbs assaulted her. The kerosene heater ticked in the cold room.

The Hebamme crossed herself and dangled the amber pendant motionless before Margaret's face. "Look into the stone, Margaret. Don't blink any more than you need to."

Margaret took in air and settled. The pendant glowed in sunlight streaming through the window. The roaring wind clattered canes of a naked rose bush against the side of the porch.

"How old is Danny, now?" the Hebamme asked.

Margaret thought for a moment. "He's almost seventeen, already," she said. "Seventeen in July."

"What else?" the Hebamme asked, taking one of Margaret's hands.

"There are spots of blood every month even now, this late. I lost one already, years ago. Before it was even a baby. I bled with that one too, but I wasn't sick to the stomach like now. Not since Danny." Margaret lowered her eyes.

"Well, let's see what we can find out." The Hebamme scooted closer placing her hands firmly one on each side of Margaret's face. Bare tree branches swept against the roof line.

"Now let your eye go soft, Margaret, but keep it open. Don't look at what you can see." Concentrating intently, the Hebamme leaned forward and began reading Margaret's eye. The astonishing blue iris was rimmed in gold. It pulsed faintly in the changing light, undulating around the black center. The women leaned closer; staring into each other. Sharing each other's breath.

In the Hebamme's eyes, Margaret saw a golden field at harvest undulating in the wind, stretching to the blue, blue sky on the steppe of Russia. The tall grain pulsed in eddies, changing with the light.

Two women worked side by side. The only sounds were the sweeping of their scythes, and the clattering of the stalks as they set the bundles. Overhead, a bird of prey, its wings flapping darkly, soared high in the deep blue.

But now Margaret's eye was turning. Though she willed it straight ahead, Margaret's right eye turned outward to the corner.

The Hebamme readjusted herself, staring deeply into Margaret's other eye. As she entered it she glimpsed a family in a horse-drawn sleigh at night, the mother staring straight ahead. Now images were coming faster, a woman throwing golden grain while chickens swirled, a bear on two legs beating his chest, a young man and a beautiful woman running naked into the sea.

Outside the sunlit room Annie drew her knees to her chest and took the puzzle out from the breast pocket of her bibs. Her older brother, Danny had made it from three twisted sixteen penny nails somehow joined together. How was it Danny had separated them with just a few twists of the wrist? Annie laid out the puzzle in her palm. Where the three twisted nails were joined she imagined three heads locked together. "How can I get away from you two?" One nail asked, as Annie shook it by the one straight leg.

"I don't like this any better than you!" the second nail complained.

" Me neither," said the third. "I need to get away from both of you." Annie tried patiently to separate them, until she jingled the nails in frustration.

Leaning close to the Hebamme, Margaret heard them coming, the jingling of horse's reins, and a terrible thunder from the low hill behind the working women. The men bore down, heads turbaned, faces and eyes dark. The whites of their eyes stood out, starkly. And their teeth.

Margaret shook, clinging to the rails of the chair. She willed herself back to the small room, to the statue of the Virgin, to the wispy smell of candle wax.   Instead, there was the acrid smell of blood.

The Hebamme stared blankly. She had fallen into the wisdom from long ago—when Hebammes performed the *Nah Tauf*, the baptism the church refused to perform on the black-eyed babies born of force and sacrilege, with the bluish spot at the bases of their spines.

Annie shivered. Just a little heat was coming out now from under the curtain. Again she focused her attention on the nail puzzle. "I just have one leg!" Said the first nail. "If one of you would loan me your leg, maybe we could walk away." Annie twisted two nails trying to free them from the other. "Ouch! Our heads are still tangled." Annie said in a squeaky whisper for the third. In a while she gave up and tossed the nails with a jingling thud on the floor beside her shoe. When would her mother come out of the secret room? She tapped her feet impatiently, waiting, anxious.

Margaret clung to the shaking chair-—again the jingling. Horses thundered into the distance.

Two women lie in the golden field at harvest. Their lilac flowered babushkas torn from their heads, their blouses ripped, their skirts splattered with spots of blood. Above, only the startled blue sky.

Now the Hebamme willed herself to stay with Margaret's eye as she backed out of the spell. A bear growled as a hawk took flight. A dragon spitting fire. A man taking a woman on a battered couch. A bunny swirling in a stewpot. She leaned forward looking deeper, not a bunny, a malformed baby girl turning in the womb. At this the Hebamme shuddered, but held her ground. It would be dangerous to lose her concentration now. She began softly chanting the *Gelobet seist du Maria* in a low voice until it was safe to slowly step away from the blue, blue eye. She stood upright and picked a packet of herbs from the wooden box in the corner.

Margaret leaned back, smoothing the soft well-washed cotton of her lilac flowered house dress.

"It will be a girl," the Hebamme whispered. "There might be something wrong with her." Margaret lost her color then, bringing her hands to her belly. The Hebamme handed Margaret the little bag of dried herbs tied with red string. "This is shepherd's purse; drink it in a tea once a day to stop the bleeding. It should help. And let my daughter Katie know right away if you go into labor, even false labor early on. And Margaret, try not to work too hard."

Margaret accepted the small bundle, keenly aware of the texture of the cloth, of the feel of the planked floor under her shoes. The Hebamme laid aside her mother's dark, fringed shawl. She was once again her neighbor's strange mother, Sofia.

Margaret pulled aside the curtain. There was Annie looking up at her with dark questioning eyes.

~1~

The landlord rolled down the driver's side window and shouted instructions: "That twenty acres behind the house there should be alfalfa," Humpy Chris spoke slowly, in a condescending tone annunciating each word as if Urs couldn't understand plain English. "And put another twenty in there by the pond, where that little piece of flax was last year." The hump-backed man was so soft and pale, the flesh above the color of his business suit oozed like vanilla pudding over topping a blue cup.

Urs manhandled the seed out of the trunk. The farmer was thickly built and grizzly with bushy dark hair and eyebrows. The knuckles on his good hand went white with effort as he lifted the awkward fifty-pound bags and caught them underneath with the thumb and single, calloused forefinger on his right. He carried each shapeless weight a few steps and let it drop with a lifeless thud near the base of the elm. Urs scowled at the back of his landlord's balding head. That puny, twisted excuse for a man. And now what was he saying about alfalfa? Any idiot could see that whole portion should be flax! What if it was another dry year? Hell, what did that leech know? That cripple who never farmed an honest day in his life. Urs hauled out another bag.

Humpy Chris produced a fat cigar from his vest pocket and slowly licked the leathery outer leaves, darkening them. He had foreclosed on this farm twice already. Now he intended to keep a close eye to see if Urs could make a go of it. By the time the cigar was lit and Chris had taken a couple good pulls, Urs was done.

The farmer stood under the tree, sweat popping out on his forehead, his thick hairy arms rigid across his chest. A haphazard stack of bags was strewn at his feet. Though one had burst open and seed littered the ground, Urs wasn't about to clean it up with Humpy Chris looking on.

Chris quietly studied his tenant's belligerent stance. "By the way Urs, I can't go on like this forever, you know. If you can't make something out of this place well, a man's got to look out for himself." Humpy Chris had already made up his mind. This year at least he'd be in charge of what was planted. That might increase the odds for some kind of profit. He let out a rattling cough, as he carefully balanced the cigar in the ash tray. Who knows, maybe he'd try to sell, if this farm didn't pan out on a share basis. "And, Urs," he called, "wipe out the trunk with that red rag there, if you don't mind."

When Urs was finished Humpy Chris gave a small wave, rolled up the window, and smoothly pulled the new '46 Pontiac out of the farm yard.

As soon as the car was well out of earshot Urs began. "*Schwienehund!*" How the hell could a man ever get ahead with some *Dummkopf* landlord telling him what to plant, threatening to kick him off the place? That flax would've been insurance." The barrel-chested farmer was shaking with rage. "The worthless cripple!"

Urs headed across the freshly plowed field to where the horses stood patiently waiting. "And I'm the one who's gonna have to pay. Der *Schwindler'll* take out for the seed before I ever see a penny, probably make a profit in the bargain!"

In his blind anger Urs nearly stumbled into the end gate seeder at the back of the wagon. He scooped up a handful of seed. It looked dry. Was there any life in it?

Maybe Humpy'd got it on sale. Maybe he'd got the seed marked down because it wasn't any good, too old maybe. Urs peeled one open. Looked dried up.

What would he do if Humpy kicked him off the place now with another mouth on the way? His face was hot with the shame of being made to wipe out the trunk. Like Urs was a kid or something. He doubled up his fist and banged the seeder. The sound of ringing metal rang out vibrating up his arms and through his bones. The horses startled and jolted. He hated Humpy Chris, with his cigars and his college education and his tricks and papers.

"*Scheiss*!" Urs had dislodged the track where the seed funneled and smashed the delicate feeder mechanism. Now it might take him the rest of the afternoon to get it going again. If he could just hurt that son of a bitch, just once, without hurting himself; if he and Humpy Chris just weren't practically married through this farm. *Scheiss*!" Urs yelled again and walked away.

All the years he'd worked as Dale's hired hand, Urs had never felt such contempt, such worry—a constant turning in his stomach. How had he gotten himself into this?

The North Dakota sky darkened and a wind started up. Urs stood motionless. Hadn't he lived just fine for almost thirty-five years all by himself? By himself he could make it. If he had to sleep in the ditch with the dogs he could make it. Urs walked off mindlessly kicking the dirt.

It was Margaret. And those kids. Four kids. And another one on the way. Why, three of them weren't even his. Somehow she was making him do it. Somehow she and those kids had him out here wasting his time planting crops that wouldn't grow on somebody else's land.

Urs buried his face in the horse's mane breathing in the salty animal warmth. All winter he had carefully planned his fields. Just enough in wheat and barley, just enough flax for insurance. The horses stamped and snorted.

 And these animals. These horses. Hadn't he groomed and fed them all winter, telling them his plans. They were patient and hardworking. Dependable. Together they could do it. Urs found himself stroking their haunches, lovingly smoothing his hand down their sides.

Urs stepped back from the animals and stared at the rough clods at his feet. The broken laces in his work boots were knotted in three dirty clumps. Urs put his hands to his head and rubbed the coarse hair of his scalp, feeling the shape, the heat, while all the time thinking of the smooth glossy feel of Margaret's hair. The baby she carried would be a son. The Hebamme had predicted it. A son who would grow to be strong and dark and healthy, like himself. A good hard working German boy. They would plant together. On their own land. No, his problems weren't really Margaret's fault. She was the one giving him hope.

Urs climbed into the wagon and opened the tool box. On a clean cotton rag he laid out the tools. He worked quickly and in silence. A little baling wire and know-how and that feeder would be working good as new.

If only life were like this machine. If only a man could fix it up and oil it and treat it right and it could be depended upon to work. And if something went wrong, you could see what it was right there in front of you and fix it up; or if it couldn't be fixed you could see that too. If only life was like a machine, doing what it was supposed to do without any complication that couldn't be figured out. Urs made the repair and stood back satisfied.

A movement in the long dry grass near the fence post caught his eye. What would that be now? Urs stood very quiet listening. Yes, there was movement there. A rabbit burst from the undergrowth and bounded away. Looking closer, he saw two gray baby rabbits lay coiled in the weeds. A few feet away a third crawled shakily. Urs had never seen a wild bunny like it before. Pure white. With pink eyes. He wiped his greasy hands on his pant legs and picked up the quivering bunny. Setting the tools aside he unfolded the clean rag, wrapped the rabbit, and placed it deep in the pocket of his denim coat.

Just a few rounds left. Time today to finish up the spring wheat. Urs searched the dark, low, distant hills first plowed, then 'tiled and now planted. It was over two weeks since he and the younger boy, Wayne, did that piece to the north. Urs couldn't see a thing sprouting. Not a hint of green.

But what could he do but keep on plodding along like the horses, like his own father and his father before him? First in Germany then Russia, and now here. Always putting down the seed. Always building something up to hand down. Always having it taken away.

Not this time, Urs vowed. This son would be the third generation to farm the prairie. "Third time's the charm," he whispered. With each round of the tractor he repeated the old saying like a rosary, like a prayer. *Erste Generation: Tod. Zweite Generation: Entbehrung. Dritte Generation: Brot.* First generation, death. Second generation, hardship. Third generation, bread! A muscled wind started up and though it wasn't cold, a chill shot through him. Urs brought the horses and the wagon to a halt as he removed the yellow fuzzy work gloves from his bib pocket. Margaret had adapted the right one to fit his mutilated hand. Carefully he pulled it over the giant finger.

Deep in Urs's coat pocket, the rabbit trembled. Urs peered inside. It had squirmed out of the rag and nested on top. Shockingly white against the dark fabric.

As team and wagon moved across the field the spreader resumed its circular motion, flinging the grain with a steady whirr. The steering wheel remained cold in his hands even through the gloves. In spite of Margaret's adaptation, the solitary finger was hard to keep warm. Urs raised and wagged it now and again in an effort to increase the circulation. From a distance it would have looked as though Urs were greeting a succession of neighbors on the road to Drake. Any one seeing him would have been hard pressed to determine his mood as he greeted each few feet with the giant nodding finger.

The sky was blue and bright, but on the horizon thunder heads were building.

~2~

Humpy Chris drove the blacktop county road towards town. What did people see in this god-forsaken country? Drab and ugly, not a sign of life anywhere. The only movement was the racing clouds and their shadows streaming across barren fields.

Chris wasn't in the habit of seeing beauty in the landscape. He'd trained himself to look for farms in poor repair, fields overgrown with weeds, bank statements that showed unmet mortgage payments, or the county list of back taxes due.

A gust of wind blasted the side of the Pontiac making the car vibrate. Chris tightened his grip, keeping an eye on the trembling cigar balanced in the ash tray. All during the Depression there'd been wind like this. Those had been good times, the times that everything changed, including his luck. He'd picked up first one little farm and then another. The more rundown and desolate a place looked, the easier it was. Chris sank deeper into the plush upholstery. Even the crops had changed. Without rain they were overrun with thistles and wild onions.

What would make a man want a life like that? Chris shook his head, unbelieving. Why even the milk took on the stench of onions. At an ice cream social with Juanita, there had been a new flavor—-onion!

A single tumble weed danced the road in front of the car. Chris's hands tightened more, remembering what he'd heard: some damn fool brought that awful weed with him from Russia. Russian thistle. Now it skipped across the road spewing seed everywhere. They'd even made a song about it. Romanticizing a weed! Chris shook his head. Gene Autry sung it, if he remembered right. Something about tumbling along with the tumbling tumble weed. What nonsense! But wasn't that weed part of the change that brought him luck? His lucky weed maybe? Chris knocked off the bright glowing end of the cigar saving a good portion for another time.

Another thistle danced out of the ditch catching on a fence wire. He recalled clearly how dust had gathered on the thistle stuffed fences so hard a man could walk right over the top. Farmers hacked them out in desperation, wrapping their legs with layers of rags for protection from the barbs. Funny, how things turned out. People that wouldn't talk to him when he was a boy suddenly begged to talk to him then. Every curse he ever suffered boomeranged back to those who'd made them.

Usually Chris didn't let himself think of his early life. Born crippled, in a hardworking farm community, he couldn't measure up to those other boys his age.

Chris turned off the blacktop onto the pavement. He had been his folks' only child and they wanted to do what they could, considering. Would he have it any different?

Living at his spinster aunt's in town he got his education. At home his parents answered the neighbors' questions with smiling masks, nodding that he was doing well, that it was the best place for him--like other folks might talk about a relative in the state insane asylum or a poor relation in the county home. Chris didn't like thinking of that. But it all turned out to his advantage didn't it. Chris had learned how to protect himself from jeering cousins and neighbor kids.

Chris smoothed his hand over the nappy fabric of his blue suit coat. He showed them in the long run didn't he. The only man from Drake who went to the State Agricultural School in Minot. The only man to earn a Bachelor's degree in business and guile to make tenants of them all.

Over the years, Humpy Chris had built up his protective armor. Take this Pontiac, for example. Dumb farmers, 'tiling at the god-forsaken soil. On his behalf. So be it.

But there was a satisfaction that came from something more than the money and the power. It was a satisfaction that rose from getting a man such as Urs: a strong, healthy man with a family and a pregnant wife, to do his bidding. Chris could make him squirm.

Yes, by now Humpy Chris felt quite safe, quite satisfied. By now he was sure they all envied him. But Chris imagined that what they envied him most about was his beautiful wife, Juanita. She was the most cherished scale in his armor. The bejeweled plate that protected his heart.

Just then, a strong gust nearly stripped the wheel from his hands.

*

A few wispy strands of glossy brown hair slipped from the practical braid hanging down Margaret's back. A basket of eggs hung from her arm. The loose gray-green sweater only hinted at her budding pregnancy when the changing wind pressed the cloth to her shifting form. Lagging at Margaret's side was Annie, her youngest.

Even from a distance though it was Margaret's eyes that were her most dominant feature. They were bright blue and calm, challenging anyone who dared to look into them. Those who did saw bottomless wells and felt themselves going down and down, forever falling, never quite reaching the sparkling blue. Most preferred to turn away.

Below Margaret's cotton house dress a pair of brown, men's wingtip shoes, the toes stuffed with paper, stepped quickly. She wore them almost constantly since her third month of pregnancy. They were the only shoes that fit. The shoes originally belonged to her first husband's brother, Phil Borgen.

Nine years have passed since Phil started into town with that load of Easter chicks dyed pink and yellow. They never made it to the Ben Franklin store. Phil had wandered lost in the vast whiteness of a spring blizzard. The temperature dropped fifty degrees in thirty minutes.

They didn't find the horse 'til summer, his harness in tatters, rotting in the gully behind the Fassbinder's place and though the shoes had never been worn, they didn't fit the artificial feet sent from Minneapolis. Now, under Margaret's care, they were still serviceable--the only shoes that fit since her feet had swollen so.

Annie took Margaret's hand as the two climbed the rise to the porch. Puffs of dust rose with their steps. Wingtips Annie thought, trying to match her mother's steps. What a strange name for shoes. Could it be they could make a person fly?

Leaning against the rail of the porch stood Margaret's oldest daughter, Liz. Margaret directed her gaze at the girl.

"Liz, go get about ten good-sized potatoes and a half a dozen carrots and bring up one of those sweet onions to the right of the door." Margaret forced her voice above the bursts of warm wind. "Now don't bring up one of those yellow onions from the back, Liz, you hear me? You know Urs don't like strong onions, even fried."

Liz looked up dreamily. She'd been copying the words of a popular song on the yellow sheets of a lined Big Chief tablet. She let out a sigh, placed a cigar-box toy wagon on top of the tablet, and started for the cellar. Gusts of tepid wind ruffled her sun-streaked hair.

"Annie," Margaret bent, shouting above the wind to the dark-haired girl at her side, "go down to the smoke house and bring up the last of that summer sausage."

At six Annie was big for her age. A hint of sunburn pinked her round cheeks. The girl veered from her mother's side and plunged head first into the wind.

Rounding the corner of the house her entire world opened up. The barn sat heavily with the shed to one side. The row of elms waved fitfully. Their new leaves, turned inside out showing silvery undersides, were rolled to hollow throats awaiting rain. Annie clung to the side of the house.

The fields beyond lay muted in the dull browns and grays of early spring, with splashes of white or bright green in the dead dry grass at the side of the field road and in the ditches. Sudden gusts flattened the brown overgrowth and sent cloud shadows searching over the land like lost ghosts. Among the racing shadows she saw spotted ponies with flashes of brown arms about their necks. And what was that sound? The beating of hooves? No, it was her own heart. Annie shuddered, clinging closer to the house. In the other direction, sat the pond collected melting snow: its thin skin pulsing goose flesh in time with the wind.

As Annie passed the lilac bush, the place cleared at its base reassured her with its clean earth and little, fencepost sticks. Earlier, she'd scraped away the dead grass with a flat board exposing this earth to the sun.

Annie wanted more than anything to farm. To help her father with the spring work. Her hopes had risen when she heard Danny would be gone a month, but nothing came of them.

The closest she had come to farming was to take out a thermos of coffee, and this secret labor at the base of the bush where she copied her father's work in miniature as best she could. Seeing it now, the memory of the earth returned to her hands. This little place lay nearly hidden below the leaves that were just beginning to bud.

Annie studied the bark of the bush's many-forked trunk following it down into the dark earth. Did the root plunge straight down like a carrot, she wondered? Or did they spread wide in a pale, tangled mass? Annie lagged a bit before leaving this protected pocket to reenter the windy world.

From where she stood, the smokehouse seemed far away. Far and dark and cool. She plunged onward with a quicker step. A blast of dirt prickled her face and bare arms. The stubble of last year's field corn made her think of the steel brush she'd used to scrub down the planks after butchering. Her hand reached out as if to touch it. They planned to slaughter again soon. She'd heard her father talking. Annie shivered and turned, continuing down the path. The thought of going in amid the hanging meat frightened her, but it thrilled her too.

Opening the sagging door, a surge of rich, strong spices overtook her. It all came back to Annie then: the animals stripped of their skins, the boiling heads, the gelatinous pink meat and fat gouged from the cheeks. In that one powerful surge she remembered, too, helping her mother mix the grainy spices and the sensation of the hot, smooth meat on her hands that chill October day.

Cradling the sausage, Annie returned solemnly to the house. Wind whipped her short cropped hair into her eyes. The landscape blurred. Wiping the tears and holding back her hair, a flock of blackbirds rose, only to be absorbed by the stretching fields. Overhead the sky was empty. At the earth's rim the low sky was streaked with rain. The wind surged the other way, pulling back her hair, for an instant offering the feeling of flight.

Then she saw it, through half-closed eyes, near the outhouse. The curved spine of a dragon rising above the long dry grass, its dark snout rested on the rotting stump. It was nothing like the glowing stained glass dragon at church, belching orange-red fire, St. George's gleaming sword thrust through its black heart. This one hid in the shadows. This dragon was hard to see and sly. It helped if she didn't look directly at it. During a more gentle gust it moved ever so slightly. The waiting beast appeared most clearly, though as an afterimage with her eyes slightly shut. This impression she nurtured until the wind snatched up a handful of sand and flung it against the sheet metal roof of the shed. Annie hurried on with her sausage.

~3~

Margaret bent over the cook stove placing the cobs. She was pleased there were still live coals from lunch time. Holding her back where it hurt, she blew them to flame.

Next, she brought a chair to the high shelf behind the stove. Opening the covered box she added fresh water to the bowl in the bottom and began turning the eggs laid out on the steel mesh tray. They were slightly tepid to the touch.

Fifty fertile eggs she'd taken during the past week from those hens, along the north wall, who wouldn't roost. It had happened once before—the nests infected with lice. Margaret was able to manage it with dustings of lilac powder, twice a week for a month. This year taking care of the problem was easier. The farm extension man recommended DDT, and it did the trick with one good dousing.

Margaret sprayed again, a week later, just to make sure. The man at Bukenmeier's hardware had told Urs it would keep down insects of any kind. He threw in the handy pump for nothing. Margaret had treated the screen doors, too, to keep down the flies.

One by one Margaret turned the eggs. Each one was like holding the smooth, fragile head of a new born baby. A few new chicks she would use to build up her flock from the winter. (She had lost eight good layers.)

"Ehre sei Gott," she whispered softly turning the last egg. The planting was halfway done. Urs had worked twice as hard with Danny gone, with just a little help from Wayne. Her little garden by the house was almost in. Even the field garden had a good start. With Annie's help, they were nearly finished with the stooping and spading, with the covering of the seed potato's white finger eyes. Yes, things were going well. She was almost afraid to think it. *"Man soll den Morgen nicht vor dem Abend loben,"* don't praise the morning 'til night comes, her mother once said.

Suddenly her stomach clenched with anxiety. Margaret swallowed a chocking in her throat. Why had she lied to Urs about the baby? She would have to tell him sometime.

There had been no premeditation. The lie jumped out as if it were on a spring that she had tired of holding down. And when it did, the words gave her a pleasure, a secret satisfaction. Remembering, Margaret let go of her anxiety. She had a knowledge of her own. Something Urs didn't share and couldn't take from her. A weapon she could hurl when she chose. Her secret. He had backed out of their argument about Danny immediately when she said it: "The Hebamme predicted a boy, Urs, a boy swelling from your seed!"

Holding her back, Margaret stepped down and put away the chair. Annie had pulled out the crate and was making soothing sounds. "You'll love that poor bunny to death." Margaret said "Let him rest now."

Annie's eyes flew to her mother's face; the tender lettuce leaf in her fingers changed that fast into a kind of poison. Was she feeding him too much? Was she holding him wrong?

"Albino, I think they call it when something is born all white that way," Margaret said. "I heard they can't see very good."

"If he can't see good, I'll help him. I'll see for him," Annie said. She almost reached for the bunny where it lay curled tightly in the hay, before she stopped herself. The bunny looked like the Christ child so white and serene in the manger at church on Christmas Sunday. Annie softened her eyes then, remembering Mary looking down at what she'd done. Behind Mary flamed the dragon's breath.

Annie thought then of Urs coming home earlier from the fields. By the time she had arrived breathless at the field gate, the two black and white speckled dogs were already there waiting, squealing in their high animal voices. From where Annie stood, Urs's shape blocked out a portion of the sky.

"I'm gonna fong your vambee." Urs spoke to the dogs, hugging one from behind bringing it onto two legs. He rubbed its belly energetically.

Through he greeted the dogs with these words nearly every day, Annie wasn't sure if they were German or English or some made up language only her father knew. Today, no sooner had Urs "fonged their vombees" than he shooed them away, remembering the bunny.

His cheeks were wet when he retrieved it from his coat pocket and scooped Annie into the protective crook of his arm. The wind had stopped, and a gentle rain just begun.

For a few moments while he led the horses, with the dogs leaping wildly all around, Urs pulled Annie into his lonely center. Annie remembered how his dark eyes crimped at the corners when she'd asked where bunnies went when it rained.

Annie returned the crate to behind the stove. Her father trusted her with the bunny and now was she hurting him?

*

In the machine shed, Urs removed the blanket he kept over the car's hood, and dusted the freshly washed Ford Town Sedan, both inside and out. Urs had bought the car second-hand when he married Margaret, and though by now it was fifteen years old, he kept it in good repair. The car shone black with bright chrome accents. Urs caressed the elegant curve where the fender met the running board.

Much as he loved to drive, it still irked him, the thought of the errand tomorrow to get Danny and then waiting around at the Borgen's house in town 'til time for the dance. And that the letter from Allen telling Urs where to go and when. That irked him too.

"Danny'll be right there at the Feed and Seed around noon," Margaret had said. "I took the letter to Father Weaver after confession and he read it right out, just like plain talking."

Urs had pressed his lips in irritation. You never knew what a woman might run off and do or say, such as running to the priest with their business.

Urs wasn't sure what he thought of Father Weaver. A few years back he started using English in church. A good German church and he was talking English. Even the prayers he said in English. Why, Urs wasn't sure God understood the language. In this house at least, he made sure they prayed in German.

Maybe it was on account of the war. Two wars now. But, like him, the Germans around here came from Russia. Didn't his people leave Germany for Russia a long time ago with the promise they wouldn't have to fight any crazy wars? When they tried to make them they left.

But not talking German in church, that was going too far! Even in Russia they hadn't tried that one!

Urs blinked and saw that he'd been rubbing the same patch of fender for so long that a small scab of rust had broken off exposing the bright steel underneath a like wound picked open. His bad hand throbbed.

Urs seldom noticed his hand at all. It was almost as if the missing fingers had never been there, as if he had never been a baby lying tightly swaddled at the edge of the field during harvest, his father high on the mower while his mother followed with the rake. The machine had gone right over him. The horse miraculously stepped around the brightly colored bundle. The turning wheels passed above where he lay hidden in the tall grain. Only the rhythmically sweeping blade caught the three tiny fingers of his outstretched hand as he lay reaching for the sun.

When Urs's mother heard the scream and saw the bright flapping flesh, she tore off her kerchief and wound it tight. At the end of each day, she'd soaked the tiny mangled hand in salt water until the skin closed over. In North Dakota or in Russia where she'd been born it would have gone the same way: there were no doctors to call.

Urs walked around the car to check the tires and to admire the shining curves. Then he shut the shed door and turned to the house.

As Margaret approached the table with a steaming bowl, Urs looked up, his eyes resting on her belly. His gaze held the same odd blend of pleasure and anxiety it assumed in the mornings, when Margaret in her night clothes, with Urs's jacket across her shoulders, lit the candles and began chanting. Before, Margaret's rituals had always galled him, but now Urs had softened. He sometimes thought of her as a holy vessel.

When Urs first started coming to see her in town, she hid these rituals as best she could. Always, when he entered her house, she feared the faint waxy smell of candles would one day give her away.

He had been seeing her quite some time before he happened to open the door to the little pantry. The room wasn't much more than a closet really, the thin linoleum worn through in patches where her knees pressed as she rocked and chanted; where through half-closed eyes candle flames reflected points of light on the jars of sauerkraut and pickled chicken's feet. The shelves were decorated with bits of ribbon and saints in gilded frames. And there at the center of the widest shelf, taped to the back wall and surrounded by tinsel, was a photograph of her first husband, Lars.

When he saw the room, Urs had been furious and when they married Margaret gave it all up. She gave up the ribbon and the tinsel and of course the photograph. She gave it all up except for this little time in the morning, chanting with the clicks of her rosary.

After the death of Lars, Margaret had remained for the most part cloistered in the little house on Second Street. It had taken two years for her to remove the blankets from the windows, to make over the curtains her sister-in-law Gracie Borgen had brought by and to return to church.

That was when Urs Wagnor began eyeing her. Though the children sat huddled about her on the wooden bench, he hardly noticed them. He was aware almost singly of Margaret, the young widow on relief. And of the muffled yearnings of his own body, and of something else, like a forgotten song.

Margaret in turn gradually became aware of Urs Wagner's interest. She began noticing his bulky strength and patient, hovering attention. One night after bingo, he worked up the courage to make his move.

The winds had been merciless all month. They had nearly cleared the land of snow, driving the fine white dust into the ditches and into the coats of the animals. With a penetrating force, the winds drove the cold dry powder into the very land.

That Sunday night, after bingo, Urs kept his employer, Dale, waiting a few moments in the car before he appeared outside the driver's window.

"You go on without me," Urs shouted into the crack above the rolled down glass, pulling up the collar on his coat, hunching down away from the wind, "I got another way home."

Dale smiled and gave Urs an exaggerated wink. "Don't do anything I wouldn't do!" He had been watching his hired hand's patient attention to the young widow for some time now. He saw each Sunday as Urs's eyes intently followed Margaret to the communion rail. He saw the pleasure on Urs's face as the widow tipped her head and closed her eyes taking into her pretty mouth the holy flesh. Sometimes when Dale's wife was in the kitchen out of ear shot, Dale would begin. "I hear those Eigler girls are a lusty bunch." Or in the barn before the hanging teats, "They say once a woman has had the taste, she can't turn it down." Dale extracted from the cluster of emotions Urs felt, the driving one, the one long buried that made him toss and burn at night.

Urs had been Dale Swanson's hired hand for more than fifteen years by that time, and though they labored side by side, Dale never let Urs forget his inferior position. Hoping to be noticed, hoping to be appreciated, Urs always did more than was necessary. As Dale's sons moved forward through the Christmases and Easters they grew until they established their own farms and businesses, while Urs remained. That Sunday night after bingo if Dale had known it might cost him Urs, he most likely wouldn't have given his permission.

Instead, Dale had rolled down the car window a bit more and shouted hastily over the howling wind. "Tomorrow we got to bring in the last of the hay if those cows are going to make it, so don't be too long." Then he withdrew a flask from his inside coat pocket. "Here have some of this, keep you warm."

After a few quick gulps, Dale was off, driving down the only paved street in Drake, the wind twisting and distorting the puffs of white that rose from the exhaust in the near darkness. Urs shivered standing alone in the empty street.

When he got back to Margaret, she was covering the two smaller children with heavy blankets. They lay sleeping, wrapped and bundled between the side boards of the small sled. The oldest boy, Danny, stood beside his mother with a glazed look. He had sprung from sleep in that way children sometimes do without fully gaining consciousness. In a moment she had him seated in the back of the sled, sleeping once again.

"Let me pull the sled for you." Urs said it awkwardly, gruffly, fortified by the blend of liquor and desire coursing through his blood. At the rough command, Margaret automatically stepped aside.

The sled floated easily over the ice-glazed grass of the churchyard. Both Urs, a bit ahead, and Margaret behind, hunched into the wind wrapping their scarves up around their noses as protection from the stinging snow.

"I was going three ways in that last game," Urs turned slightly as he spoke. "I almost had the pot three different ways." Suddenly, the sled became heavy as the metal runners strained against the pavement. A spark flashed.

Danny sat bolt upright in the sled. Where was he? Why was it so cold? Who was that strange man? Oh yes, he remembered him now. He had seen him before.

They continued down the side of the road in silence. It was lucky for Urs that he walked ahead, that his scarf hid most of his face. For with each few steps his mood swung and his expression with it. Sometimes he grinned so much that his eyes teared and his cheeks rose so, he could hardly see. His mind held no thoughts at all. Instead, there was a kind of joyful exaltation, just barely contained.

In a moment though, his face would fall as the energy drained away, as doubt replaced exhilaration. His only awareness became the straining need that throbbed inside him. It was all that kept him going, that and the thought that had crept into his mind. "She's lonely," he muttered, forcing one foot before the other. "She's lonely," he said just below hearing, over and over with each step. "She's lonely and she wants a man. She'll want me." He clung to that thought for the courage to go on.

Margaret, for her part was merely grateful to be relieved of the sled and for the quiet place in Urs's wake, somewhat protected from the wind.

When they reached the small house, Urs opened the door for her, as one by one, Margaret carried the sleeping children into the house. When it came Danny's turn she stood him on his feet. Urs followed as she led the boy, limp and stumbling, to the clean bed the children shared. Danny's eyes were open. He lay looking out with calm from the small bedroom off the kitchen while Urs stoked the fire for the night.

An electric light burned overhead. "Thanks for helping me with the children and the fire," Margaret said. Her red, woolen scarf hung loose around the collar of her coat. She still wore her mittens and boots. "Maybe I'll see you at bingo again some time." She guided Urs toward the door where she smiled and said goodbye.

Urs turned and put his arms about her clumsily. He pressed his face next to hers whispering hoarsely. "Aren't you even going to ask me in to sit for a while?"

Moving his body like a heavy, slowly closing iron gate, he forced her into the little living room. Urs took an aggressive lead in the quiet dance. "Now let's not wake the children." He swallowed and smiled, though tears were running down his face.

There on the sagging couch he had his way, both of them still in their coats and boots. Afterward, when he stole back out through the kitchen, he noticed through the open doorway to the little bedroom, Danny staring calmly.

Then Urs found himself standing outside the warming house, in the bitter, blowing wind.

By the time he'd walked the three miles back to Dale's farm and entered the little room off the kitchen, his face and lower legs were numb. Where the buckle boots rubbed his shins were bright, red rings of flesh, chapped raw.

But in spite of the cold and the chapped legs hadn't everything gone well? Hadn't everything gone just as he had hoped? He answered yes, both times but when he pulled down the covers and climbed into bed there swelled in his chest such sadness.

~4~

"Shall we say grace?" The family responded to Margaret's question as if it were a command. She made a wide slow, exaggerated sign of the cross, kissing her fingertips before touching her forehead, and bowing her head. From the others, there was only the quick flicker of hands. Then, Wayne, whose thin arms stuck out of last year's cowboy shirt, bowed his head. And Liz, who was coming with the coffee, supported the wobbling pot at the lip and bowed her head. Annie let her swinging feet hang still and bowed her head. Even Urs, who didn't like taking directions, let his large rough palms press together and lacing the single finger among the others, bowed his head.

Margaret spoke softly and rhythmically those simple German words with the rest mumbling along. As her lips formed the sounds she experienced the lifting up of something inside of her. It was as if something had been wadded and wrinkled all during the day and as she prayed it was being lifted and smoothed like the clean white cloth at a wedding banquet.

When Margaret finished, she watched Urs lift his empty cup to Liz like a begging child.

"Get that letter from the chest, Wayne, the one from the Borgens." His voice was unnaturally soft, with the pleasure of the hot liquid at the back of his throat.

Wayne rose slowly, thumbs in his pant loops, and started off in his practiced cowboy swagger.

"Get, getta move on."

Margaret knotted her hands just above the subtle mound of her belly as if they might protect it from Urs's irritation. There they fluttered like sisters, fussing over an infant's cradle.

Urs read slowly and silently, his lips stumbling across many of the words they met. The page trembled in his grasp. What little skill he had brought both pride and shame. Hadn't he been taught that only a cheat needed to know how to read? Der Schwindler, who couldn't just say out loud what they meant but had to sneak in other stuff that wasn't really part of the bargain or change the words later so they didn't mean anything anyway? Just as in Russia, here only the sick or the crippled went to school. Those that couldn't work. Someone like Humpy Chris.

"You're sure August's boy is coming now?" Urs put the letter aside, wanting to go over it all again.

"Yes, he's comin.' Wayne talked to him about it on the way home from school." These straw men were an agony for Margaret. It was as if Urs were looking for a reason not to take the trip to Minot. But they had to go get Danny. All the arrangements had been made.

"Did you tell him to be sure and milk 'em dry? I mean all the way dry? You know that white face will get infected just as sure as anything if he don't milk her all the way dry." Urs addressed Wayne.

"Yeah, I told him all that. He'll be over right at milkin' time." Wayne had recently taken to looking past Urs when they spoke, and letting one shoulder hang in such a way as if what Urs had to say wasn't important.

"You look at me, young man, when I'm talking to you, you hear me?"

Wayne's chest fell beneath the faded cowboy shirt. His face grew pink, the thickets of pimples, even pinker.

"And leave him a note about tending the bunny, too," Urs said.

Margaret held her breath. Urs seemed to need to do it. He didn't like the Borgens, she knew that of course. They were Norwegians, Margaret's first husband's people. "Wegers," Urs called them, and "Stidtler," to boot.

"Those Wegers"! he'd rant. "Didn't they all come to this country with bags of money? When times were bad, didn't they all move into government jobs, administering all the New Deal projects?" Whatever administering meant, except worming their way into things because they could read and because they could speak good English. All the honest work in the world didn't do a man any good then.

Urs had shaken Margaret hard that time he came back from the bank when they said they couldn't make the loan. He wasn't one of "those people," he'd said, those "Wegers" with their pens and notebooks and figures. He supposed her first husband, Lars, could have got it couldn't he? After all, wasn't he one of "those people?" Not even Catholic. No wonder he did what he did.

And there was the time Urs started in about Phil Borgen. When the county gave him that little job at the courthouse because Phil had lost his feet and hadn't been able to work.

Winter had come early that year. Urs had to dig out the barn and the lane was drifted higher than the horses' shoulders. He worked three days just to get it opened up so he could get those few eggs and that little cream to town. When he got home hours after dark, he burst in with the cold, whiskey on his breath and a half-finished flask in his coat pocket.

"Now that cripple's got it made," he announced. "I heard he's got a sit-down job at the courthouse! A pencil pusher! Can you imagine that! Getting paid good money for making chicken scratching on a paper! Next, he'll be owning half the county like that cripple Humpy Chris!"

Margaret had planted her feet and glared at him with the full power of her blue, blue eyes. But like now, she clamped her lips in a tight line, swallowing the hurt. If she could just keep Urs calm. If she could just keep him calm and going along without getting all wound up. Margaret went over it all again. Phil and Gracie Borgen were expecting them. They were welcome to spend the night if they wanted. Hadn't Phil wrote the letter himself? See here where he even added their phone number in neat little scratches at the bottom. Margaret pointed at the numbers, saw them start to swim. Her eye had turned nearly to the corner again.

Annie watched her mother's eye drift. Something about how her shoulders raised and slid back just then, made her mother's chest look like a shield. In the splintered light of sunset coming through the window, her mother shone bright. Annie thought of St. George. And the dragon. Wouldn't a person need a shield if they had to fight a dragon? Or shoes with wings? Was the beast still there in that special place? Would it be dazzling now from the recent rain, its dusty spines washed to life? She wanted to leave the table and run to it. She wanted to learn the dragon's powers and share them with her father. But why would her mother have a shield?

After supper Annie slipped outside and went to the special place. But the dragon was gone. There was only the stump and the dead curving spine of the fallen tree. To the side of the rotting stump a few sprouts shot up from the living root. Then, in a flash, greenish-white root fingers reached out, snaking below the ground, a zig zagging, living net reaching out.

*

Danny wiped away the steamy fog on the medicine cabinet mirror at Allen's brother's house in Minot. His looks surprised him. Danny's arms and shoulders had filled out, a dark shadow traced his jaw line. He had changed a lot in one month.

That first week Danny tripped and stumbled under Allen's watchful eye. It was all so new and they expected him to know.

"How did he think it was done?" the regular hand, Günter questioned, opening the medicine box and withdrawing the device with a smirk. "The same bull servicing so many cows all coming due in the same month?" But Danny had never heard of artificial insemination before, and the rubber vagina both startled and confused him.

"Maybe you thought great storks swooped down in the middle of the night, the new calves in their beaks all wrapped in blankets," Günter had joked.

Danny put a little water in his mug and watched the soap mound as he stirred it with his brush. Yes, he'd been quite the greenhorn that first week or so.

But how was he to know. The few times Danny'd seen a cow calve before, both he and Urs had merely stood by watching, or more often than not simply found the calf the next morning curled beside its mother in the corner of the barn.

Danny applied the soap in a circular motion to his blond whiskers. He gazed into the mirror as he raised the razor to his sideburns. It hadn't been easy those first weeks.

Was he man enough, Allen and the others seemed to be asking? The unspoken question hung in the air, implied with every word and gesture. Danny's confidence had plummeted.

Danny began smoothly shaving the side of his face. Rinsing the blade, he went on remembering. The jeering men and his own ignorance weren't the worst of it. Evenings, after supper he would go alone upstairs to the starkly furnished room and single cot.

He grew homesick, at the same time knowing he had to somehow stick it out. From below would come the sound of the others laughing and talking. The radio would be tuned to Amos and Andy, or the Grand ol' Opry.

Quitting wasn't an option. His mother needed him to do his part, the family needed the money. The sounds of the laughing men that filtered upstairs only increased Danny's loneliness. His mind raced with dark thoughts.

As much good as he was at calving he might just as well have stayed home. He summoned up a picture of that other life: the comfort of a familiar routine. What would Urs be doing he wondered? Maybe just starting the planting, if the ground was thawed enough.

Danny would wrestle the single blanket, twisting fretfully. He convinced himself he wasn't really needed at home either. Urs could handle that little land himself if he really wanted to and even Annie could start taking over some of the chores. He used as proof the fact that he was right here at planting time.

Danny rinsed his face and patted it with Old Spice. He shivered with the cooling sting. Sometimes, when the moon had gathered clouds at the curtain's edge, meaningless incidents had reeled before him. "You're the man of the house now." The last words his father had spoken to him rang in his ears. "My little man, my little man." How many times had his mother said it. But even those incidents he had counted as successes, had deflated under his critical eye.

When the house grew quiet and the others were asleep, his thoughts would only become darker. Hadn't his own real father been basically worth nothing too, when all was said and done? Pacing the room, Danny's spirits fell with his steps. Wasn't there some great flaw that ran through them both? Briefly the rosary in the box under his bed had beckoned, but it offered no consolation.

Though Danny had longed to be somewhere else, he could not conjure up a single picture of where that might be. Instead, the lonely room seemed separated from all the world, encased in a bubble rising into the cool night sky, turning endlessly with the moon.

Danny patted his face with the towel and rinsed out the sink. He shook these dark memories away. Once again he admired his reflection in the mirror, flexing his muscles. Those uncertain times were surely gone now. Just the thought of her had saved him.

By the second week at Allen's, she began coming to him in his sleep. At first just her face, and then her full lips, her dark beauty. Those dreams gave him courage.

As the days passed Danny held the memory of her in his mind. His skill with the calving increased and his confidence returned. The violent births and sexual force that filled the barns by day gave way to tender dreams at night. Without those dreams he never would have made it.

Danny dressed quickly and left the bathroom. He would be seeing her in just a couple of days. Sunday maybe. Would she realize how much he'd changed? That he had become a man?

~5~

Standing before the car swelling his chest and arching his back, Urs waited until all eyes were on him. He inserted the iron crank into the fitting and cranked. Then, he ran back and forth adjusting the choke and directing Margaret to reach over with her black dress pumps to depress the throttle. "Push it right away when you hear it catch, you hear. No! No! Now try it again. That's it! That's it!" Urs's eyes sparked with the plugs and when the engine finally caught, a steady good humor surged through him. This morning the weather was clear, the car was shining. Now, Urs looked forward to the trip to Minot, to getting Danny, seeing the Borgens and to the dance at the hall. The Six Fat Dutchmen were playing according to the poster at Bukenmeier's store in Drake.

Urs drove down the back roads painstakingly slow, "so as not to bump anything the wrong way," as he put it. For Margaret this was torture. She had thought of the car as speedier transportation. Every pothole they eased through at a snail's pace, every soft spot they cautiously avoided, ground away at Margaret's patience. All she could think was that Danny was already there. Maybe waiting out in front of the Minot Feed and Seed right now.

Looking out the car window, not really seeing the monotonous landscape, Margaret brushed a bit of lint off her coat, before letting her shoulders sag. She'd had such high hopes for Danny's education. But what now, with him missing so much school….Margaret tensed with anger. Urs had rented out her son without even consulting her! A deal struck in a bar! Going over it now, all Margaret could think was how unfair it was. Danny had always been so smart. So like his real father.

Turning onto the blacktop, Urs handled the car easily. He understood the lay of the land and the gusting wind. Margaret appreciated the speed and skill. As the wheels hummed, the sun rose higher in the sky.

Margaret opened the buttons of her coat and smoothed the fabric of her dress over her belly. She thought of the baby growing there, her secret child. She was glad not having to worry about Urs bothering her in that way now. After about the third month, when Margaret was really sure beyond a doubt that she was pregnant, she and Urs had come together less and less. They both had been taught this was best for the unborn child, though Margaret knew this wasn't true.

Feeling safe, there were times when she woke in the dim light and felt a certain tenderness for Urs. As his chest rose and fell with slow breathing, there would be an innocence about the curve of his shoulder. She saw him as a young boy, unhurt. Urs seemed lighter then, some of the heaviness gone. Nights like that, she would lie in the quiet moonlit room and recall how his eyes sparkled that time he told about the tricks he'd taught a dog at one of the farms where he'd worked as a boy.

In their darkened bedroom, Margaret sifted through their shared life, stringing together the occasional smiles, remembering the times he had shown real concern for the children. Even his hard working drudgery, she imagined, might be evidence of some deep inexpressible love. Those times Margaret suffered under the weight of her secret. As if the secret was pressing down, making it hard to breathe. Should she wake him and somehow find words to tell him?

Once, Margaret tried. Wanting to wake him gently, she reached across to cover his shoulder, tucking him in tenderly, as she might a child. When he didn't stir, she wrapped her arms about him, folding herself into the contour of his form. But before she knew what happened he was on her. Easily sparked to passion, before she had a chance to look into his face. Before she had a chance to speak.

Afterwards, there was shame and anger. "What's the matter with you, woman?" he'd said. "Why do you want to start something like that, in your condition?" Margaret closed to him then, holding tightly to her secret. She was glad she had it to herself, this wicked power.

Margaret glanced over at Urs, crudely bent before the steering wheel. How bulky and out of place he looked, driving an automobile and dressed in town clothes. So unlike her first husband Lars. Margaret focused on her swollen feet. She couldn't remember that they had ever swelled like this so early. Her knuckles and wrists were swollen, too. Flesh bulged around her wedding band. Any more swelling and she'd have to take it off. Could she get it off even now?

Wayne, Annie and Liz were crowded together in the back seat, with cream cans between their legs and dozens of eggs stacked behind. Annie sat in the middle. Feeling small and squished she lifted herself higher and knelt, settling on her heels. Now, she could see outside to the passing low, narrow hills that strained upward from the floor of the flat plain. Their rocky spines showed bone-white against the faintly green skin of the earth.

Urs turned onto the state road, fitting the Ford Sedan neatly between the high concrete shoulder and the painted line. He was considering the eggs. They would bring more at the Feed and Seed in Minot than they ever got at Drake. The difference might pay for the gasoline.

Suddenly he leaned forward, squinting. Up ahead was something new. Something standing straight up in a perfect row, electric poles! Urs marveled. The REA'd come through here already! Urs studied the farmhouses as he passed. They all had yard lights and even wires running out to the barn. He'd heard they had plans to get electric up his way in a year or two. If only there was some way he could buy the place.

There would be the money Danny'd give him. Half of fifty, they'd agreed. It had been easy to hire out Danny. And next year Wayne would be old enough too. How much money would it take he wondered to make a down payment? If he showed he could build the place up, surely that would help. Maybe this year, he thought, suddenly optimistic. If the alfalfa got a good price and the wheat came in heavy, maybe he'd be able to build up a nest egg, make Humpy Chris an offer. Hadn't he already slowly, and steadily, begun to build the place up? Maybe not by making much money but how could he control the price of wheat? Hadn't he and the boys drained some of those mud holes and put in the pond? Hadn't they cleared out a good garden spot for Margaret and sunk the clothesline posts?

Urs removed his flat cap and tossed it on the dashboard. He ran the fingers of his good hand through his thick, curly hair and shook out his shoulders like an optimistic fighter getting ready to step into the ring

Why, every field had been spread with manure.   With hard work couldn't just about anything be made sweet and productive? With the sun lighting his face through the windshield, Urs smiled remembering the old saying: *Beten hilft nichts, was wir brauchen ist Mist Praying* is of no use, what we need is manure!

"*Gott im Himmel*," Urs whispered, "help me make it happen." He squeezed shut his eyes, the closest he ever came to praying.

Seeing him smiling so with tears running down his cheeks, suddenly Margaret let go of her hard feelings. She saw her husband not with hope or anger, but just as he was. Just a hardworking farmer dressed in town clothes on his way to Minot to get the boy he'd taken in as a son. And as far as Danny went was it really Urs who was holding him back? Margaret's face went hot with shame. As far as Danny's chances for graduating the eighth grade, wasn't Urs the innocent? Wasn't it she herself who for three years hadn't even thought to send him to school?

As the car approached a drooping wire, a row of blackbirds dipped and swooped in a crazy contest with the approaching vehicle. Urs slowed and his dark eyes followed them until the specks disappeared against the distant fields. The land was wonderful here. All along the bottom the faint fuzz of green softened the landscape between the brown borders of last year's wheat stubble.

Now if they just got a little rain out his way. Things could look just as well there in no time.

Annie tucked one leg under, trying to get comfortable. Looking straight ahead, between her parents, she could see the passing fields and the road going on ahead. When they passed a row of poplars, there was a slight change in the light and Annie saw that the windshield also held the reflection of what they'd passed. Annie concentrated on one scene and then the other--what was coming up and what was gone. She purposefully tried to mix the images, holding them together, superimposing one on the other, trying to make some sense of them. But the scenes moved and changed so quickly she could not maintain her bearings. Annie had the dizzying sensation of going forward and backwards at the same time. When she raised herself a bit there added to the confusion a bug splattered image of herself, in some dimension not quite here. Not quite now.

*

Danny paced the wide painted porch of the Minot Feed and Seed, watching for the car. To the side of the steps his boss, Günter and three other hands were having cold ones in the shade. "Come on down and get yourself a beer," Allen Schmidt hollered up at him.

"What would my mother say, if she came to get me with beer on my breath! It isn't even noon!" Danny laughed, smiling at the drinking men.

"Yes it is! Allen hollered back holding up his watch. "Five after!" Laughter rose from below the porch where the men were drinking.

Then he saw them. As the family got out of the car Danny swooped down the steps towards his mother's open arms. Her coat flew open and the subtle changes in her shape startled Danny. A kind of resentment and the undefined thought that she was wearing out tightened his jaw.

"Danny, my little man all grown up!" He gave himself to her gathering arms, his heart singing, as he had accepted this one more intrusion.

Could that really be her brother Annie wondered? Danny seemed different somehow. There was a dark shadow running along his jaw line and a crease between his eyes. Then he smiled. It was him all right. Better than ever. Annie rushed on ahead.

He had a flat cap with a bill, like her father's, only cocked more to one side, and a pair of new blue half pants made out of some kind of silky material. The gleaming white shirt showing through the V in his sweater. Why what had she been thinking? He was fine. He looked great. Like someone out of a mail order catalog.

"Well who's this here, if it isn't Annie the nanny goat." He lifted her high, his sweet, clean breath on her cheek. "What you doing wearing a dress?" he asked, twirling her as her feet climbed the sky.

Urs was cautious about leaving the car, checking that all the doors were locked and sizing up the situation. Allen Schmidt, his hired hand and four others Urs didn't recognize were leaning on the high porch at the near end, using it as a kind of stand up bar. They threw empty Pabst bottles into the bushes.

A strange way for grown men to dress, he thought, especially coming to town. Their get-ups were almost identical, with wide brimmed hats and boots like those displayed in the window of Paulk's shoe store. They were German, Urs mused, but somehow odd too. Maybe it was that they were Lutherans... as well as being from clear up by Anton. These thoughts coupled briefly with Margaret's worrying complaints about Danny's welfare. Perhaps it hadn't been all foolishness.

Urs stepped forward extending his mutilated hand to Allen Schmidt. He enjoyed the bit of flustered hesitancy he could evoke from grown men in offering it. When Allen regained his composure Urs learned they were going into breeding bulls. Dirt farming just wasn't worth it in this forsaken country, not with the money they'd pay for champion bulls out in Montana. Urs shifted his feet uncomfortably. Who did Allen think he was drinking beer in the middle of the day, having life so easy? When Urs saw Margaret fussing with the picnic things on the hood of the car, he took the excuse to check if she was scratching the paint. Then he noticed the flat.

How could it be? The tire showed very little wear and hadn't he put the car on blocks all winter just so this wouldn't happen? Anger built like thunderheads. This whole trip into town was probably going to cost way more than he'd get out of it. Urs threw open the trunk with such furious force the Ford shuddered. He saw right away the jack was missing.

With contained fury, Urs lifted out the crates of eggs, the cream, the spare tire. He was aware of Allen Schmidt and his boys watching, lounging and drinking behind him. If it had been Wayne he could have spent his anger and had it over with, but not trusting the job to him, Urs had checked and rechecked the spare himself. It was he himself too, who had laid the jack at the edge of the drive while he'd rearranged the load. Urs pulled his thick shoulders up as another empty bottle clinked in the bushes and laughter rose from somewhere beyond the steps to the porch.

"Danny, you get those nuts off that flat and I mean right now!" Urs spit the words in a bolting whisper. Danny set to work at once, not asking about the jack or why he was handed the crescent from the tool box instead of the tire wrench. It wasn't until Urs backed up to the rear bumper and muttered his instructions that Danny saw what was intended.

Urs had turned his face from the drinking men. He burned red with their insolent presence, too proud to ask for a jack. Urs worked with such speed and restraint that even his angry voice was controlled in such a way as to avoid attention. The men in fact might not have noticed at all if it weren't for the explosion of sound that released from Urs's mouth as he compressed his determination, anger, and strength into lifting the car.

In the instant he held it, Danny worked furiously to interchange the tires. Urs had caught the attention of the loafing men as they gazed on disbelieving. As he lowered the car, the spare intact, a murmur of genuine appreciation rose all around.

"My God, what do they feed you boys south of town, bear meat and thistles?" Allen's voice rose above the others. For a moment Urs hung onto his sour mood, but gradually he recognized the appreciation being thrown from all sides. His eyes lighted like a wick set aflame.

Easily he was coaxed into a beer as the men slapped his shoulders and squeezed the corded muscles of his back and arms.

"No wonder that boy of yours is such a good hand," Allen said. "I could use a hand like him anytime. You got any more where that one came from?"

"I got another one just like him, and even the girl there'd put a lot of men to shame," Urs boasted, "but the one in the oven there, is going to be the dinger of them all."

Margaret flushed red. Should she tell him the truth right now?

"No need to be embarrassed, Margaret." He gave her arm a little squeeze misinterpreting her crimson face.

"What about me?" Annie stepped forward standing as tall as she could. "I'm a good hand."

Everyone broke into laughter. Urs smiled, ruffling Annie's hair.   By the time the discussions were over Urs had promised the two boys to work as hands and Liz to help with the cooking. Annie was assured they needed her to stay home and help with the farm.

When some of the men went into the Seed and Feed for cigarettes, Urs found that he had stumbled along behind them. Once inside, he stood awkwardly before a rotating wire stand of flower packets. He turned the rack self-consciously.

Urs had seldom seen such a glorious display of brilliant color in one place before. Flower seeds. He removed a packet and stood absently feeling the hard little lumps through the paper.

Zallias. Weren't Zallias the kind Margaret had been so crazy about when they first put in the garden plot? She'd wanted a border of them inside the row of rocks.

"Can I help you with a packet of flower seeds, sir?" The boy who helped out on Saturdays startled Urs with his question.

"No. No. What would I want with flowers?" Urs stuffed the packet back in the rack, glared at the boy and went out mumbling about who would spend good money for decorations and adding that a man couldn't live eating flowers.

Outside some of the men smiled and slapped him good-naturedly again making comments about his strength. Wasn't it a beautiful day after all, the sky clear and the temperature just right? And the spare tire looking good as new on the elegant town car.

Annie proudly escorted her dad to the lunch laid out on the pink bedspread. As the family passed around the sandwiches and potato salad, their talk bounced between the flat white side of the

Feed and Seed, and the towering grain elevator that nearly scraped the blue, blue sky. Only Urs sat reflectively quiet, hardly knowing what he ate, with the fullness of the moment caught in his throat, like a half-starved baby on a full breast.

~6~

When they got to the Borgens, the family came out to greet them. Philip waddled ahead of the others in that distinctive way he had acquired along with his artificial feet. "Yah, they stood there with their eyes rolling;" Urs said, recounting his feat of strength. "Wanted to know what I ate.

"You got that medal?" Big Gracie pointed with her chin at her son Hank.

"It's right here in my pocket. I said I'd give it to him didn't I?"

"Well, tell 'em what happened, Hank," Big Grace ordered, but then didn't wait for Hank to respond. "You know last fall when Hank was sick at fair time and Wayne did the Bronco Ride for him? Well, by the time the fair was over, Wayne still had the best time. Those 4-H guys doing the judging never even knew it wasn't Hank.

Hank brought out the shiny medal and dangled it for all of them to see. "First Place" was engraved near the top. Nearer the center was printed "Youth Bronco Busting" and under that "Hank Borgen." As he dangled the medal, just a bit of white fur showed between his fingers. "What's that other thing there?" Annie asked.

"This?" Wayne opened his palm and lowered it for her to see. "It's a rabbit's foot. For good luck." Annie was horrified. Was it real? Had someone really cut off a rabbit's foot? How could something like that be good luck? But he did win the first place medal.

In the living room big Gracie passed around pictures of little Gracie's confirmation at the Lutheran Church. Liz looked at the pictures for a long time before passing the yellow envelope to Annie.

Little Gracie had on a white dress with puffy sleeves and a white rose pinned on one side. There was another photo with all the girls that were confirmed together. They all wore the same thing. There was a photo of the boys. And one of the boys and girls together. Annie shook the yellow envelope to see if there were any more. A row of negatives slipped out. Holding the flexible dark strip to the window Annie saw that the pictures were all backwards and inside out. Did that have something to do with being Lutheran?

In a while Little Gracie and Liz retreated to Little Gracie's bedroom. They closed the door after themselves. Annie knew what that meant. Outside, she stood very still listening. She heard Lizzie ask, "You like to do der Schottische?"

"Lizzie, let's not do the schottische tonight." Little Gracie answered. "We should do the jitter bug or swing dance. It's so swell, Lizzie. We can practice if you don't know how." There was a quiet space and then Annie heard. "And try not to say dis and dat and da all the time, if you know what I mean. I don't want people thinking you're not American."

Another long silence. "I'm not really German." Lizzie said, lowering her voice. "Or only half German at most."

Annie held her breath, shocked.

"American really." Lizzie went on. "I'm a Brogen too, just like you."

Annie wandered away, thinking. What did Lizzie mean not German? How could her own sister not be German? Suddenly Annie had to pee.

In the bathroom, Annie flicked on the electric light. She flicked it off again. The shine and sweep of pipes and gleaming fixtures made her forget her purpose. She turned the faucet marked with a C. Under her hand water gushed out with tremendous force and then trickled all the way to a dribble. The dribble reminded her, she had to pee. She'd just let go when her cousin, little Gracie, burst in. "Why don't you lock the door?" she asked in what Annie thought was a snippy voice. "I didn't even know you were in there." When she left, seeing the bolt, Annie got off the pot and locked the door. Now her investigations began in earnest.

She redirected her attention to the mirror over the sink. Closer inspection revealed a latch on its side and that the mirror was a secret door. Using the toilet as a step, she climbed up into the sink. Behind the mirror was a secret compartment with three shelves. The top held a razor, a mug of soap with a brush, some amber liquid and a tablespoon. On the middle shelf were a lipstick and a small bottle of perfume. In a heap at the bottom was a pile of toothbrushes and some store bought toothpaste in a tube. Annie squeezed a little onto her finger. It was sweet. Much nicer than the baking soda she used. The lipstick was blood red. Annie unscrewed the lid to the perfume and dabbed a little behind each ear. The spoon from the top shelf was sticky with something sweet. The handle was worked silver with a cluster of grapes at the end. It had a smooth, heavy sensation in her hand. Why were these secret things hidden here? When she looked into the spoon she saw herself upside down.

"Are you still in there?" It was Little Gracie outside the door again. Annie panicked, flustered. "Hurry up, will you?" Annie thrust the spoon into her dress pocket and shut the secret door. When she flushed the toilet, it sucked down the slightly yellowed water and the dab of tissue with surprising noise and force.

Back in the living room the overhead light was blazing. Except for the smell of beef roasting in the oven, a person would have no way of knowing it was nearly supper time. Big Gracie was tugging Wayne by the shoulders, and holding worn overalls and half pants and patched shirts before him. "I guess I held 'em too long. If only I hadn't forgot to bring them to the wedding."

Wayne hung back embarrassed as Big Gracie pulled him to the center threading his arms into shirts that were too small.

"Hank's not much bigger than Wayne right now," Margaret asserted eyeing the two boys.

"Come here now, Hank. You stand back to back there against Wayne." Big Gracie dragged them both to the center of the room.

"Why a half an inch, I think that's all there is between 'em, if that. That boy of yours has sure shot up. Tall, like all the Borgens."

"Annie, let's see if some of these clothes fit you," Urs called from the deep overstuffed chair. Annie walked to the middle.

"Well look it here, she's growing like a foxtail and just as skinny." Big Gracie turned Annie by the shoulders, looking her over. Annie could feel the spoon caught edgewise in her pocket. "Her birthday was this spring wasn't it? Don't tell me she's seven already."

"Just six," Margaret offered, "but I've seen kids eight don't look as big. Got Urs's big bones." The grape on the tip of the spoon showed just above the edge of her pocket. Annie wondered if they saw it. If they thought she had stolen it.

"And look at the size of those wrists!" Philip leaned forward from the davenport, his elbows pressing his knees. "And those feet! They say you can tell how big they're going to be by the size of their feet. Like with dogs."

"Now look here," Gracie rummaged through the box and came out with a blue flannel. "This shirt is practically new. Phil got it at that Sunshine sale over at the Woolworth's store. Got it for a quarter. It was almost too small already then, but for a quarter you couldn't pass that up." Big Gracie rummaged through the box again. "Here, you might just as well try on these corduroy half pants too. Let's go in the bedroom there. There's a big mirror. You can see how you look and then show your mom and dad."

Annie's mind rushed ahead. In the bedroom she'd put the spoon under the bed. Annie was easing herself toward the bedroom door, the flannel shirt covering the pocket, pressing the spoon into her thigh when Phil called her back. "Here, you might just as well try this jacket too and make an outfit of it."

Big Gracie picked up the entire box and pushed Annie into the bedroom ahead of her.

"I can dress myself," Annie protested, but Big Gracie paid no attention.

"Arms up now, honey." Annie felt the spoon release from the dress pocket. She waited for the sound of it hitting the floor. Instead it landed in the corner of the box of clothes at her feet. Gracie pushed her skinny arms and legs into the outfit and turned her around to the mirror for a look. "That's just fine," Gracie said as she stepped back for a better look, and then on impulse, took the cap from the hook on the backside of the door and set it on Annie's head. "Oh, you're beautiful," she said and with a "TA DA!" and flung open the bedroom door.

"Come on out here and let us have a look at you." Phil coaxed.

Standing before the group Annie's head reeled. Then she remembered to be relieved that she was rid of the spoon.

"She looks just like a boy!" Little Gracie laughed. She nearly screamed it out.

"She does look like a boy, just like a boy!" Liz took it up, pointing.

Annie flushed. Nothing wrong with looking like a boy, she thought. Better that than like those two cream puffs.

"Come on over here," Margaret held her arms wide. She pulled Annie to her, straightening the collar, pulling down the shirt, talking low, just to Annie. "That shirt looks real nice. By next fall it'll fit just fine. And that brown plaid just picks up the color in your eyes."

"Why she don't just look like any boy, Urs. She looks just like you!" Phil's discovery darted between father and daughter.

"He's right!" Big Gracie exploded, seeing the resemblance. "I do believe you've got yourself a son."

Annie's emotions in the past few minutes had been in such a tizzy that she hung onto this one idea with satisfaction.

"Here we all thought we were going to have to wait 'til fall to see a little Urs, and we had one right here all the time. Go over there and stand by your father, Annie. Look there, Margaret, isn't she just a picture of Urs. He must have looked just like that at her age. I'm going to get a photo of those two. Now that's all."

The two traipsed out onto the porch and under Big Gracie's direction Urs sat on the front step with Annie balanced awkwardly on his knee. Annie cherished the feel of her father's form through the back of the plaid flannel. His arms encircled her, and their smiles were recorded forever.

At supper that evening in the middle of a glass of buttermilk Annie remembered the bunny. It awakened in her a surging guilt: first for having forgotten all about him for so long and second for realizing he might be freezing to death. He might even be dead. Just because the weather was nice here, that didn't mean a thing about how it was at home. Hadn't she heard the men say that just this afternoon?

"I've got a bunny named Buttermilk." She spoke up tentatively at the table set up out of planks for the kids on the closed-in porch.

"Buttermilk, what kind of a name is that?" Liz teased.

"Buttermilk's a good name. They're both white and smooth. And he likes it too. When I dipped my fingers in buttermilk he licked them clean." Little Gracie and Hank, showing the mildest curiosity at what might develop, slowed their eating. Annie lowered her eyes. She was just aware of the squeaking sounds her wiggling cousins made on the orange crates.

"Anyway you can't feed 'em buttermilk." Liz just wouldn't stop. "Buttermilk will kill 'em. Anybody knows a little bunny like that will die if it drinks buttermilk,"

The crates stopped wiggling. "That bunny's too little." Liz went on. "If you get 'em away from their mothers that little they can only eat Dutch, and the Dutch clover isn't up yet. Anybody knows that."

Annie started gulping her buttermilk, hoping against hope that her sister would stop.

"It looks like you love buttermilk." Liz said with a sly smile. "To drink, I hear it sure tastes good with roast rabbit!"

Annie put her head down, and stared at her potatoes. Her eyes got hot and wet. Then she remembered the furry little rabbit's foot in Hank's palm. Her food turned pasty on her plate.

*

At the dance hall Annie worried and sulked, feeling all alone. Was the bunny lonesome too? Liz and little Gracie whispered and elbowed each other, giggling and nodding, leaving Annie out completely. Why should I care, Annie thought. They look so stupid. Both with the same dirty blond hair and little mouths pressed back into their faces.

Then it dawned on Annie that they had the same last name too, Borgen. She never thought of that before. She was the only real Wagnor.

When the older girls left their seats, Annie's desire to spy on them lured her out into the balmy spring night. Once outside, Little Gracie and Liz abruptly slowed. A full moon was beginning to rise. The two older girls immediately focused on the parking lot where a cluster of boys in army uniform stood smoking cigarettes.

"That's Elsie's brother Gunter, there," Little Gracie nodded to Liz, "the taller one. Isn't he cute?" Little Gracie nodded in his direction.

The exaggerated beat of a polka vibrated the planked wall where the girls leaned just a few feet from the boys. One smiled at Liz. Had he winked? Annie silently looked on unbelieving.

Lizzie folded her arms tight across her chest. There was a tension in her shoulders. Her arms had goose bumps. Annie saw her sister in a whole new way. In a way she didn't quite understand. Lizzie glanced coyly at the boys. From inside the hall dancers yelped when they kicked up their heels.

Three older girls paraded by in starched skirts and cinched waists. One of the uniformed boys threw down his lighted cigarette and let out a long, low wolf whistle.

Annie gasped, giving herself away.

Gracie screwed up her face speaking in a furious whisper. "Annie, what do you think you're doing out here? Go on back inside and leave us alone!"

Lizzie stepped away from the pulsing wall with a shiver. Her arms relaxed. She seemed happy to see Annie. "I s'pose they'll be missing us inside," she said. "Especially with Annie here," Liz took her little sister's hand. "Let's go back inside, Annie. I'm getting a chill."

Annie was thrilled and confused by her sister's sudden tenderness.

Inside the hall, the dancing had begun in earnest. Annie's father jiggled her on his knee while his face got hot with whiskey. The more he drank, the more he wanted to dance.

Before he'd married, Urs seldom had the courage to ask anyone, but with Margaret at his side, his eye roved about the room. He started out with Big Gracie, leaving Annie feeling small and vulnerable on the cool square leather of the chair.

Seeing her there, Danny pulled her onto the floor and hopped her around to "Roll Out The Barrel." How good it was to have him home.

By 10:30 Margaret had spread out the pink bedspread in the corner for the child sleeping in her arms. She covered Annie with her coat, and for the rest of the evening Annie lay unawakened by either accordion or laughter as the waxed floor spread with sawdust beat beneath her.

*

Urs drove even slower back to the farm after the dance. They were all here now, packed together under his care. In the back, Danny held Annie in his arms. At his side was Margaret. Wayne lay sleeping with his head in Lizzies lap.

For Urs, time seemed to have melted away. There was no tension to be anywhere else. His hands lay slack on the steering wheel. The steady purring of the engine reminded him of the feeling he sometimes had when he removed the harnesses from the horses and was rubbing down their great trembling shoulders after a long day. In the damp skin stretched tight across his temples, the music and liquor of the dance pulsed faintly.

The moon pouring its light over the North Dakota plains made even this drab time of year take on an unearthly glow. Last year's dried prairie grass, straggling along the roadside and the fence lines, caught the light for a moment and then let it go, transforming the edges of the fields into magical borders of some holy place. Between, the dark earth lay open to the seed.

As the town slept, Urs passed silently through Drake. Only the streetlights glanced back. On the high ground just out of town, he realized how soft and black the night had become. A falling star left a tail of brilliance for an instant, as if some velvet curtain had been torn, momentarily revealing a silver land beyond.

Sometimes from within the shining grass, the headlights caught the eyes of some night animal: a skunk or badger, or down on the flats, coyotes. Seeing them, Urs slowed even more, feeling the black Ford town car and himself to be one more night creature scurrying along with shining eyes.

The full, round moon was beginning its descent. Beside him Margaret's head was flung back. Her face and hair shone silver. Her arms lay quietly apart. Her legs. Her mouth. Through the open coat the silky fabric on her belly shone and when Urs caught sight of it, he glanced away quickly, embarrassed. The sight of Margaret's belly made him look at the moon, and when he did, it became a round hole in the velvet night.

For a brief instant he felt as if he could grasp those black edges and with his strong arms raise himself up and through, into the brilliant land that lay beyond.

~ 7~

As the car pulled into the yard, the sun was peering over the pink rimmed horizon. All but Annie who lay slumped asleep in the back and Danny who was parking the car in the shed, stumbled blurry eyed toward the house and into the cold kitchen carrying boxes and crates and empty cream cans. Danny, with Annie in his arms, followed, staggering up the rise to the house. He pulled the pink chenille bedspread up around her face enveloping her like a large baby. The bedspread was worn so thin that here and there showed through the tanned flesh of Annie's arms.

The farm had changed since Danny saw it last. Snow that had been beaten into great, hard, wind-driven dunes, had now receded to meager patches. Just a narrow strip bordered the house on the north in the shade under the eave. The pink blush of color was fading in the sky and drew his eye unobstructed out across the prairie. The entire place had opened up, grown somehow.

How different he felt now. One week at Allen's learning everything the hard way and the next week, he was the one called on when things went wrong. She had given him the courage to succeed, just the thought of her, Juanita.

For new born calves and freshened cows, Danny seemed able to foresee what needed to be done. Towards the end, Allen himself was having him assist at deliveries. Danny had put together a kit of all the things they might need. But it wasn't just the clean ink bottle of tincture of iodine, or the ready gunny sack to rub down the new animal that impressed Allen—routine things. Danny had a knack for treating the unexpected. He could neatly and quickly clear a calf's throat of mucus if need be, or push on its chest just so if there was any difficulty with the breathing.

Remembering these times, Danny inhaled deeply extending to full height. The very air seemed full of promise, and Annie's weight in his arms was like nothing at all. Monday he would be back at school. Back with her. He might see her today! At church. Then, something about the angle of the light, the chickens beginning to stir, or the early morning sounds of the cows ready to be milked, shoved another thought forward: He didn't always save the calf. Not always.

It was barely night, not a week ago, when Allen had climbed the steps to Danny's room. A young heifer was having trouble. For seven hours the two worked together side by side, barely saying a word. The swollen, straining, animal quivering under Danny's touch, her eyes dull, her tongue dry. Why she was little more than a calf herself.

"Come on now, girl," Danny had encouraged time and again, pulling on the spindly wet legs; but her hips were too narrow. Towards the end she wouldn't even drink.

Allen withdrew a slim flask from his breast pocket and offered it to Danny. "She was too young," he said. "I knew she was too young when I bred her, but she was prize stock and it was my last chance with that bull."

They had to cut it out of her. As Allen handed Danny the bloody pieces, it was only the thought that it had to be done that kept him going.

When all the chunks of the dead calf were removed, unexpectedly behind it, still in the sack, was its twin. It too, was dead of course by then. Danny had staggered under its lifeless weight cradling it to the floor. At the last minute it slipped from his hands and the membrane tore away. There in the early morning light was a perfect fetus all clean and smelling sweet, as if waiting for him to blow it to life. How sweet it was. How tender and sweet. And now, with Annie in his arms, tears sprang to Danny's eyes.

A breath of wind teased the edge of the bedspread where it dangled from Annie's shoulder. It wasn't cold, but out of instinct she drew herself into him.

Once inside the dark kitchen, Danny eased Annie onto a kitchen chair where she stirred a little and then slumped once again asleep. Her dark hair parted in a crooked line exposing the scalp.

Danny surveyed the familiar kitchen for the first time in weeks. The flour sack curtains he'd seen so many times he no longer saw them, now stood out as they had that first day his mother hung them. How dingy they had become. The tiny lavender flowers faded to gray, no longer matched the scalloped edging of the oilcloth shelf liners Margaret had so carefully cut and laid. And the pump that squeaked at the bottom of each thrust, how it grated uncomfortably like the phonograph needle caught in the groove of one of Gracie's new records going over and over the same thing.

Urs, who'd kindled the fire and changed clothes, had gone out to the barn. Margaret and Liz had begun putting away the provisions purchased in Minot. The activity and chatter were intrusive, suddenly senseless to Danny. And he hadn't noticed before how crammed in everything was, how there wasn't enough room. It annoyed him that his mother didn't seem to notice or to care. Here everything would always be just the same, or in time become a little dingier, a little more worn. He tensed the muscles in his upper arms, and thrust his elbows out to each side testing the space. Was there room enough here for him?

"Well, I guess I might as well get started with the milking," he finally managed. At least that would get him outside.

"I don't know if I mentioned it before or not," Margaret began, "but all the time you were gone that red heifer hardly gave a drop of milk." Margaret expertly pulled the string, opening the cloth flour bag. "Wayne got kicked half way across the barn the first time he tried to lay a hand on her, guess he doesn't have your touch." Margaret opened the tin flour safe and emptied the bag.

Danny was only half listening, but the vague hostility that had him a moment ago was gone. As he reached for the door a genuine burst of laughter broke from his lips.

At the kitchen counter Liz, enveloped in a cloud of white, vigorously scooped flour into the speckled enamel bowl. "*Kooga*! You'd think my brother was the Czar of Russia." Danny could see there were other, specific words, too, trapped in her throat that she thought it best not to let out.

With short quick strokes Liz cut in the lard. The crispy flat cinnamon dessert had to be made just so. A delicate blue tracery rose on her thin wrists and climbed the insides of her arms as she exerted herself in the mixing. Margaret shooed her away then and took over. Though exhaustion weighted every movement, she felt complete: he was home. Now she could sleep again at night. With Danny gone she'd felt a part of herself strained nearly to the snapping point, as though the blue cord that had tethered him once, like the one coiled in her now, had never been cut.

Tired and relaxed, Margaret stood before the spiced dough, transfixed in the moment. The trip to Minot had replenished those extras they'd been able to do without and now for the first time in months the smell of cinnamon and orange peel mingled with the slow heat spreading from the stove. The delicious odor of Kooga took her to another time as Margaret's eye turned.

Kooga baked in the kitchen oven. It was Christmas. Her mother, her father, all of them were still alive. It was crowded; there had been the cousins, and aunts and uncles. They sat in a circle in the little living room, when with the tinkling of a bell, down the snow swept path she came. Down the path swept clean of snow she came, until she knocked at the door. When her father opened it little Margaret couldn't believe her eyes. There stood *Christkindla* carrying the tree. Her face was hidden under a veil that hung to her shoulders. She was dressed all in white with wide ribbons each a different color draped from her hat to the edge of the bountiful hooped skirt. What a sight to behold!

Then the other one appeared. Her dark shadow, *Pelzanega*. His coat, black and furry, his dark hat pulled over his face. A wild thicket of black whiskers spread over the collar of his coat. In one hand was a switch of willow branches and in the other a black cloth sack. Once he'd bagged the bad children, he'd go off to the deepest part of the forest, leaving them at midnight where they'd never again find the way home.

And between the two of them they knew everything. In a gentle voice Christkindla told how Margaret shared her egg with her twin Maryanne when there wasn't enough to go around, only to be countered by the deep dark voice of *Pelzanega*. "It was Margaret who broke the plate brought all the way from Germany and then from Russia found in the bottom of the kindling box." How her heart had jumped when he'd said that.

On it went for each of the children, and there was squealing and threats and crying until magically the presents appeared from under the hooped skirt. Then the two were a couple, turning round and round.

Tannenbaum, O Tannenbaum, sung faster and faster clapping and clapping until the dancing couple once again disappeared back down the path and into the night.

Standing in the kitchen before the fragrant *kooga*, Margaret realized just then how much Christkindla seemed to enjoy dancing with the fearsome black one. Even all these years later she was surprised but, questioning the memory, found herself nodding in confirmation. Yes, it was true. Margaret put the last crimp in the dough and wiped her fingers, shiny with lard, on the front of her apron.

The sounds of clanking utensils and closing cupboard doors stirred Annie from where she sat propped before the table. Her eyes blinked several times before they focused enough to take in the warming kitchen and came to rest on the stove. A swell of anxiety rose, and she hurried to the box behind it. With closed eyes she listened. No sound whatsoever. Crouching down, Annie counted to seven and looked.

The bunny was still alive. It lay quaking in the corner huddled among the shredded rags. Annie tucked it inside her sweater leaving a slight fringe of fur showing below the tight knit ribbing at her waist. Encased there, the bunny still trembled, not strong enough to protest, its cold nose nuzzled into her stomach. Then it sucked, a strangely satisfying sensation just below her breast.

Under Liz's supervision Annie heated a little milk and sat at the table, dipping her finger as the bunny licked. Annie was getting hungry too. Occasionally with mild interest she looked up to see what was being prepared for breakfast. Not much, since only she and Urs would eat. The others would be taking Communion.

Though Annie longed for the day when she would be allowed to join in this Holy ritual, her father's resistance to it intrigued her as well, and his insistence that the others observe the ceremony to the letter. How could he survive, Annie wondered, when everyone from Father Weaver to her mother agreed that it was necessary for life itself? Could he have entered into some secret pact with God. Or the dragon?

~8~

It was Margaret who led the family into the cool entrance way, dipping her first two fingers into the holy water and making the sign of the cross. At every possibility she genuflected, until finding her way to the favorite pew. By the time her knees pressed the kneeling block through the nylon skirt of her Swiss-dotted Sunday dress, her face was calm and her senses satiated with the low sound of whispered prayer, the scent of candle wax and the gleam of metal and polished wood.

"I believe in one God, Father Almighty, maker of heaven and earth and of all things visible and invisible." The words came in a gentle rush. They held none of the urgency that had accompanied them after her first husband died, when she'd murmured it continually.

Then, Margaret had lived in that little place on Second Street. That was the time when she covered her windows by day with the same blankets that covered the beds by night. She wore dark colors. Ate little. She had maintained a thread of sanity by saying the Apostle's Creed over and over, in Latin, in English, in German, in languages never spoken before. Frontward and backwards she said it. For Lars, for his soul and her own.

In time, Margaret returned to the confessional on her knees, begging Father Weaver for forgiveness. There, she collapsed in shame, sobbing for mercy. She admitted trading her love of God for the love of Lars. For Lars had been a Lutheran and for Lars Margaret had given up the one true church.

Eventually, Father Weaver brought her back into the fold. She would not be excommunicated. The three children were properly baptized in a private ceremony.

But still she wondered. Was it wrong to pray for Lars? What had stopped her from confessing that part to Father? Margaret's obsessive mind twisted in confusion.

One cold sunny morning in December she'd tried to wash the windows to let in the light. A thin sheen of dirty water froze to the glass, swirling like smoke from her candles swirled, like the smoke from the incense.

When Lizzie would wake, Margaret turned the child's attention to the red ball she kept in the bottom of the bed stand. She tried to focus the toddler, Wayne, on the bright yellow bird made from ribbon saved from her wedding bouquet. The yellow bird hung from a string above his padded box by the stove. But sometimes her eye would turn and the bird would fly away singing through the sky with the ribbons trailing.

Once a week she'd call Danny to the kitchen to start him on his rounds. On winter mornings, puffs of breath showed white as she spoke. She would take out the stub of a pencil. Sharpening it with the knife, she was careful not to cut away more than was necessary. The 5 & 10 gave them away every year at Christmas. She meant for this one to last a full year. She wrote on a corner torn from a grocery bag 3 oat. "Look here Danny, this says three pounds of oatmeal. 1 coff. "And this here is, one pound of coffee," Margaret pointed with the pencil. She knew the two-pound cans were cheaper, but how could she get that much money all at once?

Margaret looked up from her broken scrawl. "After you cash the check Danny, go to the 5 & 10 for candles. Get three long ones like Father Weaver uses on holy days." 3 candls, she penciled in, and 1 Bolnie. "One pound of bologna Danny, now ask the butcher when you get the bologna if he has any extra soup bones or liver or tongue."

Danny would bundle himself against the cold. First, last year's summer jacket tight across the shoulders and over it the winter wool Father Weaver had set aside for him. Next, Danny would wind a white cloth around his neck, tucking it in his collar so it would add warmth but not be seen under his father's old scarf, layered over with a handsome fold across one shoulder. Last were the mittens of different sizes and colors. He pulled them over pudgy hands.

As soon as the children were occupied, Margaret would steal into the small dark pantry and begin. The words of the Creed were a palpable thread, each one touched by her mind. "I believe in One God, Father Almighty, maker of heaven and earth, of all things visible and invisible." Sometimes then, the ground fell away, and she would reach for her rosary, something solid in her hand. "Holy Mary, mother of God, pray for us sinners now and at the hour of death." Falling away and away, she gripped her beads as if they were all that connected her to the earth, as if they were all that connected her to her life.

As she prayed, Margaret was no longer aware of her son preparing himself. She no longer heard the toddler humming in the box by the stove as he batted a yellow bird. She no longer heard Liz rolling the red ball across the floor back and forth, back and forth.

Those days, when Urs Wagnor found an excuse to come into town to deliver the milk or to pick up some feed for the chickens, he paid special attention to the widow's small house. Sometimes he imagined a mild heat escaping from the open door when Danny left, and he felt a yearning or thought he smelled something baking sweet and crusty.

As Danny threaded his way through the small town, following the ghostly puffs of his own breath, it was his feet that got cold first. Sometimes in the course of business, man and boy would meet, Danny stomping his feet in the 5 & 10 while Urs with his big frame looked frightful amidst the miniature glass dogs and bins of tiny rubber dolls with painted lips. Though their eyes never met, they became aware of each other in this way: Urs of something small and frail and cared for and Danny of something strong and powerful with thick coats and socks.

That was the time Margaret kept her door closed. She had moved within her house as candle smoke moved, always in rhythm with her chanting, a ghost chanting. *"Ich glaube an Gott den Allmaechtigen, den Schoepfer des Himmels und der Erde."* For her it worked. Now, years later, Margaret moved through the rituals of the church with an easy, familiar grace. The kneeling and rising, kneeling and rising, made something inside her feel like an all-seeing hawk effortlessly riding the updrafts, seeing all, both in heaven and in earth

From the kneeling block even Annie noticed the heightened grace of her mother's gestures. It was as if entering the church opened some dimension that lay hidden. Annie thought of gazing into the pond at a fuzzy green stick, only to suddenly see a bird take flight. How amazed she was that a creature of the sky had been captured there in the quiet water.

Sandwiched between her mother and father, Annie grew quite uncomfortable. She removed one glove when she heard the annoying sound of Lizzie pretentiously clearing her throat. This was her signal that Annie had done something wrong. A bell tinkled and from among the plaster saints the priest appeared. He wore vestments of the darkest purple trimmed in soft white fur. At his side was Tony Schultz awkwardly swinging glowing incense in a silver burner. Scented wisps floated outward and Annie strained to catch the thinning trails. The burner was decorated with delicate flowers climbing the brightly shining pear-shaped sides. Annie's gloved hand searched her pocket remembering the stolen spoon.

"Santos...Spirituous Santos..." Annie tried her best to follow along. Sunlight streamed through the colored glass behind the altar.

There, loomed the Dragon. Nothing like the dragon she had seen by the outhouse. This one reared up on his back legs, fire snorting from his nose, belching from his mouth. Sunlight enlivened the flames, the green scales, St. George's white, white horse. Annie's eye could barely hold the color, the brightness.

Annie knew that St. George was theirs. Margaret said St. George was her grandmother's church in Russia and in Germany before that. "It goes back and back," Margaret said. "St. George is ours, and the Princess Sabra, and the dragon too, though his father was Evil and his mother Darkness. He was Wickedness itself."

With a sudden blast from the huge pipes behind the organ, the air vibrated. The choir sang.

But why didn't St. George stay after he killed the dragon? Why didn't he stay with Sabra, that's what Annie wanted to know. The light from the stained glass lent the room a dreamlike quality. Annie located the blue of the princess's dress. She was off to one side and small. If he was such a good German man then why did he leave? Could it be that he loved dragons more than princesses? The church grew hot. Annie was having trouble getting enough air.

Margaret began her procession to the communion rail. Though this was forbidden, Annie felt herself rising as well. She curled her hands under the edge of the pew and held on.

Her father fell to his knees. The colored sunlight streamed. At the communion rail, her mother grew suddenly younger, flushing pink, eyes rolled back, tongue extended.

Annie felt herself rising, floating above the others, mingling with the incense and the chants, the streaming light. Then, at the base of her neck, began a faint rumbling, cool and dark. Something just beyond the edge of her vision, just beyond the reach of her hearing was weighting her down.

The heavens clouded. Sabra, St. George and the Dragon no longer glowed with life. Electric lights reflected off the leaded panels, dull and identical. Annie could see plainly they were only glass.

The sound again, a rumbling. Was it real? Yes, certainly, a low wet growl coming again and again, tightening her stomach. Annie's chest heaved to take in air. The back of her neck grew more uneasy.

Turning around, she saw Humpy Chris, his chin resting on his folded hands. Slick with sudden moisture, Annie's ungloved hand slipped where she grasped the bench.

At her side her father's face was heavy and unmoved as a dumb child. From out of his breast pocket he drew his hanky and blew his nose with a honk. This simple gesture made Annie feel both sad and safe.

~ 9~

In the vestibule after church Humpy Chris rocked on his heels, with his beautiful wife Juanita at his side. She wore a blue, fitted, linen suit, with matching pumps and small veiled hat. On her wrist shone an emerald bracelet, a gift from her husband. Her figure was trim and she stood out handsomely on the rose colored pile of the carpet.

Danny, tall and handsome himself, in his white Sunday shirt and tie stood staring at her as people gathered round the couple. Juanita smiled and nodded, acknowledging his presence.

*

In a small German Russian Community like Drake any visitor might find a name like Juanita remarkable. In this place, where people and events were sifted over and over for anything that was different or new, surprisingly, no one seemed to notice. The presence of this dark-eyed beauty or even the sound of her name might have been a source of irritation. Such was not the case. The name Juanita rolled off the tongue in German dialect as well as Hilda or Shelestigar or Ethel. When Juanita was growing up, the girl's peers didn't realize it wasn't German. Their mothers and fathers had let it settle in, not remarked upon, a little at a time over many years.

It was the year the public library was built when Juanita's mother, Marlys, ran off. Most people said it was someone from the construction crew, though work on the building had barely begun.

By the time Marlys quietly moved back in with her father, the shanties where the workers lived were already torn down. The town appeared to be exactly as before. The only indication that two years had passed was the new brick library on Main Street and the dark-haired baby girl wrapped in blankets and very seldom seen. The young mother lived very properly, taking care of her baby and her father's house. She dressed inconspicuously and aged quickly.

Juanita's grandfather raised the child as his own, running the hardware store and taking an active role in the Knights of Columbus.

As time went by no one seemed to remember Juanita wasn't his. His wife had died years before and the town seemed to forget that she ever existed. By the time Juanita entered St. George's elementary school, people were willing to forgive the strange name, the thick black hair and the dark eyes. They no longer noticed. By the time she was in high school, it took a stranger to see it, or someone who had been away. Someone like Humpy Chris.

So, to Christopher Nielsen the idea of a deformed humpback seeking out the most beautiful girl in the town was not altogether unlikely. Even so, how could he have hoped to be the answer to her prayers?

*

Now, in the church foyer, Danny could smell her perfume. She gazed briefly into his eyes. Though she appeared calm, he sensed the blood pulsing through her thin wrist. Her emerald bracelet glittered. Then, his own blood pounding, he regarded the man at her side. How could it be that they were married?

One would think she could have chosen any available man in Drake.

But by the time she was in high school, Juanita had been beautiful. Sometimes in the evening after supper, when her grandfather came across her, Juanita had a faraway look, homework ignored, strewn about the kitchen table. She day dreamed of strong hands and smooth muscular shoulders and blue, blue eyes. When she became aware of her grandfather standing over her, her faced burned.

But at the time Juanita didn't care for the boys of her town. The brittle reality of their ungroomed hair and ill-fitting clothes broke the ethereal quality of her daydreams. Crisp winter nights in bed early, she preferred to hear them calling to one another and laughing in the distance. She was disappointed when she recognized a voice.

Then there appeared a new boy in town, Sorn. He didn't hang around with the other boys his age. He dressed in pleated slacks, ironed shirts, and a snappy blue fedora set cockily to one side. He swaggered a bit when he walked. Juanita had heard he'd quit school and moved here from Makoti taking this job in his Uncle's drugstore. Juanita and her girlfriends occasionally stopped at the soda fountain there on their way home from school.

One afternoon Juanita was the last to take her money to the cash register. Accepting the coin, Sorn quickly returned it and curled his fingers around hers. He gazed into her eyes as his hand squeezed hers.

When Juanita's grandfather returned from work that evening he looked at her curiously. Again her face burned. How could he know?

Another day Juanita went to the store alone. Sorn was unpacking merchandise. He smiled and said, "Follow me. I have something to show you." Sorn led her to a corner in the back room. He pushed the length of his body against hers and placed his hands over her breasts. Juanita pushed his hands away and ran from the store as if it were on fire.

For weeks she couldn't forget. Didn't want to forget.

A look of disappointment spread from the tight lips to the sad eyes of her grandfather's face. How could he know?

Sometimes, on her way home from school Sorn would stand in the doorway of the drugstore watching as she crossed to the other side, her face crimson. He knew there were other ways home from school.

Gradually, she began stopping in again with girlfriends. Sometimes she mustered the courage to throw back her head and smile when he looked her way.

One day she again entered the store alone. Blocks of gray linoleum shone in the empty aisles. "I've been waiting for you to come back." Sorn whispered at the back of her neck . Juanita followed him again to the back room. This time when he touched her, she kissed his mouth. His hands again found her breasts, the insides of her thighs.

After the incident with Sorn, Juanita had suffered with guilt and the fear of being found out.

Juanita avoided her grandfather. The silent dreariness of her mother made her angry. Fear entered where a terrible battle waged.

She never went to the drugstore again. At confession each week, she could not bring herself to share her shame. Her sin compounded, while at school and with friends, she grew fearful and anxious. Determined to make it right, to cleanse herself of earthly sin, she developed a twisted theory. She calculated that her short-comings were in some way due to her beauty. That beauty attracted evil. It was evil.

Juanita plunged herself into reading St. Theresa, the mystic nun. She prayed hard and often in an attempt to force her youthful energy to higher realms. Gradually the lightheartedness of a young girl gave way to someone sullen and serious. While the other girls wore their hair bobbed, she pulled hers back, twisted into a bun. Still she was beautiful.

No longer did her daydreams take soaring flights that made her head spin and her heart pound. She shunned what was light and young and bright, developing a taste for fruit past its ripeness. Juanita no longer skipped or danced with her cousins. But her slow, purposeful walk only become more graceful, more alluring.

Juanita threw herself into helping her mother clean the house and the church. She developed a fondness for leftover flowers from funerals or weddings, keeping profuse bouquets at her bedside with brown petals smelling too sweet, tinged with rot.

To the community at large she only seemed to be maturing. Her grandfather was pleased—my responsible, serious Juanita. Other parents pointed to her as an example. Though these changes intimidated the boys her age, older men were shaken by her beauty. Her walk was queenly, her eyes a bit sad. Only her mother was disturbed.

But Juanita found she could not erase her sinful thoughts completely. They wound round like a gauzy shroud, tightening, tightening. She prayed for a solution.

Then one day home from college, Humpy Chris stood in the specially tailored suit in the church foyer as he did now. Juanita had been repelled by his ugliness. He was the answer to her prayers.

Margaret stood waiting to shake the priest's hand. She would not be put off from her usual church routine, though she sensed Urs's patience was wearing thin. She wanted to approach Juanita, but she could see that would be impossible. Would Danny be able to take the tests, she wanted to ask? Could he get the diploma he'd more than earned? Margaret knew they were cracking down on country schools. In the last couple years students were even required to attend during spring planting. As Margaret studied the stylish woman from across the room she, too, wondered how Juanita and Chris could be man and wife.

The wet spring day they were married, Margaret had been young herself. Only the baby, Danny, sat between her and Lars on the church bench. Margaret had kept her head down, ashamed to have Father Weaver see her. She had told herself she had nothing to be ashamed of. But she was ashamed.

It was the only time Lars had been in St. George's Catholic Church. The wedding was a huge affair. A special band from Fargo was hired for the wedding dance. The celebrations lasted three days.

Juanita had barely graduated from high school but already carried herself with the poise and certainty uncommon to a girl her age. In the crowded church her grandfather guided her firmly down the aisle. She spoke her marriage vows softly and directly with the determination befitting a girl being received into the nunnery. In that brief silence that followed, a soft sharp sigh escaped from her grandfather's lips.

Contrary to appearances Margaret knew now, as she stood in that same church, that Juanita hadn't married the man at her side for money. Margaret was sure of that. Humpy Chris didn't really have much at the time, though it was rumored he had somehow benefited from the misfortune of others when the stock market crashed.

Perhaps this was the first time Margaret really looked at Juanita since that day of her wedding. Margaret felt she somehow knew Juanita. Though the women's paths seldom crossed, there had been that one time. Margaret seldom thought of it now. Their eyes met briefly in recognition.

Margaret had always assumed Father Weaver had talked to her. He knew how bad off Margaret was. He knew she had that one last thing of value. It was winter when Juanita came to Margaret's little house in town. The young widow sat before the coal box, counting out the pieces for each day of the week. Her hands were black when she answered the knock at the door.

All during the discussion Danny looked on, leaning into his mother. When Juanita made the offer, Margaret rose expressionless. She filled the basin and carefully scrubbed her hands before retrieving the ivory box from the little altar in the pantry.

Juanita had seemed to understand how much it meant to Margaret. When she took the box and held it to the window light, the translucent, delicately carved flowers glowed. From the little bedroom could be heard a ball rolling across the floor and hitting the wall again and again. It would be Lizzie waken from her nap. In a few moments she stumbled into the room still holding a red rubber ball in one hand and rubbing her eyes with the other. Seeing Juanita she stopped and joined her brother silently watching.

"Is this enough?" Juanita had asked. She gave the impression she would have liked to let Margaret keep the box and take the money, too. But it couldn't be done that way. Not for either of them. Twenty dollars she gave Margaret. Probably more than Lars had paid for it in the first place. Margaret needed the money.

"What's your name, young man?" Juanita smiled at Danny, trying to lighten the mood. "Here's something for you to share with your sister." She brought out of her coat pocket a Hershey's chocolate bar and placed it in his hand. His eyes were very bright and blue.

Margaret told herself she wouldn't have sold it to just anyone. She wouldn't have sold it to Humpy Chris. Before that day she would not have considered selling it to his wife. But the man and wife weren't alike. From what she knew of Humpy Chris, he was nothing like this woman.

"Danny," Urs was tapping Danny on the shoulder, "bring the car on around. It's time we got home."

While Danny brought the car, Urs stood self-consciously rooted to the rose colored pile rug. He noticed the way Humpy combed a few hairs over his balding head. What kind of a man was he anyway? It galled Urs the way the neighbors and even the priest formed a cluster around the couple. And what was that funny smell. Cologne? Was the man wearing cologne? Was Humpy Chris even a man?

Urs looked down at his hand. It angered him more, the sight of it, connected somehow to his own unnamed fear that kept him following orders, trying to please, trying to be appreciated. Urs knew he needed his landlord's approval. But more than needing approval, Urs suddenly realized, he needed to feel safe.

Then there was Danny, placing his hand on his mother's arm. "The car's out front now, Mom. It's time to go."

Margaret realized she had been staring. The women were both staring. Margaret quickly looked away. She felt for Juanita a strong, sad, surge of kinship.

~10~

Annie pulled the covers up over her head. They'd had a feast. A special Sunday dinner of tender honeyed ham and for dessert the *kooga*. All because of Danny. From her bed, she heard Liz and Danny doing the dishes. There was the clattering of plates and silverware and in between some kind of code they knew.

"Alabama?"

"Montgomery. The cotton state."

What did this strange way of speaking mean? Annie felt disoriented. Were Danny and Liz grown-ups now? Was there something going on that only the grown-ups knew, but weren't telling her?

"Arizona?"

"Phoenix," Danny said, "place of few or little springs."

Under the covers Annie was cupped against the bunny. One hand was cold, raised above her head, almost as if to ward off a blow. She pulled it in and snuggled deeper. An old memory began haunting her.

There appeared in her mind a cold star filled sky. But under that, there something else, something bad that was her fault. Something about foxes and a rooster, and a broken house.

In that memory, or was it a dream, had it been her fault they were taken to a broken house with foxes in the cold. Could this house be that place?

On her fingertips, Annie smelled the *kooga* and the Dutch clover she'd been feeding Buttermilk. The two swirled together, more colors than scents: orange and green. Swirling together, orange and green. There were no foxes here.

Annie floated in and out of consciousness. She only remembered snatches of what had actually happened.

From that other time three years ago she remembered mostly only the cold. How cold it had been when they'd loaded up everything they had into the runner sled and hitched the horses. It was night by the time they got here, the stars a million bright promises flung across the sky. Annie had juggled to and fro, seated on the floorboards half asleep, wrapped in blankets and held between her father's knees. All the way he spoke to the horses in a hopeful voice. This is what Annie remembered, and what she clung to. The rest of it, she tried to avoid it as though it were a hungry dog following her around, when she had no food.

Margaret had sat silent in the sled, eyes riveted ahead, while her throat ached with unspoken words. Why was he doing this; sitting there talking to the horses as if nothing were wrong, pretending they were on their way to a church social?

And when they opened the door, bringing the lighted lantern to the dark, broken house, there had been a den of foxes. At the sight of their glowing yellow eyes Margaret's thoughts ran, as a dreamer caught in a nightmare runs. What was the matter with him? Was he crazy or something bringing a family into this in the middle of the night, in the middle of the winter?   From a corner she took a ruined broomstick, half its shaft gone, and went after the foxes, driving them, hissing at her, into the night.

The first things she brought in were the three prized chickens and the rooster, indignant in his cage. Would they be safe here? They were all she had left of the flock she'd so carefully tended, all that was hers. Margaret carried the cages stiffly, her mouth compressed, and set them behind the cold stove.

She spoke only with her hands as she slammed a crate down and with her feet as she kicked the door jamb and traipsed back to the sleigh for another. The barns are sound! The barns are sound! No wonder Urs had so much to say about the barns. Oh he was too good to ask for help, wasn't he? They could have gone to Phil's in Minot at least until there was heat, at least 'til they found out if the water was good!

Sound barns, as if the stink of manure was a prize deserving a special roof over its head. And now it had come to this. He'd set out on the word of Humpy Chris; like stepping off a cliff in the middle of the night, taking them all with him.

When everything had been brought in and was piled haphazardly in the kitchen, Margaret's energy gave out. She sat down not knowing what to do next.

Urs tried to get a fire going, but there was no dry kindling. In a fury he dumped the contents of the boxes on the floor and ripped them up. Still the cold wood wouldn't catch. Wind whistled down the flue. Smoke billowed out into the room.

Margaret and the children dragged out a shapeless mattress to the kitchen floor and put on as many of their clothes as they could find. All night they huddled together under blankets and coats. The room only grew colder. Fine snow sifted through the cracks in the window above where they lay, while the wind cried like a lonely animal rounding the corner. Frost collected on the floor, its white breath stealing through the mattress.

Urs didn't go to bed at all. He carried in sticks of wood and stacked them behind the stove to dry. The lantern flickered in the draft, making crazy shadows of their belongings, scattered and heaped every which way. Was it his fault they had to move, that Anton Eisenzemmer's son was getting out of the Army next spring and would be farming that bottom 350 himself? Hadn't Humpy Chris said there were plenty of others who would be glad to rent this place on a share basis and if Urs wanted it he'd better get out there right away?

Why it was a stroke of luck they had anything at all; that he'd even heard of its being repossessed. Urs groped about in the unsteady light looking for bedding or anything he could wrap around himself for warmth. For most of the night he sat motionless, head in his hands, beating back failure as best he could. He'd made it all right, through worse than this already. But here the cold wind took up a chorus: Could he do it again? Could he?

How many times could a man come back to life? Could he carry it all on his own back, a load that pressed his face in the mud, and still see the sky? Urs got up and stomped and shook these thoughts away before wrapping himself and sitting down to blow on his hands. The only sounds in the room were the steady breathing of the sleepers and the caged chickens re-positioning themselves, fluffing out their feathers. Quietly Urs emptied one of the larger boxes and placed it upside down over their cage to cut the draft.

They could do it, Urs paced. In the spring they'd have a big garden and Margaret could start up with her chickens again. And Annie, he'd make her a little sand box to play in, where Margaret could keep an eye on her while she gardened. Maybe they'd get a duck or two. Urs sat down uplifted a bit by his efforts.

For a while in the middle of that long night he saw the farm buildings all cleaned and painted. He saw crops coming in strong and full harvests. Maybe this wouldn't have been the farm he'd have chosen for himself, but he could make it do. He would make it do. Twice failed, he could still make the effort again.

But by the time the first light of morning seeped through the cracked window pane, he wasn't sure. If he just didn't have this family, these people who expected so much from him. If it was just him he could make it anywhere. He could curl up with the dogs in the ditch!

So Urs sat in the icy room, talking in a voice nearly audible until the light from the lantern grew dim and the heaps of clothes and the torn boxes emerged from the darkness. A thin skin of dazzling frost lay brilliant on the walls and floor and upon the table.

From where the family slept came the steady sound of breathing. Annie's small half-opened hand extended from the patchwork of towels and bedding and coats that covered them. Quietly Urs knelt and returned it to the covers. He saw then that Margaret was awake.

Her blue eyes were soft. Slowly she sat up, the covers falling from her shoulders unheeded. Her back pressed through the dress and sweater, to the frosty wall. She looked around disoriented. In the night had the foxes moved things around? Then, the question she had carried in her thighs and arms, in her every move and gesture for years sprung from her mouth. "Urs, why'd you marry me?"

In the thin light, the words flew out before she'd had time to catch them. Though Urs tried to avoid her eyes, there was no place to go. She asked it again. Without a trace of anger, without pity, without anything. She simply asked once more. "Urs, why did you marry me?"

Urs's head snapped back as if he'd been slapped. "Oh you had it so good before I came along, didn't you? You had it so good eating oatmeal and potatoes every day and living on the welfare."

Under the covers and coats was Annie, cupped against Danny. She had been lightly awakened when her father first touched her hand and the shroud of sleep kept slipping from her as they spoke.

"So you want to know why I married you, do you? Well, I'll tell you why. I'll tell you though you know God damn well why I did." Urs's hard finger poked Margaret's chest. "If that Lars of yours hadn't blown his brains out, he could be taking care of you now. So I wouldn't have to."

Annie was fully awake. Her father's voice made her wince and her arms wrapped themselves over her head as if to ward off a blow. Even so she was unprepared for what she heard.

"Do you think I need you? You were pregnant weren't you? It was Annie and the hope for a son, you know that!"

Margaret fell against the wall, staring quietly. She was tired, more tired than she had ever been. She didn't have the energy for anger. Instead she merely glanced up once again at Urs.

At just that moment her eye turned. In the undulating blur of his form, with the blankets and coats wrapped about him Margaret saw a beast tottering on two legs. When her eye locked on his, she saw the deep pain he hid and his eyes brimmed.

"Margaret, I never would have gotten a woman like you if it hadn't been for Annie," Urs whispered, sorry for what he had said. But before he could shape another word of submission the rooster crowed, a very loud sound in the cold room.

The afternoon sun slanting through the window awakened Annie.

Had it had been her fault, she wondered now, their being taken to that broken place in the middle of the night, in the middle of the winter? Was this house even that place? This house with Buttermilk and her farm under the lilacs and the kooga and Danny back after being gone and the spoon clutched to her heart just now, her thumb in the depression of its bowl?

Annie watched as the shaft of light from the window highlighted dust particles like the bold beams from heaven on the church missal. Could that cold broken place be here, where the spider lived on a post of the windmill by the livestock tank? Where just last week, she'd watched as he spun his orbed web from the post to the lip of the tank to a stick floating at water's edge? Where he'd tied together with filmy threads the sky and the water, the earth and the sun?

The house was quiet.

In the living room Urs lay slumped in the big chair sleeping. His face was calm, his breath even. As Annie watched, a picture of the small field at the base of the lilac bush opened in her mind. Perhaps it was paying off. When was the last time she had seen such contentment on her father's face? She rubbed the bowl of the spoon with her thumb. And now there was this, too. The spoon was meant to be hers, she felt sure. Her secret. She fingered the raised clump of grapes before withdrawing her hand from her pocket and reaching out to touch the sleeve of her sleeping father's arm.

Outside, the tiny field encircled with broken sticks beckoned. She would have liked to go to it immediately, but instead began circling the house, her eyes probing. Where were they all? Sneaking as quietly as possible she scrunched down small. If only she could disappear completely, like the dragon. The outhouse door was fastened from the outside. Were they all sleeping, after the big Sunday dinner?

A cloud of dust rose from the fenced corral, to the side of the barn. It was Wayne. He had Star prancing in a circle. He talked to the horse holding out his hand, saying something Annie couldn't quite hear. Star raised her right front hoof and he offered her something Annie couldn't quite see.

Suddenly, there came a voice singing, high and clear. "Blue were the skies and blue were your eyes, just like the blue skirt you wore. Come back blue lady, come back. Don't be blue anymore." It was Lizzie, on the front porch. She had set up the ironing board there, and stood before a blue cotton school dress with a faraway look. The front door was propped open to let in a cooling breeze and so she could bring out the hot irons, without disturbing Urs.

Where would Danny be? Annie looked out searching the pasture. Only the blind eye of the pond glanced back. He must be upstairs, sleeping. Her mother must be sleeping, too.

Satisfied that no one was close, Annie began her secret work. Near the bush was the toy wagon Wayne had fashioned from a cigar box. It had lain forgotten in the ditch at the side of the lane until Annie freed it from the partly frozen mud and rinsed it off at the pump. Seeing it now her mind leapt as the idea focused.

Annie stole back into the house to get the knife. Yes, there was her mother sprawled on her parents' bed. Lizzie sang softly. Her back to Annie she swayed, gliding the hot iron over her favorite skirt. A sweet smelling steam rose from the clean cotton.

At the base of the bush Annie sat for a moment with the sun on her lids. Back and forth, back and forth she sawed the diagonal notches in the soft wood at the side and back of the wagon with the sharp knife. When Annie finished, Lizzie was no longer singing. She could no longer hear Wayne either.

The stillness held her as Annie fitted the handle of the spoon diagonally into the slots of the wagon. With the heel of her hand she pressed the spoon's cup into the dirt. The process required just the right amount of pressure, just the right speed from the wagon. The well packed earth curled away from the spoon. Yes, the plowing was going well.

The silence was broken by the sound of someone walking across the floor of the upstairs bedroom and descending the steps. Her first impulse was to run, to protect the realness of everything in her mind from questions that would spoil it. Like the dragon. If you looked right at it, it just went back to being dried grass and a stump and the new growth. There was a hesitation of the sound of footsteps in the kitchen, before the back door quietly opened and closed. Annie drew into the shade of the bush. Her little field lay exposed in the sunlight.

Annie stopped her work and watched from her shaded circle. There stood Danny in his shirtsleeves. There was a stiffness across his upper back and shoulders. He held a new black oxford in one hand; in the other a soft brush flicked back and forth finishing the shine. He seemed worried, until he saw her.

Annie slipped the spoon under the edge of her trousers. The knife lay in plain sight.

"Well, well, what is it you've got here now?" he asked. His shadow fell over the little field.

Always before Annie would have told him, but now she felt sure he wouldn't understand. "Oh nothing, Danny. I'm just playing." Annie kept her eyes to the ground.

"Why, Annie, you going into farming? What'er you raising there?" If Danny would only go away. He was ruining it. How could her special work, work with him watching?

"Nothing," Annie answered, her eyes tracing his shadow to where it curved up at the edge of the house. There, just below the jagged crack in the foundation were three green claws of bright moss.

"I got Wayne's wagon. Promise me you won't tell him I got it." Could this be Danny, so stiff and worried looking? Where had he gone, her Danny? "Promise me you won't say nothing about this or he'll just kill me. I know he will." There were the green claws and Danny's shadow, and the cracked foundation.

"No, I won't say anything." Annie had spoken with such startling sincerity, it took Danny aback. "Don't you worry now, I promise." Danny touched her hair and left her, his shadow trudging at his side. Then he re-entered the house as silently as he came.

Later that evening, before bed, Danny sat in the big chair off to the side reading a book on North Dakota history. Annie climbed up into his lap. There on one page, was a drawing of Lewis and Clark with a huge grizzly bear in the background. "That's the first grizzly they ever saw, Annie, right here in North Dakota. It was over eight feet tall." It had a huge square head with coarse black hair.

"Are there still big bears like that around in the woods?" Annie asked. Black hair covered the grizzly's arms and tree-trunk legs.

"No, Annie, that was a long time ago. And besides, they didn't see it around here." But Annie wasn't convinced. The picture of the bear seemed so familiar.

Annie turned and twisted in Danny's lap, trying to find the familiar hollow where before she fit just right. "Are you sure there aren't some of those bears still around here?" Annie asked.

"Annie, now stop bothering me. Either sit still or get down. I need to study this, now."

Why was Danny's voice so harsh, so not like him? And why did he seem to have bones sticking out where they hadn't before? Annie waited patiently and didn't wiggle, but the old comfort never came. She retreated to the cool planked floor. Could it be that this wasn't Danny at all? Could it be that some other boy that only looked like him had returned from Allen's ranch? She positioned herself on the rag rug at his feet, and traced the cracks between the painted planks. Maybe the real Danny had died. Maybe if Wayne and Liz went there, too, to help with the cattle drive like they were talking, they wouldn't come back either.

There were holes in the bubbled, painted cracks between the floor planks. Annie pressed her ear and listened. Cool air rushed up. It came from somewhere under the house. A whispering.

"Annie, come out here. I want to show you something," her mother's voice called from the dark kitchen. Margaret sat at the kitchen table, incubator to one side. She removed the lid exposing the precious eggs. "Come here and light the candle for me. Let's see how these little chicks are doing." Annie thrilled at the prospect of striking a match. She scraped the phosphorous head on the sandpaper. Light and heat exploded and then a steady glow. When the wick took, she proudly shook out the flame.

"All right now, Annie. Let's take a look." Margaret held one of the eggs a few inches above the candle flame. "Come close here now, Annie, see the little chick growing inside?" Faces side by side, mother and daughter peered carefully into the backlit, glowing orb as if it were a crystal ball. "See there, Annie, that's the head." But as Margaret turned the egg, two heads appeared. "Oh no, something's wrong!" Margaret suddenly snatched the egg away from the flame. "Go get the slop bucket, Annie. Once in a while they don't turn out right."

The next egg was fine. Margaret spiraled it slowly, showing Annie the little feet, the big eyes, and the beating heart. But

Margaret had lost confidence in showing the eggs. After the second one, she sent Annie away.

By the time Margaret finished her inspection, she'd added nine eggs to the slop--deformed or not fertilized at all. Was it the infestation of bugs? Tomorrow Margaret would pump the cloud of spray around the nests again.

~11~

Over the door hung the white sign with black lettering, North Dakota Rural School #46. The frame building had been painted just that fall, but it still had the raw look of rough lumber. Along the perimeter to the north a thin wedge of ice feathered to mud. On the south stood a crab apple tree, with a few pink swelling buds and leaves that were just beginning to unfurl. Danny squatted there in the thin shadows. With his thumbnail he clipped off a crown from one of the bright green plants that traced the edge of the building. It was Russian thistle, at this young stage a delicate, many crowned, lovely plant. He began thoughtlessly peeling the scalloped leaves down the stem.

While he watched the first softball game of the spring in the field where the mud had finally dried, enough anyway in the middle, to mark off the diamond and set up bases, it might as well have been a stage play with him, a person in the audience, interested yet not an actor with part. The cheering girls, most of them anyway, sat along the top of the rail fence like colorful song birds. Only three hadn't joined the others: His sister Lizzie, who couldn't stand to miss a chance to play ball, was running for a high fly off Joe Krueger's bat; and Martha Hoogenburk, who didn't care much about clothes or bathing, was sliding into third; and Edith Bloomer, who stood off a ways fluffing herself waiting for Danny to turn up. She would have had something to say, he was sure, about his new oxfords and pressed half pants. That and she'd be ready with a dozen conversation openers: I hear you hired out, up by Towner, Danny. I hear you went to the dance in Minot.

Danny leaned with his back against the school house, pressing his frame into the weathered siding, thinking how flimsy the wall was that separated him from her—and, too, what a formidable distance it was.

When the first bell sounded, he made sure to be the last to enter. Juanita Nielsen stood with her back to the class composing at the blackboard. A soft rectangle of light lay across her shoulders lighting up a shining blue-black curl that had fallen from the others to the nape of her neck. Before her flashing hand grew the rounded script accompanied by those little gestures of hesitancy and excitability that he had recalled so often lying on the cot in the spare room at Allen's place. How many times in the past month had he remembered her criss-crossing the room as she was now, only discussing Thoreau or Wordsworth. How he had missed those moments when her mind seemed to leap ahead with sudden insight and the small cleft in her chin would try to keep up with the pace of words flooding out of her mouth.

Now he followed her neat ankles sidestepping in front of the blackboard and her hand sweeping across it, marking the pattern of her thoughts. Then the chalk suddenly lifted, and she hesitated before replacing it in the tray and turning to the class.

"Would the class please come to order and rise for the saying of the pledge."

Danny stood. His hand rose to cover his heart. When they finished and had taken their seats once more, Mrs. Nielson centered herself again before the blackboard and looked directly at him. "Would all those studying for the eighth grade exams come up here to the front of the class?"

There was shuffling and bumping as the more elementary students went to the back. Danny was immediately thrown into confusion. He stood, extending a well-shined shoe as if testing the strength of the pond ice the first day after a hard freeze. He continued forward. Was he being allowed to join the others and take the tests in spite of missing a month of school? Humpy Chris was after all a member of the school board. Was she daring to go against his rules? But here she was, facing him squarely, and with an accepting smile of approval, she nodded for him to be seated with the graduating students.

Edith Bloomer, in the row in front of him, peeked once over her shoulder and winked. The backs of her arms had pimply little bumps. A pucker of flesh swelled from the edge of each tight-fitting sleeve. Danny stole a glance at Mrs. Nielson. Her clear skin shone in the brightness of the room. He pulled the new oxfords under the desk, knowing suddenly it was sheer foolishness to make a point of them. He must be careful not to mention anything about the calving at Allen's. The less said about his absences the better. It would be their secret.

On the blackboard, Mrs. Nielson had written the major headings that would be covered on the exam: Math, Science, Literature, Geography, History. She would assign each eighth grader one or two topics to be expert in. Most country schools allowed the students to work together on exam day and they usually all ended up with identical answers and they usually all passed. Juanita certainly expected her eighth grade candidates to graduate as well. Only Danny had more than the allowed absences, and he was her very best student. If there had been enough books to go around, she would have sent one with him during the time he was farmed out.

Hadn't she had help when she least expected it? From Chris of all people! As a member of the school board he made sure she got this job, this little building. Now she felt it was her own school, where she was respected and admired, a welcome relief from— home. Her life with Chris. Ironic wasn't it? Like with snake bite, the antidote made from the poison.

As she framed herself before the blackboard, sometimes Juanita thought of herself as standing in a doorway. With the darkness behind, she felt she was coming out of small shadowy room. From another time.

Inside that room lived her grandfather, and her mother, and her husband. The room was close and musty. On her night stand, her Book of Saints beside a bouquet of rotting flowers. At times it seemed the room contained the entire community. Dense fine webs connected them all. She couldn't see what was in the darkness under the bed, or beyond the window. Inside that room she wandered in the dim light, entangled in a dense gauzy shroud.

Here in rural school #46 was another whole world. The one she'd been promised in Bismarck where she'd gone for teacher training. The one Wanda had shown her.

How they'd laughed together when they met on the train to Bismarck. The woman was from California! Had wanted the experience of teaching a few years in the "Wild Lands," as she'd called North Dakota!

Wanda had found it quaint that some of the teachers taught in languages other than English, unbelievable that others punished children for speaking their mother tongue. She marveled that rural schools didn't hold classes during spring planting or harvest; and laughed at the anti-garb politics that disallowed priests and nuns from wearing their religious clothing in state supported schools, here, where good teachers were so scarce!

Juanita had never known a woman like her. Unmarried and independent. Outgoing and happy. Happy! She was writing a book about her experiences here. Planned to return to Sacramento after the school year. The two had sat head to head on the train for hours, discussing books they'd read. The movie Wanda had seen: Showboat. The books Wanda would send to her new friend, written by independent women: Gertrude Stein. Willa Cather. Virginia Woolf. Books full of ideas that eventually made her life with Chris seem a prison and this cramped schoolroom seem a spacious unpredictable universe.

During eighth grade study period, Mrs. Nielson worked with the younger students. Passing Danny's desk she handed him a note with the words "Danny Borgen," written on the outside in the familiar script. Danny's heart jumped into his throat. Carefully he opened the paper smoothing it before him on the scarred surface of the desk. Glancing down, he read the words: "Would you please stay after school for a few minutes this evening. I need to discuss something with you. Juanita."

Juanita. That was her name. Juanita.

He'd borrowed her dictionary one day and there it was in the familiar rounded script just inside the cover. Juanita. It was beautiful sounding. Danny's blood was banging, but he felt strangely calm too. And handsome. And better than him…Humpy Chris.

It was the summer before their marriage when Juanita first really became aware of Chris. When he quietly cruised the Midwestern nights in his recently purchased Buick. At a band concert in City Park he'd caught sight of her when the cluster of girls rose from the grass in their colorful cotton skirts. At first glance she stood out sharply from the rest. Her thick black hair and dark eyes made the others look pale and watered down. She carried herself regally.

At the insistence of her mother, Juanita was at the band concert with her girl cousins. Her grandfather was away in Minot on business for the store. With a few exceptions nearly the whole community had gathered on the park lawn. Throughout the evening, girls had managed one by one to drift away from their parents until they formed this little group. In the dim twilight of the sultry summer evening, some had pushed up the sleeves of their blouses exposing bare forearms. They let their shawls drop displaying smooth rounded shoulders. Two removed large floppy hats, and used them as fans. The girls seldom had a chance to display themselves in this way. Always in church or at a wedding dance or a well supervised social, they were under the watchful eyes of parents, or the sisters, or the priest. That night the deepening darkness, the sultry heat, and the expanse of open land and sky made them giddy. Giddy and daring. Fireflies twinkled in the bushes. Crickets sang.

A tall blond girl passed around a magazine clipping from the bottom of her handbag showing Betty Davis, a long cigarette holder in her hand, her large eyes beckoning, half closed. Another girl secretly fingered a tube of lip rouge deep in her pocket.

By the time the music ended, the moon was up. The girls rose, unfurling upward in one's and two's like the bent grass where they'd sat. They giggled and whispered. Only Juanita remained aloof.

When the little group broke apart, young voices sang in the night air calling good bye. Waving hands flashed in the light from the street lamps. As the girls went their separate ways, in a matter of minutes, only Juanita and her cousins vied for position on the sidewalk and then on the moist dirt path at the side of the road. They walked in silence, each lost in her own thoughts. Once, Juanita stumbled on a half-rotted log by the side of the path. It overturned and reflexively she bent to set it right. There in the moonlight she touched its slick moist underside and glanced the quick scurrying of shiny wet things. Juanita shuddered, thrilled.

About a block from her home the group split again and Juanita was alone. She had almost reached the front step when the dark shiny car silently eased past. Though she didn't see the driver, a glint of moonlight through his already thinning hair left the impression of someone tall, someone strong.

That night Juanita prayed to Saint Theresa not to be drawn from God's path. She renewed her commitment to a life of dedication.

Long before morning she sat up suddenly in bed. Had she heard the fading sound of the sleek Buick rounding the corner into the night? Who might it be? Again she imagined someone tall, and strong, this time with blue, blue eyes.

The following week she heard Humpy Chris was home from college with a shiny second hand Buick. The rumor was affirmed that Sunday, as he stood between his parents on the sidewalk after church, in the specially tailored suit like some distinguished foreigner. For some reason the sight of him made her feel like a child entering a room where adults were talking and something heard or half heard was hushed and left hanging in the air.

When he caught her eye, instead of looking away, she held his gaze, smiling briefly before turning to follow her grandfather and mother down the walk to their parked car.

~12~

In the front row, Danny openly watched her.

Juanita in turn, studied him. His chest and upper arms filling out the freshly ironed blue cotton shirt. His slim waist. Trousers neatly creased. Black leather shoes shining.

Here! Now! This boy become a man. Overnight! Blue eyed, and young, and strong. Head erect. Alert. She stood dazed.

Suddenly Juanita felt foolish. She would never write and tell her friend Wanda about this. A student. Half her age! Unless she mentioned it as a joke. Unless she merely joked about Danny's swooning infatuation.

When the final bell rang and the students made their way out of the classroom, there was Danny. Invited to stay.

All afternoon, Danny could barely concentrate on his studies. What could she possibly want to talk to him about? Was she going to tell him he might as well stay home? That this might as well be his last day?

He watched as Mrs. Nielsen rummaged through her drawers and stopped to make a notation on her calendar. Danny held his breath hoping for the courage to stay calm and manly. Jerry Schmidt was the last to gather up his things and leave. When the door swung shut, Danny's mouth suddenly went dry. They were alone.

Danny pulled himself tall and laid one hand atop the scarred surface of his desk. He could hear his classmates bridling their horses or starting home on foot. Still his teacher took her time, gathering some books and getting her coat and purse from the closet. The nearly empty room seemed cooler and darker, now that the others had left. From the school yard their voices mingled as they led out the horses. A fly buzzed high at the window.

As his teacher approached, her eyes went soft and deep looking directly into Danny's. She took the seat in front of his and turning around, laid her open arms on his desktop. Danny smelled a light perfume. Never had she been so close. Never had they been so intimate.

Juanita began, almost in a whisper. "Danny, I can see how much getting your eighth grade diploma means to you, how much it must mean to all your family." Her words were unhurried, she smiled. "I don't think it would be right for you to be refused because of being farmed out. Not when you're such a good student. I'd like to help you if I can." She took his hand and squeezed it, resting her other one on top.

Danny's blood banged in his chest. Gently, what appeared to be almost absentmindedly, she began stroking his arm.

He held her gaze and lifted his free hand to touch her shoulder. His hand grew damp through the thin cotton of the dress. "With your help I could do anything." Danny swallowed hard.

"We'll see, Danny." she said softly. "We'll see how things go." She could feel the muscular curve of his forearm and the beating of his pulse under her hand. "We both know you wouldn't have any trouble passing the eighth grade exams. And as far as the time you've missed goes. Maybe I can alter the records. In fact I've been thinking. You might want to give the High School Graduation test a try."

Danny was so astonished he could not answer. Dazed, happy, disbelieving, Danny felt he might break into tears, but he didn't back away. Instead, he placed one hand on each side of her face, leaned over the desk, and lightly kissed her on the mouth.

Juanita felt an astonishing freedom. Of something loosening and slipping away. The filmy white shroud of her mother's shame, of her grandfather's expectations, of the dogmatic saints, it was all unraveling.

For a moment they sat in silence. His teacher rose slowly. How blue his eyes were. How blue! Juanita felt like a schoolgirl herself. "Perhaps though, you should spend some extra time after school, or in the morning early, to make up what you've missed." She found herself speaking softly, "If I tutor you, we could probably get you ready. Sometimes they'll let country schools give the test if they have an exceptional student, and he's old enough and the teacher thinks he's ready."

Outside, already bridled, stood Rider at the hitching post where Lizzie had left him. In a daze Danny untied the reins and thrust his foot into the stirrup. Swinging onto the mare, he nearly threw himself to the ground on the other side. He felt so light. So free.

Danny urged the horse down the lane and onto the dusty road. Nothing could stop him now. Crouching into the mane he pushed her faster. He dared to imagine leaving the farm. Of rescuing Juanita from Humpy Chris. Of going to some place far away with her, of creating a life of his own, a life for both of them. Faster and faster Danny urged the racing horse. The both of them panted, but Danny only pressed the mare more. She was wet and hot and Danny'd grown hard where the animal bounded wildly between his thighs. There sprang from his throat a shout.

Then, just ahead, snaking up the back road, swirling out of the ground toward him, was a lengthening column of dust. At its head was a dark shiny Pontiac. As the car approached Danny saw, hunched over the steering wheel intently looking, the pasty face of Humpy Chris.

Chris glanced up just in time to see a light-haired, blue-eyed boy galloping on a chestnut mare. He swerved the car at the last moment, to keep from hitting him. What was the matter with that kid anyway?

Although Chris had barely seen him, the face lingered. Was his expression one of blazing joy or of shock at evading death? Humpy Chris drew a fresh panatela from his inside pocket, licked it thoroughly and placed it between his lips. He had just settled back again against the dark plush seat when an uncomfortable nagging of having forgotten something rose to his consciousness.

What was it now? The appointment with his lawyer? No, that was Tuesday. Humpy Chris tried picturing his calendar, and the list of things he'd made in the margin, that needed attending. He drew a blank.

He pulled the car to the side of the road searching his suite pants for the sterling silver pocket lighter. He clicked it open and puffed the cigar to flame. Chris sat leisurely for a few moments getting back his breath. He rested an arm out the window.

Juanita would be waiting for him at the school gate.

She could wait a little while. Keeping her waiting now and then was good for their relationship. Sucking deeply on the freshly lit cigar he burst out coughing. When it stopped, that feeling of forgetting something still hadn't subsided. He eased the car back onto the road.

He saw now that whatever was nagging at him had a quality different from the usual business appointments and everyday transactions. Whatever was trying to rise to the surface of remembering was tinged with melancholy, pulling in the direction he resisted most. Had it something to do with Juanita? The car was barely moving. He picked up the speed.

Chris drew thoughtfully on the cigar. By now he had reduced their relationship to business concepts. To terms of efficiency and investments-concepts he understood, that were easily dealt with. Although he kept the reins of a few small businesses in his hands, and many farms as well, he prided himself in managing their marriage as well as any of them.

Chris handled the car cautiously. How inconvenient it was to come clear out here. Luckily Fred's Garage had returned her car earlier that afternoon. Now it was parked curbside, in front of the house. Monday, she could resume driving herself.

Chris knocked off the growing ash. Yes, he understood their relationship. He knew her well. Chris let the smoke out pleasurably. And no one could accuse him of being insensitive. He knew she was often dissatisfied, bored, unfulfilled. So he placed in her path just enough satisfactions to sustain her.

At first it had been the gifts. The most expensive dress or the finest emerald bracelet.

Chris continued on the country road without noticing the landscape. He was remembering the lovely enameled opening egg. A Faberge, made for the Russian nobles. He'd found it at a farm auction of all places. The seller didn't even know what he had.

Chris lightly turned the cigar, the glowing end just touching the lip of the ash tray. It didn't take him long to learn these gifts had to be displayed in order to earn their full return.

He began arranging little escapes for her into the bigger world. The first, he recalled, was when the Museum of Fine Art opened in Fargo. At the time he never would have guessed how much he would grow to enjoy these little forays himself. He saw to it that they got an invitation to the champagne reception.

In the weeks before he told her how the most important people in the state would be there. The most important people in the arts.

He had primed her to a pitch. Everything must be perfect. Her hair. Her clothes. Her jewelry.

Actually he cared nothing about these things. They were so much pretentious fluff. But he hoped by playing to her romantic fantasies he could keep her. Keep her happy. Keep her with him. Keep her trying to please, or at least getting along.

Chris smiled thinking of it. When the time came, he paraded her on his arm in the custom-tailored satin gown while she trembled with excitement.

He'd felt at ease in the company of the governor, the director of arts flown in from Washington, D.C. She lowered her eyes when men looked at her and blushed charmingly. Chris savored the remembering. Perhaps he'd enjoyed the event even more than she. He could stare down anyone in the room. The young artists and musicians he waved away like so many hornets swarming around ripe cherries. Although Chris could not actually picture these memories, he savored their texture, the feeling of power and territory, possession and control.

Chris maneuvered an especially sharp turn in the gravel. And he was proud of himself, too. Proud that even those most satisfying feelings didn't entrap him. He knew enough not to encourage these fleeting friendships. Not to try and hang onto relationships with the outside world. These forays could only work as a stimulant if used sparingly.

Chris never entertained in his own home, and the activities he chose usually involved a hefty monetary contribution. He considered these contributions investments well spent, a tidy bit of business with no further obligation.

Chris nodded in agreement with himself. The cigar between his fingers was no longer lit. He stubbed it in the ash tray. He was approaching the schoolhouse gate, where Juanita stood waiting in the sunshine with a stack of folders under her arm.

How lovely she was. The sun and wind on her face gave her the fresh quality of a schoolgirl. When he leaned over to open passenger door, she flashed a smile. She was beautiful. Chris could hardly believe she was his. Chris turned the car around and headed toward home. They didn't speak for some time, but he was keenly aware of her presence. The smell of her excited him. He was proud. Proud of her. Proud of his choice. But it hadn't always been so smooth.

Those first months, he'd half expected some magic. In their honeymoon bed he'd been shy, hoping for some deep surprise, some profound and intimate acceptance. Enchanted by her beauty he'd imagined her kiss transforming him. But, she'd cringed under his touch. And in their intimacy she never gave evidence of having discovered in him anything hidden. Or precious. Chris drove in silence, still thinking, glancing now and again at his wife.

His latest offering had been this job as a teacher. Was it more of a risk than he'd bargained for? The job had so many variables. So many variables that seemed to be getting out of control. Even the things that worked so well before. Was he losing his grip?

Again he looked at her. Trying to see her as an investment. Trying to cancel out her beauty. She sat with her hands resting on a stack of folders a faraway look on her face: content, satisfied. And he couldn't help it. Beautiful.

But he couldn't let that overtake him. Enchant him. Chris remembered on the train coming home from the charity concert in Grand Forks, she'd had that same look though she hardly sat with him at all. She talked with a woman, younger than herself and a teacher, too, about books he hadn't read. She seemed to know her already, though Chris couldn't remember meeting her. They'd laughed and made little jokes he didn't quite understand. The women embraced when they parted and promised each other to write. And to send books. The next day, Juanita hardly acknowledged the new yellow silk blouse with the hand-made French lace.

 Up popped that feeling again. No, it wasn't that incident on the train. That wasn't what had been bothering him all afternoon. Something else. What was it now? Chris brushed the feeling aside and settled down into the monotony of driving. Hadn't he learned in his other investments not to put too much into any one of them? Didn't any business or enterprise only absorb only so much upgrading before it began the disappointment of diminishing returns? Best to keep them on the hungry side. Well fed projects tended to become lazy and demanding. Yes, perhaps he should make some slight adjustments.

Chris fancied himself a realist. He could play the game and keep on winning if he just kept track of things and saw them as they really were. Even the painful could be used to his advantage- if he worked it right, if he kept control. He knew she thought of those other men and acquaintances. But long ago he'd learned that if she dreamed of other men in their darkened bedroom, so much the better. If his arms could become young and strong and well formed, why complain? Over the years he learned when to let out the silken leash a bit and when to take in the slack.

Juanita smoothed down the cotton skirt over her knees. She smiled quizzically. Was the smile for him or had she been thinking of the teacher friend on the train? Or a passage from one of her books? Was her smile for some imaginary lover? Chris noticed printed on the top folder of the stack she held in her lap the name, Danny Borgen.

"So how did your day go?" Chris finally spoke.

"It looks like all the eighth graders are going to graduate. I have one student though who is very bright, started first grade late so he's older than the others. I might just ask them to send down a high school exam. With a little help, I believe he could pass it. Danny Borgen's his name." Again, Juanita gave him that smile

"Borgen...Borgen...I know that name from somewhere, don't I? Norwegian, huh?" Chris asked, glancing again at the folder. Did that name have something to do with what he was trying to remember?

"I'm not sure." Juanita replied. "He's one of Urs Wagnor's wife's boys. By her first marriage. The oldest one I think."

Humpy Chris pictured once again the tall boy with the eager face on horseback. Was that the Borgen boy? Chris was just about to make some comment about not living until graduation if the boy didn't watch where he was going, when he experienced again the deep sad pangs of remembering.

He realized then that the nagging feeling of having forgotten something he'd had all afternoon didn't have anything to do with Juanita after all. It was before Juanita. Way before Juanita. The memory was from deeper. Much deeper. From when Chris was still a boy.

Could it really be the same or did the face just remind him of it? How long had it been since he'd even thought about the golden boy? Long before this man he had become. Even his name had been different.

*

David Christopher Nielson. His parents picked out the name one hot summer night during their courtship. That night they sat as they did every Friday, legs stretched out on the porch floor, backs identically grooved with the clapboard siding of the white frame farmhouse. They spoke softly, a chorus of crickets just beneath their voices.

His mother, Sarah, was tall and thin with a spotty complexion. The edge of her skirt was pulled to the side and tucked tightly around her leg all the way to the shoe.

They sat on the porch for the coolness and to get away from her younger brothers and sisters. And because her father would not allow the courting couple to leave the house.

For the most part they'd been pleased with each other those evenings, each feeling they had done well, maybe better than could have been hoped.

Whatever might have been missing, whatever little compromises they might have been vaguely aware of, were more than compensated for by the excitement they felt at the idea of starting a family, and the name they'd picked for their first son. David Christopher Nielson. The very sound of it rounded out their union and made them feel complete. It brought to their minds the image of a strong young man with blond hair and very blue eyes. He would be their golden boy.

Two years later when her time came due, Sarah labored hard for three days. The baby was positioned backwards in her womb. When he was born, in addition to the hideous hump, his back was broken. Chris wasn't expected to live. They gave him the name anyway. David Christopher Nielson.

But that name never settled in. The boy never learned to wear it even awkwardly, like an ill-fitting set of clothes. Instead, over the years it gradually gave way to other names. He became "David," and then "Christopher" and then "Chris" and finally "Humpy Chris" (behind his back). The original name seemed to have an identity of its own.

Where that other identity came from the young David Christopher never knew, but as a boy it was always there shimmering beside him. Sometimes he would slip into the space it occupied, a perfect fit. The golden boy. When someone called "David," that other image always came first, strong and clear and blue eyed. The boy he should have been. Those times, he was genuinely startled if he caught sight of his deformed shape reflected in the dusty glass of a shop display window or when he met his glance in the sink mirror as he raised his head after washing up for supper at his aunt's house in town. He would pause then and stare at the overweight boy with the thick mass to the side of his neck, the lifeless hair and the unbelieving soft brown eyes.

~13~

Urs was waiting in the barn when Wayne and Lizzie arrived. He wasn't in a good mood. "I expect you kids to have that pasture cleared by night fall. Annie and Margaret are out there now. And where the hell is Danny?" Urs had been having trouble with the seed drill, a Minneapolis Moline he'd hooked up to the tractor.

In the small pasture near the barn, Queenie was hitched to the stone boat while Annie and Margaret cleared. Loosening a fair sized rock, Margaret picked something out of the dirt and rubbed it clean with her thumb. "Look here, Annie, an arrowhead. Put it in your pocket for luck. People who made it lived here a long time ago."

Urs had been adamant about putting this land into production. He was determined to have his way about the flax, even if it meant pasturing the horses along the side of the road and in the margins between the fields, even if it meant buying the seed himself.

Together mother and daughter hefted a large rock and let it fall, banging to the wooden bottom of the stone boat. Considering the size and number of stones, it was doubtful this piece of land had ever been farmed. When it was full, Annie climbed on top sweating. Margaret signaled Queenie. She leaned against the sled as they rested a bit. "Annie, what do you think of a new baby coming?"

Annie lifted her shoulders with a questioning shrug. "I don't know. A new little sister? When she's old enough, I'll teach her how to farm. "

Margaret sharply pulled-in her breath. Her stomach tightened. So Annie had heard. She thought for a moment before answering. "First when the baby is little we'll have to take good care of it. Feed it when it's hungry and rock it when it cries. You can be my helper,

Annie. It will be a long time before it can learn to farm. We don't really know yet if it will be a girl or a boy."

"But I heard the Hebamme. She said it was a girl." Annie fingered the arrowhead in her pocket. It was flat and cool and sharp edged. She liked the feel of its bumpy bite against her finger. Annie only saw the top of her mother's head and the bulge of her belly as she looked down from high on the sled. "Didn't you tell Dad? He thinks it will be a boy."

Margaret stood thoughtfully for a moment. "The Hebamme isn't always right, Annie. Sometimes she can't tell. She just guesses." Then, pushing herself further. "It's best not to say anything about it at all. Keep it under your hat, alright? For all we know your dad might be right." Margaret wiped dirt from her hands onto her apron. Was she entangling Annie too, in her lie?

Then, from high up on the load Annie was distracted. She saw something she'd never seen before. Rocks of a uniform size formed a large circle. And what was that at one end? Was that a head and there opposite, a tail? Suddenly she saw what it was... a turtle! There were dark holes where one foot should be.

"Oh, Momma, look there's a turtle in the rocks. Come up here and look. See, the head there and the tail and feet?" Annie barely contained her excitement pointing as if she had discovered a new world.

Margaret was glad to have the subject changed. She stood on tip toe, following Annie's gestures. Yes, the pattern of rocks did seem to be in the shape of a turtle.

"Annie, my father said once it was Indians' land around here. Indians made the arrowhead. He said sometimes they put the rocks in shapes like that. There was a turtle like that only a lot bigger, over by the lake, by where we used to live." Annie's thoughts ran wild. This was part of that other whole world only Annie knew. A whole world it must be. And this was a part she never knew was here. Right here! Her mother had seen it too.

By the time Danny rode into the yard, Margaret was working in the garden. Wayne and Lizzie had taken her place and were digging out stones and loading them. Annie was in the field too, gesturing in a panic trying to make them stop.

"Indians made it a long time ago," Danny heard Annie screaming. There were tears in her throat. "It's magic. Leave it alone!" Annie was replacing stones, saving the picture of the turtle.

"Shut up, Annie. Stop that now." Wayne dragged her forcefully back as she wriggled out of his grip. "Now, unload that sled! Right now Annie! Don't you have a brain in your head?" He walloped her on the backside. "Now get moving!" Danny stopped for only a moment. What was this all about?

"Danny! Danny!" Annie screamed. "They're wrecking it. They're wrecking the turtle. Indians made it. It's magic!"

"You better get out there and give Urs a hand." Margaret said as Danny approached the garden. "He expected you home a long time ago." Danny hesitated, caught for a moment between seeing to Annie and getting to work. He hurried to the house.

By the time he'd changed clothes, Annie was working alongside Wayne and Lizzie, wailing as loud as she could, letting the tears flow. Snot hung from her nose and she hiccupped and twitched trying to get air. Now the turtle was ruined and Danny didn't even stop to see what was wrong.

"Shut up, you big bawling calf," Lizzie commanded. "You big baby."

Danny joined Urs where he stood studying the contraption he had rigged between the seed drill and the tractor, in an attempt to make the planting a one-man operation. Urs glowered. "Where the hell have you been?" Then without waiting for an explanation, "Get on that seed drill and get this seed in the ground. If we have to work all night, we're going to get this in. This weather won't hold forever."

The last thing Danny wanted to do now was get Urs more upset. With Urs on the tractor, Danny sat on the cold metal seat of the drill lowering and raising the depth of the seeder at the end of each round. Danny's movements immediately fell into the familiar rhythms. With horses only one of them was needed to plant. Now with the tractor it took them both.

Back and forth they made the rounds; Danny did his best to pay attention through the monotony. Soon he found himself trying to keep Juanita from his mind. He brought his attention back time and time again to the work.

Then from where Danny sat he could see Urs's idea. The three-bottom seed drill had been made to use with horses, the driver on the seat working the levers with one hand and maneuvering the horses with the other. That had always been a trick for Urs considering his hand. Now Danny saw that the three-bottom duck foot could be rigged for use from the seat of the tractor. Urs had attached a rope and pulley system of sorts in order to operate the levers from where he sat. It was an innovative idea and would have made the operation much simpler. But Danny could see the problem too. The rope was frayed and fuzzy here and there, where when it went slack, got caught in the machinery.

Danny knew better than to compliment Urs on his ingenuity or to offer a suggestion. In Urs's mind wouldn't a suggestion seem like criticism? Wouldn't he take a compliment as some kind of back-handed comment about his hand? Danny swallowed his frustration. Always walking on eggshells, trying not to upset Urs. Danny was sick of it.

Then a new kind of thought sprouted. No wonder Danny and Juanita understood each other. Were made for each other! Didn't they both live with someone with a weakness, a flaw, that everyone could plainly see, but they who were closest had to pretend not to? Was it like that for Juanita too? Did she spend her life walking on eggshells too? That was no life for her or for himself! They deserved better. They deserved each other and, dare he think it, loved each other. That realization took Danny's breath away. But it made sense, didn't it?

They continued planting for almost an hour before Urs turned off the tractor, took down the canvas water bag and swallowed a long drink. He offered the water to Danny without looking at him.

But Urs had settled down considerably. The vibrations of the motor and the rich smell of the opening earth had eased the tension.

"Danny, go tell Margaret to have Annie bring us out a sandwich in an hour or so. I want to get as much done in daylight as we can. And stop by the machine shed and take that cable off the hay rack. Coil it up and bring it out here. I'm going to change out that damn rope. Bring a lantern too, and extra kerosene. Hurry up now."

*

Annie was excited to go so far from the house so late in the day. She'd followed the sound of the tractor to the windbreak, carrying her gifts: bologna sandwiches, canned chokecherries, and a thermos of coffee. The trees had all put out buds and some were leafing out. Tiny chartreuse shapes unfurled in bright contrast to the watery blue sky. The land rose and fell in subtle swells. All the way she planned in her head, to tell Danny about the turtle in the field, how she'd seen it first, how she meant to make one herself, smaller, at her little farm under the bush.

And then she saw Danny riding behind Urs on the tractor and, too excited to wait, she set the jar of chokecherries down and the lunchbox, too, and waved and shouted herself hoarse until the motor stopped and Danny jumped to the ground and walked over.

"Annie, don't be distracting me when I'm working with machinery! I could lose a thumb or my whole hand even, just like that," he said, snapping his fingers.

On her way back to the house Annie turned every few steps to watch them back at work. Danny no longer followed on the seed drill but worked at covering the furrows by hand. Near the pond there came a place where she could no longer hold them both in her line of vision. Danny lagged so far behind that she'd have to turn in order to see him. A sadness rose in her throat. If they would just come closer together. If they would just come close enough for her to see them both at the same time, without having to choose. A swath of Dutch clover bloomed at Annie's feet. She picked a few for the bunny.

Annie turned again to the pond and its slick, smooth, shining skin on the belly of the earth. It was lapping gently up and down, up and down like slow breathing.

Then, from somewhere on the water, came a splashing sound and movement. Annie stood absolutely still. From the shadows, two brown birds floated low in the water toward each other. The underside of their necks flashed white. Pointing and dipping their bills they began shaking their heads. Annie watched, not moving. They swam side by side raising their upper bodies from the water-- wings slightly lifted.

Suddenly the pair darted forward, dancing across the surface nearly to the center of the pond. Annie let go her breath. "How beautiful." she whispered.

Then, she had that feeling. That funny scary feeling but peaceful too. From that day she tried to swim alone. Before, she'd always clung to Danny's neck as he kicked off stirring the muddy bottom. But it had never been enough. Annie had always longed for the clear water at the center and of floating free.

The day Urs found Annie and pulled her from the water, he'd struggled to land himself. He'd never learned to swim. On the grassy bank, he hit her back 'til red welts appeared. Water gushed from her mouth. When she sat up gasping, stunned and startled, Urs shook her hard. *"Nicht tun Sie jemals wieder*!" Don't you ever do that again! His voice was tough and loud as he pointed with the one giant finger. *"Sie Glueck lebendig zu sein*!" You're lucky you're alive! Lucky I even saw you! Urs was shaking. Tears welled in his eyes. "Don't you ever go in that pond again. Do you understand me! Do You!" Like a hammer blow, Urs was exhausted. Bone Tired. Dripping wet, he leaned to Anne and took her face in his hands. Suddenly there was tenderness.

Strange, through it all Annie didn't cry. Afterwards, she merely sat quietly. Pulled from the water Annie thought, this is how it feels to be born. Everything wet and new. Even her arm was shining, and her father's eyes. But there was something else, too. Something she had seen under there, down under the water.

"Now the birds are looking for it too," Annie whispered softly to herself standing very still watching and remembering. "I saw it real good. I really did. At first it was kind of blurry, a flat round disk like thing. But then it uncurled. A snake came out. I was afraid then, afraid that it would bite me. While I looked, the head steadied straight up and I saw it was really a flower. A very pretty pinkish flower. I thought it was a snake, but it wasn't. Cause the head opened up. The head was a flower.

Again the birds were splashing. "And now the birds are here. Dancing on the water." The light was almost gone. A chorus of frogs rose as the birds disappeared into the marshes. Water was gently lapping at her feet. Barely moving. Shining. Breathing in and breathing out. Annie started off toward the farmyard, the stone arrowhead weighting her pocket.

~14~

Humpy Chris pulled the car into the driveway and got out to open the garage door. Juanita went in to start dinner. Their house was a two-story brick one, modest when considered against some of the fine homes in Minneapolis or Fargo, but still the finest in a town like Drake, where extravagance was frowned upon, considered wasteful, disgraceful, even. No family in Drake had enough money long enough to give up frugality. Those who had managed to put away a tidy sum, kept news of their good fortune to themselves.

Humpy closed the garage doors and collected the newspaper before entering the front door. In the kitchen Juanita placed the macaroni and cheese hot dish along with the whitefish in the oven. It had been prepared earlier by Mrs. Jensen. When Juanita began teaching, Humpy agreed to have the woman do the grocery shopping, prepare the dinners and pack the lunch box. She kept a grocery list on a nail inside the cupboard door but Juanita seldom added anything to it. Each day Mrs. Jensen left the evening meal covered with wax paper held in place by a rubber band, in the Frigid-aire for Juanita to put in the oven.

Throughout the dinner the couple barely spoke. They sat across the table from each other, neither able to think of anything to say. The only sounds were the discrete chewing and the clink of silverware against china.

Afterwards Chris went to the living room with his coffee to read the paper. Mostly local news. The price of cattle, hogs, wheat, the weather forecast. The sky grew dark. There was a slight draft from around the windows. Coldness spread through the room. His feet grew numb in the shiny dress shoes and thin socks.

Chris crumpled the paper and returned to the kitchen where Juanita was finishing up the dishes. "I'll be down at the store for a while," he said.

In a moment Juanita was standing alone, with only the sound of the car easing out of the driveway, and the hum of the new electric Frigid-aire.

Humpy liked going to the jewelry store alone at night. It was one of the few places he truly felt at home. The fire of the gemstones excited him and he liked being surrounded by things of value that he owned. He also liked the privacy.

All his life Chris had been more or less alone, although it wasn't until he started college that he'd actually had any privacy. At home his mother fussed over him constantly, waiting on him like a little prince or a fragile invalid. At his aunt's house in town he'd slept on the living room davenport. Every morning after he heard the discordant squawking of her treasured cuckoo clock, he would rise to fold the bedding while his aunt came walking through making her way to the kitchen where she stirred oats into the boiling water.

All his life he never knew when someone might come walking through. He'd felt invaded. At school though he'd been excused from most sports and showering too, they did insist he "dress out" for physical education. He did it quickly, choosing a locker away from the others, doing his best to hide behind the door. Sometimes, one of the boys would walk through and shut the locker, exposing Chris to the others. Some pointed and laughed while others looked away. Though these indignities made Chris feel small, so small he wanted to disappear, nothing shamed him like the doctor who made him stand naked under the glaring lights, examining. The mirrors on three sides Chris avoided desperately.

While living with his aunt, Chris learned to fortify himself against the teasing town kids and at her insistence studied hard. He did well in school and on his own, learned the basics of classical art and music. Those years he still glimpsed the golden boy, who he was meant to be, the boy Chris still thought through some miracle of medicine or magic, he might become. His birthright.

But in his nightmares the young Chris was pursued. Pursued by people dark and barrel-chested, with dirty fingernails and overalls. People who said "*Dis*" and "Dat" who spoke a bastardized English and bastardized German. He shrunk from the skinny arms of his mother and the averted glances of his father. He kept his mind's eye straining for that other shining boy the others couldn't see.

Humpy Chris pulled the Pontiac into his spot at the front of the jewelry store and turned off the lights. How much he had changed since then. And though life had been better in college, he had to earn that better life. With courage and luck he had. Humpy unlocked the door to the store and secured it again upon entering. The lighted glass display case filled the room with an eerie glow. The clump of keys made a jarring sound as he released them on the glass.

*

By the time Chris entered college, David Christopher Neilson had become Christopher. After the first semester, he invested a portion of his scholarship money in the stock market, for at that time Christopher was living for nothing in the attic bedroom of his business professor. A room of his own for the first time.

Near the end of his sophomore year, in that airless attic room, its wallpaper blooming with stains, Christopher began to feel secure in his privacy. There he came to terms with himself.

The school year was nearly over and spring had come in strong and early. Why shouldn't he take off his shirt and work at his study table in this heat? Like any other young man at the university? He could hear the teacher's family downstairs listening to the Victrola. What was it now? Something Baroque. Bach? Oh, yes, Magnificent. That was it. Chris smiled, pleased to have identified the piece.

Standing away from the window and the mirror, Christopher took a deep breath. Now he would do it. Yes, like any other young man at the university in this heat. He unbuttoned and removed his shirt. No one would bother him here, he reassured himself, trembling.

Only on Tuesday did his teacher climb the steps with The Wall Street Journal. It came by train, already outdated. Together they poured over the prices of the various stocks.

After World War I, the bottom fell out of the wartime grain prices and banks were closing. Early on North Dakota farmers were plunged into the Depression. The stock market on the other hand was doing very well indeed. Although Christopher didn't have enough savings of his own to make a purchase, his teacher had been investing for some time and allowed him to piggyback on his purchases in return for Christopher's amazing luck at picking stocks.

But that was only on Tuesdays, Christopher reassured himself standing before the mirror. This was Wednesday. His teacher wouldn't be creaking up the stairs today.

Christopher removed his undershirt and stepped out of his trousers and drawers. Up until that moment he had only undressed for a hurried sponge bath or to change quickly from one set of clothes to another, and of course for the doctors. Christopher stood before the full-length mirror with the explicit purpose of looking at himself. The book he had found lay open on his study table.

He'd returned to school a few days early during Christmas break and had wandered the library, devoid even of the sounds of students turning pages and scratching at their notebooks. And there in the dusky stacks he'd discovered it quite by accident.

Anomalies and Curiosities of Medicine

Being
an encyclopedic collection
of rare and extraordinary cases,
and of the most striking instances
in all branches of medicine and surgery,
derived from an exhaustive research of medical literature
from its origins to the present day
abstracted, classified, annotated, and indexed.
with
296 illustrations in the text
and 12 half-tone plates

After reading the title page, heat rose to his ears. Beads of sweat broke out across his brow and upper lip. He had to have it. The assistant librarian sat in the main entrance, near the door. How could Christopher bear the look on her face when he checked it out? How could he write his name on the card under that title?

The place was deserted. Lucky, yes, wasn't he the lucky one. No one was there to see him open his briefcase and place the book quickly inside. At the coat rack, the assistant librarian paid no attention as he put on the long wool coat, the cap and scarf. She didn't watch as he bent, slipping his shoes into the black rubber six buckle boots.

Outside, a shocking bitter wind. The streets vacant. There was very little snow. A dead mottled gray stretched from horizon to horizon interrupted by the great holiness of black, leafless trees.

That winter the cold sank into the ground freezing pipes, killing hibernating insects, squirrels and prairie dogs. Northern pike, walleyes, and perch froze solid in the lakes. The sinking cold killed spring bulbs and young flowering trees.

Nearly every night that winter, after his studies, Christopher rolled over in bed embracing the book, pulling up the bed covers. He left just enough of an opening in the blankets to feebly light the pages with their grainy photos.

Chapter 1

Genetic anomalies;
Ministration; vicarious and compensatory,
from the skin, from the breasts, from the extremities,
in men
impregnation without completion of the copulative act,
artificial impregnation, conception with deficient organs,
children of different colors.

While he read, the sound of his breathing manifest in whitish
yellow puffs that lingered for a moment and then dissolved.

Chapter V
Major Terata;
Monstrosities;
artificial production of monsters, triple monsters, double
monsters, Hindoo sisters, Siamese twins, Porcupine man,
Elephant man, Snake boy.

Those nights, Christopher had half expected to turn the next
page only to see a picture of himself naked, tripled, before the three-
way mirror. Tricked by the doctor.   Though he knew this couldn't
be, each disturbing page made him ask: Was he one of them? A
morbid fascination kept him at it. He reached up from the covers to
turn the pages. Immediately his hand had grown cold.

Chapter XIV
Miscellaneous surgical anomalies;
Marvelous recoveries from multiple injuries;
recoveries after injuries by machinery,
with multiple fractures,
recoveries from high falls, high dives,

operations on the extreme young and old.
Repeated operations,
Bill Roth's marvelous operation,
self performed surgical operations.
Chinese foot binding, manufacture of cripples, castration,
mutilation of the genital organs.....

Christopher had looked in detail at each fantastic violation of nature. He had imagined the texture of the scaled skin. The curve of each twisted limb. He grew to like the book. He kept it under the edge of the bed, hidden, even in the privacy of the attic room. He had paged through it nearly every night.

Then, months later in the heat of a spring night, he stood before the mirror. By force of will Christopher beat back those twisted images, those scaled textures. Now, he told himself, he was over all that.

Before the mirror, at first he did not allow his gaze to fall anywhere but on his face. It was neither ugly nor handsome, the brown hair thinning already a little on top and growing low on the neck. The eyes were large and tilted a bit downward at their outer corners, the nose, slightly bulbous. Sweat collected on his brow and at the temples. He attributed it to the heat.

Christopher was having difficulty turning his head and so leaned forward, bowing to his reflection. The sloping ceiling of the close, airless attic room would have bent him if he had not already been bent in the womb. He lifted his eyes to study the raised right shoulder curving sharply in and the massive hump. Slowly he let his eyes drop. There was considerable webbing at the neck, giving the appearance that his head sat on his shoulders. Sweat collected there as well.

From the waist down Christopher looked perfectly normal. His hips. Sexual parts. Thighs, legs, and feet. "It's not so bad," he whispered to himself in the sultry room. He practiced different postures. "It has a kind of beauty of its own," he whispered.

Then, he was a child again. The old lady at church seeking him out and giving his hump a strong rubbing until he felt a surprising restful comfort as she followed him down the crowded isle. "It's for luck," she'd smiled down at him when he turned, questioning with his eyes.

Remembering, Christopher reached up and gave his bare hump a firm rub. As he stepped back into his trousers, his hump and the one hand were warm with the luck.

Later, when a carriage stopped in the street below he jumped up from his worktable and put on his shirt.

*

Chris turned on the jeweler's light at his worktable in the back room of the store. Here, he often went without his shirt and his trousers too, when the evenings were hot. Sometimes, he imagined eyes peering under the pulled shades as he puttered around in his boxer shorts.

Chris went to the safe where he kept his favorite stones. He seldom looked at them anymore. Although they had little of the character or value of the more recent additions, they still retained a special feeling.

When Christopher started at the university, he had been shy and studious. He lived like a pauper investing every penny into stocks. Those years, with the help of his teacher they'd done very well.

But it was his junior year when he really came into his own. He gradually awakened to what he felt to be an astonishing fact. People had a hard time telling him no. Especially people who wanted to appear kind or fair. In time he learned to use this knowledge to get what he wanted.

Humpy Chris opened the little black pouch he'd removed from the safe. He'd even managed to get these. They had started it all.

His third year at Minot State he created the Future Business Men's Club with his teacher as faculty adviser. Minot was an agricultural school and teacher's college; not many students signed up. When Christopher ran for treasurer, no one else was nominated.

He had a hard time believing how easy it was. Anything at all he wanted, all he had to do was find the right person—those who seemed embarrassed in his presence, or overly helpful—and ask. If possible, they always saw to it he got his way. It was like having magical powers.

As a fundraising project, he secured the contract for senior class rings. With stocks he could double and triple his money but with jewelry, he learned, the pay off was tenfold—as it had been with those silly rings. Especially with no overhead. Nothing to it.

The next year he invested his own money for the senior rings, a pittance compared to what the students paid, and that's where his money was when the stock market crashed. Most of the students made regular payments, but a couple in the end couldn't pay the remainder. Was that his problem?

Gradually Christopher underwent a change in style. He began wearing specially tailored suits, bought a used Buick. Funny how clothes and cars attracted much longer streams of people, in positions he had once respected, who would let him build on his success, even at their own expense if he just pushed. They honestly seemed unable to resist him.

And then the girls. They too seemed to need to prove something. He'd ask one out to a football game or school social, and sometimes later end up in the car with her along the river.

Oddly, only two seniors failed to make the last payment on their class rings. Their fathers were bankers and their rings had been ordered special, each embellished with a half-carat diamond.

Humpy laid out these very stones under the single light at his worktable. They didn't have the value of much of his collection but all the same, how they shone. How they sparkled in the light.

Those stones and the profit from the rings had been his first big break, and after graduation, he had started this little business in Drake. This small jewelry store. Juanita even helped out for a time when they first married. But selling engagement rings, and wedding bands, during the Depression, barely covered expenses. His real break came in another way: land.

When the bad times came, working closely with the bank, Chris had picked up one little farm in foreclosure for a song. Commodity prices had gone through the floor, banks closed, stocks were worthless—but turned out the lady at church had been right: he, Humpy Chris, had been lucky.

The politics fueling the luck were crazy; he'd had to be smart, too—farmers unions and cooperatives sprung up overnight, rising out of the old North Dakota Socialist Party. It was the waves of Norwegian immigrants who were behind all the trouble. Many had been long shore men, union members from the docks of Norway who brought with them their organizing skills and socialist ideas.

By 1932 those ruffians formed The Farmer's Holiday Organization and elected the populist William Langer governor of the state.

Chris shook his head remembering. Nothing had been predictable or secure. But exciting?—you betcha. There were imposed moratoriums on mortgage foreclosure sales, embargoed shipments of grain and the capitol building in Bismarck burned to the ground. Policies and politics changed overnight. There was so much turmoil that the state had four governors in seven months.

Then in the midst of all that chaos, Chris had that one real stroke of luck. He had followed the changes closely and made his move at just the right time. There was nothing those farmers could do about it. Five farms each one dependent on the others, like a house of cards, just fell into his hands. From then on it was easy.

Chris rubbed his palms together warming to the memories of his luck. They had been small farms owned by local German farmers, but it had been a Norwegian organizer who had the poppen-amie scheme that brought them all down. Not much more than a kid really, sticking his nose in were it didn't belong. Why Chris hadn't been much more than a kid himself. He sat back in the chair, suddenly tired, struggling for breath as though he was drowning. As though he'd been struggling to stay afloat all his life.

Chris had been fiddling with the stones, hardly seeing them. Then, that feeling seeped back again. That disturbing feeling he had in the car, while he drove out to get his wife. Was it the memory of his youth that brought it up? The golden boy? Was it the memory of that straight, strong, blond haired boy a-horseback?

Chris shook his head to clear it of these thoughts and leaned into his stones. Then it struck him. Wasn't it about the time he acquired these diamonds, when the presence of that perfect shimmering twin dimmed from view, evaporated? Wasn't that when his name had changed again? To just Chris.

Now at middle-age, he was Mr. Nielson to his face, though he knew that in every other reference people called him Humpy Chris.

But wasn't he rich? And didn't he have for a wife the most beautiful woman in the county? And the way he looked, hadn't he accepted it over the years, even used it to his advantage? And those dark beasts that chased him, hadn't he left them all far behind? Chris arranged the stones once more on the velvet pouch. A starburst. Then a square like an acre parcel. Then a circle. Like a noose. How they shone.

"I'm rich" Chris whispered in the empty room. He liked the sound of the word though it was one he normally didn't say out loud and certainly never in the company of others.

"I'm rich" he whispered again, aware of the full ripeness in his throat, the slight movement of his lips. And though he never wore diamonds himself, here with the shades drawn tight and the back room dusky and dark except for the single jeweler's spotlight, he lost himself to the sparkling stones and the private joy they glinted back at him.

In a little while, he returned the gems to their velvet purse, quietly listened to the tumblers as he spun the combination of the safe and after picking up the keys and locking the shop securely climbed into the Pontiac and headed home to seek out his wife.

~15~

From the bedroom window, Annie saw the lantern swinging as Danny and her father worked the crest of the hill by moonlight. When the two men came in from the field, they sounded happy parking the tractor and stomping the dirt off their shoes on the porch. "*Harte Arbeit gibt guten Schlaf*, Danny." Annie could hear the smile in her father's voice as he repeated the familiar expression. Hard work makes good sleep.

They all were sleeping well when the king birds started their chatter. Then came the hoots of an owl. On hearing it Margaret rose, lit a kerosene lantern and made her way to morning prayers. As mourning doves began their soft cooing, daylight seeped color into the vast North Dakota sky. Danny and Wayne dressed and headed to the barn. By the time the meadowlarks were trilling, everyone was up and about their business. Lizzie and Margaret had breakfast on the table--dumpf noodla, eggs and bread.

After breakfast, the boys hauled out the gasoline-powered washing machine from the corner of the kitchen where it had been stored, while Liz followed with the broom, sweeping where the smell of oily dust lurked all winter. Annie followed Urs as he collected a five-gallon can of gasoline and a tarp, while Margaret ran here and there smiling at the progress, anticipating once again doing her laundry in the open air.

All winter that closed-in human stink made Margaret a claustrophobic. Cold nights they'd used pee buckets. The soot of coal and corn cobs and cooking grease had coated the white enamel paint of the kitchen. One week ago today, Margaret had aired the quilts and blankets on the clothes line and opened all the windows and doors to let in the fresh air. But this was the Saturday she waited for. When she could do the washing outside.

As the boys rounded the corner struggling with the machine, Urs and Annie lent a hand. They all heaved in unison lifting it onto the platform, manhandling it into position.

Then, they stepped back, ringing the platform in silent satisfaction. The morning sun shone from their folded arms and open faces. Even Urs, usually so dark, shuffled side to side with spring birds circling in his mind. Clinging to them all was the sweet, salty smell of physical work.

Then they all went their separate ways attending to their chores.

Annie stood before the kitchen window doing the breakfast dishes. Those moments of quiet, peaceful satisfaction were so short. She put the plate down and stood once again in silence with her arms folded. It seemed to her that they should all go back; the whole family should stand again smiling and silent ringing the platform, admiring their efforts maybe all morning and well into the afternoon. But no they couldn't do that. Urs and Danny had to take the cream and eggs to Drake. And there was the garden to be weeded, and the washing. And the dishes, too, Annie supposed, reaching again for a submerged plate. She was surprised to find how cool the water had become.

The kitchen was becoming unbearably hot. On wash day the cook stove was hard pressed to keep up with the demand for more and more hot water, and now that the flies were out full force, in spite of her frequent spraying, Margaret insisted the door and windows stay shut. Luckily most of the work could be done outside. Only Annie suffered in the heat.

"Move on back out of the way now, Annie." Lizzie's arm trembled with the weight of the kettle. Very carefully, she poured the scalding water over the soapy dishes. "You got way too much soap in that dishwater. I'm gonna tell Mom you're wasting." Liz tipped the pot to the last dribble before filling it again with cold water and replacing it along with the rest of the pots and kettles and buckets that were being heated on the stove. "Now don't you wait for that to turn to cold pig slop. Dry'em just as quick as you can stand it." From the open door she offered this one more bit of advice before hurrying out with another steaming bucket.

Annie dried the dishes without thinking. From outside came the put, put, put of the washing machine. On tiptoes, Annie watched. A disjointed crack ran down the window glass.

Margaret was threading dripping clothes into the wringer. The rollers pulled swiftly and smoothly until Margaret jerked to the other side of the cracked glass. Annie tightened her hold on the plate in her hands. It seemed to her, her mother's fingers were too close. Could that dangling strap from her apron get caught and pull her mother through, squeezing out her blood like soapy water?

Annie gripped the plate tighter nearly snapping it in two. Her mother repeated the motion again and again. Annie shut her eyes and willed Margaret to the edge of the platform. Annie willed her mother to stand as she was earlier, with folded arms strong and safe with the family all around.

Lizzie stormed into the kitchen with a flurry of activity. She immediately put away the stacks of dishes and utensils strung out along the counter. Annie kept one worried eye on her mother. The rhythm of her work continued at a steady pace.

 Lizzie clattered and banged. What was she up to? She was on a rampage, working fast and furious. Normally her older sister made the most of these moments when her mother wasn't watching. At the very least, she'd slow her pace and sometimes even prop up her feet and page through one of her three cherished movie magazines.

But, today she hummed something fast and jazzy, working uncomplainingly, eagerly. By the time Lizzie hurried back outside to finish hanging up the clothes the kitchen was swept, the dishes put away and the dish towels drying on the hook.

Annie followed, curious. At the clothesline Liz bent over the basket piling her shoulders high with wet towels and shirts and socks. She took them from her shoulders one by one shaking then with a snap. Annie offered to hand up the clothes pins, but this only slowed down Liz's well coordinated and much practiced skill.

Annie stood watching with admiration. In a few moments there was a growing row of gently waving colors, emerging as if by magic from the thin wire. Every so often between the bending and the snapping and the hanging, Liz would pause, letting some damp silky fabric billow cool against her face and arms. Annie saw this was Liz's kingdom. It was as if she owned the very air where she worked. When Annie stepped inside her circle of power she could smell it. A dark salty smell that belonged only to Liz.

And all around her it was blue. Blue jeans, blue work shirts, blue overalls, blue coveralls. Blue shirts. Blue dresses. Blue half pants. Blue interspersed with the dresses made from the delicately printed flour sacks and the white: underwear, slips, socks, undershirts. Behind her was the blue, blue sky.

Today, the air felt of sure spring. The threat that winter might sigh one last chill breath had diminished over the past week until now the day shimmered. They were going to meet the neighbor kids on the high plateau between the farms for baseball. Flocks of sand hill cranes, mixed with a few whoopers, flew overhead searching out nesting areas.

The high plateau was flat on top and about a mile from both families' property. It bordered on the road and rose above the surrounding, faintly rolling, hills. On the east was a deeply eroded gully. At its mouth the ground was littered with ashes and blackened cans and broken bottles.

As the children approached, the plateau loomed before them like some huge shaggy beast grazing on the gentle plain. Its sides were covered with long brown grass interspersed with patches of Russian thistle. Where the prairie met the sharply rising ground, the children staked the horses, and started up on foot.

Annie began the climb lagging behind her brother and sister. She surged upward trying to catch up. Last year's dry and matted buffalo grass rose to her knees. She struggled up a slope too steep to have ever seen a mower.

Annie concentrated on digging in with first one edge of her shoe and then the other. Twice she slipped. Her face was hot and her breath quick with trying to keep up. Then up and up she climbed in the final effort.

When Annie finally broke the crest, she was taken aback with what she saw. Here there was very little grass. The flat surface had been constantly swept by winds and scoured blowouts dotted the surface.

She was far, far above the prairie floor. The land and sky, two rolling plains stretched away and away until they met in the far distance. The air itself seemed of a finer texture as a breeze cooled the film clinging to her face. Empty seed pods and the long dry grass on the hillside at her feet rustled and chattered and nodded in the breeze. Annie listened. She could almost pick out a word here and there, but the voices whispered just beneath the edge of hearing.

For a few moments Annie had difficulty orienting herself. The land she knew so intimately was hardly recognizable from this panoramic view. Those sloping interruptions which seemed so obtrusive in her daily life were now gentle breaths rising in succession into the distance. There at the base of one stood a few tiny cows. They looked as though they had been carved from soft pine with some sharp tool and then carefully painted. Off to one side a miniature tractor chugged silently.

Gradually, through the maze of stripes and patches of pasture and field stubble and dirt she retraced her path. There, not nearly as far as she would have thought, could that be the house and barns? The kitchen window glinted. If she waved her arms would her mother see her?

Hot with climbing, the seed pods chattering at her feet, a sensation of power rose from Annie's stomach. By raising her hand at arm's length, she could blot out the farmhouse altogether. How insignificant it all looked. The farm that dictated the pattern of their lives was drab and unimpressive, with its details obscure and the powerful presence of the family scattered. Against the wide space of browns and blues, the farm's absence was hardly noticeable. Annie heard herself calling as a power rose up and out of her open mouth. A long slow sound like ooooooohhhhhh spread with her breath and was carried by the wind. Then she stood in silence. The wind was blowing backwards.

~16~

Margaret appreciated the time alone. She brought in a basket of dry laundry and sat at the kitchen table folding the cool, sweet towels. When was the last time she'd worked at such a leisurely pace? In spite of what Margaret had felt when she first came to this farm, now it was home. Maybe more her own home than any other place.

She looked about the room. Margaret was almost satisfied with its appearance. The calico curtains had faded a bit, but she was saving flour sacks and had enough material to start new ones--a slightly different pattern, but also with the tiny purple flowers.

That first year, Margaret had fashioned the farm as much as possible after the house she'd shared with Lars. She scrubbed and painted and hammered, but it didn't work. The crudely planked floors of these small rooms looked silly in rubbed wax. In that Urs was right; porch paint fit them fine.

When she and Urs laid out the garden, Margaret tried again to bring back a bit of the life she'd lost. The patch of overgrown prairie to the side of the house, she envisioned as her old garden as viewed from the upstairs bedroom. She'd unfolded a sketch for Urs to see how she hoped the new garden would look.

"These white rocks around the edge, what's their purpose?" Urs had asked, unbelieving.

"It's just rocks painted white. To make it look nice." Margaret said.

"The porch needs whitewashing before a bunch of rocks. Where do you get your ideas, woman?"

"But I'll be doing the gardening." Her lame argument rang empty against his good sense.

"And what's this?" Urs said pointing to her drawing of poppies and daises along the path leading to the house.

"They're perennials," she argued, "giving pleasure for years, and only bought once."

"We can't eat flowers," had been Urs's response. "A good field garden is all we need."

"But with a little garden by the house, we'll have rosemary to sprinkle on the *salzkartoffelm*." Urs liked his *salzkartoffelm*. "And in the fall I can trade tomatoes with Katie for apples. We'll have *Himmel uhd Erd*," heaven and earth: apples, potatoes with bacon in one dish.

"Don't get so fancy, Margaret. All we really need is an acre of potatoes and a few rows of cabbages. Get off your high horse."

"I'm not arguing against potatoes or cabbages, but if you want sauerkraut the Weisskohl will have to be tended to and kept shaded."

"The best way to a man's heart is through his stomach." Margaret took the old saying seriously.

Margaret smoothed the towels, folding and stacking them in a neat pile. She got her little house garden, all right. Even got Urs to help put it in.

Urs had got into the area with a horse and two-bottom plow. The space between the clothesline and the corn crib was too tight for the tractor. With spades they'd chopped the turned furrows and shook off the matted grass.

Before that day Margaret hadn't thought there was any physical work Urs couldn't do. She'd never thought of him as being crippled. When a rock appeared too large for his grasp, Urs had scowled and pointed with his chin for Margaret to remove it. As if he were merely ordering her about.

She'd stop shaking the sod then and maneuver the heavy boulder to the edge of the plot. But as the morning progressed, Urs let down his guard. When one large boulder fell from his grasp, Margaret hoisted it to the garden edge without a word. Color rose to Urs's face. "You mind your own business shaking those clods," was his thanks.

By afternoon, he forgot his self-consciousness as they spread the whole area with seasoned manure and mixed it into a fine level bed. At day's end they arranged the stones culled from the plot, neatly and naturally, around the garden's edge. Margaret was surprised to see that Urs had been right. The stones didn't need whitewashing. They were fine in their natural colors. As if the whole thing had just grown out of the land.

As Urs and Margaret started to the outdoor pump, Margaret reached for her husband's hand. At her touch, Urs stiffened. The giant forefinger was hard and calloused. The nail was caked with dirt. As they walked, Urs focused on the feel of Margaret's fingers wrapped around his one.

At the pump Urs had eagerly grasped the handle, pulling with strong regular thrusts while Margaret bent, washing in the shiny liquid spurts.

Over the years the garden, the kitchen, the clothesline had become hers, just as they were, almost in spite of herself. Hers and Urs's. Margaret smoothed out the dish towel, enjoying the clean fragrance of cotton hung in the open air.

From where she sat, Margaret could see the carrot tops and new lettuce popping through the earth. Why, last year the house garden had almost produced more Weisskohl than they knew what to do with.

When the final towel was neatly stacked, Margaret took out the funnel and filled the pop bottle with water, stopping it with the corked sprinkling head. With an easy rhythm she sprinkled pillow cases, shirts and blouses, before wrapping a damp work shirt around the stack.

Now, for a nice lunch while the laundry settled. She'd use her special plate, making it something nice, while she had this time alone.

From the cupboard, way in the back, she pulled out the cardboard box. She thought of it as her box of sorrows and joys. Like saint's relics, guarded in the holiest of holies, or cemented into chambers, or displayed behind smoky glass.

Setting it on the table she rummaged through it. There, was the bone-handled folding-knife that belonged to her father. And there, the photograph of Lars, from her altar in the pantry.

There too, was her twin's fringed shawl from their first communion. The pink roses still bright, had been the only color in her otherwise white Zumnachtmahlrock, her first Holy Communion dress.

Margaret unfolded the shawl and smoothed it in her lap. What was that there underneath? Oh, the fuzzy pink slippers. Margaret hugged them to her chest.

Nights in their upstairs bedroom Lars had given her gifts: perfume, the music box of carved ivory, a plush robe of lilac velvet, satin bed sheets, these slippers. Margaret fingered them. The worse their finances grew, the more impractical and extravagant his gifts became.

Those nights, Margaret had disjointed dreams of climbing up and up to a gilded place where lovely white birds leapt from a golden sill, falling, falling as they sang in the vast blue sky. Then Margaret would step to the golden sill. Her turn to leap. Whether to death or to freedom, she never knew.

Margaret hugged the slippers to her chest. In the end the gifts had only made her feel worse. Why did he insist on giving her extravagant gifts while their world unraveled?

Margaret slapped the slippers against her thigh. Slapping out the dust. She should be wearing them. Especially with her swollen feet. Margaret set them aside along with the haunting memories. She put her mind back to making lunch.

There was the carnival glass plate she was searching for. But seeing also the balsa wood box, she collapsed again into reverie. Instead of the plate, she lifted the wood container come all the way from China. She could no more hold back her memories than the screen door could keep out a spring breeze.

The wooden box had tidy Chinese letters on the side, like little pictures. What did they mean, she wondered, turning the box slowly? It had contained the music box. Now there was only this, the balsa wood box it came in.

Inside it was the letter. Margaret had forgotten she'd put it there. It had come into her hands as such a surprise. In such a roundabout way.

That first winter in this house, when Margaret was cleaning out the junk and piles of paper left in the bedroom closet, she'd happened across it. It was only by chance that this letter was in the stack of papers that slipped from her hands and scattered across the room like a deck of cards. Picking up the pages, her heart stopped. There was the name Lars Borgen written in her dead husband's hand. She would recognize that signature even if she couldn't read another word.

Margaret had lowered herself to the bed, stumbling over the words. A pale sun shone through the frosty window. So this farm had been the one! So, Franz Hofbrau had been the one Lars had talked into it. The only farm that was owned outright. The farm that was supposed to save all the others. And in the end it, too, went to Humpy Chris.

Margaret had been dazed, the paper trembling in her hands. How strange that this farm should come round to them after all. The frosty window beside the bed shuddered and pinged as a ground blizzard began flinging dry snow. And how right, she thought that the piece of land that caused Lars'ss undoing would come back round to help support his own. Ice crystals shone like broken pieces of mirror, each holding a reflection of her Lars.

That was the day Margaret began laying claim to this place. That was the day she began thinking the farm belonged to them. That it was meant to be.

Now in the warming kitchen, Margaret smoothed the page, tracing the signature as she had done that cold morning. It felt somehow comforting. The comforting breath of Lars seeping through the years. She felt him looking over her, looking out for her and the children. Margaret held the paper to her face. Was that the faint smell of Lars? After all these years?

The peeps of the chicks behind the stove, encased in their shells, brought Margaret out of her reverie. What was she doing sitting here with the lunch to be made and the ironing to be done?

Margaret replaced her box of treasures. Before closing the curtain, she picked out the carnival glass plate. Staggering with dizziness she rose grasping the cupboard.

This was the third time today. Twice, as she stood over the ringer, the sky swirled and the earth had tipped. Margaret slowly lowered herself into the chair. Carefully, she set down the plate.

She never had this dizziness with any of the others. And the swelling. Margaret raised her heavy legs and placed her feet side by side on the chair facing hers. Now she nearly always wore the black oxfords she'd inherited from Phil. None of the rest of her shoes fit. She pressed the puffiness of her ankle with a thumb. The white mark it left took a long time to disappear. At least the bleeding had stopped. Since visiting the Habemme, Margaret had at least one cup of the special tea every day.

Remembering the Habemme brought a surge of guilt, knotting her stomach. She should have gone into town with Urs. To go to confession. To confess her lie and wash away the offense. But could she even confess to Father? Father didn't like women going to the Habemme, with her dark powers, outside the church.

Oh, why had she lied to Urs? How would she tell him the truth and why she'd done it? Why had she done it? So she could know something that he didn't? So she could be the gatekeeper, and he the fool? Was that the reason? Maybe if she had gone to confession.

But Danny had insisted on going in with Urs. He was the one who insisted on a chance to kneel within the darkened box to murmur his secrets.

From the stack of folded towels Margaret took one and began polishing the carnival glass plate. Its reflection lighted her face. Danny. Her little man. Always the one she could trust. Sunlight danced from the plate, it's iridescent sheen pulling her into the changing, dizzying center.

Margaret traced the raised flower border, affirming the solidity of the plate. Danny had won it for her at the fair, years ago. He had been so young. Barely up to her shoulder. Walking with her all over the fairgrounds, at once showing it off and protecting it. So excited. So proud.

Margaret set the kettle on for her special Habemme tea and began preparing a grilled cheese sandwich. She crossed herself and spoke in a clear, quiet voice. "*Alle Augen warten auf Dich, Herr.*" The eyes of all wait upon Thee. But as her hands went about their business her mind worked at unraveling the knot of what had gone wrong.

~17~

Adam Bosch had come on horseback after supper. The German Russian farmer stood awkwardly in his overalls, hat in hand. "Could he please talk to Lars in private?"

Lars shut the door to the little parlor. His mother, Karn, looked uneasily over her crochet. Each squeak of the old woman's rocking chair jarred the nursing baby in Margaret's arms. From the parlor came the faint murmur of bastardized German.

"Could he please read. Foreclosure notice.... could he please explain."

From behind the stove the chicks peeped in their thin shells. "*Und du gibst ihnen ihre Speise zu Seiner Zeit,*" and Thou givest them their meat in due season, Margaret prayed, but the past kept pressing in on her.

"Governor Langer is behind us, Ma, it will all turn out ok. These farms will be saved."

"What do you know about politics, Lars? These people and their problems are none of your business."

"*Und du gibst ihnen ihre Speise zu Seiner Zeit,*" and thou givest them their meat in due season, Margaret repeated, concentrating on her prayer. Had the old woman been right?

"You're getting sucked into something you can't control, Lars. It's dangerous."

Margaret didn't understand it all but the strange words still rung in her mind, drowning out her prayer: WPA, the CCC, grain embargoes and farmer's unions. Mortgage loans and the forgiveness of loans.

After Lars helped Adam, rumor had it he knew some magic secrets. Tricks with papers and numbers. Slowly the farmers had begun to think he could save them all. Lars began believing it himself.

"*Komm Herr Jesus sei unser Gast,*" Margaret's voice rose above the peeping chicks.

"Wilfred Kohler came to the office, Ma, with the first communion picture of his boy. Yesterday the boy was drug by horses, Ma. Got tangled in the reins. They don't have money for a doctor."

"Charity begins at home, Lars, they have their own people."

"Ole's your own brother isn't he, Ma? He's working on a plan, I tell you."

Lars was upbeat with the German farmers. "Ole's going to finish the Governor's term, Lars reassured. "He won't let us down! I know Ole. He won't let us down!"

"*Und segne alles was Du uns bescherest hast. Amen,*" and then silently Margaret added as she always did, "Jesus and Mary, help save Lars's soul and forgive me for my sin."

Ole couldn't stop the unlikely chain of events. When Governor Langer was driven from office, the populist movement was thrown into confusion. But Lars had still believed. When records of land ownership were lost in the state capitol building fire, and Easterners began buying up big tracts of foreclosed farmland, hiring back the original owners as hands, Lars still believed.

When Ole did briefly take the reins of governorship, he lost his nerve. In a few months, Thomas Foodie was elected to replace him and then, just as quickly, was disqualified.

Margaret slowly chewed her grilled cheese sandwich, without tasting.

Some said Lars started going a little crazy then. He began loaning his own money until there was no more money to loan. He tried convincing his mother to mortgage their place. "Just to help them through? Just 'til this thing is over?"

His mother's chair, squeaked anxiously. "I told you not to get involved in this! Why they're not even your own people!"

Though Margaret's plate was empty, she couldn't remember eating. Had any of her chanting and praying saved Lars's soul? Had God forgiven her for deserting Him, for loving Lars too much? Would she go to hell for Lars? Margaret took a breath and sat a moment looking about the kitchen, quieting her mind, fortifying her faith.

She rose and rinsed her plate.

Another thought crept into her mind. Margaret let go the plate with a clatter. Wasn't it a sin to share a bed with a man when there was no love?

Suddenly all of her precious possessions seemed like cheapened junk. Hadn't her marriage to Lars been for eternity? Or didn't a Lutheran ceremony count at all? Would they be joined again in heaven? And what about Urs? Had God tied them together for eternity? Margaret glanced at her reflection in the window pane. She saw a spent woman.

She sat for a while without a thought when, riding a light spring breeze through the screen door, came a wispy scent from another time. It swelled the room. Her eye was turning. She grasped the window sill, struggling to hang onto the present.

Across the eastern sky, unfurled her little sister's shawl. Margaret's twin. The thinning clouds were drawing her face with hollow eyes. Little Maryanne was hot with fever, her teeth chattering. Maryanne's first communion shawl spread over the top of the blanket. It had flowers bright pink with leaves and vines twining under the light of the lantern.

A young Margaret rolled closer to her twin, leaning in to hear Maryanne whisper, "Pick the chokecherries by the creek for both of us, sister. And when you sing the *Gegruesst seist du Maria voller Gnaden and say the Bekennntnis des Glaubens* say them for me, too." Little Margaret shivered in the tiny bed imagining the hollow sound of those Ave Marias and Apostles Creeds she would say. Lying next to her, her precious little twin went cold.

Margaret shook herself and broke from the window. She heated the irons on the cook stove and set up the ironing board: she turned on the radio. Billie Holiday sang her sad song. "In my solitude,"

Margaret set down the iron and listened to the haunting melody, the haunting words. She could almost feel Lars's hand lightly touch her shoulder. She could almost smell the scent of him, and feel his breath lightly on her cheek as he led her in the dance. Margaret rode the song back into that other time to the years they spent together in the big Victorian house.

Margaret had never known such a life before or since. The hardwood floors shining with wax and lemon. The electric lights and radio. The table set with linen and china. The sachets of roses and lilac in the drawers. And there were the books. Shelves filled with them.

Margaret turned the pillowcase on the ironing board, remembering. On winter afternoons her mother-in-law would sit in the parlor, an elegant finger pointing to the page as she read aloud to Danny. Many a time Margaret had stopped her work then to stand in wonder at the sound of the old woman's voice. Danny could read some even then, and understand it all. German, Norwegian, and English. Did he remember any of it now?

Shaking out another pillowcase, Margaret recalled how on sunny days back then she would open all the upstairs windows, flooding their bedroom and the little nursery with light and air. They had the top floor all to themselves and from there she could look down on the laundry in the back yard. The lines looped up the little hill dotted with apple trees. The garden was bordered by flat round stones painted white. Beyond the furthest corner sat a hive of bees.

For Margaret it was like a fairy tale. Five years they'd lived there. Five years out of a lifetime. When Lars died, the old woman didn't want Margaret in the house.

After Phil had the accident with his feet, the place was sold. The old woman moved in with her married daughter in Minneapolis.

Margaret returned the cooling iron to the stove and carried the stack of freshly ironed sheets and pillowcases to the bedroom. There she stripped the bed, exposing the gauzy mattress cover. The lilac satin sheets from that other life winked through where the gauze was frayed and worn thin. She quickly made the bed.

At the old place, sometimes she would stop her work briefly and thread a colored ribbon through a lace sachet and hide it somewhere in the bed. And she would daydream as she did now.

They'd had it so good. In bed at night they had had it so good. So good sometimes they hardly slept at all. Often they would fall into their native tongues and, though at first they didn't understand each other's words, there was nothing wrong with their communication. Had all this been a sin?

Margaret slapped the pillow into shape and covered it with the spread. Back in the kitchen, although her hands resumed the ironing, her mind stayed in that other time. Lars had worshiped her with his hands. After the children were all asleep, sometimes when she'd let loose her hair, his hands would tenderly touch her breasts, her thighs. Sometimes when the plush robe fell to the floor she wondered if her skin glowed. She welcomed the cool night air coming in the open window, before climbing into the great feather bed. Had all this been, against the laws of God, evil?

"So how'd your day go?" Urs stood in the doorway, back from Drake now, from delivering eggs and milk with Danny. His eyes were glittery, tracing the curve of her belly, the fall of her hair, her breasts, before settling on her face.

Margaret caught her breath. The iron had grown cold in her hands. "Oh, okay," she answered. Her face burned with shame. It was as if he had come upon her making love to another man.

"What's the matter?" Urs asked. "Is there something wrong here?"

Margaret's first instinct of shame was followed closely by anger. Not anger at anything Urs had done, but just for his being there. Just for Urs being himself.

The thick, stocky man stomped across the room and turned off the radio. "Do you think money grows on trees, woman? They don't give batteries away for nothing, you know. Urs's face lost its glitter." He thrust his hands deep in his pockets as he hunched before the living room window, irritated. "How long's the windmill been on the blink?" he asked, pointing in that direction with his chin.

In the silence that followed Margaret heard someone chopping kindling in the wood pile. Danny. Making himself busy. Staying out of the way.

When she didn't answer Urs went on. "You can see from here it's not working. I can't be everywhere at once you know."

From the wood pile came the rhythmic sound of Danny's work, as he set each piece on end and split it into smaller and smaller sticks.

At the window Urs's eyes were tracing the land, searching. Not finding what he sought, he went on, to no one in particular. "With this heat, and the ground sucking up the water like a sponge, the cows will need to drink when they come in from pasture. How do you expect a cow to give milk when it can't find water?" There was the clatter of slender sticks from outside as Danny dropped them into the bottom of the kindling box.

"And where is Wayne?" Urs wanted to know. "Not here! What, did he have to be watched over like a two-year-old? The way he'd tied down the tarp on the washing platform, the first good wind and it'd be over in the north forty." Margaret's cheeks were as hot and red as if they'd been slapped.

Urs stomped out of the house.

Did he know her shame? She stood before the window watching Urs traipse off to the windmill. There, too, was the last of the laundry waving in the open air. The only sound was the crack of dry wood splitting as Danny resumed his work.

Outside she hurried down the clothesline, releasing the blue jeans and overalls, gathering them into her arms.

Suddenly she was spinning. The sun grew dark. As cool and dark as the inside of the confessional. There was a sensation of floating and then more coolness as the fresh, stiff clothes fell from Margaret's arms. Little sister Maryanne swam through the sky, the flowered shawl trailing behind. Margaret dropped to her knees. Something worse than turning away from the one true church was twisting in her mind. Something worse than trading her love for God for the love of Lars.

Had Lars'ss suicide been her punishment from God?

Then, Danny was there helping her up. Helping her to the house. "It's nothing, Danny," she reassured him. "I must have tripped." Leaning onto his arm how much he looked like Lars!

Margaret brought her hands gently under her belly, relieving the pressure of the downward pull. Looking intently into the face of her son, she asked. "You're the one, Danny. Are you sure everything's all right with you? Your extra studies with Mrs. Nielson every day after school, plus all the help around here."

Danny took a step backward, startled. Color rose to his face. "Sure, Mom, everything's fine with me. Everything's just fine."

The dogs started up. Wayne and Liz were bringing in the cows on their way back from the high plateau where they had gone to play ball. Near the barn Lizzie helped Annie slide down Ryder's rump.

From near the livestock tank there rose a jarring ringing sound. Again and again, Annie heard the harsh clanking sound as her father worked marooned alone on a little hoof-dimpled island near the windmill. He was bent in such a way that Annie could see only his legs and his torso and his swinging arm. He had no head.

Beyond her father stretched a lumpy field. How separate it was from the farmyard. How separate from the little hoof-dimpled island. And in the other direction the chicken coop. How different with its smooth, well-beaten earth. And the barn was so separate too, so apart from everything else. From where Annie stood, it looked as if pictures of entirely different places had been pasted together haphazardly side by side.

How could it be? All these separate places and pieces. All these separate feelings? How could she have just this morning blotted it all out with the palm of her hand? As if it was all just one little place?

Annie approached the fallen tree near the outhouse. Her uneasiness grew. Wasn't that where she had seen the dragon? She began stomping down the high dry grass near the broken trunk. She could smell the green. Beneath the dry overgrowth, fresh shoots of buffalo grass, needle and thread, June grass and wild currants were taking hold, their runners creeping along the ground. In a few moments Annie's hair was damp with sweat. No, the dragon wasn't hiding here.

Annie shaded her eyes. Maybe it was out there? Far out there, where the land rose to meet the sky. On the high plateau. Hadn't she found its lair when she was playing outfield and went to retrieve the ball?

~18~

The older kids hadn't let her play, not really. They stuck her in the backfield and didn't give her a chance at bat or any other position. Annie had lain on her back looking at the clouds most of the afternoon. Only a couple grounders had come her way, and then they didn't trust her to throw in time. When Lizzie and the neighbor boy Joe got into a fight about whose turn it was at bat Annie looked on with interest. Lizzie stepped up to the plate and held her ground. Joe threw the pitch. With the power of anger coursing through her, she hit the ball with a tremendous smack. Annie had sprung to her feet. When the ball finally hit the ground it continued to roll fast in

Annie's direction. The child ran as hard as she could to prevent it from going over the edge.

Annie almost stumbled into it. She almost lost her footing and tumbled headlong into the gaping trench of charred and rotting garbage. A few stunted trees and bushes lined the banks. That hidden place exposed under full sunlight made her head ache.

"Hurry, hurry! Go get it, before it gets lost," Liz screamed, face flushed. Annie had stood frozen. Where was that ball? She didn't want to go down in there. Hurry up now, Annie! Get the ball, you little dummy! Get the ball!" They were all yelling at once.
In the bushes on the steep bank, there was movement and a slight noise. Was it the ball, still rolling? Or was it something else? A rat maybe? Or a snake? Or something else... slimy and spooky? Was that the ball there at rest by a charred tire?

Annie descended into the ruined trench. She had no choice. It was narrow and steep and farther down, shaded even at this time of day, Annie stumbled on wet cardboard. Grasping the cold, wet, stinking layers, down and down she slid. Deeper and deeper past rotting garbage, past Indian villages with smoking fires, down and down past the thigh bones and three toed claws of ancient beasts and into the slimy belly. Annie opened her eyes. She stopped her slide by grasping a stunted oak and setting her feet. All around her, there was ice. How could it be at this time of year, with the day so hot? Ice. Glittering like forgotten treasure of some dragon's lair.

"Get the ball. Get the ball. It's right there--right there over to the right," Lizzie shouted from above.

Was that the ball there? Not much farther? Hung up on a bed spring? Annie stared deeper into the gaps between the twisted, rusting metal. A glinting lace grew between the wires. Ice crystals. Like twinkling gemstones. A cold, hard treasure among the rot. Annie returned her eye to the grayish ball as she carefully made her way. If only it would stay put and not roll deeper.

By the time she lunged and grasped it in her hand, the others were all ringing the horizon above her.

"Throw it here. Throw it up here," Liz demanded. But Annie didn't want to throw it. Didn't want to chance the ball wouldn't make it and roll back down. Looking up she grew dizzy. Annie leaned into the side of the bank trying to keep her balance. Looking down, to check her footing, there, staring into her face were the icy eyes of a stiff dead dog.

The others saw it, too. It was reddish with matted hair, a white spot on his nose. "Hey, Annie, got a new pet?" the neighbor boy Joe teased. "Here, Red; here, Red," he taunted slapping his thigh. Slowly, Annie made her way out clutching the ball. She tried not to look back at the red dog with the white spot. When she emerged and stumbled forward so glad to be up, she had taken a deep breath of relief.

Yes, that must be where the dragon hid, in his liar up on the high plateau. Annie didn't like remembering. No the dragon wouldn't be here by the stump and fallen tree. Annie headed to the porch, passing the lilac bush. There she saw the overturned cigar box wagon nearly hidden under the leafing branches. There lay her magic possessions...the spoon along the wagon's length, and the arrowhead at the back. Her little field was barren and smooth. Then, Annie noticed, there at the edge of her cultivated kingdom, where the wild grasses began, an outcropping of delicate pasque flowers: a bouquet of tiny blue flowers with yellow eyes. The first to appear every spring. Immediately Annie began singing as her mother had taught. Singing more flowers into existence. Singing the crops to grow strong in the fields.

"Komm schoepferischer Geist, Du, der du Troester und Beschuetzer genannt wirst, bist die groesste Gabe Gottes, Lebenskraft, Feuer, Barmherzigkeit, Salbe fuer die grosste Gabe Gottes, Lebenskraft, Feuer, Barmherzigkeit, Salbe fur die Seele." Come Creating Spirit, You are called Comforter and Protector, You are God's greatest gift, The power of life, fire, mercy, and the ointment for the soul.

In the kitchen Margaret folded and stacked the overalls and bibs in three piles. She tilted her head, listening. Was that singing?

Margaret's hands stopped their work. Yes, there it was again a clear, sweet, earnest voice. *"Gabe Gottes, lebenskraft, feuer, Barmherzigkeit."*

The power of life, fire, and mercy. Yes, Annie. Yes, it was Annie, knowing all the words, singing just as Margaret had taught her. Her little Annie. Suddenly it occurred to her that Annie wasn't just her child. Annie belonged to Urs as well. Yes, he loved Annie, too.

Annie took a breath and stepped up onto the porch. Perhaps the first flowers of spring would bring back the Danny she knew. He'd hardly been around since school started again and when he was home, he seemed to float like a spider letting itself down on a thread, tethered to something only he could sense.

Annie quietly entered the kitchen, letting the screen door close slowly. Margaret smiled, looking directly at her child.

"Annie, were you singing just now?"

"Yes, Mom, for good luck, for God's help."

"Well, it sure sounded nice," Margaret said, as she lifted a stack of folded clothes and handed them toward Annie. "Take these on upstairs to the boys' room for me."

After supper that evening, Urs cleared away a little glass dog sitting on a crotchet doily and dusted the surface with his shirt sleeve. From the bedroom he brought out a wooden crate, filled with parts of an old clock he'd found in the garbage trench a while back. A pioneer clock, hauled out in a covered wagon, and thrown in the trench when electricity came to town. These clocks were durable, Urs thought to himself, the only ones that still worked after the bumpy ride. Urs examined the pieces. They'd been removed from the clock's body and except for the spring and the chain and the chimes, were made entirely of machined hardwood. A few were cracked or broken but all were smooth and balanced to the hand. Perhaps with some pegging the clock would work again. Urs laid out a few pieces. He worked with the same patience as a man who loved jigsaw puzzles.

Annie quietly watched from the doorway. Every so often her father would bend, returning a piece to the crate and trying another. Thick, dark hair stuck out every which way around his blocky head. Thick, dark hair curled up each forearm. Even the top of his blunt single finger, curled with dark hair as it nudged the wooden pieces into place.

Margaret in the easy chair basted a zipper pulling the thread to arm's length with each stitch. This time of day Wayne and Liz finished up the dishes with softer voices. Now Danny had joined Wayne, stooped before the radio, listening.

"There will be a slight possibility of rain tomorrow in the Northern Plains," rose the crackling voice. Urs paused raising his head, listening. And then...."It's a beauuuutiful day in Chicago, and I hope it's even more beautiful wherever you may be." The announcer drew out the word beautiful as he did at the end of the program. Was it always so beautiful in Chicago?

Still wearing her apron, Annie carried the rabbit cage to the front porch. The sky glowed with swirling oranges and pinks. The air was cool and intoxicating, arranging and rearranging the clouds; breathing life into the world. Had the little pasque flowers helped to grow her crop? Had she sung her field to life?

Annie went there and set down the cage. The delicate pasque flowers vibrated blue in the slanting light. She threaded a few branches of unfurling leaves through the chicken wire netting. A pungent green smell pricked her nose as Buttermilk stripped the tender heart shaped leaves. Clusters of tiny budding blooms were knotted to tight, fragrant, purple fists.

Annie laid out her magical possessions. The little field was still barren. Nothing had come up. What more could she do? Her bunny stirred round and round in the cage. A wire bowl of freshly mashed potatoes. Then, the ticking of the little hard poops hitting the metal bottom.

That would do the trick! Farmer's gold! Annie shook out the dark droppings. The sliding bunny jolted, frantic to right himself.

"It's okay, it's okay," her voice soft, righting the cage she threaded through a few more branches.

Annie hitched her finger horses to the cigar box and inserted the spoon. The pasque flower nodded. Back and forth, back and forth her finger team pulled the wagon, mixing in the little dark nuggets. She encouraged her horses with song. With song, she encouraged the earth to become fertile and the clouds to bring rain.

Looking up, she saw an astonishing pink bordered the blue-black sky. How long had she been working? The sun barely peeked above the horizon.

Darkness seeped into the low-lying places. A barn owl flapped from the loft, beginning his evening hunt. Annie cocked her head listening. A snoring rose from the ditches followed by stuttering croaks. Had she ever heard those sounds before? Meadow frogs were beginning their spring courtship.

As Annie trudged to the house, her long shadow dipped and rose with the contours of the yard, a dark rope holding the farm yard together. To one side hung the cage's shadow, a lantern flickering, as the bunny moved.

At the step, Annie made a deep pocket of her apron and placed the bunny in her lap. A murky darkness covered the gentle swells of land. Only the tree tops were lit.

The chicken wire cage sat empty at her side. A few dark shapes swooped against the glowing red line in the western sky. Bats probably. A cool breeze billowed her pant legs.

Annie scooted to the very side of the porch step. It was time to go inside. But she didn't want to. She wanted to sit very still, with the bunny sleeping between her legs. She wanted to disappear with the light. To fade into the porch, hearing the night sounds and watching the bats and feeling the fur. She wanted to become this twilight night.

In a while her father came out. Annie didn't speak and he didn't seem to notice her there. He just stood looking out. A hint of pink and a few swirling clouds. Annie watched him quietly.

Sometimes when he turned, his face lit with the glow from the kitchen and sometimes he would turn so that his face was dark with the coming night. Annie held so still, she barely breathed. The bunny between her thighs slept.

In a little while, her father went inside. A wishing star was falling in the sky.

Her mother loomed large in the lighted doorway. "Annie, come on in now. The water's hot and it's time you got washed up for bed."

~19~

Urs lifted his feet high, stepping carefully, before placing his Sunday shoes safely inside the car and slamming the door. "Why don't you come on by this afternoon?" August Krueger called as he approached.

Urs rolled down the window. "What was that?" A light drizzle had collected on the glass and the beads formed small rivulets as the glass descended.

"I said, why don't you come on over. Katie's still got a few combs of honey she's been saving for you folks." The brim of August's hat dripped, his shoulders hunched, as he thrust his hands deep in the pockets of his Sunday suit. "Maybe we can play a hand of pinochle."

"Oh, I don't know." Urs looked up squinting through the partially opened glass. "That barn of ours could use a good cleaning, now that the damn thing's almost empty."

Margaret's brow furrowed. Urs hadn't said a word to her about cleaning the barn. In this drizzle? He certainly hadn't gotten permission from the priest to work on Sunday! Just an excuse not to go visiting. Margaret leaned, directing her voice through the window. "I got a couple dozen eggs set out for you folks, I been meaning to bring by."

August's quick green eyes saw that this didn't do much to persuade Urs. "Urs, to tell the truth," he tried again, lowering his voice, head cocked, leaning closer. "I'd like your opinion on something if you've got the time." A drop dangled from his hat brim and fell with a splash to his shoulder. August had been planning to talk to Urs for some time now and guessed he didn't mind getting a little wet. He waited.

"I can't say for sure, August. What is it you want to talk about anyway?"

Though August didn't consider himself the man Urs was when it came to machinery or animals, he did pride himself on knowing how to handle people. "It's business, Urs. A man can't go discussing business in the church parking lot. We need, *mit jemandem unter vier Augen sprechen.* If you can make it, come on over any time. Like I said, I'd like your opinion on something."

So he wanted his opinion did he, speaking privately among four eyes? Urs raised his chest a bit and fumbled with his tie. "Oh yeah? What's that August? You think you got gold or something in that little ditch back behind the silo?"

"Now Urs, in some things it's best to talk it over before you make your move." August could see he was getting somewhere now. He had Urs in a good mood. He tried a more direct approach. "You know I respect your opinion." Urs's eyes brightened. "Come on by after dinner anytime. We'll be home."

All during Sunday dinner Urs let Margaret talk him into it. "It'll do us all good to have some conversation for a change," Margaret prodded as she passed the dishes of food to Urs.

Urs didn't answer. He sat at the head of the table unceremoniously shoveling in the potatoes, chewing the meat off the chicken leg. It was hard for Urs to take the day off, to just sit around doing nothing at somebody else's place. Even though there wasn't much more he could do here for the time being. It was hard for Urs to relax, to give up his worrying. "*Eie gute Arbeit ist suss wie Zucker,*" good work is sweet like sugar, he said licking the grease from his fingers. That was his argument for staying home.

Lately, his worry was different. It had some hope in it. Urs wanted to succeed. He wanted to succeed more than he had ever wanted anything in his life. So much it scared him.

Margaret rose and began clearing the table. "That comb honey of Katie's sure would be good on pancakes. And Urs, those herbs Sofia gave me to help with the baby. I'm almost out of them. Katie said her mother left some at the house to pass on to me."

Urs took another drink of coffee. Maybe it wouldn't hurt to take the day off. After all, this drizzle was what they really needed. Now that the seed was all in what more could he do? He sat thoughtfully finishing his coffee. The barn could wait. And August had wanted his opinion on something. What was that all about?

"Ok," Urs conceded. "We can go on over for a while but I don't want to be sitting around there all afternoon." In truth, nothing could have kept him from going, now. Might not Sofia's herbs help assure a healthy baby boy?

When the family climbed back into the car, the drizzle had stopped. A thick fog roped through the ditches and thinned across the flats. Urs switched on the head lights the last quarter mile. Even so, he could barely see beyond the edge of the road.

Now what was that coming up out of the ditch? Urs swerved to avoid the oddly colored shape. Short legs and a foot long body. What could it be? Urs brought the car to stop.

Why there were two more, quickly making their way across the road. Was it some kind of lizard? Black with yellow stripes. Wayne jumped out of the car and ran into the ditch trying to catch one, but it moved surprisingly fast when startled, wiggling out of his hands.

"Look how funny they are," Urs was smiling now. His eyes crinkled with happiness. "Look at those funny little men all dressed up in striped overalls. They come by this way every year"

"Baby dragons!" Annie exclaimed. "I never knew dragons could have babies!" Tiger salamanders were only visible for a few hours after spring rains, when they had a mania for crossing roads, returning to wetlands to mate.

The rest of the way to the Kruger place Annie tumbled the idea of baby dragons in her thoughts. Maybe she had had the wrong idea about dragons. Were there mother and father dragons, families of them?

At the Krueger place Annie hung in the doorway between the closed in porch and the kitchen trying to make up her mind. She didn't like being there, but she didn't know where else to go. The older kids were outside where it was damp and chilly and it looked like the grown-ups were just going to play cards. Annie crossed her arms grasping her elbows. This was where she sat that time Katie's mother, the Hebamme, was here. That time the Hebamme read her mother's eye. Annie stood paralyzed by indecision, watching the grownups.

Katie and Margaret went to the cellar for beer, while August arranged the table and chairs. "I just can't believe what they're saying, Urs, can you?" August asked, scooting a chair into place. "About those death camps?" August was getting excited, talking faster and faster. "All those half starved people made to work 'til they gassed them to death?"

Annie shuffled her feet. What were they talking about?

"Do you think it's true, Urs? I seen pictures of it in the Life magazine. Katie got Edith's old copy. Everyone's talking about it."

The color drained from Urs's face. Surely this wasn't what August wanted to ask him about.

"Germans aren't that way, though, Urs. We know that," August went on, getting more worked up. "I just can't believe it, even if they do have pictures. They say Germans were gassing those people to death, and burning them up in giant ovens. No German would do that."

"I heard about that, too," Urs frowned. "I don't believe any of it." Urs crossed his arms in front of his chest, and stood with both feet firmly planted. He held back even considering the idea, though he knew even a German man could be cruel. There were those times when he was farmed out as a boy.... But he didn't like to think of that either. Why was August bringing up this? Urs didn't want to hear it.

"But look here, Urs," August went to the bedroom and retrieved the magazine. "Look at these pictures." August opened it up to the dog eared two-page photo spread and laid it on the table.

"You can't tell what kind of man it is by looking at a picture, August, you know that." Urs wouldn't look. He maintained his stubborn stance, feet set on the freshly waxed linoleum. "We don't know what really went on over there. I heard that when Heinrich's boy, Markus, got home from the army, he told it different," Urs said. "Markus said, his company went to one of those places where those people were locked up. When Markus got there, whoever was keeping them locked up was nowhere around. He talked to one of those guys that was almost starved to death and he talked German, just like you and me, August. Jews talk funny don't they, not good German talk like us?"

Urs took in a deep breath and continued. "We don't know what went on over there, August, even if they do have pictures. You know what the Russians were doing to us Germans, what Father told us about." Urs was visibly upset. He looked down at the magazine in spite of himself.

"Look here August, they're skinny, yes, half starved to death, yes, but look at those faces. Jews look funny don't they? Not like us anyway." Urs's eyes stopped on the picture of a boy, about twelve or so, on his knees, his striped uniform in tatters.

The sad dark eyes looked out from the page directly at him. This couldn't be a Jew or a Gypsy, could it? Urs stopped talking-- stopped breathing. The haunting sad brown eyes, the shaved head. The look of hunger? Was that a picture of himself as a boy on his knees begging for soup? When they'd shaved his head for lice and doused it with kerosene?

For a panicky moment, Urs didn't know who or where he was. The stunned man embraced himself, arms tight across his chest, holding himself together.

"Germans are honest, hardworking, people," he suddenly announced, "and devoted to God. This can't be true."

"Now that's enough of that crazy talk!" Katie said. The two women stood in the doorway, both with a quart of homemade beer in each hand. "Margaret, you get the glasses and August you put that magazine away and bring out the cards!"

"August, did Urs tell you what we saw coming over here today?" Margaret interjected. "The funniest little animals, crossing the road. All dressed up in striped overalls, weren't they Urs?"

Annie backed up further into the closed in porch, hiding. She wasn't sure what the pictures were about, but she knew it was something bad. She thought about the new gas oven at the Borgen's. Had they said those people in the magazine were gassed to death and put in ovens?

Tip-toeing backwards, Annie passed through the curtained doorway entering the hidden room Katie's mother used when she was the Hebamme.

The room was dim and swamped Annie with its many sharp confusing smells. Here, the Hebamme had read the iris of her mother's eye.

There was a statue of the Virgin on a small altar with many objects Annie didn't recognize. Two empty chairs sat facing each other. Here, she knew the Hebamme had told her mother that the new baby would be a girl. And that her mother should drink the special tea every morning.

Annie shivered. The whole business gave her an eerie feeling. Annie wouldn't have been surprised to see a striped baby dragon coiled at the feet of the Virgin.

Annie rushed through the curtain and out of that magical place. The statue of the Virgin bothered her. Somehow she looked different in that little room from how she did at church.

All at once she wanted very much to find the older kids and to feel the earth beneath her feet. Annie wandered around the farmyard, until she heard them laughing and talking from inside the barn.

Annie brushed away the twigs and dry leaves at the base of a large oak and sat down watching the barn door waiting for them to come out. She liked the feel of the ground beneath her.

In a few moments, the door opened. Coughing and sneezing, the older kids dragged out a few pitiful, dusty bales of hay. Though they saw Annie sitting there, they ignored her. What were they up to, Annie wondered? Then they were gone, back inside the barn.

Annie leaned against the tree looking up. A rising mist clung to the leaves. The clouds were thinning and the sun shot through here and there. There was some kind of bird, a robin maybe, flying back and forth to a nest he was building. Then Annie noticed the rope. It was tied to a high thick branch and hung straight down to where it curled on the ground.

Then there was the banging of wood on wood and barn swallows erupted from the eaves. Danny appeared in the dark open mouth to the hay-loft high up on the barn wall. He had flung open the small, high door.

When Danny's eyes adjusted to the sudden light, he was looking down at Annie. The sight of her, head thrown back, paralyzed him for a moment. Danny had been so distracted lately. He hadn't really seen her for days. How small she was, and sweet.

"Hey Annie, what you doing way down there?" Danny concentrated on seeing her, but with the dust particles hanging in the sunlight, and the barn swallows startled into flight, and with her head thrown back like that, instead Danny's thoughts turned to the dim light of the closet, to the open dress. Dizzy, Danny felt himself weaving in the high doorway.

Rudy came out of the barn and grabbed the knotted end of the rope stretching it over the bales to check the distance. Satisfied, he tossed it up. "Hey, Danny! Here you go, Tarzan." Danny leaned out of the opening and on the second try made the catch.

~20~

The next thing Annie knew Danny jumped. As she jerked in terror, the rough bark poked her back through the thin sweater. Danny's hair was pressed back by the force of the fall, his face a blaze of joy.

He was thinking of her. Always thinking of her. Two pressed wild roses fell from between the pages of his history book. In front of the class, her folded arms cradled her breasts; everything she said had another, secret meaning.

Not until the arch of his swing turned once again upward did Annie understand that Danny was holding the big knotted end of a rope. The thick branch where it was tied, lowered and raised, disturbing the nesting bird.

Again up and through the mist he swung, and then back. Outward and back again. How beautiful it looked, and dangerous. On the final outward swing, Danny threw the rope free and landed in the pile of sagging bales.

Wayne, Liz, Joe, Rudy, one by one Annie watched them all take their turn. Each time one jumped, Annie's heart fell, only to soar again with the rising sweep of the rope.

Then, Danny stood once again at the open mouth of the loft. He was remembering that time. That first time. While the last of the students left, Juanita and Danny began cleaning the blackboards. They worked side by side in silence.

When the room was empty and the last of the talking and the clomping of the horses faded, Juanita asked Danny to go into the narrow coat closet and get the attendance book. It would be in a folder on the second shelf.

Danny left the door open for light. He was on his knees, going through the folders, when the light diminished to a narrow strip. He could smell her perfume. He sensed her moving towards him. Then she was on her knees beside him. Her hand on his.

"Oh, Danny," she whispered, drawing out his name. Her hands were one on each side of his face. Her hands began pushing back his hair, caressing the back of his neck. Then, they were in each other's arms, the thin cotton dress all that separated him from the curve of her hip, from her thigh.

Annie saw Danny concentrate his expression and jump. More forcefully than before, he flung himself out, hurling farther than any of the others. Down he soared in a powerful arc, through the mist and back again, his feet climbing the coarse face of the barn.

It was like a dance, even that first time. He never thought of what to do. If he had, he would never have had the nerve. Danny moved in a dream. Doing a dance whose steps had been set by destiny, a dance made for him to do, with her. It was all motion, gentle and restrained, going deeper and deeper into unthinking, until her dress was open and her soft breasts heated his hands, their tips hard in his wet mouth.

Once, he saw the strip of light from the partially opened door. Once, he saw her face, head thrown back, black hair cascading, soft on his face, soft and silky in his hands. Her lips were slick with wet. They were the only two people in the world.

There, on the coarse face of the barn, Annie watched as Danny pushed off again and again, plummeting higher and higher with each thrust. When Danny'd reached the highest point, and was all but invisible through the fog, that clear holler burst once again from his lips.

Annie covered her eyes. Had he lost his hold and was floating out and up tumbling head over heels into the sky?

She had drawn him down to the hot moist secret places. He tasted the sweetness, drawing out the longing. And when he couldn't stop. When he couldn't stop himself, he waited, barely hanging on to the pounding of his heart. He waited for her turn in the dance. Then, they were dancing together, faster and stronger and louder, in time with their pounding hearts, until Danny cried out, "Ahh, AAAhh," loud and clear. Tears sprang to his eyes. How could there be joy like this?

"You're wonderful, Danny" she was saying. "Danny, you're wonderful."

Annie watched amazed as down again Danny swung in perfect control with lightness and radiance. By expertly dragging his feet, he broke his momentum and once again stood on solid ground.

Annie sprang to her feet and began clapping. Oh, how she would have liked to try it herself. How she would have liked to climb the sky and float through the mist. She would move with that same perfection, suspended between freedom and fall. The muscles in her arms grew rigid with the imagined strain of hanging on.

Suddenly Annie felt very foolish standing next to the oak tree, her hands spread rigid mid-clap, while the others looked good-naturedly on.

Beautiful as the wild swinging looked, she feared the power and pleasure that transformed her brother might consume her. If she jumped, perhaps she'd never come back. Out of fear and embarrassment and the chance they might ask her to take a turn, Annie wandered back up to the house.

Inside, August was dealing. On the table were four half-empty glasses of beer. Urs shuffled his feet uneasily letting wisps of small talk drift by unnoticed.

"Oh, I don't know if it really makes much difference or not, when it comes to farming," Katie turned to Margaret, "Karl never got his eighth, and I can't say it hurt him none."

"Maybe you're right, Katie, but since we don't have a place of our own yet, it seems like some kind of education wouldn't hurt." Couldn't Katie see Margaret was trying to convince Urs? You'd think Katie could give her a little help. "For all I know Danny won't even be going into farming," Margaret continued. "And they say it's getting so a man can't even get a job at the hardware store without somebody asking to see his eighth grade diploma." Margaret's voice rose as she looked over at the men.

Urs pretended to give Margaret a cool glance and buried himself further in his cards. He was thinking about what had happened yesterday in town. It tickled him no end.

Though Margaret didn't know it, she was wasting her breath. Urs had already joined her in the matter of the graduation for Danny. Urs wiped down the sides of his glass with his good hand, leaving long dripping lines in the film.

Urs had already been in a good mood when Danny's teacher approached him. He was heading down the sidewalk on Main Street, hands thrust into the pockets of his overalls. Earlier he'd had a drink at the tavern, and he'd struck a lucky deal with the superintendent of the county farm regarding the price of Margaret's eggs.

"Congratulations. Congratulations." It was a woman's voice from behind, slightly breathless with trying to catch up. Urs immediately dismissed the idea she might be speaking to him. "Mr. Wagnor... Mr. Wagnor, is that you?"

Urs stopped abruptly and turned around. The schoolteacher, Juanita Nielson, nearly stumbled into him. He steadied her, grasping the back of her arm through the soft mohair sweater. Spun rabbit fur wasn't it? It sure was soft. Immediately he pulled away. Urs hadn't had a chance to wash up, since he unloaded the eggs and cream. Her cheeks were flushed and she smelled like flowers.

"Oh, I'm so glad I saw you," she said, holding his astonished gaze. "I just wanted to thank you for seeing to it that Danny finished out the year and for letting him stay after school, to make up what he missed."

They fell into step, and began walking together. Urs swelled out his chest. If she didn't mind about the overalls, he wasn't going to let it worry him either.

"You must have taught that boy a thing or two" she continued, "cause it looks like he's going to graduate highest in the class."

Urs couldn't stop the wide smile that broke on his face. She was beautiful. There he was right on Main Street in broad daylight with this beautiful woman. The wife of the landlord yet!

"The graduation will be the evening of June fifth, I believe it is. You'll be there won't you?" Urs's eyes shined so they nearly overflowed.

"What's that? The graduation?" he stumbled, "Yea, we'll be there I guess."

"Oh, good," she said turning to him full faced and giving his arm a little squeeze that sent his nerve ends tingling. "It'll be so good to see you again."

Urs stepped lightly as he continued down the street alone. He'd parked near the hardware store and as he passed the window he noticed a rack of flower seeds in packets on the counter. Zinnias, wasn't that the kind Margaret always liked so much, or was it nasturtiums?

With a breezy air of good feeling so unlike him, Urs entered the hardware store and bought one each of the brightly colored packets.

Now in Katie's kitchen, with his cards fanned out before him, Urs reached for the half-empty glass of beer and drank it down.

Annie loitered without speaking behind her mother. "Annie, you come over and stand by me. Be my lucky charm," Katie pulled Annie to her lap.

"Now what do you think about that?" Katie asked, fanning her cards, a colorful court of kings and queens and princesses. "What do you think I should play?" Annie stepped forward and pointed to a blank faced beautiful Prince.

After selecting a different card, Katie seemed to forget all about Annie, though the woman's fat arm still encircled her waist.

"Well, I suppose if a person was thinking about moving into town then maybe all that education would be alright," Katie gestured in disgust, releasing her hold on Annie. "To tell the truth though, it seems like a person with any brains would be more interested in finding out what kind of worker a man was than how many years he spent sitting in a school house." To Katie, just the idea of moving into town seemed somehow unwholesome. She put down her card with a snap.

Margaret folded her arms above the rise of her belly. She wasn't getting anywhere.

Annie soon tired of listening and wandered aimlessly into the living room. She crumpled in the chair by the window. What was Buttermilk up to, she wondered, looking out into the damp day. Was he ok? Was he lonesome? Annie wished he was here. She sat looking out into the clearing gloom, imagining the bunny quivering in her lap, the soft fur under her hand.

The table had been cleared and was reset with stacks of bread and coffee cups and slices of cheese and bologna and sausage.

"I sure am getting tired of that Krogstad bunch making a fortune off us at threshing time, aren't you, Urs? I hear that Case machinery's got all the McCormicks and Model 55 Fords beat to hell. What do you think, Urs?" Urs fiddled with the flimsy china coffee cup rocking it back and forth with his strong finger and thumb. Would August ever stop beating around the bush?

"Look it here, Urs." August sucked in a breath of air. His voice wavering. "I got something to show you." From the bottom of the sideboard August brought out a dog-eared paper, and spread it on the table between them.

Urs sat straighter, with the knowledge that he was about to find out what this skinny, green-eyed neighbor had been pussy footing around about all afternoon.

"Last February's Prairie Farmer's got a combine in it that'll take the place of a binder and a threshing machine and about twenty good men and three wagons all at once. And at a pretty reasonable price too, considering what it'll do." August located the illustration and smoothed out the paper turning it to face Urs.

"The extension agent says down in Illinois and Iowa they're using them all the time. Don't even need a threshing crew to come in or nothing. With the kids helping, I figure between the two of us we could do the job ourselves, and when we're done we could even hire out. Old man Larson's got one and I hear it runs the Model 55 Ford right into the ground."

The two men sat at the end of the table, their heads almost touching as they leaned over the page. Stalling for time, Urs took a sandwich from the plate. Now and then he rose from his chair to see more clearly, dropping crumbs as he did.

Here was an idea Urs liked. Think of what it'd save him, not having to bring in a crew. Over the years that would sure add up. And they could hire it out. Use it to make money on the side. But how could he even think about it? Maybe if August made a down payment and Urs put in more than his share of the payments.... 'til they got evened up again. But how could he even think of it? Especially now that he was thinking about trying to buy the farm.

But then again maybe his luck was changing. Maybe this was part of it. It was the baby. Just knowing his son would be born in a few months made him see things different. See possibilities he'd never thought of before. Urs's giant finger followed the gears and pulleys and chutes in the illustration spread out before him. There was the blower and the grain hopper, way up front.

"Does it have a weighing and counting apparatus?" Urs asked, this time tracing the path the cut stalks would take. It looked ok.

"I went over last Saturday and had a look at old man Larson's. You don't suppose we could drive on over there again this afternoon, do you?" August had carefully laid it out, planned his tactics for this battle of wits. "I sure would like to hear your opinion of the machine." He sat back in his chair half holding his breath waiting to see if Urs would bite.

"Here, Urs, have another glass of beer while you think about it," Katie pressed. The pendulum clock chimed once from the sideboard.

"My gosh it's 3:30 already," Margaret interjected. "I sure do hate to eat and run, but we got to be getting those milk cows in."

Just then the older kids came stomping up onto the porch. Katie strained to see that they wiped their shoes on the rag rug she'd made for that purpose.

It was the two men along with Margaret and Annie who finally piled into the car and headed down the lane. The older kids were left to have some lunch, to help do the dishes and bring in the cows on their way home.

Urs left off Annie and Margaret by the mail box at the end of their lane. Then he and August headed on over to the Larson place to inspect the new machine.

~21~

The fog had cleared completely and by the time the men arrived the sky had lightened considerably. Before they were out of the car old man Larson was coming down the walk, smiling with his hand extended. With a minimum of small talk he showed them out to the machine shed where the gleaming combine was displayed like some holy relic. Each gear and pulley shined with oiled vanity. The body had been waxed like a new automobile.

A sour taste rose in Urs's throat. He believed in conscientious care, but a piece of farm equipment, like a pair of work boots, took its value from durability and practicality, not shine.

The machine was hooked up as if the old man intended to start threshing first thing tomorrow morning.

"That sure is some piece of equipment," August crooned. "I hear when it's running full out it sounds just like a song." The three men stood around the machine in their Sunday clothes like suitors come courting.

With very little encouragement August had the old man up on the combine wiping off the seat. As he pointed out the efficiency of the well-oiled parts, the sprinkling of broken vessels across his well padded checks and bulbous nose lent him the glow of a bridegroom at the altar.

Urs walked around the machine slowly, inspecting each individual part. When the old man started the motor and adjusted the throttle, the gears and pulleys were set into motion. Urs stepped back to take it all in. His mind sped and changed gears along with the motor. All his worries about the seed, and the weather and his frustrations at not owning his own farm, faded. Not only did his mind follow how the grain would proceed through its complicated journey, but he held on to all the previous processes weighing them against each new one. He listened carefully picturing how each part would respond under the resistance of actual work.

As mind and know-how took over, even his hopes disappeared. His own possible stake in the machine, he forgot completely. Here was a puzzle, complete unto itself, divorced from anything he'd ever thought or hoped. Urs forgot the old man, smiling and lovingly patting the levers. He took a more critical look, analyzing where the stress points would be and if the engine could really power the whole operation. Then, he very carefully brought out the ironed and folded Sunday hanky from his pants pocket and wiped the oil and grease from his fingers.

When the old man saw that Urs had completed his inspection, he cut the motor and sat back awaiting his admiring response.

Urs came out of his trance, shaking his head. The idea that he was about to comment on a man's own pride and worth never entered his head.

"I hope you've got plenty of spare belts for that band cutter...and if I were you I'd take off that feeder altogether. At that angle it won't last the season." Urs let out what he thought with graceless honesty.

The color drained from the old man's face like a rejected lover.

"Well, that looks like a honey of a combine to me," August spoke up quickly, trying to repair the damage. "It sure would be nice to bring in a whole crop without having to pay a threshing crew."

"That outfit might be cheaper than a Model 55 Ford, but it'll never do the work a Model 55 will do." It was as if Urs couldn't see the hurt and anger on the old man's face; as if Urs couldn't see how August was trying to soothe him with his smiling.

"Well, I've got other business to attend to." The old man's eyes excluded Urs. He spoke directly to August. "A man's got to keep up on the latest. With these new synthetic belts and alloys a man that can't think ahead won't be farming at all in a few years." He said it like some kind of official pronouncement and with the final words nodded his dismissal. He climbed down off the tractor then and went into the house without a backward glance.

All the way back August didn't say a word. When Urs let him out at the cement walk, he didn't so much as turn around and wave. Had August expected him to lie? To say what he saw with his own eyes, wasn't so? There was a man who wanted to be tricked. Couldn't he see that machine wasn't what it was cracked up to be? It was no Model 55 Ford that was for sure. Why did he even take him out there to look at a piece of junk? Just because it was cheaper?

It's a good thing they didn't go in together. Urs couldn't go into business with a man like August who wanted to go living on false hopes. Well hope wouldn't make the mortgage payment. After all hadn't he wanted it, too? Hadn't Urs hoped there would be some way they could have worked it out?

That's what a man gets, Urs thought, as anger beat red beneath his brow. People. You couldn't depend on them. Not like you could a machine. With a machine a man could see right up front if it could work or not. When it came to people, a man tries to do a favor and ends up getting treated like a piece of shit. Be better off just minding your own business and keeping your nose clean.

He could do just fine without August Krueger. That wasn't going to stop him. He'd have that farm. If he had to farm out the older kids so they'd have send the money home, he'd have it.

When Urs arrived at his own yard, he couldn't remember driving home. One thing was for sure though, he wouldn't be speaking to August Krueger for a while.

*

Only a few high clouds broke the sunlight as Margaret and Annie made their way down the lane to the house. Margaret fingered the blue cloth pouch of herbs. Annie was thinking of Buttermilk. And the little field by the lilac bush. When mother and daughter reached the gate to the house, they separated, going about their individual business.

Annie brought the cage with her bunny to the base of the lilac bush. Luscious clusters of color and fragrance greeted her. A million little buds had burst open overnight, each one a four-pronged star, a holy cross. A good sign, she was sure. And the little field? The light rain had destroyed some of her rows, but they could be easily repaired.

Annie positioned and repositioned her magical things. Buttermilk clawed and scampered in the cage. Annie couldn't get him to settle, not with tender leaves or little flowers. Then she remembered what Liz had said. The rabbit was albino. Annie studied the frantic animal. Yes, he kept turning from the light. His pink eyes couldn't tolerate bright daylight.

Briefly, Annie remembered the night she and her mother had been candling the eggs. Before she'd thrown the egg into the slop bucket, her mother said the chick couldn't survive if it hatched out funny like that--with two heads. But just because something was born different, didn't mean it would die did it? Couldn't it be born different and be better? Like Jesus? And Mary too? Annie scooted the cage under the shade of the bush. The bunny settled.

Satisfied, she sat without moving with her eyes partially closed. The sun on her lids, the cool earth damp beneath her. The only movement Annie felt was her breath under each nostril, cool and then warm. Breathing in--breathing out.

Suddenly, in a frenzy of clucking and fluttering the chickens started up. Among them stood her mother on the well packed earth. Seeing her there, washed in sunlight, Annie saw this as her mother's one true image. As she always was and always would be.

Margaret wore a loose cotton house dress even on Sunday now. Over it was what was left of one of Urs's shirts, tied around her waist by the arms. It had been Urs's Sunday shirt and Margaret had kept it that as long as possible. It was shocking white even now, and though she had patched and whip-stitched the cuffs, the material grew too thin. Too thin to find a portion to piece together for a shirt for Annie, or for patch work, or even to be of much use when Bloody Mary came to visit. But since she started the herbs at least she didn't have that worry for a while.

Cradling the coarse grain in the folds, Margaret dipped her hand and then lifted it in a graceful gesture to scatter the feed. It spilled golden in the shafts of sunlight. All her concerns and worries fell away. Margaret took on a confident satisfied look; as if she were surrounded by a huddle of undemanding friends. There was a gentle rush of power as the chickens scurried at her feet. A few new yellow chicks were big enough to join the hens. They scuttled crazily, their initiation to the earth, to the sunlight springing from between the retreating clouds.

Annie pressed the toy wagon, turning the spools neatly over the miniature field. Waiting to begin. Waiting to make sure she was alone. Annie hummed as she waited. "Rummmmmm," she said each time she breathed in. "Sou," she repeated each time her exaltation touched her protruding lips.

At Margaret's feet the kernels scattered in time with her dipping hand. A leghorn pecked away at a slower hen who came too close to a coarse nugget. Annie saw this gave her mother pleasure. And that soon her eye would turn. And she would dance. In a golden swirl of dust she would dance, and that would be Annie's time. The spoon glinted, calling Annie to her work. But she waited. Watching her mother.

Taking the tails of the ragged shirt Margaret pulled them one at a time, sifting the feed through the strained cloth. The chickens rose up in a white flurry all about her. Annie knew now that her mother's eye had turned so far into the corner she could no longer see. That Margaret was dancing, blind to this world as she remembered.

Margaret had only been seven. It was the Sunday of her first communion and the snow swans had risen up white all around. It was a miracle.

Maryanne, her twin was still alive. They were all still alive. Mother. Father. Jack. Freddy. All of them, still alive. It was Easter Sunday. The little twins' First Communion. They tied their shoes around their necks as they made way down the muddy path. Three miles home from church they learned years later when Urs measured it with his Ford.

It was spring. Even the sand hills turned to mud in spring. All the little ponds were full, like kettles brimming with water, brimming with life.

Margaret's Mother, Eva, walked behind, threading her way around the softest mud and most obvious puddles. The careful choosing of her steps; the awkward hesitancy, the intent concentration reflected the pattern of her thought. Easter Dinner. We always had a feast for Easter dinner. And now the twins' first communion too. Just a few potatoes left. Not to blame him, but how could he do that? How could he do that to himself, to the twins? Not having meat was nothing compared to that. Missing Holy Communion on Easter Sunday! On the day his daughters partook of the holy sacrament for the first time!

It had been a bad winter. A very bad winter. Fifty below zero for weeks at a time. And the wind!! Cattle and hogs froze to death in the pastures and barn. They finished the last of the canned goods a month ago.

Eva avoided a narrow rut. If only we'd been able to put the garden in a little earlier. Even the lettuce would be a week yet. Eva muttered to herself, shaking her head. There was the hand full of seed corn held back. And the dried peas. They would help some. They were soaking in the blue enamel dish on the window sill. But there would be no meat. How could there be a feast with no meat? No meat. No meat. This softly spoken phrase gave rhythm to her step.

That long ago time when the family threaded its way home from church, Margaret's father, Matthias, sat in the chair by the cold stove, going over what had happened. How could it be that he missed his own daughters' first communion? He'd wanted to go. More than anything, he'd wanted to go.

Hadn't he painted Freddy's shoes white, so Margaret had a pair too when she took her place by her sister at the rail? And the little white veils to cover their heads, hadn't he been able to come to terms with them too, though they were made from a portion of a curtain sheer passed already through many hands?

Matthias rose from the chair and began pacing the room. The winter had been too long. Too cold. There'd never been another one like it. Holed in for weeks, without so much as a footprint in the snow to show the world contained another living person, they ate up the last of Eva's canned goods. He'd brought the five remaining chickens into the house finally, after chopping out a path through twelve-foot drifts hard as cement.

The livestock froze to death on the hoof or huddled together in the barn. Just that one brown milk cow made it. By the time spring broke, that's all there was left. She was so skinny. They tried to get her to drink water. The kids picked the first patches of grass that sprouted. They brought it right to her. She was a sister, they said. She could make it.

Only Matthias saw she'd never give milk again. She was way past that.... sick....dying. But they kept her hanging on.

The night before Easter it came to him. Yes, they would have their Feast. They would have their celebration for the girls. At least the dying milk cow could give them that.

And now his sweet daughters were taking First Communion without him. Matthias left the kitchen and began walking aimlessly in the sunlight of the yard. How could it have all turned out like this? He stood in a daze, looking at nothing as he went over what had happened the night before.

It was late already by the time he talked himself into it. After all, this surviving milk cow was the last thing they could claim of any value.

He did it while the family slept. Tomorrow would be a new day. There'd be meat. And his daughters' first communion. A feast for Easter Sunday.

Afterwards the brown milk-cow lay crumpled at his feet. There was the sigh of putrid gas as his knife plunged into the hot cavity. The barn was quiet. Quiet as no barn should ever be.

When he slit her open, the putrid smell brought a rush of liquid to his mouth. What did he expect? After all the cow was sick. Maybe he'd have to throw out the organ meat. Tomorrow he'd see if the guts could be cleaned and saved for sausage casing. What did it matter as long as they had their feast.

He worked by moonlight. Moonlight dappled through the open barn door. There was the sound of something tearing. And then silence. And then the sound of tearing again, as he used his knife to skin her out. Moonlight dappled the flesh as he pulled back the skin.

At first he tried to wipe away the patches. He told himself the dark patches were nothing. Just the dappled moonlight coming through the open barn door.

When morning came and the family woke he was cursing God and burning the carcass of the dead cow.

They went to church without him.

Matthias sat in the chair by the stove staring at nothing. She had been full of worms. The flesh was full of worms, putrid smelling and half rotted. He shook the image away, composed himself and chopped out chunks of snow and ice to heat water. At least they would have hot water when they returned home, to wash their muddy feet.

Annie watched as her mother swirled to some ancient dance. Annie would begin her work. She fitted the handle of the spoon into the diagonal slits through the corner of the wagon. As she pressed her palm, her first two fingers raised, she curled their tips to the ground. Here they pranced and pawed, those two giant work horses King and Queen. More powerful even that those in the picture on the poster in Drake. The lead pair of twelve teams pulling the beer wagon across the dusty window of the Pines. They reared and pranced, ready for their work.

This while Margaret was dancing out her past on the well beaten earth of the chicken yard. No meat. No meat. Her mother, Eva, had taken up the chant on her way home from church. She was gaining on the twins. Her steps hurrying with her thoughts. Just a few potatoes left. And the young dandelion and thistle. And the vinegar. There was a little flour and sugar and the sourdough starter. She could still make Zwieback. The two onions lay in the root cellar.

Margaret's twin Maryanne had been at her side. The twins ran ahead cutting across the unbroken prairie, rising and falling as they raced across the dunes. Away from the beat of their mother's step. Away from the memory of their cursing father. Rising and falling, they ran toward holy reconciliation, and the glory of their first communion.

When they climbed the highest rise they reached for each other's hands. As they breached the top, a hundred snow geese took to the air at once. A flock of snow geese engulfed them rising up. All white. Their communion dresses floating, white. The girls were flying.

Margaret's mother threw the first rock. Then Freddy and then Jack.

When the family came into the yard they were singing. *Komm, schoepferischer Geist!* Come, Creating Spirit! It was a miracle.

From the small box on the table by their bed Matthias had got his blue handled knife and locked the blade into place. There were three in all. He cut off the heads and slit open the bellies. Eva dipped the birds in the scalding water. There were greens with vinegar. And Zwieback. It had been wonderful. A miracle. A feast.

*

Annie surveyed the completed work. She carefully lifted the spoon from the slots and returned it to the weeds along the very edge of the house. Then she placed Buttermilk's cage in her lap.

Her mother's dancing stopped. Just a faint dust of golden grain still clung to the white over the rounded curve of Margaret's belly. The chickens gathered behind as she made her way to the dark entrance of the coop. There Margaret quickly disappeared inside, a few bright chicks trailing after her.

From against the flat horizon Annie spotted Liz approaching. She was shaking the dirt from a head rag, waving the red flag against the open North Dakota sky. Dangling the cage, Annie ran to meet her. She fell into step and together they climbed the rise to the house. As they walked in silence, Annie couldn't see the spoon at all. She couldn't see it, but she knew exactly where it lay hidden, in the grass, just below the window.

Margaret, carrying her basket of eggs, called for them to come. Peering in to where her mother pointed, Annie saw the two. They lay away from the other eggs, placed carefully side by side. Their shells were as thin as the veined skin stretched across the pulsing belly of a new born baby.

By the time Urs drove into the yard, the boys had started the milking. Annie watched from the porch as her father removed a cloth from the glove compartment and wiped off the dash board and all the seats before painstakingly rolling up the windows and locking the doors. His climb to the house was consciously controlled, but it wasn't until he stomped onto the porch, that Annie recognized all this as anger.

Urs took his usual posture, hand raised to shade his searching eyes. With a faint growl he pulled air deep into his lungs. The sun soaked his great chest through the dark Sunday suit.

Then a welcome sigh released from his tense form and Annie thought she saw something wispy and dark rise above his head like a quivering ghost in the afternoon heat. Beyond where he stood, a haze of a green fuzzed like fine hair on the belly of the earth.

Her father removed his suit coat and hung it over one arm. "I'll give the boys a hand with the milking," he said. And then he turned to Annie, "Get that bat of Danny's, Annie, and the ball under Wayne's side of the bed. Let's play a little softball before dinner." Her father smiled as Annie jumped to her feet. A sturdy little farmer herself in striped overalls, Urs thought fondly as she raced to do his bidding. Then Urs caught the screen door before it slammed shut and went into the house to change clothes.

~22~

"Ladies and gentlemen, Superintendent Krostad, my beautiful wife, Mrs. Nielson, future graduates…." Humpy Chris nodded to each while making the recognitions. He continued with a speech that was decorated with Latin phrases and high sounding quotes from Longfellow, Shakespeare, Tennyson and others. Almost in unison, the farmers folded their arms over their chests and settled back in their chairs. Whenever Humpy Chris glanced up from his notes, fewer eyes looked his way.

Urs wore the same expression he had when he huddled under a tree or in a shed waiting for a short summer shower to pass. Now what was it Humpy Chris was blowing so much hot air about? "...Ladies and gentlemen...future leaders of the community." Urs picked up a word here, a phrase there. Humpy looked to him like a squat frog or a lumpy toad--his words buzzing around like shiny green flies.

Margaret leaned out to the side in order to see the backs of the graduates. Her feet hurt, but she didn't dare slip them out of her shoes. It had been a struggle to get them into the red pumps, but it was Danny's graduation after all. She did her best to listen to the speech, but the growing baby inside her was so distracting. Readjusting her gloves Margaret rested her arms on her belly. When the baby moved, poking out an elbow or heel, she eased it back in. She wondered, did Urs ever notice the baby's movements. They could be seen now if someone really looked, a little nob poking out now and then.

There it was again. And Margaret was pushing the baby back inside, pushing her daughter back in, pushing in her secret.

The baby took up so much room, sometimes Margaret felt there was hardly any left for her. Like her lie, she thought suddenly. More uncomfortable every day. A surge of bile rose in her throat. Margaret swallowed it down.

It was against her nature to be holding so much in. Even in the case of Danny. Margaret held in what she knew. She had avoided the matter of his missing so much school. Though it churned in her stomach, she didn't speak of her concern. She didn't want to draw attention to the fact. It was something more that she swallowed. Turning to poison with holding it in.

With all the times he had come home late or gone early he must have made up the work by now. Today she would find out and that would be over at least.

Chris paused for a moment and loosened his tie. His face took on an oily sheen. Margaret didn't like looking at him. Who could tell what the man was thinking? Maybe, he intended to withhold the diploma and make an example of Danny. Margaret tried telling herself these fears were silly.

Again Margaret leaned out looking down the aisle. From the back, the class members looked almost identical in the black choir robes borrowed from the church. Margaret had wanted a new suit for Danny, but she saw now that it hardly mattered. The robes covered them to the calves.

Only halfway through, Humpy Chris had lost most of his audience. He didn't care. Why, most of these people probably wouldn't even know what he was talking about anyway. He went along with his prepared speech automatically. As a representative of the school board, he gave the same one at all the little schoolhouses in this district.

As his eyes roamed down the row of graduates Chris tried identifying each of them. There was Edith Bloomer. She would probably have been selected valedictorian. And next, the oldest Schmidt boy. Humpy owned an interest in their farm. When he came to Danny his eyes rested there as the man studied the boy.

Danny returned his gaze looking back deeply, thoughtfully. The boy seemed to be listening. To be considering Chris's every word. Who was he now? So much taller and more grown-up looking than the others.

Was he the boy Chris had seen on horseback at the side of the road? Maybe that was it. Each time Chris looked up from his notes, their eyes met. And those eyes! How blue. And how straight he sat in the black robe, his shoes set out carefully before him. David, Humpy thought, I believe his name is David something. The dignified boy distracted Chris so that he lost his place. He stumbled a bit and then just kept talking. No one would probably notice the difference. Regaining his place on the note card, Chris picked up the pace. The words just kept coming.

The next thing Chris knew the schoolhouse room and the rest of the audience blurred. He found himself speaking earnestly. Just to Danny. "You can get ahead. You can attain your dreams if you just put your mind to it. Take a chance. Don't give up...."

Chris felt as if he and the blue-eyed boy were alone together. As if they were seated at a common table, discussing a common investment... partners somehow...."Don't expect to have anything handed to you... take what you want...." Chris felt a surge of kinship, as if Danny were a son, or a brother.

Then very suddenly, Chris was exhausted. He had nothing more to say. The humped man reached into his breast pocket and automatically withdrew the cigar, rolling it between his fingers. He was about to place it between his lips when the room full of dressed up farmers broke once again into his awareness. He laid the cigar down in the little lip at the edge of the podium.

Chris pulled out the note card from the back of the stack. "And so ladies and gentlemen, we salute this graduating class of 1947 for what they have already accomplished and for what they surely will accomplish in the future." Chris stepped from behind the podium and weakly bowed his little bow from the waist. How his back hurt.

Picking up his cards and papers, suddenly Chris's eyes welled. In spite of the relieved sighs and the applause, he felt fleetingly very sad and very lonely. As though he were returning to his seat after having received Holy Communion at a special mass, for an old and dear friend he'd only recently learned had been dead for a long, long time. Chris hung his head. His hump, as if it had a mind of its own, danced behind him as he returned to his seat.

Mrs. Nielson, in a shiny navy rayon dress with a big lace collar, took her place at the front of the room. One by one she called off the names of the graduates and they came forward to receive their diplomas. Danny was the last.

Mrs. Nielson stepped forward lightly tapping the rolled up diploma on her hand. It was tied with a lavender ribbon. "And now, I would like to announce the name of our final graduate and the valedictorian of the eighth grade class." Mrs. Nielson lowered her head and when she brought it up again she was beaming. "But first I'd like to tell you a little bit about this young man. I think he's proof of what qualities it takes to succeed. He proves once again that anyone can do well if he works hard, sticks by his commitment and has a positive attitude....Add to these qualities courage, kindness and dedication and you have the valedictorian of the class of 1947, Danny Borgen."

Mrs. Nielson took a step forward and, when she handed him the diploma, instead of shaking his hand as she had the other graduates, she gave him an affectionate hug and said, "Congratulations, Danny. May your future be bright."

Both Chris and Mr. Krogstad rose and motioned for the dazed young man to accept their extended hands. When his wife had announced Danny's name, Chris felt rejuvenated. He was pleased at having recognized something special in the boy.

Of course it would be him, Chris thought, as he returned the steady shake, looking into those bright blue eyes. He felt genuine camaraderie. Perhaps this was another one of the pleasures that came with growing older, with relaxing a bit and letting down one's guard.

A committee of mothers led by Edna Bloomer removed the podium and began setting up a makeshift plank table draped with cloth. In a matter of minutes a bowl of punch appeared. The table sagged with cakes and strudels, Rullkucha and spicy pepper cookies, Pfeffensse.

Margaret had brought kooga and it was set out on the carnival glass plate Danny had won for her so long ago. How nice the table looked. There were even flowers. Roses. Where could they have come from? It was too early for roses. Margaret bent to smell them.

She was enjoying the occasion as much as anything she could remember. The room buzzed with conversation as the graduates dispersed. Danny stood gesturing and talking in a cluster of students around Mrs. Nielson. He spoke with such poise, now and then giving his teacher a cheerful glance.

From across the room Margaret watched. He looked so different in the black gown and yet so familiar. So tall and grown up, like a priest, she thought. Danny could be a priest! He was smart enough. How she enjoyed watching him. He was so handsome. So animated and expressive. What a young man he had become! With a surge of realization it occurred to Margaret that she had been younger than Danny when she married Lars. Lars himself had been only a year older than Danny right now!

In the back corner, Liz was helping Pam and Edith step out of their choir robes. People had hardly had a chance to see their new dresses. The three girls joined the group around Mrs. Nielson.

Annie circled the impressive table of sweets. Everyone seemed excited and chattering.

Only Urs stood off to the side awkwardly shuffling his feet. He hated crowds. And being cooped up inside so long. What was Margaret doing standing there staring anyway? Wasn't it about time they got home? Urs crossed the room, and leaned in the open doorway.

It was a balmy June night. From where he stood, Urs saw Humpy Chris outside, all alone thoughtfully hunched over the tiny flame of his pocket lighter as he held it to his cigar. The crickets had come up. The air vibrated with their shrill ringing.

Watching his landlord Urs suddenly felt quite superior. How silly Humpy Chris had looked, making his pompous speech, his fat face glistening, his hump jumping in agreement with each point. Urs would never stand before a group of his neighbors like that, his voice cracking with emotion, his eyes welling. Urs moved into the doorway to take another look. Humpy Chris had moved deeper into the school yard. If it hadn't been for the lighted cigar in the darkness Urs might have missed seeing him altogether. Urs could hear him though, even above the crickets.

The man was bent forward coughing violently, the bright point of red held off to the side. It occurred to Urs that Humpy Chris looked like he was sobbing. A deep, forgotten feeling constricted Urs's throat. He cut off the feeling immediately. Why Humpy Chris looked like nothing so much as a big baby, sobbing uncontrollably.

When Urs turned back to the noisy room Mrs. Nielson approached. He stepped out of the way so she could get by, but she stopped in front of him.

"Urs Borgen, it's so good to see you.... Don't you look fine on such a fine occasion." Suddenly, Urs didn't know where to put his hands. "Won't you join me at the table for refreshments?" Should he walk in front of her or behind?

Urs broke into an awkward smile. "That's more like it," she said, guiding him toward the table. "You're one of our prize guests this evening, you know."

Mrs. Nielson was high with color, but she moved so smoothly, spoke so effortlessly, it was as if she were playing a part in some high school play. Chairs had been strung out in a line along the walls where some of the adults were already balancing their plates. Led by Margaret, the family was halfway through the serving line.

Wayne and Annie were heaping their plates with cookies and pieces of German chocolate cake. Liz was sandwiched between the two boys, swishing her taffeta skirt and talking to Danny. "Let me see the diploma, let me see it." Then she held up her hand hiding a loud whisper. "After all, you wouldn't have got it if I hadn't covered for you."

"No! No! Not now!" Danny pulled it out of her reach. "I haven't seen it yet myself. Besides it'll get dirty with all that chocolate on your plate. Wait 'til we get home."

Mrs. Nielson guided Urs into line near Margaret. Urs enjoyed cutting ahead of several neighbors.

"Oh, come on, Danny, come on now. I won't hurt it." Liz reached for the diploma.

Smiling playfully, Danny held it above her head as if he planned to hit her with it.

Mrs. Nielson stepped forward. "Danny, now you take real good care of that diploma. That's a very important piece of paper." The teacher shot a glance at Liz. "In fact Danny, why don't you let me take care of it for the time being. I'll put it up for safe keeping."

Edna Bloomer was serving at the reception table. "Congratulations, Danny," she said handing him a cup of punch. "What do you plan to do now that you've finished the eighth? Going on to high school in Drake I suppose." Edna Bloomer's white gloves climbed half-way up her plump arms. The woman had expected her daughter to be selected valedictorian.

"Gee, I'm not real sure just yet," Danny stammered.

"Now you take some of this kooga," Margaret insisted. She was too pleased to let the woman irritate her. Edna Bloomer knew Danny couldn't go to high school, and Margaret knew the woman thought the award was wasted on Danny. That it might have done her daughter's future education some good.

"Whatever Danny decides on you can be sure he will be a success. He's such a good worker...." Mrs. Nielson answered for him smiling with an artificial brightness that no one seemed to notice. She tapped the diploma lightly on the makeshift table. "As for now, I'm hoping his father will let me borrow him for a couple days next week. To help get this school house packed up for the summer vacation…and the desks sanded and varnished for next year."

She turned to Urs. "Do you think you could spare him a few afternoons?"

"Yea, I guess so, if you need him." Urs was startled into answering.

"It's a deal, then," Juanita Nielson said, extending her hand.

Urs looked down at his shoes. The tops shone, but he could feel the hole in the sole with his toe. Shaking hands with men, he was used to, but with a woman? And one this pretty? Then, hardly knowing where to place his finger and thumb he took her small white hand in his and shook it enthusiastically.

When they'd all had their fill of sweets and the conversation dropped off, the families began gathering their things. Many of the children had gone outside and were playing No Bears are Out Tonight, in the darkness. Their sing-song voices could be heard teasing imaginary bears as they rounded the schoolhouse. Margaret was collecting her carnival glass plate when Mrs. Nielson drew her aside. "I have something for you," she told Margaret. "I've been going through my things and I thought maybe you would want this." Juanita handed Margaret a box wrapped in white tissue paper tied with lavender ribbon. "It's a gift for you in honor of Danny's graduation. Something just for you."

Immediately, the box took a familiar weight and proportion in Margaret's hand. She looked deeply into the teacher's face. "Thanks," was her troubled reply. She placed it into her pocketbook and closed it with a faint snap.

When Margaret stepped from the confines of the crowded schoolhouse the far reaching prairie seemed unending. There wasn't much moon, so the vastness was more felt than seen. A light tepid breeze breathed on the back of her neck and her legs in the sheer silk stockings. Margaret could smell the fresh new green from where the row of poplars whispered. The air vibrated with the sounds of crickets and children. "No bears are out tonight. No bears are out tonight."

While the kids got into the car Margaret stood a moment looking into the darkness. She made out the hopeful glow of kerosene lights from a nearby farmhouse.

Inside the car Margaret eased her aching feet out of the red pumps. She felt tired, but so contented. It had all gone right. Margaret couldn't remember ever feeling so proud of anything in her whole life.

"Danny, I always knew you had it in you. That extra time at school these last weeks sure paid off. I can't tell you how proud I am." Margaret made this little speech rather hurriedly, wanting to finish while Urs turned the crank. Then the motor caught, Urs settled in beside her--all that could be heard was the chugging of the engine.

Urs turned on the lights, illuminating the ruts and dried clods, before maneuvering the car around and down the lane. As they bumped along Margaret's purse fell off the seat to the floor boards. In the dim lights from the dash, there lay the red pocketbook, fallen open. Her gift, wrapped in the white paper, had tumbled out. Normally she would have picked it up immediately. It was just for her, Juanita Nielson had said.

But maybe, Margaret thought, the ivory box was something she no longer wanted.

"Danny," Urs shifted down, looking ahead into the darkness. "Don't worry about what I said to the school teacher tonight."

"She looked like she was having such a good time I didn't want to.… Of course, I'm not sending you out on no charity case packing up books. Not while Allen Schmidt's got greenbacks in his pocket he's willing to hand out to kids."

Danny sat straight as a board in the back seat. "But you promised her. You shook on it." The words sprayed out like hissing liquid released from a shook-up bottle of Coca-Cola.

This time Urs turned around when he spoke. "You're getting awful big for your britches, young man. Sounds to me like you need to get knocked down a peg or two.…" Urs turned back to the road. "If you think getting some dumb eighth grade diploma means you can start mouthing off to me, you got another thought coming. I won't take you messing around with my plans, you understand. I won't take it!"

When they got to the farmhouse Margaret couldn't get her feet back into the pumps. But nothing was going to spoil her pleasure, not Urs, or swollen feet, not anything. "Now, what am I going to do, Annie?" Margaret laughed. "My feet grew two sizes this evening! Swollen with pride I guess. Run in and get those fuzzy pink slippers from under the bed. I don't want to snag my stockings going barefoot up the cement walk."

Annie hurried ahead of the others. When she entered the silent house, she heard the faint peeping of the unhatched chicks from the incubator on the shelf behind the stove.

"We can't help them." Margaret told her fretting youngest daughter, before bed that night. "They need to be strong enough to fight their way out of their shells or they can't survive."

~23~

At first Urs thought maybe it was some kind of trick. At first he thought that she was going to try and make him do something he'd feel sorry for later. So he held out. But it didn't turn out that way. By holding out he'd got what he wanted. What he hadn't even thought of getting.

Urs and the two boys were shoveling out the barn when he caught a glimpse of her through the open barn door. She was driving into the yard in that little black Chevy Coup. "What in the name of Christ?" Urs said, steadying the shovel before him, and taking a hanky from his pocket to wipe his forehead and the worst of the muck off his hands and fingers.

She pulled right up to the side gate and got out. Then she opened the gate and started down the cement like she came visiting at Margaret's kitchen ever day of the week. Well, he'd see what this was all about once and for all. This time she wouldn't trick him into saying he was giving Danny up to work for nothing.

"You boys get this place mucked out now. I got business to attend to." Urs set the shovel aside and hurried after the woman.

By the time he got to the gate, Margaret was at the back door asking her to come on in.

"Just a minute," Urs interrupted. "I'll take care of this, Margaret." Urs set his face, and strode down the walk. He didn't care that he smelled of manure.

The teacher turned and seeing Urs smiled a greeting. "Oh, Mr. Wagnor, I was so hoping to see you."

"Well, come on in. Come on in and have a cup of coffee." Margaret scowled at Urs from behind the screen door, standing her ground. "Whatever you need to discuss you might just as well come in here and do it."

"This'll do just fine right where we are." Urs folded his arms across his chest. His feet seemed planted in the cement.

"Thanks anyway, Mrs. Wagnor," the teacher nodded. "Mr. Wagnor's right though, no need taking up too much of his time."

Urs stood unmoved, rounding over his folded arms.

"What I came to say is this," the teacher began slowly addressing Urs. "I've been discussing what I mentioned to you, about Danny helping with the books and shellacking the desks. I've been discussing it with the school board and...." Urs took a quick small breath and opened his mouth to speak. But before he got a word out she began again.

"Well, I been discussing that with the school board, and we could use help getting all the little schools in the county packed up and ready for next year. Some of the books and desks need to be moved around--and to make a long story short, the board would like to hire Danny."

The expression on Urs's face hadn't changed one iota all during the teacher's speech. Now Urs stepped forward, arms still tightly wrapped around his chest. "I'm afraid Danny's not available for any other work at all. He'll be working for Allen Schmidt the next three weeks or so, driving cattle out to open range." Urs's manner was arrogant, his face stiff.

The teacher looked down. "I can see why. He's a good worker." She began slowly stroking a scarf tied at her throat, looking up at Urs. There was a nervous tightness around her mouth. "The school board has authorized me to offer him five dollars a day with a hundred dollars minimum if he finishes the job on time."

She lowered her eyes again, her hand still on the scarf at her throat. She waited a moment as if gathering her thoughts and then added, "Of course they didn't want me to say it right out front the first time we talked, but I can see now this might be my only chance."

This news took Urs completely by surprise. But he had been so guarded and so set to resist her that his expression didn't change even now.

The woman studied him thoughtfully. She was holding her breath, and then--"I might throw in a bonus of twenty-five dollars myself if he does a good job." Her hand fell from her throat.

Though he still stood stooped over his folded arms Urs broke into a wide grin.

"Don't you think, Urs, we can come inside now and discuss this over coffee and Rullkucha?" Margaret, standing patiently through all these tense negotiations, asked from the other side of the screen door.

And so it was done.

*

Wednesday morning Margaret found Annie packing.

When she first heard of Allen Schmidt's cattle drive, Annie'd wanted to go, too. Wayne went around singing every song Gene Autry ever knew. Liz told her of cooking over an open fire and of sleeping out under star-filled skies. And when Annie heard that Danny wouldn't be going, she grew more determined than ever. I'll take his place she announced. Annie had even saved space to one side of the box for Buttermilk's crumpled chicken-wire cage, but her hopes were a blind, racing horse straight at a barbed wire fence.

"Annie, honey, now what do you think you're doing?" Margaret leaned into the door frame. She was beat, bone tired--up since before daybreak supervising Wayne and Liz, making sure they had everything they needed and that it all fit in one box each. There had been arguments over neckerchiefs and a bracelet and their rosaries and prayer books.

And now here was Annie, with that fierce look, filling a cardboard box of her own. The whole routine had been upset. Why, it was almost afternoon, and the separator hadn't been cleaned.

"I'm going," Annie said shaking two clenched fists.

Margaret shuffled into the room and sat on the edge of the bed. "Come on now, honey. I know you want to go, but you'll be farmed out soon enough."

"I'm going," Annie said insistently. Her voice cracked as she repeated her declaration. A dry burning rose in her throat. She squeezed back the tears and began arranging her box more determinedly than ever. Little dry heaves shook her chest and shoulders.

For a minute or so Margaret let her be. Then she started, slowly rubbing the little back. "Annie, I'm sure Allen could use you." She was talking soft and low. Margaret could feel the tense muscles climbing along each side of the little spine. "I'm sure if he found out what-all you could do he'd be glad to have you out there on that cattle drive." Margaret worked her fingers where she felt the tenseness. Annie slowed her organizing. "But now, Annie, we need you here. We couldn't do without you." By now Annie sat hunched over the box, her arms resting at her sides. "With Liz and Wayne, and Danny too gone most the time, how could we do it all?"

"And, Annie, I'm not feeling real good a lot of the time, myself. You know I've been getting tired out real bad lately. Annie, I need you here to help out."

From the empty space in the bottom of the cardboard box rose a dull drop, drop, drop. The dry shuddering had turned to deep wet gasps. Margaret pulled Annie to her. "I'm really sorry, Annie, but we can't let you go right now. We need you too much here at home."

Annie dried her cheeks and reached out to embrace her mother. The heaving had subsided to wrenching little hesitations.

*

Overhead a clear blue sky arced from horizon to horizon. Green grass higher than Annie's boot tops flicked like bent pages of a book quickly released, each time she took a step. The sun caressed her shoulders and a mild heat radiated from the dark earth beneath her feet. This was the first time Annie had been trusted to bring in the milk cows by herself, the first afternoon since the older kids had left. Annie stopped to watch Pet and Sport work the cattle into a cluster and turn them towards home. She believed that the two herding dogs could do it without any human help at all. That they knew the time of day. Each afternoon promptly at 4:00, they lay whining on their backs, tails beating the dirt, anxiously waiting for the signal.

Wayne had trained the dogs to herd, though it was Margaret who had chosen these two from the litter. She first saw the five, eight-week-old pups snuggling together in a pile of gunny sacks in the corner of the little shed August Krueger used for storing hand tools.

Margaret had lifted each one by the back of the neck as she looked it over carefully. She hefted it for weight and noticed the sex. She stroked the fur checking for thickness and glossiness and fleas. Margaret had always been the one to pick their dogs. Even as a child she'd done it for her own dad. The ones who didn't make the cut, her brother Jack had hauled to the creek and drowned. Margaret hadn't made a mistake yet. August, Urs and Katie milled around behind her as she set each pup aside separately and watched the way he moved. She looked for any indication of bone problems or trouble in the hip area.

She wanted them to have a certain standard of health and looks of course. But it wasn't size or sex or even general health she was most interested in. It was their ability to handle cattle. How smart they were. It wouldn't be 'til she opened their mouths that she made her real decision.

August, Katie and Urs had stepped out of the cool shed to the sunshine. Alone, Margaret carefully opened each mouth and looked inside--for the black roof. Two identical pups had it. She chose them without a moment's hesitation, passing up the biggest, as well as a handsome male. When she'd made her selection she brought them out to where Urs and the others stood waiting in the sun. If they had asked, even Margaret couldn't explain why these were the ones. She only knew the hidden black marking showed them to be strong and easy to train.

That was the last thing Margaret had to do with them. She never liked dogs around the house and wouldn't allow them beyond the gate. Urs took the pups from her and carefully placed them in the bottom of a gunny sack. From his pants pocket he took a small coil of twine and securely tied the bag shut.

Wayne had taken them under his care immediately. Before the wagon arrived back home he had untied the sack and the two pups were biting at his fingers with their small sharp teeth. If he could have trained other dogs, as well as the ones Margaret had selected, no one would ever know.

And now, for a few weeks anyway, Annie was in charge. She was the one who gave the whistle that sent them racing out behind the barn heading for the pasture. For a while at least they answered to her.

Maybe it hadn't been so bad having to stay behind alone after all. Her mom had been right. They did need her.

Pet circled around a stray. The dog suddenly dropped on her back haunches and rushed. The errant cow trotted back towards the herd. Annie felt satisfied. Her mom had been right. She was needed. She could do the work.

Real work made Annie feel stronger. Smarter somehow. She'd dragged the post hole digger all the way beyond the silo yesterday afternoon where her dad was working. All by herself. Even he had showed surprise that she could do it.

"*Arbeit adelt*," work ennobles the soul, Urs had said, smiling.

And the more real work she did the more she forgot about the other--at the base of the lilac bush. After all wasn't she really helping with the farming now? What good could that be? Annie picked up her pace. In the air, just above the ditch brush ahead, hung a swarm of gnats. She headed deeper into the pasture to avoid it.

But she'd always had a special feeling about working in her pretend little field. Like it was something she was supposed to do. Like praying. Suddenly Annie felt guilty.

But everything was so good lately. That was no excuse was it? Like not saying your prayers when you didn't have any problems.

Like not believing in God. Annie bumped right into the swarming gnats. One got in her eye.

That afternoon Annie wasn't the only one out in the fields. Earlier Urs had hooked up the cultivator in anticipation of the days ahead. Just puttering, really. Since the crop was all in, but not up all the way yet, there wasn't much more that he could do. When he finished he drove the tractor back into the machine shed. It was so nice out, he thought he might as well survey the land. Give things a good looking over.

Of course Urs knew already how the crops were doing. But he just had to visit them again. To reassure himself. And while he was at it he might just as well try to locate those markers. He might just as well find out if that point on the map corresponded with where that little painted stake had been. And if he could locate the others. And if they really did define the boundaries of the farm.

As he headed off across fields, he could hardly control his pace. His heart banged with excitement. Urs wanted to run in the open field and leap into the air like a boy. Like the boy he never was. Like the boy he never had a chance to be. His brother Harold had farmed him out after their parents died. Farmed him out to Lawrence Reisinger, assuring Urs what a good German farmer their farmer was?

A stationary steam engine had been set up in the middle of the wheat field to run the machinery. At ten years old, Urs was dizzy with the heat and the intense noise and the dirt. He'd been in the group that threw the cut hay onto the belt. Though his hands were big for his age, they weren't as big as a man's. A blister rose where the fork handle rode between the thumb and finger of his bad hand. All morning the bundle haulers gained on him. Though he worked as fast as he could, the pile at his side grew larger.

The sky was darkening. Flying chaff and dirt from the wheat found their way into his eyes, and nose, and throat. His ears. And clung to the hair of his arms. All morning the men had been cursing and calling to each other from the flat beds. The teams whined in terror at the noise from the machinery.

Urs was a little behind the others as the men came in hot and tired for lunch. Tables were set at the edge of the field and spread with steaming bowls of Suppen and Grundbeeresalat, potato salad, Sauerkraut and Wurst, crusty loaves of hearty Russian Borodinsky.

Urs was approaching the table with the others when Lawrence Reisinger singled him out.

"What do you think you're doing here?" Urs's stomach knotted. Oh, God, what had he done wrong now?

"You get down there and water those horses. You hear me? You'll eat when I say you'll eat... When we're done. Do you understand?"

Urs started towards the teams still harnessed to the flatbeds. His stomach leapt with anxiety and hunger.

The sky was threatening. Urs could feel the rain coming.

The boy unharnessed the horses and led them to the water tank. The knotting in his stomach eased. Wasn't he more comfortable here than with the men? With men he never knew how he'd be treated.

He'd been farmed out since his folks died. At one place they kept him like a pet. They'd never expected much work out of him. He didn't trust that any more than working here.

It was hot. And humid. Unbearably humid. Overhead, a darkening layer of clouds pressed down. Urs was so thirsty. So thirsty and sticky. His head still had the odor of kerosene. The horses crowded around the water tank. Urs elbowed for a place.

Water never tasted so good. His lips grew cool and wet, his eyes closed with the pleasure. With bent head he could hear the mare sucking noisily at his side.

What he felt for the horses maybe couldn't be called affection. It was more like kinship. Or maybe it was just the knowing. If a horse hurt its leg it would limp. After it ate it shat. The boy liked the knowing.

Urs dipped his head in the cool water of the tank and rubbed his shaved skull, before beginning the job of harnessing the teams again. By the time he was done, the men had finished eating. They sat around the yard while the women cleared the table.

Still hungry, Urs was drawn to the fringes. Lightning danced in the distance. The sky was growing darker. Urs knew if it rained they'd have to stop threshing. He knew this crew wasn't cheap. That they could hardly be paid to stand around waiting for the weather. He'd heard Lawrence worrying about it all week.

"You like soup?" Lawrence grabbed a handful of Urs's shirt. "You think you'd like some of that soup?"

It was *Pellkartoffelsuppe mit Speck*. There were new potatoes no bigger than marbles, and fresh peas and new carrots, all in a thick cream. Bits of crispy bacon were crumbled on top. It smelled wonderful. Lawrence held the bowl in front of Urs's face. "Here take this spoon. You can eat as much as you want." Urs stepped forward, digging in eagerly. Faint thunder grumbled through the sky.

"What kind of manners is that? Did you see that, boys?" Lawrence spoke louder increasing the attention of the others. "He didn't even say grace, and he wants to eat right out of the serving bowl! Come on over here, boys." Lawrence motioned to the men sprawled on the grass, picking their teeth. "Let's teach this kid some manners."

They made him get down on his knees. The men stood around laughing and coaching. "Don't forget to say your prayers."

They had him on his knees with the soup bowl balanced on his heels behind his back. He held the spoon in his bad hand.

"You can eat as much as you want," Lawrence prodded. Another took it up. "Go ahead, aren't you hungry?" By the time Urs maneuvered the spoon around to his mouth most of the soup had spilled.

"What are we going to do with him? He doesn't know his prayers... He wants to eat out of the serving bowl.... And now he spills his food all over his clothes...."

Urs shut his eyes and shook away the humiliating memory. But when he did he saw the face of the boy in the Life Magazine on the table at August's. Urs found himself staring into those sad brown eyes sunk in deep hollows.

~24~

There wasn't any reason for that kind of remembering. Now, maybe his luck had changed. Now, maybe if he could just have something to call his own, for once in his life. Something maybe to hand down to a son, like a good German farmer would do. That kind of remembering only hurt him--confused him. After all it was a beautiful day.

Urs was headed east, between the fence and the ditch bordering the road. He kept a strong steady pace bringing himself back to the present. The dark earth was moist and giving under the foot, but not muddy. Urs's hands curled loosely at his sides. He came to a patch of foxtails, just beginning to fluff out green. Urs thoughtfully pulled one and stuck it between his teeth, chewing lightly. Tasting the sweetness. A light wind rose and fell.

Urs was approaching the end of the field. The flax was coming in strong and thick, just like he knew it would. But more and more his eyes fell to the ground. He found himself kicking at the weeds where he thought he'd seen the stake before. Prying with his eyes, darting his gaze. But what difference really should a stake make to him? Why would it matter just exactly where the boundaries ran? After all, the land wasn't his.

He found it easily, at the edge of the field along the fence line, where he remembered it. So he was right--it must be a boundary marker. This would be exactly that point marked on the little map in the shoe box under the bed.

Urs scraped away the dirt from the stake, with his shoe. It was a square wooden stake painted red. There were numbers on the side. And letters. The same ones he'd seen on the map.

Satisfied Urs turned, heading west, retracing his steps. He felt good. Contented in a way. Like the world had some order to it, some boundaries that were sure and known. He crossed the lane to the house and followed the fence line again, continuing west.

It seemed like things were starting to fit together, like the pieces of that old clock he worked on. Even things that before he wouldn't have paid much attention to, now seemed all to point the same direction.

Urs slowed his pace. This section was all in corn. The dark leaves were just opening, curling upward. For the first time since planting, he could really tell where the rows were. Urs enjoyed the orderliness of the design emerge, first the straight lines north and south. And then the diagonal. And when he stepped into the field looking the other way, east and west. It reminded him of green soldiers marching, or a band at a Fourth of July parade.

Right about where the road ran out, Urs started looking for the next marker. Along the fence line. Where the creek cut through. That next stake must be right in through here somewhere. When he saw it, where the fence poles petered out on the creek bank, a surge of heat rose to his face. He bent over it, smiling and rubbing his hands together. Another small wooden stake, this time in a patch of bare gravel that washed down the bank. Who could explain the rush of joy?

Urs removed his cap, rubbing his head through the thick, black hair. How could he feel so good? He'd been afraid to even hope for so long--but when Danny explained the papers, it sounded like there was a way. One of those laws still on the books from the thirties, when Governor Langer and that bunch was in the state house. First rights to refusal, was it?

Urs continued down the creek bank, lost in thought. Thinking over how everything seemed to be falling into place. Of course after that deal with the teacher, there'd been the problem of telling Allen. Since there really wasn't any way to get a hold of him on such short notice they'd just hoped he'd take Wayne and Liz anyway.

Even that had gone better than Urs would have thought possible. Of course Allen was disappointed that Danny wasn't there, but he had to admit Margaret did a good job of smoothing it over with the *rullcoka* and coffee, and apologizing so.

When Wayne told Allen the story about how he won the medal, that didn't hurt any, either. Allen had roared with laughter and pounded his fist, nearly spilling his coffee and told Wayne he really needed someone who could ride. Urs smiled thinking of it. And Liz had charmed him too. She wore a pair of blue jeans and a pretty pink blouse, looking rosy cheeked and ready to work, her hair done up in a ponytail. By the time it was all over, everyone was in a good mood. The kids loaded their boxes in the truck bed and piled into the seat beside Allen.

Allen stuck out his hand to Urs through the rolled down window. "There's no hard feelings about Danny, Urs. I can understand a man can't let an opportunity just go on by. I got a feeling these two here are gonna do just fine."

When Urs got to the northwest corner, again he hunted the marker stake. He paced up and down the fence line. Back and forth dragging his feet. Suddenly it occurred to him that it wouldn't be here. The creek angled some and he had used it as a guide as he'd chugged along with the old F-20 pulling the two-bottom, just as he had now.

That would mean the stake was west of here, yet. Across the creek. Maybe even as far in as those big cottonwoods. For a minute he thought about giving up the search. What difference would it really make where all the markers were? But something about it wouldn't let him alone. The thought of hunting it down exhilarated him. He had to know.

Urs hurried back down the side of the field. When he got where he could see the corner he'd found already, he stopped. Letting it out of his eye for an instant he hurried down the creek bank, rushing through the water and back up the other side. Again his eyes found the point. He lined himself up with it as closely as he could. Then, spreading his arms straight out, exactly parallel to the way the fence, ran he began going straight north. With his arms spread wide, he looked like an overgrown boy who had never given up the childhood dream of learning to fly.

Urs saw now that the northern boundary must be quite a ways from where the creek cut though. With his arms still stretched wide he went crashing through a clump of gooseberries, hardly noticing the stickers. There was something about finding the stakes. And defining this land. Defining it exactly. And making the new path.

When Urs came north far enough to be back in line with the fence again, he began stomping down the grass in a widening circle. A noisy gray squirrel leapt from branch to branch in the cottonwood above him, claiming the territory himself. By now Urs was way west of where the creek ran through. Way west of where he stopped farming.

Maybe he'd gone too far. All this couldn't be part of the farm, could it? Urs began dragging his feet through the rank growth. Just then he heard the thud and felt the toe of boot hit the third stake, smack dab in the middle of a patch of wild roses. Urs stomped his feet, flattening the old canes and fresh shoots.

It protruded only about three inches above the ground, was painted red, and was perfectly square from the top. When Urs saw it his heart jumped. It was just a marker, he told himself. Just a marker to a farm that wasn't even his. So what if it indicated Humpy Chris owned a bit more land than they'd supposed? In spite of what his mind said he felt this by rights was his. As though he'd discovered it. Urs looked around.

This patch was wild land, with big cottonwoods and gooseberry bushes and wild roses. Maybe never been cleared. It would take a lot of work to make it farmland. If a man owned the property though, it would be worthwhile all right, to put in a little bridge out of 4X12's and take the tractor over here. There'd be stones to pick and buffalo bones too he saw now, but it would be worth it.

Standing in among the big trees with the sun filtering through in bright patches and the meadowlarks darting through the sky, it occurred to Urs that it was wonderful just the way it was. A chattering flock of goldfinches rose from the glowing meadow. Yes, it was something wonderful that belonged to him, that he hadn't even known he had.

Urs emerged from the wild land as if he were coming out of a dream. He felt as if he'd found something he'd been looking for all his life, like another part to his very own body. A part that he could do things with he hadn't even thought about. Urs couldn't have been more surprised if he'd looked down at his dangling hand and seen all the fingers growing there.

Urs splashed through the shallow creek, ignoring the damage to his boots. And there on the other side, struggling up the rocky bank, a box turtle, with its highly arched, bright green dome. A good omen, he thought. He would buy this farm one way or another. Now he felt sure it was meant to be.

Urs paced the fields of wheat all along the north boundary. Just that one little patch was a bit thinner, where the water had a tendency to sit. Otherwise, it was coming in strong and thick. And there in the corner, right where it should be, Urs found the final marker.

Satisfied beyond reason, Urs headed back. When he got to where the wheat bordered the alfalfa and the pasture, he bent, spreading the barbed wire and expertly slipped through the strands.

When he was able to see beyond the brush at the fence line, he found the alfalfa was coming in just as he hoped. A fuzzy mat of lighter green, even and thick. It made him think of a woman somehow, or a young girl with curling hair.

Urs slipped through the fence and started along the pasture towards the house. He thrust his hands deep in his pockets looking from horizon to horizon. Now he could really see exactly what land was his. How he loved it.

Annie swerved into the pasture up ahead of him. He stopped to watch. She was bringing in the cattle. The dogs were expertly working under her command. Yes, she was part of his plan too. In a few years it would be just her and the little one and him and Margaret. He waved to her and called out her name.

Now, Annie saw him too. She stood waving back, waiting for him to catch up. "Annie, you got those dogs doing just right. Just don't let Sport get 'em running. Have her bring 'em in nice and slow. Nice and slow makes the milk sweet." Annie melted under the unexpected compliments. She reached out and curled her fingers around his big one. They started home together.

"She won't run 'em, Dad. Wayne already broke her of that." Her lightly curled fingers trustingly clung to his. Their high-top work boots swished through the pasture grass.

Just then a disturbed wild prairie chicken rose in flight. The hen had a nest in the grass along the fence where they stood. The movement momentarily broke Pet's attention. The dog approached, head down sniffing. "You get on back to those cows," Urs pointed speaking sternly.

When she was back again among the cows, Urs brought Annie cautiously to the nest. It was well hidden near the fence post. Gently pulling the grass aside they looked in. There was a single chick, very fluffy and brown, peering up at them.

Urs felt Annie's fingers squeeze his own.

Oh God, how could he get his hopes up so high again? Hadn't he always been knocked down? But he wanted to hope. Annie kept steady at his side. "What do you think, Annie? Look like a good crop to you?"

Annie stayed in perfect rhythm at his side, her two steps to his one. If things went right for him maybe he could still be the kind of man he always wanted to become. A good man. A good German farmer, with his own farm and his own family.

"It's going to be the best crop yet, Dad, I can just tell by the way it's starting out."

"You think so. Annie? You think we're really going to hit the jackpot this time?" But of course it was too early to tell. One year it started out just like this. The crop just got better and better until the hail ruined it all right before harvest. It came down as big as baseballs shredding the corn, wrecking everything. Another time it was the grasshoppers. Oh God, if you would just let it be OK this once. Just this one time.

Swish, swish. The grass bent under their boots. A good man. The kind he always wanted to be. "You're all I got now, Annie. You going to help me get in the crop?"

He squeezed her hand. If the older kids could just help him now too with the money, he would pay them back. Not because he had to, but because he wanted to. A good man. A man in control of his own farm, his own family. A man who could afford to help out kids that weren't even his own blood.

Urs smiled down at the girl at his side. The hair that lay along her pale scalp was wet with the heat of keeping up. It gave off a sweet dusty smell. Near the windmill a slight breeze set the blades to spinning. It fanned the birch trees into movement, turning the new leaves, hinting at the silver undersides.

And everywhere he looked, as far as he could see it was green.

*

Urs and Annie watched the rabbit in its cage on the porch after milking. "Look at those ears, Annie. Do you think you could wiggle your ears like that?"

In the kitchen, Margaret was mixing up the dumplings. Each time her spoon hit the side of the bowl the rabbit pricked his ears.

"Look at that. Look at that." Annie pressed her hands to her cheeks, and looked out over the tops of her fingers, laughing. The two large white ears were quivering in anticipation of the next clink.

"Too bad Wayne's not here. He can wiggle his ears like that. Annie, you give it a try." Urs held back her hair, while she mimicked the bunny, puckered her mouth, nodding her head each time she did. "No, Annie. Your ears! You got to concentrate on your ears. Now try it again." Again, Urs held back her hair. This time Annie flexed the cords in her neck.

"We got to have Wayne demonstrate. Just as soon as he gets back."

Margaret lifted the lid and carefully spooned the soft dough into the boiling pot. "Ok, Annie. It's about time you came in and set the table. Just bowls and these little plates with the Jell-O should be enough."

Some days, since the older kids were gone, Margaret made a light supper. Tonight, *Leberknoedelsuppe*. Now, she felt safe in finishing up most of last summer's *Eingemachtes*, the preserved foods that had filled the pantry. The garden was doing so well. It looked like in a week or two there'd already be new onions, and carrots and radishes.

Tonight, she was serving a Jell-O salad with *Mochonye Yabloki*. Each glistening portion of the preserved apples was laid out on a new lettuce leaf from the garden and the whole thing decorated with a dab of mayonnaise.

While Margaret said the prayer aloud, Urs's eyes roamed the table. The soup was in the middle, with the dumplings puffed up round and high, just the way he liked them. There to the side was a plate of Margaret's heavy dark rye bread sliced thin. And the butter. His eyes came to rest on the fancy little Jell-O salads.

Wasn't that just like Margaret? For a man they seemed silly. Lacy-like. Each one on its own individual plate with a leaf of new lettuce fringing the jiggling pink square with sliced apples. Urs looked at his wife. Her eyes were closed, her pretty mouth forming the last words of her prayer. Her face looked peaceful. Margaret hurriedly made one more sign of the cross.

When their eyes met Urs looked down again. There was the Jell-O salad. "Looks like you're already getting fresh lettuce out of the garden?" Suddenly Urs recalled the packet of flower seed he had bought on his last trip to Drake with Danny. Nasturtiums, the man had said. The picture on the front of the packet showed the flowers had a lacy edge like the lettuce.

"Just these few leaves," Margaret commented. "Not enough to make bacon and wilted greens but it's coming up good." She was dipping out the soup. The largest bowl for Urs, first. Three large white dumplings floated on top. She placed it before him and started in on Annie's.

Urs bent, alternately slurping the soup and biting at a thin slice of rye bread quivering in his hand. Maybe he should go get that packet of flower seeds and give them to Margaret. After all, what good would they do on the high shelf in the machine shed?

"It's quiet around here without the older kids isn't it?" Margaret had her soup dished out, too, now and had begun eating. "I guess Danny won't be home 'til later. When Mrs. Nielson picked him up this morning she said they'd be working at the school in Drake. Maybe 'til dark. I'll hold a little soup out for him."

"The quiet's kinda' nice for a change," Urs answered, only half listening. What would it hurt if he just went out after supper and brought in the pack of flower seeds and threw it on the table and said, Here, this is for you.

"Yeah, I guess we should enjoy it while we can, cause when this little one comes along, it'll be an end to the peace and quiet for a while."

Urs mopped the last of the soup with his final piece of rye. "Oh, that's right." He was blushing. "I guess that's right." Urs smeared the dab of mayonnaise over the little square of Jell-O.

He had cut through the lettuce with his fork and was just about to take a bite when suddenly Urs rose from the table and hurried out the door. In a minute he returned with the packet of flower seeds in his hand. "Margaret, I forgot to give these to you from the last time I went to town." He laid them by her plate while she looked up in astonishment. Then, he pulled out his chair, sat down and resumed eating as if nothing had happened.

~25~

The house was quiet, clean and empty. Humpy Chris sat at the dining room table, hands tented as if he had caught a hummingbird in flight.

She should be home by now. Even if they had worked late, she should be home. Chris furrowed his brow, breathing heavily. If he spread his palms, would some hovering thought he didn't want to have, escape and burst into his awareness? The clock chimed seven. His elbows startled, crumpling the white crotched table cloth on the polished wood, bringing him out of his musings. Instead of following his growing uneasiness, Chris told himself the feeling was only a growing concern for the safety of his wife.

Maybe she hadn't allowed enough time to drive out and back to the Wagner place. That must be it. He'd tried to convince her it might be a problem. That any teenager right here in town would do just as well closing up the school for summer. Well, she could trust Danny, she'd argued. Besides, his family could use the extra money. One of her charity cases.

The tablecloth shirred away as Humpy Chris shoved and leveraged himself up out of the chair. Her car had been out in front of the school house late that morning. Chris had been by the bank already and the jewelry store. He had just made an estimation of his total worth, when he'd thought of her and got the urge just to drive by. Just to see what she was up to, even if they didn't speak.

She'd been laughing, bringing in a load of books. That Borgen boy was helping. The morning had felt of spring. The sky blue and sunny. Everything was fine. Even the aching in his back that was almost constant lately, had let up. He didn't think she'd noticed when he drove by. She hadn't looked up.

Humpy Chris folded into his armchair in the living room. He immediately began coughing violently over the standing chrome ashtray to the side cradling the butts of two fully smoked cigars. Ashes plumed and drifted. Maybe the penicillin wasn't working any more. Dr. Hanson had said sometimes that happened.

Lying on his side, in Dr. Hanson's little brightly lit examination room, Chris had stared into the mirror. He'd wanted someone to talk to, but he'd made out it was just a routine visit. That he was just interested in the state of his degenerative disease.

Contrary to what you thought, Mr. Nielson, the hump hasn't grown larger at all. It's just that the vertebrae are getting brittle with age, wearing down on the edges, causing them to fold over onto themselves.

And the cough?

The doctor had placed the stethoscope on Chris's sunken chest. Doubled over like that makes it difficult to expand the lungs to their full capacity. You know we've been down this road before. Your lungs have a tendency to collect excess fluids; and when that happens, as you know, there is always the possibility of pneumonia.

Then the needle prick and the doctor delivering the news along with the antibiotic: people could become immune to what was once good for them.

It was getting dusky out already. Maybe he'd see what Mrs. Jenson had left for dinner. Probably another one of her modern one-dish meals.

On the bottom shelf in the Frigidaire was a tossed salad and the cake pan covered with tinfoil. It had a note stuck to the top of it. "One hour at 350. Keep foil on." He lifted the edge. A cut-up chicken on a bed of uncooked rice with a thick pasty sauce smeared over the whole thing. The spring on the oven door whined, snapping shut.

Where could she be? Maybe she'd had a flat tire on the way home. Or slid off into the ditch. Most farmers didn't have phones out that way. That's what Humpy Chris told himself. But that bird-thought was back, that whirring in his ear. He'd better drive out there and see what the problem was.

Outside, Humpy Chris heaved until the garage door slid up. He didn't know what hurt more; his back, all the way down to his legs, or his chest from the coughing.

She must be between here and the farm, he reasoned. Stuck, trying to wave someone down. But instead of going out highway 10, he turned left at the corner and drove very slowly by the Skyline Cafe. He could see through the lighted window that there was a woman sitting alone at the counter. Then he saw it was Ila Johnson. She worked there as a waitress sometimes.

The Pines Tavern was right down the street. Of course she wouldn't be there. Not alone anyway -- and no man in this town would dare to take her there, even if she dared him. It was dark inside. All he could see was the light from the juke box. Humpy Chris slowed the car.

He'd heard about a woman who had worked the Pines tending bar for a while. She'd had a room upstairs. Left after a few months. Was the room still there, he wondered? Did anyone ever use it now?

Humpy Chris pulled up to the curb and turned off the switch. As his eyes adjusted he saw two men hunched over their beers at the bar, and the bartender hovering, wiping something over and over. Then, one of the men must have told a joke. The bartender stood back laughing, his cheek shining in the dim light. But of course Chris wouldn't find her here. He didn't expect to find her here.

Maybe she'd stopped at a friend's. Who were her best friends anyway? She really didn't have any but the woman she'd met on the train. What was her name now? Teaching in the southern part of the state if he remembered right. From California wasn't she. But what could that teacher possibly have to do with his wife not coming home? Chris thought about going in for a drink. But he didn't know those men.

She must be on the road somewhere between here and the farm. Off in a ditch. Or changing a tire. Or flagging someone down. Humpy Chris pulled out his timepiece. Almost nine o'clock already. How long had he been staring into the tavern? The two men were no longer sitting at the bar.

Chris started the engine and pulled out onto Main Street again. Of course there was the Saylor Hotel over in Minot. But that was over an hour's drive. He'd heard of women sneaking over there with men. Of that one married woman. Her husband had found her in a room, in a bed, and shot the man she was with. Her, too.

Why was he thinking such things? But if he didn't see her on the road between here and the turn off to the farm, he would already be part ways there. Part ways to the Saylor Hotel in Minot. But, when Humpy Chris got to that intersection he turned off the state highway onto the dirt road to the farm. She must have run into trouble out here. Probably walked back to a farmhouse. But wouldn't they have changed the tire for her and sent her on her way? She must have hit something. Hit a pothole and slipped into the ditch and banged up the car. Maybe even hit a dog or a rabbit. They probably decided to come out and work on it in the morning and, since they didn't have a phone.... But, then again, he hadn't seen the car yet. His eyes searched the darkness on both sides of the road. Where could she be?

Humpy Chris reached into his inside pocket and withdrew a cold half-smoked cigar. He hoped he would recognize the driveway when he got to it.

Things looked different after dark. He squinted into the distance. Was that something there, just off the road? No, nothing. Was this the right way? He'd really only been out here a few times. Never after dark. Humpy Chris snapped open his pocket lighter and clicked it to flame. He held it before the dead cigar, breathing deeply. Immediately he coughed. How the coughing hurt! He felt his ribs might crack.

Humpy Chris slowed the car. Wasn't that it up ahead? Yes, it looked like the place, the way the farmhouse set on the little rise, with the barns and outbuildings to the side and the wind break to the other. He slowly turned down the long lane. His headlights swept the barn and the outbuildings and the parking area to the side of the house near the gate. The black Chevy Coupe was nowhere to be seen. Even the family car must be parked in one of the out buildings.

Inside, a single lamp burned. Not much activity. Everyone must be in bed. No, there was someone there in the lamplight pulling the curtain aside, looking out. But it wasn't Juanita, he could see that much.

Margaret rose and pulled the filmy curtain aside when the headlights of a car lit the farmyard. She hoped it might be the teacher's car, bringing Danny. But no, it wasn't her car.... Though she couldn't see it clearly, Margaret knew the shape was wrong. Probably just someone using the driveway to turn around. Sometimes drivers from town got lost out here. They thought the county road should go all the way through and, when it didn't, they used the driveway to turn around.

Margaret returned to her darning. The kerosene lamp contained her in its circle of light and lent the room a bit of warmth. Where could he be? Danny had never stayed out so long before. When his teacher left him off yesterday after work, he'd said they were almost finished.

Margaret drew the thread to arm's length over and over. For a darning egg she used a fragile, burnt-out light bulb Big Gracie had saved. Each time Margaret wove the thread, her mind worked in and out creating another worry. How long could it take to pack up the books? It was night time, after all! They wouldn't have enough light to work by now. Why didn't Danny come home?

In the ashtray of his car, Humpy Chris stubbed out the cigar. He switched off the engine and sat in silence. After a while it occurred to him he had nothing to say to these people. There must be some logical explanation of where his wife was, and he sure didn't want to set any tongues to wagging. What would these people know anyway? How could they help him? She obviously wasn't here. He felt a chill. His shirt was soaked with sweat.

Margaret wove the needle in and out, in and out imitating the pattern where the sock was whole. Maybe Danny wasn't going to come home. Just a bit of the gray bulb still showed. Why did Mrs. Nielson insist on hiring Danny to help with the books anyway? And the pay, why did she offer to pay him so handsomely? A corner of the pierced ivory box was visible from the bottom of her sewing basket where Margaret kept it hidden. Whenever she saw it she felt the pangs of hurt and betrayal. Now why had the teacher given it back? A sinking certainty fell from her racing mind to her heart to where the baby rested. With a final stitch Margaret closed the hole.

She let her hands fall slack. She could just feel the weight of the burnt out bulb inside the sock, resting lightly between her legs. But what was she thinking? Of course Danny was coming home. How crazy it was to even think anything different. Margaret drew the fragile bulb through the sock cuff and carefully placed it on the top of the sewing machine. Why, Juanita Nielson must be twice the age of Danny. Not that much younger than herself. It was just her imagination, Margaret told herself. The mind worked in strange ways when you were alone in the dark. She smoothed out the sock on her thigh. The mended part hardly showed.

The sound of Urs's heavy breathing rose steadily from the bedroom. Margaret folded her arms and rocked back in the chair, waiting. The little circle of light cast by the lamp lit the tops of her hands, folded in her lap. The tops of her shoes. A portion of the throw rug at her feet... On the ceiling, a little circle shone brighter where the chimney threw its form. The lamp lit the underside of the window sill and, above it, the ghostly glass. Though the days were lengthening now, beyond that small circle, all was darkness. Margaret thought of the baby inside her. It usually comforted her to think that coiling colored cords were attached from her navel to the heart of each of her children, a bright pink one tethering the baby inside. Tonight, even that didn't work.

Margaret's lips burst apart with a soft sigh. She picked up the light bulb and shook it, listening to the slight tinkling sound. Holding it to the lamp light, she looked for the part that was broken.

Humpy Chris started the car and turned around. The headlights swept the room.

As the car swung, Margaret felt the baby move. For a moment she was blinded by the light. In that blind moment something snapped inside of her and floated free.

All was quiet. She listened for the car. It had gone. She couldn't even hear Urs's steady breathing. All was still. No movement anywhere. Margaret couldn't feel her own heartbeat. And her womb? More still than any womb should ever be with a living child.

But Margaret only had thoughts for Danny. She placed the sock on the table and blew out the lantern. She suddenly knew he wouldn't be coming home. A trickle of sweat ran between her breasts. Danny was gone. Why hadn't she seen what was going on right under her nose?

As Chris drove back to Drake he fought the urge to drive on to Minot. There had to be some other explanation. He had never even heard a rumor that there was another man. But who would tell him? Hadn't he seen her himself, working, loading the car with books? There was no other man! She worked alone with just the boy.

No, she wouldn't be so stupid as to jeopardize her position. Her life was too easy. Too comfortable for that. Too secure. A diamond wrapped in velvet.

Without thinking, he parked in front of the jewelry store. The little light he left on in the back room gave the place an eerie glow. He inserted his key and opened the door. The rows of rings and strands of pearls behind the glass counters reassured him. The street outside was empty.

Humpy Chris went immediately to the safe and knelt, hunched forward like a thief listening to the tumblers, as he spun the dial. There, waded in the corner was the velvet pouch, empty.

She was gone. He knew it then for sure.

By the time he got home it was nearly midnight. The house was filled with smoke. He coughed convulsively while opening all the windows. Mrs. Jenson's chicken was charred black.

~26~

In Margaret's kitchen, darkness came up all around, cool and sharp at the base of her neck. The only thing visible was the red glowing rings outlining the iron pot hole lids. Then the quiet and stillness was broken when a burst of flame shot a cleansing blast rattling up the stove pipe.

Margaret had to do it. Though she could hardly see in the dark room, she had to open the little curtain and get the candle. She lifted the iron plate and touched the wick to the glowing coals.

" und an Jesus Christus, seinen eingeborenen Sohn, unsern herrn, empfangen durch den Heiligen Geist...." Margaret knelt before the candle in the drafty room. "One Lord Jesus Christ, the Only-begotten Son of God, born of the Father, before all ages..." She

said it slower, in English this time, concentrating on the rhythm of her words. Still, the darkness was there at the base of her neck, cool and sharp.

Margaret shivered. She felt cold and dead. Deeper and deeper she sank into that other time. The children had been flying through the house--Danny, six, Liz, three. Her brother Jack's house, banging the back door, letting in shocks of November cold. Only Wayne had been too young to join in. The padded box used as a traveling bed was on the floor behind the pot-bellied stove in the living room.

The dinner hadn't satisfied them fully, that chain of North Dakota farm folk linked by blood and marriage vows, and promises. "At least we're eatin'. Better'n you can say for them that got up and moved to Minneapolis." It was Jack, Margaret's older brother, talking.

"Don't know how much longer we're gonna be doing that. Sure wish this deal would go through. When did you say they were going to make their offer, Lars?"

Jack had asked him that same question three times already that afternoon.

All eyes were on Lars then. Liz on the floor in front of his chair, rolled a softball to him, back and forth, back and forth. Her legs were spread wide to help make the catch. Each time he returned the ball, he leaned forward in the chair. "Any day now, any day," Lars said, bending and then straightening as he rolled the ball. "I expect they should be making their offer sometime next week."

Danny came from behind, putting his arms around his father's neck, draping himself over his shoulder. Back and forth, back and forth rolled the ball.

Margaret's sister's man, Hans, had been wedged in the straight-backed chair by the radio. Hans tipped back, arms folded across his chest, rocking on the two back legs as he spoke. "Missy threw out ten dozen eggs yesterday. Fed'em to the hogs."

"The A&P's only offering four cents a dozen." Hans went on. The men nodded agreement. "That Charles Ogelesbee on the radio figured it all out. Just buying the cartons and haulin'em into town we'd lose. That's if we use horses and don't have to put money out for gasoline. Like I said before, you can come on over any time and get all the eggs you want, long as we got 'em." He looked to Lars.

Lars could see they all wanted him to go over it again, to reassure them. He had to do it. Lars rose to his feet with great effort, brushing off his pant legs with one hand while grasping the ball in the other.

"Let's play some more, Daddy. Don't stop playin'. Roll me the ball." Liz hung on to her father's pant-leg, weighting him, holding him to the earth.

Lars bent and scraped a spot of dried snot off the front of Danny's shirt, with his thumbnail. "What you got all over the front of your shirt?" The young father looked into the round sweet face, into the serious blue eyes that reflected his own.

From the kitchen rose the sound of the women doing the dishes. Lars tossed the ball lightly to Liz. It bounced on the floor with a thud missing her outstretched hands. All eyes followed the ball and then went back to Lars. Margaret was standing in the doorway to the kitchen holding a dishtowel and listening and watching.

Standing before the men, Lars began slowly. "If we just stick together, we can beat this thing." The familiar words sounded dry and empty to Margaret's ears. "Where one of us standing alone wouldn't stand a chance, a group of us has some power, some control." Lars rubbed his face with his hands. He had dark circles around his eyes. Looked beat.

The men didn't seem to notice his exhaustion, how their dread drained him. Tension left their joints as they settled back in their chairs. Jack lit up a Lucky. This was what they wanted. What they needed--insurance.

"I got all the paper work started," Lars continued as if paperwork would guarantee success. "The state office says it looks like it's gonna be that piece of land. That 185 acres that comes out there along the gully on the creek....added to that worthless plateau they already own."

"Why a big chunk of that Hofbrau farm never could be farmed anyway. The sides are so steep in through there, a man couldn't get a horse and a plow, let alone a tractor up there. Perfect for a dam. And a little lake...." Lars went on. "We got to fight back. Stand up for what's ours. What have we got to lose?" Lars tossed back his shock of blond hair, running his fingers through it. He paced the room looking at each man encouragingly.

"Hans, you would have lost your place already if we hadn't 'a worked together. Wouldn't ya?" Lars continued.

Hans nodded.

"And you, Jack. They'd already signed the foreclosure papers and everything, hadn't they? Couldn't wait to get their hands on your land. It was just us all working together, that saved you. Got the court to reconsider, when we came up with the money. It was just 'cause your friends were willing to stand with you, that we even had a chance. Now, you at least all got seed to plant. And some hope."

Lars sat down in the chair by the stove, rubbing his hands together, leaning forward. His voice fell into the familiar rhythm. His eyes caught fire. "I tell you the CCC wants that 185. They're planning on putting in a state park there. They're going to pay good money for that piece. Put those CCC fellows to work."

"None of us owe much," Lars went on smoothly, convincingly. Sounding like he was a farmer, too, who couldn't make the payments. "Just a few hundred dollars and we'll all have clear deeds. And when they buy that piece, Franz Hofbrau's share will be way more than that place was ever worth. Way more than he could ever get for it without our help. The WPA wouldn't have known Hofbrau even wanted to sell if we hadn't brought it up. Would they? Would they, now, Jack?" Jack shook his head. "They hadn't even considered the place 'til we suggested it. By next week, we'll all be home free and clear, with next year's seed in the granary to boot."

When Lars finished, the men sat lax in their chairs. The room was quiet, except for the sucking sound Wayne was making from his little bed in the corner by the stove. Lars rose up out of his chair and gave his back a twist until it popped.

That Thanksgiving afternoon, Lars's words had just kept coming out. The dead dream had kept unfolding as if it had a power of its own.

If she had only paid more attention then.

Margaret stared straight ahead into the candle flame. She pressed her temples with her fingertip. "Blessed art Thou amongst women, and blessed is the fruit of Thy womb, Jesus...." Her knees pressed through her cotton dress to the cracked kitchen linoleum. If only she had really paid attention to what was going on right under her nose.

There was that day when Lars had come through the door whistling, but his eyes had avoided hers. He set his lunch pail down on the table and went out again to the garden. Something was wrong. Something was bothering him. Margaret saw that now. Why hadn't she been paying attention? But then something deeper rose up within her like a cleansing fire. She had known something then, hadn't she? That he was covering something up with the whistling and his silence. If she had only asked what the trouble was. If she had only talked to him--made him talk to her! But no, she hadn't wanted to know, had she?

He must have found out through his job with the WPA--that they wouldn't be buying the Hofbrau farm, after all. That all the meetings and letters and phone calls to Bismarck had done no good.

And so he had stood in Jack's living room that afternoon and said it all just as if he still believed. Better than when he still believed.... It would have been so easy....a performer, gesturing and reciting a memorized script, not trying to convince anyone anymore!

They made him do it. Margaret recognized now that she too had made him do it. And as Lars went on, they were lulled--comforted. They all liked the fact that he always said it just the same...that he spoke so easily...so naturally.

"Lydia, is that kitchen table cleared off yet?" Jack had yelled out to the kitchen. "Get out the cards then...." and then to everybody in general. "What do you want to play?"

"I'm not playing at all unless we're gonna listen to Ogelesbee. He's coming on in just a few minutes now. At three-thirty." Hans had occupied the seat by the radio all afternoon as if he'd come early to a popular movie and was afraid everyone might not fit into the theater.

The men moved the table into the living room and turned on the radio. "This is Charles Ogelesbee talkin' and I know a lot of you out there are wondering what you have to be thankful for this Thanksgivin'." They played seven-up. Half a penny a card. The women mainly stayed on the fringes, attending to the kids and talking.

"I tell you Roosevelt's a day late an' a dollar short. He's trying to heal pneumonia with an aspirin." Ogelesbee kept up his steady crackling chatter.

Lars kept winning. After the first couple hands he could see Jack was riding his manhood on the cards, but no matter who did the dealing it seemed like Lars just kept winning. He swept the pennies into a pile and began placing them in neat little stacks.

Lydia brought out the quart bottles of homemade beer. The women circled the playing table paying more attention to the game. Margaret sat on the wide arm of the easy chair where Lars sat.

Even between wiping the kids' noses and breaking up fights, she could see Lars wasn't playing his cards. But they kept dealing him the hands and he kept on winning about half the time anyway.

"There's people making a killing off of your misfortune, I tell you. Buying up your farms for nothing. Closing on the property you already paid for double, counting interest." No one was really listening. The radio was just background, like the crackling of a cheerful fire.

Lars half-heartedly gathered in the small pile of coins. These men had trusted him. After all, he wasn't going to lose his job, was he? He wasn't going to lose a farm.

Then Lars started holding and passing and paying. Holding and passing and paying. Letting each penny snap down onto the table. Shuffling quick at the end before anyone could figure out who had what. Finally he only had one little stack of coins about five high.

By then the kids had finished churning the ice cream. They put away the cards for German chocolate cake with ice cream and coffee. The men still wanted beer.

While Lydia brought out the cups and saucers and the spoons, Margaret stepped out on the porch to get more beer and a little fresh air.

In a moment Lars was out on the porch too, his arms around Margaret, kissing her on the lips, the neck. A shot of pleasure rushed through her bringing a wave of heat and color to her face.

She had this. No bank could foreclose on this. Margaret set down the quart jars and kissed him back, drawing herself up into his embrace. Inside, the men were calling for the beer. She went back in.

Margaret set two cool sweaty bottles firmly on the table and uncapped them. She held the golden liquid to the light and smiled and nodded to each man, before touching the lip with a faint clink and filling each out-held glass. As she concentrated on pouring the beer into each glass, she didn't notice Lars moving behind her.

The sound of the shot shattered her pleasure. Wayne startled in the little bed, crying.

They found Lars behind the closed door of her brother's bedroom off the kitchen. The barrel of the .22 rifle in his mouth. Lydia picked up Wayne. Patting, patting. Once he was quieted, the only sound in the house was Charles Ogelesbee blaring over the speaker. His prater meaningless, sounding tinny over the crackling speaker, mocking them. "We need to clean house. Vote 'em out. Vote the whole bunch of 'em out." What meaning did all this have, now?

The radio had stopped. A pulsing silence had beat against the walls. When Margaret had staggered back out of the bedroom she saw that Hans had gripped the brown plastic radio knob hard between the coarse thumb and finger of his right hand.

"Heilige Maria, Mutter Gotten, bite fur uns Sunder jetzt und in oder Stunde users Todes, Amen." Holy Mary, Mother of God, pray for us sinners now and at the hour of our death, Amen. Margaret blew out the candle, cupping it in her hand.

A faint light was rising in the sky. Margaret stoked the fire and set on the pot for Urs's coffee.

~ 27~

At first Chris had fumbled around the house knocking into furniture—moving things from one place to another--leaving things lay. Juanita had been gone a week, but sometimes, when he came into a room, a photograph would be left on the davenport, or her comb by the sink, or her dress in the middle of the living room floor. How did these things get there?

Chris knew he needed someone to talk to. To have someone help him sort this out. But who would that be? And wouldn't he look like a fool, not knowing where his wife was. No, he didn't want to air his dirty linen. And if the kid was missing? Well, Chris wasn't ready to face that. He didn't want to hear that his wife had run off with a kid, a student yet. He wouldn't be made a fool.

But, maybe he could talk to the priest. Hadn't the priest taken vows not to tell anyone? But no, he wasn't really a religious person. Besides, it was Saturday. Wouldn't the priest be busy with confession? And, didn't that Wagnor bunch always go to confession? He didn't want to run into them, did he? But he did want to find out if the boy was there.

Chris finally got up the courage to call Father Weaver. He traced the huge pink peonies on the wallpaper, Juanita's wallpaper, as he listened to the rings. Two shorts and a long. Two shorts and a long. Two shorts... He knew the operator would be listening, and probably one or two others would be rubbering on the party line, but it was the only way he knew to find out if Danny was still around.

"Hello, Father? Church Sunday? Oh, I wasn't feeling so good. I'm curious though, was that oldest Borgen boy, Danny, I believe his name is.. Was he there, at church?.... I need to talk to him about this work for the school board. Didn't want to waste my time driving out to the farm if by chance he wasn't there...." There was a long silence on the other end of the phone.

"He wasn't there? Are you sure, Father?.... None of the family was there? No, you don't need to bother. I'll be going out there myself.... Yes, I'll let you know how they're doing. If anything's wrong.... Yes, I know it's unusual for Margaret Wagnor to miss church.... OK, Father. OK..... Good bye, Father."

Pacing the quiet house Chris conjured up a plan. They were renters after all. He could kick them out! It was true, normally they wouldn't pay 'til the crop came in....but after all, the land belonged to Chris, in spite of what the papers said. Why, Urs Wagnor probably couldn't read or understand those papers anyway.

The next morning Chris started out to Minot to see his lawyer. Pulling out of his driveway, he fortified himself with the injustice of it all. "Oh, how did I get myself entangled with people like this....? I can't support all the human trash in the world.... They'd suck me dry! They are sucking me dry!"

Chris was past the Phillips station, about a mile out, before he was aware he'd left town. He should have stopped for gas. Only a quarter of a tank. Was it enough to get to the lawer's in Minot? Shouldn't he turn around and fill the tank? "Oh, I'm losing my touch," he mumbled to himself, "and those people are the reason. People like the Wagnors or the Borgens or whatever their names are. People who can't be depended on even to act in their own best interest. Ruled by whim! Superstition! Ignorance! How can a man win or even play when half the deck is wild!"

Chris flashed on the last concert he'd taken Juanita to in Minneapolis. More than a year ago, now. They'd sat towards the front. But it wasn't music. He and Juanita had argued over it on the way home. It was supposedly some modern thing. Jarring and unpredictable. There was a clarinetist who looked right at him during the performance. He'd made the instrument squeal and jab and then looked right at Chris. When he put it down his smirk enraged him.

Chris shifted down as he passed a slow moving tractor. His hands were trembling. If there just weren't these kind of people always making his work so hard. People who refused to amount to anything. They were like that new kind of music. Doing silly, crazy things that didn't make sense just to upset people like himself. Just to upset people like himself who only wanted to plot out the best course for a community, not just for himself but for all of them. Raise them all up.

Did she end up choosing one of them? One of them, over him! Some ignorant little piece of arrogant dirt who could probably fuck all night. Of all the ignorant farmers. Of all the stupid over breeding, stubborn pieces of human garbage, this family must represent the worst.

A truck came up behind him, honking to pull out of the passing lane. What was Chris doing, driving down the wrong lane? The closer he came to Minot the more uncertain he became. He just wanted to defend what was his, but this self-fueled anger only wore him down. What really could he do? Urs Wagnor didn't owe him a thing until fall--unless he broke their agreement in some other way.

Chris was almost to Minot when he turned around at a dirt road and drove back home. The thought of driving any farther only made his back hurt--only made him feel more tired, more helpless. Anyway his lawyer always seemed so busy. Though he talked politely, it always seemed like his mind was somewhere else. The eviction wasn't really what Chris wanted to talk about anyway, was it. Really there wasn't anyone he could talk to, was there?

As Chris lowered the garage door coughing overtook him. How his back hurt. He called Dr. Hanson and set an appointment for the next day. He could talk to him, at least, about his back.

*

Lunch was over and so were dishes. Not time yet to bring in the cows. Annie curled among the new ferns, her eyelids drooping. The day had been so very hot. She found this spot among the early ferns, on the side of the house where it was cool. Annie was just able to see through half closed eyes. In the distance the pond sparkled.

How cool it had been when she and Danny swam there. How cool pushing off the muddy bottom, floating to Danny, or drifting weightlessly near the shore where swirling mud rose in columns. She had grasped nameless slippery things, soft curled leaves dissolved at her touch.

Annie woke to find her mother shaking her. Waking her from that cool shady place that smelled of moss and ferns. Or was it her father once again flipping her out of the pond onto the muddy bank, banging her back like a little drum --water surging from her throat and stomach, coming out her nose. Why was he so angry?

No, it was mother, having trouble walking, face contorted. She grasped her stomach, legs set wide.

"Annie, go get your father! He's over there to the west. You know, where he put in the corn." Margaret pointed with her chin, her face contorted. The talking stopped. In that small quiet space, Annie heard the whine of insects.

"Go on now, Annie!" Margaret's face flushed red and damp with sweat. Water was running down her legs, wetting her socks. She flung her arm in the direction of the creek. "Go!" Shifting her weight in the wingtip shoes made a squishy sound. "Go!"

Annie took off across the yard running. But maybe she shouldn't leave her mother all alone. The furrows in the field ahead had never seemed so deep, the dark green rows so high.

Near the creek the corn nearly reached her waist. "Father, father, where are you?" Annie licked the salty sweat from her upper lip. Sharp edged leaves cut her bare arms.   "Father, Father, Momma needs you!"

Annie stumbled. Dirt and small stones scraped the heels of her hands. She lay hot and breathless. Transfixed. Where sunlight filtered through the knife-like leaves, hundreds of bright translucent jewels were sewn throughout the matted dirt. The eggs of insects, or the seeds of gemstones. Baby diamonds or opals.

Then there was the deep, heavy clanging of iron on iron. She shouldn't have gone. She shouldn't have left her mother alone. Again the heavy cadence of iron on iron. Where was Katie? Wasn't Katie supposed to help when the baby was ready? Annie took off using the clanging as a guide.

At the source, Margaret was bent swinging a jack handle at a cast iron frying pan she had somehow managed to string over the hitching rail. The bottom of her skirt was soaked wet with blood.

Annie took the metal handle from her mother's hand and resumed banging the swinging pan. She hurled her whole weight into it. The sound rang in her head and quivered through her bones. "Father! Father!" she screamed between the clanging beats.

Margaret gently placed her hands on Annie's shoulders. "It's all right, Annie. It's going to be all right. Now you come on into the house." Her mother's eyes were calm, blue ponds, cool ponds in the midday heat.

"Let me go swimming for just a little, Mom? Let me go down to the pond, please?" For a moment Margaret appeared to approve, but then she shook her head speaking sternly.

"You come with me, Annie, where I can keep an eye on you. Get up there on the top of the chest of drawers where you can't run away, where I can see you." Margaret lifted her up with a surge of blood and liquid.

In bed, Margaret kept herself covered with a sheet and made Annie turn her face far to the left. Annie sat in her mother's view, grasping the edge of the chest of drawers, staring through the kitchen doorway. Margaret moaned. Something was under the house trying to get out through the cracks in the painted planked floor. The bed creaked and shuddered. Something was heaving its humped back against the floor. Breathing through the cracks. Something salty and wet.

When Margaret let Annie turn her face far to the right, Annie saw through the bedroom window to where the shiny pond winked.

Margaret tenderly turned the tiny lifeless dark-haired form. She placed the flat of her hand on the dark spot at the base of her spine. Not the mark of Cain, she defended. A beautiful baby. A beautiful baby girl. But tiny. So tiny. And there outside her chest between two tiny pink nipples, unprotected, her heart.

Margaret cradled the lifeless infant in one arm, while making the sign of the cross with the other. "I baptize you in the name of the

Father and of the Son and of the Holy Ghost," she said softly and clearly.

When Urs came in from the fields Margaret was seated in a clean dress at the kitchen table. Her hair was washed and brushed to dark rivers around a pale face. There was no dinner on the stove, no plates on the table. He sensed right away what had happened.

"Dead already," was all she said.

Urs hooked his single finger under the top rung of the chair back and yanked it away from the table. When the clatter of chrome legs on the wood floor stopped he thundered into the seat.

"What was it?" he demanded, his tone like a man who'd lost everything in a crooked hand of cards and was trying to find the cheat.

"What the Hebamme said."

*

That night Annie woke to a strange wailing. Was it in the house or outside? She pressed her face against the cool glass of her bedroom window.

There was the moon and a few wispy clouds and again that wailing. Low hills rose in the distance. Her eye settled on the pond, dark and limpid. To one side, standing out in the pale light, was a small grove of willows and low brush. A bear lumbered out of the silvery hedge and bent, flinging dirt and tearing at the earth, groaning. It was the same place her mother had bent that afternoon, keeping Annie away--there had been something wrapped in white.

The moaning changed to the low keening of *Das Schicksal-- the funeral lament. Das Schicksal wird keinen verschonen, der Tod verfolgt Zepter und Kronen* tragedy can't be avoided it hunts down even royal ones came howling through the moonlight.

Her father knew the truth. And so did she.

~28~

Nights since Juanita had been missing were no better than the days. Like now, Chris wasn't able to sleep. Like now, he went to bed early, only to lie on his back looking up at the ceiling.

Humpy Chris raised himself a bit and rolled over to light a cigar. He stared at the flame, watching the ethereal smoke rise and waft with the air from the open window.

What had she done? Robbed him. Yes, she had robbed him, of his most precious jewel. The jewel that gave him the confidence to stare down any lawyer, or banker, or politician in the state. There was a lonely void at the center of his being. He hated the feeling. When had she won this power over him?

Chris could barely see the smoke rising in the darkening bedroom. The long twilight was coming to an end. Still he couldn't sleep. He stubbed out the cigar and got up to use the bathroom. He flicked on the bathroom light. What day was it anyway?

He heard the clock on the mantel ticking. It must be after midnight now, tomorrow already. The days were getting so hard to keep track of.

Chris flushed the toilet and slowly got up doubled over with hacking. He coughed, bent over, all the way back to bed. He was sweating. As though he had been running. A chorus of crickets rode the breeze through the open window. He felt as though all the shadowy figures he had escaped in his past waited for him.

He tossed an hour or so more before he found himself in the back yard with both hands deep in the pockets of his robe, looking up at the stars. He studied them blankly, no longer familiar with their movement across the night sky. There was no moon.

Suddenly Chris felt silly. Why was he standing there looking up at the stars with his hands in his pockets? In the starlight, he noticed a large rock where his property bordered the empty lot to one side. He sat down. The stone immediately stole the heat from his body. How long had it been since he had slept?

Chris wrapped his arms around himself and slumped there, silently. Crickets chirped. The constellations changed their shapes. Was he awake or asleep? His eyes fell shut.

He saw a photograph of himself standing naked. The description was in Latin. If he could just make out what the words meant. He squeezed his eyes. His brow furrowed in concentration. What did it say? What kind of man was he?

A woman stood beside him. Was it Juanita? He looked more closely. No, no one else was there.

Where was Juanita? He frantically paged through the book of photographs. He couldn't find her. He was cold. Suddenly his eyes sprang wide.

It was completely dark. Where was he? Oh yes, out in the yard. He cocked his head listening. Was that a car? Who would that be, out so late? Could it be someone he knew, worried? Someone out looking for him? He didn't move at all, listening.

Chris watched the approaching headlights. But what had he been thinking? It wouldn't be anyone he knew. Probably a drunk. He hoped whoever it was wouldn't see him. Wouldn't recognize him. The car came straight through the intersection toward his house.

It slowed. Chris slipped into the bushes. He hurried deeper into the vacant lot and crouched in the weeds, muffling his cough. Suddenly his foot was wet and cold. The mud and standing water had sucked off one of his slippers.

The car slowed more. It came to a stop. Chris saw then that it was the city patrolman. There was the painted emblem on the side of the car. Above it, an exposed arm shown white through the rolled down window.

"Hey you out there." Humpy crouched lower, saying nothing. He slowed his breathing, controlling the urge to cough. The engine idled. Chris felt the cooling mud between his toes. He remained crouched, breathing as quietly as possible. Below the idling engine, was the sound of crickets chirping.

Slowly the car pulled away. Chris was alone.

Why was he crying?

Chris threw back his head and looked up at the night sky. The stars had faded. He spread out his arms and began circling. How cool and dark the mud felt between his toes. The clomp, clomp of the mud encrusted foot pounded out a drumbeat. To one horizon the sky pulsed with blue and orange. The Northern Lights.

And there were the crickets. The crickets singing all around in the grass. Small orange flames chirping in the night sky. And the smell of sweet clover. Yellow. He hadn't noticed it growing there before. Now it glowed in the sky. And the wet grass. Green tongues licked the mud between his toes as he spun. The sky surrounded him with green and yellow and the orange chirping of crickets. The sky was sheeting colored lights.

Chris stopped abruptly in recognition. He knew this jewel. How many times had he taken comfort from it? Owning it. Possessing it. Watching it throw off planes of light. Red. Orange. Green. Now he was inside it.

Chris flung out his arms. Round and round he twirled through space, his feet remembering some ancient dance. "You're mine!" he croaked. The words sprang dry and sharp. "I own you. Your beauty." The lights flickered with each word. "I tried to keep you, to love you." His breath danced across the fiery sky.

Then there were no words. He croaked and grunted while his feet padded the earth, but there were no words. There was only the dance. And the croaking. And the light sheeting in flickering greens and blues, growing to red in the distance.

Chris bent in a sudden outburst. How his lungs burned. Tears streamed down his face. In a daze he walked quietly back to the house and went to bed. As the minutes ticked away he fumbled with the blankets. Deeper and deeper he went into himself...tearing off his pride, his anger, his embarrassment and his guilt. Beneath them all lay exposed...his desire to be loved.

Towards dawn, all that remained of his revelation was the powerful urge, with every breath he took, to get up and drive out to that farm.

~29~

The speckled dogs in the yard greeted Chris at the Wagnor's, barking and leaping one on each side of the car. When Chris left town he'd told himself it was just a routine visit. Just a routine visit to assess the condition of his property. But the last few miles he had become so anxious that now his heart was racing. He pulled into the yard and turned off the engine. Now he couldn't name the reason he had been in such a hurry.

Other than the dogs, the farm was oddly quiet. No one was working in the fields. There was no movement between the barn and house. Just the dogs. They growled and circled. Humpy stayed in the car. Thinking.

Taking his time, he lit a cigar and began smoking. With his other hand he lightly rubbed the waxed wooden surface of the steering wheel--back and forth, back and forth. But this wasn't really so different than anything else, was it? You play the odds and do what you can to determine the outcome. His mind fell into the familiar way of thinking, but his heart wasn't in it. Back and forth his hand polished the wooden wheel.

Why really was he here? Especially feeling like this, so tired and run down. Sitting here slouched over the steering wheel at the end of the driveway, staring at this barn-like house he felt a kind of surrender. A strange kind of peace.

Chris put out his cigar and rolled down the window letting in a little fresh air. He looked more carefully, trying to determine if anyone was home. The farmyard was just beginning to get that run down look. Why he saw now, chickens were roosting in the trees!

It was a good thing he'd come out here today. It was a good thing he got out here before they up and left, or the place got more run down than it was now. Humpy tried to muster some enthusiasm. The logic that he had trusted all his life raced on and on without any real feeling.

Layers of fine dirt were collecting on the walk to the house. The gate banged. Was anyone here? If it hadn't been for the priest who would have ever noticed if they left? A family like this could disappear off the face of the earth and who would ever know the difference?

Hadn't all he ever wanted was to deal with these kind of people, this riffraff, on his own level? To let them keep their contracts or not make them at all if they gave them no advantage? Maybe he gave these kind of people too much credit for brains. More than once he'd shaken his head when some poor beggar signed up for impossible terms. He'd had to hold himself back from asking if the guy was stupid, or crazy. Maybe the poor beggar knew something he didn't, he'd told himself. Some way to turn a hopeless agreement to his advantage.

By now the dogs had settled down in the dirt near the gate, their heads resting on their paws. What else could he do but protect his property? But now his back ached, all the way to his feet, and he'd been coughing since before he got out of bed. Chris felt none of the usual thrill that came with announcing an eviction or foreclosure in person. No matter how his mind raced. No matter what might or might not be good for business, his heart wasn't in it.

He wouldn't allow himself to think of his real loss. Wouldn't allow himself to think of Juanita. Or the boy, Danny. Or that the penicillin no longer worked.

Chris tried to feed his waning anger. To raise the energy to go in there and let them know who was boss. He told himself it was like any other eviction. Why, he could verify the place was going to the dogs with his own eyes. Chickens were roosting in the trees!

*

Margaret sat at the kitchen table. Although the dogs leaped, barking at the car, she didn't hear. In the days since the still-birth, Margaret had grown weaker. She ate little and cooked less. Even so her breasts were huge, hard as bricks and hot with fever.

That first day after, Urs had gone through the motions. His feet had carried him out to the fields. He refused to speak, brooding dark and heavy like the storm clouds gathering. The next day his leaden feet dragged slower until on the third he didn't get out of bed.

Neither Margaret nor Urs ever left the house. Weeds were taking over the garden. The cows bellowed to be milked. At first, when Urs didn't get out of bed, Margaret tried to do it all. She and Annie. If Urs hadn't been there it would have been easier. She would have staked out a portion and kept up that at least. But all of it was too much. And there was the bleeding.

So, Margaret began lighting her candles again. She began praying in the middle of the day. She spoke in German, in English, in Latin, in languages never heard before. Sometimes she remembered Danny, Wayne and Liz, or Lars, but often she stepped into a world past them. Where she was weightless as sunshine. Where the wind blew right through.

Then, seeing Annie she would feel the old pull. She would suddenly become aware of her kitchen and rummage through the cupboards to find what there was to eat. An egg. Potatoes to boil. But mid-way through she would look out the window and fly with the birds. Fly to the far horizon. Her eye was nearly always turned. Sometimes with Annie in her lap, Margaret would grasp the child with strong talons and carry her safely to a grassy meadow where the air was cooler.

*

These days, when her father rolled in bed and her mother sat in a trance, or knelt in prayer, Annie held her rabbit for hours. Sometimes they would lie in the fine sandy dirt, a white circle within a circle. Petting. Petting. Fingering the silky fur.

One such day, Annie fell asleep cuddling like that. But suddenly the rabbit's movement woke her as he slowly hopped away. Annie made no move to get him. He stopped to sniff the little chicken wire cage where it lay discarded. Annie watched quietly. He hopped slowly towards the garden, pausing now and then. Looking back.

The dogs were watching, too. Annie had heard them growling. Their ears were pricked to stiff points. They had been trained not to come inside the gate, but Annie worried.

Since that day, sometimes Annie saw the bunny. Sometimes he ate out of her hand. Other times she looked for him for hours. She never again tried to restrain it. But the dogs worried her.

Annie was sitting in the garden between rows of lettuce when Humpy Chris drove into the yard. He turned off the ignition and sat in the car thinking. He just sat there. Then, a fire glowed lighting his face. There were wisps of thick smoke. What was he up to, she wondered? Why didn't he move?

Something white near the gate distracted her. The rabbit? No, only a piece of crumpled paper caught at the bottom of the fence. Sometimes Buttermilk did still come around. Usually at dusk. Because of his eyes. He liked the new lettuce.

The iron gate to the yard banged. The dogs rose circling. If Humpy Chris weren't sitting there, Annie would have got up and secured it. Instead, she merely clung to the idea that the dogs were trained not to come into the yard. But the gate was open. Could the dogs see the rabbit? Was he on the other side of the house where she couldn't see? The dogs settled again, resting their muzzles on their paws.

Humpy Chris opened the shiny car door. The gentle climb to the house was a tremendous effort. He spoke to the dogs in a low calming voice, closing the gate behind him, and fastening the latch. Dragging himself to the side door, he walked as if the hump on his back hung all the way to the ground. As if it dragged in the dirt like a thick tail.

Humpy Chris hammered on the door. They must be in there. The place didn't seem deserted. Still, the farm had an uncanny feel to it. Chris turned from the house, straightening up as best he could.

The door to the machine shed was wide open. He could see the old car and the hay wagon. Horses were grazing near the barn. It looked as if this family had all been going about their business one minute and the next minute, just disappeared.

His eyes examined the barn, the smoke house, the privy. They fell to rest on the garden, and Annie. They were here all right. He turned to the door and pounded again.

Annie sat watching. Not moving. Lettuce lay forgotten in her lap.

"Hey there, young lady! I need to talk to your folks." Humpy Chris started towards her shouting and lifting his arm.

Annie rose, walking fast and then running to the other corner of the house. Lettuce trailed in her wake. She rounded the corner out of his sight.

He started after her, and then immediately stopped, seeing it was hopeless.

*

Annie watched as the dragon circled the house. It stopped at the kitchen window, peering in and tapping on the glass. Three short taps, again and again. And a whispering. Three sounds in time with the tapping Wa-nee-ta, Wa-nee- ta, over and over with the tapping.

Her mother would be on the other side of the glass at the kitchen table, as she nearly always was these days. But maybe she didn't see him looking in. Maybe she didn't hear the banging at the door, the tapping at the window, the whispered Wan-ee-ta. Maybe she was gone. Flown away.

The dragon stepped away from the window removing his hat and scratching his head. He slunk around to the window of her parents' bedroom.

So, he had gotten out. He must have been there all along. Just as Annie had suspected. First, by the privy, and then buried under the house. Hadn't she heard him breathing while she tended the little farm beside the lilac bush? Hadn't she seen his green claw growing from the crack at the foundation of the house?

Again the dragon peered in the window, his hands tapping, one on each side of his face. He would be looking directly into her father's face, as he curled in bed. Her father's dark hair would be springing wild from his head. Thick whiskers sprouting from his chin. Naked to the waist, his chest and back would be matted with hair. He hardly ever moved. When the dragon stepped away from the window, he bent in a coughing roar. Was that fire? And smoke?

Annie watched as the dragon dragged himself to each window in turn, and looked in, muttering to himself words she couldn't quite hear. She maneuvered in a wide circle, sneaking from bush to tree, as he peered in. When he stomped up onto the porch, Buttermilk broke from beneath the lilac bush startled.

*

There it was again! Urs heard the sound of the insects hitting against the window as he lay curled in bed. And there again. This time banging against the door to the side porch. The sound of the grasshoppers wasn't loud but it had the power of a deadly, softly beating headache. He knew it from that time at Dale Swanson's place. That time the hoppers had overcome them, defeated them, tapping insistently, incessantly, against the window panes. But for some reason, this time Urs couldn't get out of bed.

The sound never let up. Urs tossed, trying to put it out of his head, out of his life. If he'd been still working for Dale, he'd be up already and into his work clothes. But this was his own crop. He could let it go if he wanted. Why would he get out of bed when he could lie here if he wanted? Lie here in bed and listen to them, out in the fields or lightly tapping at the windows. There must be millions of them moving across the land, eating up his crop, his life. They could have it.

At Dale's that time, at night they'd lit all the lanterns--drawing the insects to the house, away from the fields. In the morning they'd been piled thick all around the house. Three feet high some places. That must be what was happening out there now. They were tapping at the window. All the windows. And now at the door. Like a softly beating headache.

At Dale Swanson's place that time they'd scooped them into the wheelbarrow and hauled them to the ditches. They poured gasoline over them and set them on fire. A river of squirming burning grasshoppers. The ones with wings trying to fly--their wings on fire.

Urs had come up with the idea to stop feeding the chickens. Letting them roost where they pleased, eating their fill of the bugs. So that was why the chickens were out. He'd seen them roosting in the trees. Maybe Margaret did it this time. Let the chickens run free, so they'd eat the hoppers. Urs didn't have the energy to get out of bed and ask her.

And this time there wasn't anybody to make him. Even that confounded bunch of kids weren't here to make him get up. He was tired. And now, there wasn't anyone who could make him do what he didn't want to do. Urs bashed the headboard with his fist. Why should he get out of bed?

The beating at the door was still there, too loud for hoppers.

Was that the priest knocking on the door of his parents' farm-- knocking on the door to get Urs and his brothers? To give the boys to Mrs. Henderson? Why didn't the priest leave them alone? Urs heaved himself to his feet for the first time in days.

Why was that priest still knocking? Urs burst out of the bedroom and nearly leapt at the kitchen door. Didn't he know they didn't want him here? That he was too late to do his mother any good? She had held his little scarred hand begging for her final rites, but the priest didn't come; and now it was too late.

*

Humpy Chris came onto the porch and pounded the door. "Juanita! Are you in there?" There was a blur of movement from beyond the dusty window and Urs flung the door open. Humpy Chris stepped back startled and then stepped inside, without being asked.

Suddenly Urs really saw who it was. It was Humpy Chris, coming into his own kitchen with his arms folded across his chest. Was he smirking? Urs pulled back his giant fist and hurled it with every ounce of strength he had left. He hit Humpy Chris square in the chest. Hit him as if he were responsible for everything that ever hurt him. As if somehow Humpy Chris had been sitting behind some desk in a hidden room making his parents die of diphtheria, making his older brother grow mean and alcoholic. As if Humpy Chris had helped plot every cruelty Urs had suffered hired out as a boy. As if he had killed Urs's only son with his own hands. The humped man's head slammed into the partially opened door and slid to the floor in a limp heap.

Chris lay gasping, the breath knocked out of him. When he recovered some, he crawled half under the kitchen table, where he collapsed again. Urs wearily stomped off back to bed.

For hours Chris remained under the table. Sometimes his eyes were open. But other than the rattling of his breathing, he didn't make a sound. He didn't move. Sometimes Annie knelt at his side under the table, studying him. She could see that he was still alive.

*

Mostly her mother didn't seem to notice Humpy Chris. Margaret stepped around him. Or over him. Once she got the broom to sweep the floor. She started the smooth short strokes in the corner where the washing machine had been. It was soothing to watch her. Short smooth strokes. Moving the broom fluidly, the morning ticking by. When her mother got to the table and Humpy Chris, her expression grew confused. Margaret bent, poking the broom, trying to sweep him up. She tried to sweep up Humpy Chris as if he were a piece of garbage.

"Hold the dust pan for me, Annie." Margaret pointed her foot to where she wanted Annie to press the narrow lip of the metal pan. Annie placed it there, near his back while her mother tried to sweep Chris up. Margaret jabbed along the edge of his gray pinstriped suit legs as if he were a piece of garbage stuck to the floor, something stuck that might break loose.

The dragon didn't move. His eyes were wide, his lips loosely open. Where was the rabbit, Annie wondered. Where was Danny?

For a moment Annie thought her mother saw him. For a moment her mother seemed to know that what was there on the floor wasn't a piece of garbage but a dragon... or Humpy Chris. Margaret's eyes shone. "*Scheisskerl,*" shit head. The bare foot swung at the hump. Her mother backed away circling, the yellow, straw broom held sideways. Was that a snake about to strike? "*Scheisskerl,*" she repeated, loud this time, getting in a solid kick, before backing away. "Get the pitch fork, Annie, so we can get this snake up off the kitchen floor."

The dragon winced. The woman looked on in disbelief. There was a sudden clatter as the worn broom handle slipped to the floor. Her mother's empty hands fell slack.

Margaret found her way to the straight-backed chair at the side of the bed. There she hunched, moaning and rocking. It looked to Annie as though her mother felt some terrible pain or was bent over some dying invisible child.

Annie left the house--wandered aimlessly. The lilac bush was at the end of its blooming. Some of the flowers were already brown. The early sweetness now held the tinge of rot. Annie worked steadily under its branches. She pulled clumps of grass from the yard and began planting them there in neat rows. King and Queen pranced as her fingers pulled the wagon down the tiny road.

A hot dry wind blew from the south. This was not the weather for planting. Of course her little fields knew no real seed and now there was nothing to hold the soil. How could she copy her father's work when he lay in bed?

Annie began carrying water in a bucket from the pump. Overhead the sun blazed. How hot and dry the air was. Must be lunch time. Annie set down the bucket and looked out into the fields. If only she could take lunch to her father there, the sweet new crop erupting in neat rows. How satisfying it would be to carefully pour the hot coffee from the thermos, her arm trembling with the weight, her hair blowing in the wind.

Instead, Annie wiped out her little field, scattering the tufts of grass. Again, she started with the plowing. The dry soil broke in chunks away from the spoon. Hot, dry winds were crumbling her work to dust. Was it because the dragon was about? She could feel its breath moving across the land, gasping, hot and dry. It was injured now. Were these its dying breaths?

Annie wandered around the yard looking for Buttermilk. The little chicken wire cage was there by the rock garden border. But where was the rabbit? Annie didn't know where to go. She didn't know what to do or where to be.

~30~

The child stumbled aimlessly back into the house. In the bedroom her mother sat in the stiff backed chair and moaned. Her father curled in a tight knot, his face turned to the window. Under the kitchen table sprawled Humpy Chris.

All morning Chris had dozed off and on. When he would wake, he caught a word here and there. From the bedroom, Margaret's voice. "No, Katie hasn't checked on me for weeks...."

And later, Urs spoke. "Not 'til the end of July you said, more than a month away! Of course, I would have made up to August and Katie before then!"

At times, Chris coughed like he would never stop, or he would suck in air with a dry rattle. Once he looked up from under the table and Margaret was rising from a kneeling position, her back to him, skirts growing damp with blood.

Chris hardly moved--awake or asleep. Only Annie had moved quietly through the house and farmyard.

Now, in the kitchen Annie stood observing the dragon. He didn't look dangerous. More sad, really. Annie bent and began stroking the hair that fringed his head.

Chris was suddenly awake, watching her wide eyed. Slowly, Annie began talking like she might when trying to tame a wild animal. "It's ok," she started. "I'm not going to hurt you. You're ok, now. Let me see where you're hurt."

The light coming through the kitchen window had an unnatural quality. A dusky rose, though it was mid afternoon. Annie felt as though she was in the church--a dim glow through stained glass illuminating the scene. There was the dragon with the spear thrust through its heart, writhing in agony. It was conquered, with no power, now. And there, St. George, handsome and shining. And there, the rescued maiden. This time she would go with him. They would be together, leaving the dragon behind--his false powers exposed and broken, his treasure gone.

Annie rubbed the palms of both small hands gently over the hump. "There now, doesn't that feel better?" Her kindly hands moved with a firm gentle motion. He was sad and hurt now, she saw, broken like an unruly horse. Could he too be transformed?

Chris was comforted. He tried to remember the last time he'd been touched by another human being. The last time someone had touched his hump in a loving way? Even Juanita, during their love making, never embraced him. She avoided his back altogether, lying stiff and flat with arms outstretched like a suffering martyr on a cross.

From under the table Chris looked up and through the kitchen window. There was a peculiar light in the sky. The air was growing heavy, the farmyard oddly quiet. Annie stroked his back with small, strong hands. A profound sadness rose in his throat. Then he remembered, there was that time in church when he was a child-- when the old lady rubbed his hump for luck. Chris faded in and out of consciousness.

Annie's voice was a cooing now. The sweet soft cooing of a mother to her child. As Chris relaxed his legs quivered, chattering on the floor, letting go of tension.

By that time of course, he knew that the baby had been born dead--and that the neglected house was deep in mourning for the baby as well as Danny. Under Annie's gentle touch, he too became overcome with grief. As if he had some stake in the still born child-- as if the child had been partly his.

Annie continued in a sweet comforting tone. "There's nothing to be afraid of, now. You're going to be all right." Could that be Juanita, touching him so lovingly. Had she come back? Did she love him after all? Chris began sobbing, uncontrollably, then. For the loss. For all their losses.

The sobbing brought Margaret to the kitchen. She stood framed in the doorway, her skin pale...her eyes sunken. Her hair was wild and matted. Seeing Annie under the table petting Chris, tears welled to her eyes and rolled down her checks. She realized who he was—and hurt somehow. "Annie, help me get Mr. Chris into the big bed."

 "Betrayed!" Chris moaned. "I am betrayed."

Together mother and daughter worked him to his feet. "Here, let us get you to the bedroom. You need to get in bed and rest." Margaret raised him up, her shoulder braced under his arm. "Gone. Gone." Chris whispered in her ear with each labored breath. "My jewel, Juanita, gone."

Margaret's feet slipped. The earth fell from under her. Down and down, she fell clutching the door casing, in and out of the arms of Lars. In and out of Danny's helping embrace. Chris labored on top of her like a drowning man pulling down his savior. Out of Margaret's arms he slipped. Out of Juanita's beauty.

Annie looked on, stunned. Chris and her mother were on the floor in a tangled heap. Margaret beat the floor. " My God, my God, Why have you forsaken me?"

Annie waited. It seemed like a long time before Chris and her mother rose again, helping each other up. Annie brushed the dirt off his dark pants, before they resumed their hobbling way. In the bedroom Chris fell back into her parent's bed. A sigh of gratitude escaped his cracked lips. It was his first easy breath in two weeks. The buttons to his vest sprung open.

Annie wadded the corner of the bedspread. There they lay, together, Urs curled into a tight ball, facing the wall. Humpy Chris out flat, his hump pushing into the mattress, his chest high and open.

"Annie, get some water, honey. Get a glass of water for Mr. Chris." Margaret leaned over him. Worry pinched her brow.

Annie helped to raise him up. When Chris drained the glass, he breathed deeply, patting Annie's hand.

Annie returned to the kitchen. The sky, still sinister. Squeak, squeak said the pump at the bottom of each thrust, as she filled the glass again. The chickens in the trees were oddly quiet. Even the buzzing of the insects stopped. The air was heavy, stifling, pressing down.

When Annie returned with the water, the dragon was asleep. She left the glass on the little night stand. Her mother still sat in the chair at the bedside.

Annie drifted back outside. A cooler wind rose. Storm clouds were gathering, racing across the sky. Under the bush her little work had blown away. The door to the chicken coop banged on its hinges. Chickens rose and fluttered. Annie crumpled pressing her back against the side of the house. She made no effort to put right the little field.

Chickens were coming and going as they pleased. The sky grew darker. Why wasn't her mother here feeding the chickens bringing with her the late afternoon sunshine? Annie tried to see her, thinking the chicken yard all neat and hard-packed, her mother scattering golden grain in fading light.

She tried to see her dad just now be coming through the gate from the field. The dogs barking. Annie rubbed the dry dirt between her fingers, letting the powder drift. She sat there without moving. Until her breath slowed. Until her mouth grew closed and her nails long, curling over her finger tips. Until the insides of her ears filled with fur and a blinking membrane grew over her eyes.

Racing clouds stacked into dark thunderheads.

Swollen drops fell to the dust, shattering. Tears, Annie thought. And then as the earth grew dark, blood.

Lightning flashed. Thunder boomed. She almost knew what all this meant when the rabbit crossed a corner of the yard. Just as he raced to the cover of the lilac bush, rain let loose in sheets.

~31~

Rain hammers down.

Some of the roosting hens fall out of the trees and flap wildly to the hen house or huddle slick with rain, under bushes. Others stubbornly cling to their branches, side-stepping up to huddle, heads tucked under their wings, near the trunk.

Inside, Margaret in the straight-backed chair next to the bed, folds her arms and slowly begins rocking. Back and forth. Back and forth. Who are they? She'd forgotten again. Who are these two men in her baby's bed? Where are her babies? Where is the nest she had built so sweetly?

Lightning flashes, briefly illuminating the room. Oh, now she sees. There is Urs. There is Urs in bed already and they hadn't even had supper. Oh, but look there. He has a huge hump on his back. He carries around a huge hump on his back. No, it's Humpy Chris. Humpy Chris, on Urs's back. Urs can't get out of bed because he carries around Humpy Chris on his back. Where are her babies?

Oh, there they are. The twin boys sleeping sweetly. Margaret bends tucking them in, reaching over the one to smooth back the big one's hair. "Momma, I need you, momma," he says flinging out his arms.

"Go to sleep, honey. Go to sleep. Everything is all right." Margaret takes Urs's hand in hers and begins slowly caressing the coarse scar where the fingers are missing.

"Help me, momma. Help me, I'm hungry, momma." Urs tosses, jarring the bedpost against the wall, releasing his past.

"Ursie, give me your hand, honey." Little Ursie was eight years old.

His father died of diphtheria first, in the same bed the week before. Little Ursie places his hand in his mother's trembling one. She rubs the buried knuckles where the fingers were missing, feeling the texture of the scarred calluses. "I'm sorry, Ursie. I'm so sorry for your hand. It was a terrible accident. I'm so very sorry."

Rain beats on the roof, gusts with the wind. Thunder rattles the windows. Hoppers clinging tenuously to the swollen joints of buffalo grass, are stripped and washed away. The orb spider curls under the metal lip of the water tank in a tight knot. Honey bees, working the sweet clover and Dutch, unable to make it back in time to Katie's hive, are dashed to death mid flight.

Urs reaches for his missing fingers. Three tiny white fingers cut from the hand of a swaddled baby left lying at the edge of a field. Lightning blazes. Urs turns looking out the window. Tiny rivulets are running down the pane. Tiny white roots cling to the roiling earth, now sprouting high and green with the waving trees. Again all is black. Urs is digging deep, planting seed potatoes with their glowing white fingers.

Urs's stomach rumbles with the thunder. Little Ursie was hungry. The three brothers roamed the farm like wild animals eating what they could find, flour paste and raw eggs.

Urs's tongue feels for the lightly textured egg-shell. A raw egg still warm from the hen. Little Ursie pressed the fragile surface until the end popped open and he sucked.

"My babies, my babies, you're going to be fine." Margaret whispers, opening her blouse. Electricity leaps from thunderhead to thunderhead. The sky shudders. Urs's eyes spring wide. Again, his stomach growls. If he only had potatoes, like his mother made. *Grundbeerabrei.* A white rabbit hops frantically about the room.

Urs reaches once again for the missing fingers, for his missing momma. Wind gusts with the pouring rain. "Don't leave me, Momma. Promise me you won't go away." Urs begs.

Margaret bends over her infant son. "I'm here, honey, I'm here." She makes the sign of the cross performing *the nah tauf.* (emergency baptism)

A burning flash. Thunder's voice rattles the window. Ursie gave his mother his hand while she burned with fever. Greenish scabs appeared around her mouth and nose. Her voice rattled.

In and out of consciousness, his mother danced Dur Schottish, in and out of the arms of his father. In and out of lucidity. "Where's Pa?" Was it her father or husband she called for? "Take me back to mother Russia. There, we lived all together in our little *Selz dorf,* all in a circle with the church in the middle and the green fields stretching out behind. *Unsere Leute* all together."

She nodded weakly, her matted hair dampening the pillow. "Not like here, Ursie, where your land is a little square all by itself, a long ways from your neighbor's house in the middle of their own little square. Homesteading.... It sounded good but now we're out here all alone, where the church is far away and even the priest won't come."

His mother's hand burned. She coughed deeply, uncontrollably. Then, in a rattling whisper: "Take me to our *Heimatland*, Ursie. The sunflowers are blooming.."

Her voice grew angry, deeper. "Not like here, Ursie. Not like here, where even the priest won't come."

She raised her head from the damp pillow. Little pink threaded flowers embroidered on the white percale. "Grandpa said it would be hard, Ursie. He warned us." Greenish scabs grew around her nose and lips.

"They wouldn't let us leave the country with one ruble in our pocket. Not one ruble, Ursie. Just the clothes on our back and our pockets full of sunflower seeds. They told us we could never go back. When we left Pa said it would be hard:

'Eiste Generation' Steiben First generation, Death
Zweite Generation' Verlangen Second generation, Want
Dritte Generation' Brut' Third generation, Bread

That's what the old folks always said. Same here, Ursie. Same here." Tears rolled down cracked cheeks.

Out the window water falls hard. The great shining prairie rolls....the farmhouse small and alone, afloat on the vast rolling plain. His mother told of times long gone as she rubbed the calluses of his scarred hand. "We came here on a boat, Ursie, on a big terrible water...for the land." Thunder booms. "Where you bury your own, the land is yours, Ursie." Lightning illuminates the room. Urs grips the headboard. The house rolls and shakes as he rumbles his tale.

The little creek in the wild land is rising quickly. The box turtle there pulls in his head and appendages as he's carried along in the current. The nest of prairie chickens floats in the ditch.

Lightning cracks, close by. The electric smell of something scorching fills the air.

"I'm thirsty, Momma. I'm hungry." Urs cries out.

Margaret reaches for the glass of water. Her little ones are thirsty. "Here, honey, everything is going to be all right."

Ursie was hot and thirsty from working in the fields. Nudging the horses out of the way, he drank eagerly. Urs raises his head and empties the glass. The horses reared. His lips grew cool and wet, his eyes closed with pleasure. Thunder heads were threatening. What is that scorching odor? Oh, yes, potato soup, with pieces of bacon scorched crisp and floating on top.

"Thank you, Momma, thank you." There's Margaret, taking the empty glass from his hands. "Oh it's you, Margaret. Thanks."

Urs is hungry. Lawrence Reisinger stood laughing, holding the bowl of soup high above little Ursie's head.

The flashing sky momentarily lights the room. Is that Lawrence Reisinger lying next to him in bed?

"You god damn son of a bitch!" Urs shouts.

Urs strikes out at Humpy Chris half heartedly. Over and over flailing his arms. He couldn't really get a hold of that son of a bitch, Reisinger. That bastard had ended up with the farm that by rights should have been his....where Urs was taunted and treated worse than any animal.

Under the house a porcupine burrows out of the storm. He curls in on himself, nose to tail.

Little Ursie led the horse and wagon into the churchyard. Seated propped between his brothers, was his mother, weak with diphtheria, shivering with fever. In the bed of the wagon, his father, dead already. The priest was singing the Mass.

When they entered the church, the priest cried out. *"Komm nicht hier herein, bis es dir besser geht."* Don't come in here 'til you're better.

Urs sits up in bed, yelling out the priest's callous words, looking like he is awake. *"Bleibt fort und schick deine Jungs nicht zur Kirche bis die ganze Sache vorbei ist. muessen diese Sache vom Verbreiten aufhalten."* Stay away, and don't send your boys to church 'til this thing is over. We've got to stop this thing from spreading."

Thunder rumbles. "We buried him ourselves, with Ma looking on. In days Ma was dead too. No one came to help," Urs muttered. "We drug her out to a ditch and covered her up with dirt. I tried to hold up her feet. I tried to hold up her feet, but they kept slipping out of my hands. Only Harold had a shovel. Us other two tore the dirt out of the ditch bank with our hands, throwing it on her face. Her eyes were dry and sunken, staring."

Sweat soaks Urs's clothes and dampens the sheets. He shivers. "Even after we buried her, no one came.

"Finally, when it was too late, it was the god-damn priest with Mrs. Henderson!" Urs hits the wall with his fist. "Harold met them at the door.

"Harold, was skinny, seventeen years old. His dirty hair sprang from his head, he talked so hard. 'De're not gonna go live with no old couple that can't have kids. No!' His spine went hard and straight as an iron rod. His head jerked. He stared the priest down. Shouting. Pointing. 'Da're not up for adoption. I'm da oldest. De're mine!.' Harold jerked his thumb to the center of his chest. 'De're mine!' His breath smelled of father's whiskey."

Thunder growls as Urs moans his memories. "Get off a our place! This is our place and you get off of it!" Urs sits up in bed growling his brother's words. He jabs his one finger at the mound of covers that is Humpy Chris.

Humpy Chris cringes, pulling deep into the heavy quilts.

Rain roars down. At the pond, mud puppies bury themselves deeper in the silt while the surface above spikes to sharp pricks. In the meadow, prairie dogs struggle back to higher tunnels as the lower rooms fill with water.

Sitting upright in bed, Urs is laughing. "By the end of the week, we had ransacked the house, finding the last of the food.... Harold found father's whiskey. He started drinking and never stopped." Urs is laughing. "He sold the land. He sold us!" In a moment the laughter is replaced with anger. Urs resumes the hitting. He strikes half-heartedly, without any real power...at Lawrence Reisinger! At his brother, Harold! At Humpy Chris!

The trees sway and bend nearly to the ground. A newly hatched robin falls from its nest, the fragile, featherless body dead on impact.

Humpy Chris dozes off and on deep in the quilts. What is that hitting? He dreams of his ledger. What should he do with Juanita? There are the columns of credits and debits and there was Juanita. Where does she fit?

Someone is hitting him in the face. Now, let's see. Just a minute now, Chris wants to get this figured out. Get it down in black and white. Oh yes, 5,869. Now if this will just balance. How could he use this to his advantage?

Wait a minute, stop that hitting. If the hitting would just stop for a minute he might be able to get this thing figured out. Oh, yes. If that goes there, and he could collect interest of five percent there, he might be able to make money on this after all. And even if none of this works out he would have enough in reserve to bail out. He had enough other assets to more than come out of this thing ok.

There's the hitting again. It makes everything tangled. Confused. Now, which column did he decide was the credits? No, they looked more like debits. If the hitting would just stop. There. Clearly that column must be debits. That would make these the credits here. Let me see, now. No, that isn't right either.

Lightning cracks in the trees of the windbreak. Humpy Chris turns deeper into the covers, deeper into his cocoon of troubled sleep. What is that scorching smell? OH, his ledger is on fire! Chris tries smothering it out with his hands. The flames only burn more brightly, blackening the carefully ordered columns. His frantic slapping only fans the flames. His ledger curls to fragile gray ash, that disintegrates under his touch. How will he ever be able to figure out what anything is worth? How will he know what is important and what is not?

A flash illuminates the room, Urs looks in amazement. What is he doing? Who is that in bed with him? Can that be Humpy Chris? In a startled panic Urs climbs with surprising agility over his cowering bedmate and swings his feet to the floor. He sits on the edge of the bed, his face in his hands. A cooling rain falls heavily.

Annie lets her eyes fall closed, listening with relief to the steady sound of hard rain. She'd been poised outside the bedroom for hours.

Sometimes there had come from the room, the cooing of birds or suckling pigs. Once she had heard the bed scoot just a bit and then stop, and then scoot just a bit again across the floor as if it were a broad-backed hog maybe, with stiff legs. But now it rains. Cool and hard and steady. The storm is passing. lightning flashes on the horizon, thunder rumbles further and further into the distance.

The sound of the rain on the roof slows. Instead of a roar, there are patterns of sound, of raindrops drumming out rhythms. Then, it is almost quiet: just the tick, tick, tick, of water from the eaves. The wild birds sheltered there begin stirring and now, once again become strangely quiet. The storm retreats as profoundly as it came.

Annie tiptoes to the narrow crack of the partially opened bedroom door and looks inside. She can just make out the dim silhouette of a great bear sitting on the edge of the bed, head in his hands.

Urs holds despair in the palms of his hands. Silent tears splash down. The bulky man groans, collapsing again into the bed. If he could just get some rest. But there is hardly any room.

Urs wants his space. He doesn't want to feel so crowded. Urs thrusts out his elbows. He wants to stake out his own place, where no one can tell him what to do. He begins rolling Humpy Chris to the other side of the bed. Slowly. Gently.

Little Ursie rolled his mother's body into the ditch. "We wrapped her up. I tried to hold up her feet....I tried to hold up her feet, but they kept slipping out of my hands. Harold and me we kept tripping on the edge of the sheet as it came unwound. So we rolled her. We wrapped her in a sheet and rolled her to the ditch." Urs groans.

Chris is turning, rolling deep in his cocoon of quilts. Is that Juanita stroking him in the night? Are those Annie's small strong hands easing the tension in his humped back, straightening it? The night has grown silent and very dark. Chris is in deep black water. Wise strong hands untwist him as he turns in the womb.

"No one would come! Help! Help!" Urs's cry for help breaks the silence. "But no one came."

From deep in the hot, black, liquid silence Chris listens. Yes, he would have come. He could have helped.

A family of field mice creep out from the foundation of the corn crib, where they had been hiding. A heavy silence builds, deep and pure. Eerily there is no wind, no rain. The mice turn and scuttle back to their hiding place.

Chris would have come and helped. Chris would drive out to the farm in his roomy, comfortable Pontiac. He would feel an overpowering urge to get there before it was too late. As he parked the car, Margaret would have called out exhausted. "Thank God you're here, Chris! The baby is coming. The baby needs to come out, now!"

"Here, Margaret, lie down!" Chris could have supported her by the elbow guiding her to the bed.

"Lie down!" Chris instructs from deep in his quilts.

Margaret falls into the bed, exhausted.

Outside, a pure deep silence. It seems impossible the raging storm ever existed. The moon appears, partially covered by gauzy clouds.

As the kitchen brightens with moonlight, Annie lies sprawled before the bedroom door half asleep.

She awakes breathless with running. Annie'd been playing softball on the grassy plateau. Balls were rolling, bouncing, flying through the air. More and more came. And it was her job to keep them from rolling off the edge of the world. Annie lie still on the unyielding kitchen floor, listening. Behind the door, there had been whispering....cursing, prayers, and numbers. Now, only silence.

Into that profound silence, a new sound creeps. A light clicking and a thump. Another light clicking and a thump. Annie's heart bangs. She sits up, back aching with the planked floor.

As her eyes adjust Annie makes out the slow movement of a large round ball. She creeps after it. Reaching. Illusive as a ghost. She tries again, grabbing nothingness. Annie lunges. The leaping becomes frantic as the rabbit bumps into the table, the cupboard door, trying to escape.

Annie lunges. The rabbit hits the bedroom door. The door springs wide. What she sees in moonlight, stuns her.

They are sleeping. All three of them in the same bed. The hawk, the bear, and the dragon. One three-headed monster. Annie wonders, is she awake or asleep?

The trees shiver, wet with the moonlight.

A restlessness rises with the wind as it races effortlessly through the wet grass, making eddies and waves of the emerging wheat, the flax, the standing water. Lightning veins the sky.

The storm is thundering back out of the west, trailing cloudy veils and flashes in her wake. Brilliant snakes zig-zagged to the earth, snapping and cracking. The storm had only been taking a breath. A loud flapping begins as her fingers slide beneath a layer of tar paper on the machine shed roof and hurls the flapping paper to the field where it flutters weakly, caught on the barbed wire fence.

Another round is starting up. Another round of the godlike dance, with all its terrible wonder. Commanding the earth, commanding fire, air and water, she comes keening back.

Urs thrashes about in the bed. He tries to run. Away from the keening storm. Away from the singing priest. Away from his dying mother. The blankets are twisted around him. Swaddling a baby boy at the edge of a field while the sweeping blades roar over his head.

Urs sinks back into the pillow and turns to face the window. Greenish water streams down the glass. A green waterfall of ripe grain. Urs is trapped under the pounding water. The horses rear in terror at the terrible roar. A waterfall of green stalks and grain cascade before him, glinting like sparkling winter snow.

A series of gusts start up, that first boom against the bones of the house and then suck back with a shrill screeching as the nails let loose a piece of clapboard under the window. In and out, the storm breaths, screeching and sucking.... a living thing.

Margaret pants in hard labor. Again, the storm booms against the bones of the house. Margaret's breasts are hot and hard with milk. She moans and tosses in the narrow space beside Urs.

Chris winds in and out of dreams. Standing with the thick heavy book in his hands, Margaret tossed in the bed sweating, panting, moaning. And he would know what to do. He would have come just in time.

Chris flipped through the pages. Yes, there would be the pictures. Pictures of the twisted babies born stomach first, chest first, knees bent backwards first. Babies that could have been born healthy if only he, Chris, had been there to help, for Chris knows how to turn the baby in the womb so it would live. Chris exhales deeply, in and out of consciousness, in and out of dreams. Turning into the hot liquid blackness. The skin of the house shudders. Deeper and deeper into the storm Chris turns.

Then, a hush: A pause in the dance as they all hold their breath. In a moment, heavy rain drums out a terrible beat. The storm dances on the roof, flinging flashing stands of diamonds. With a roaring boom, the house begins to quake. The storm's dark skirts are drenched black, her sheeting veils of rain, falling.

Lightning cracks open the night. A flash more brilliant than any startles the bedroom to a silvery hot white. The sky shatters. In the pulsing, blazing light everything is made visible, all is laid bare.

Margaret pants heavily. Dark death falls slashing, tearing away the silken veils, destroying and renewing.

Margaret sees! The storm dances hard. Yes Margaret sees now how she clings to death! With each shiny sequined veil of pounding rain, Margaret lets loose a song of mourning; surrendering her hold on Lars, on Little Maryanne, Danny, her father and mother on all that is dead and gone. She dives deep.

Her hard breasts soften. Milk flows. Tears. All the veils tearing away.

A high, shrill wail breaks the night as the storm throws back her head, dancing herself to death, breaking her back on the roof of the house.

The sacred Latin Mass springs from Margaret's mouth as she surrenders "*Accipite ie bibite ex io omnes: hic est enim calix Snaguinis....et qui pro vobis pro nobis effudetur in remissionem peccatorum* " Take this all of you and drink from it. This is the cup of my blood... It will be shed for you and for all so that sins may be forgiven.

Margaret swaddles the still born baby in her arms. The night has grown quiet. A baby passes into the arms of its mother. Margaret lay her down. She lay her down deep, in the dark, accepting earth.

The rabbit jerks, startling Annie awake. Is she dreaming? She inhales deeply, breathing the wild animal scent, feeling the soft fur on her cheek.

Annie squints through the darkness toward the bedroom door. Are they all still in there? Thunder rumbles to the distance as the storm recedes, rattling the boards of the floor beneath her. The wind comes up again, blowing the storm to the east.

Are they still in there, the dragon and the bear and the hawk? Who would win if a bear and a dragon fought? Who would win in a battle between a hawk and dragon?

Lightning flashes on the horizon. The dragon snakes and writhes among the fitfully waving trees. Again lighting blazes. Is that the dragon rearing back, belching hot white fire? Is that the bear's thick stump-like silhouette striking with a roaring boom? Does the bear hold the dragon to the ground with heavy back feet, while his front paws claw the sky? Another growling roar rumbles away. The trees bend and sway. A flash shows the dragon down but still alive.

The trees bend and sway, nearly doubling over. Powerful wings are beating. A hawk is circling just out of the bear's reach. Annie feels its beating wings as the wind blasts the side of the house. The hawk is hunting. Her nestlings are hungry. Her eyes a piercing blue, her talons spread. Her hooked beak pierces a pulsing red stone. Or is it a pulsing heart?   In an instant, the window frames a flash holding the memory of the great bird as it soars away.

Annie is falling through space. She has been sucked into the space where the beasts no longer fight. With one hand Annie grips the thin, solid, chrome leg of the kitchen table. The shiny leg reflects a distorted image of herself falling, terrified. With the other hand she clings to her rabbit. There must be something she is supposed to do. What is it?

Throughout the rest of the night, the rabbit came and went. Now, once again it lay curled in Annie's arms. A pale sunlight seeps through the kitchen window.

Kingbirds erupt in chatter, leading as usual, the early morning chorus of birdsong. Annie raises herself on one elbow. Outside, the world is washed clean, sparkling with water and early light. The sun rises above horizon, flooding the world. Outside hens are clucking. Annie goes to the window to survey the damage. Branches and twigs litter the yard. Dead grass and debris clog the ditches, tar paper has blown against the fence posts....Hens are flapping about, clucking, drying their wings. Water stands in the low places.

But inside the house is quiet. No sound comes from behind the bedroom door. Will they ever come out?

~32~

Annie went to the corner and began working the small squeaky hand pump. She knew what she had to do. The sound of the squeaky pump in the quiet house reassured her. Annie removed her soiled overalls, her shirt and underwear, her filthy socks. How many days had she worn them? Annie washed in chilly water and patted her shivering goose flesh dry. Next, she went to her bedroom and put on a clean red and green plaid cotton dress with puffy sleeves she'd inherited from Lizzie. She stroked the soft worn cotton skirt, straightening herself before the mirror.

Satisfied, Annie bent pulling on cotton socks boiled white. She opened the lacing of her brown oxfords and looked inside. "I'm Buster Brown, I live in your shoe" rang senselessly through her mind. "I'm his dog Tide, look for me in their too." Her father always turned off the radio then, before the show started. The Howdy Doody Show. What nonsense. A waste of time. Annie quickly pulled on the leather hightops.

From the kitchen came the light clicking of nails and a thump. Again and again as the rabbit hopped across the floor. Annie understood then that everything else had just been playing. Just playing in preparation for what she would do now.

Slowly and deliberately Annie began gathering up her things. At the lilac bush--the spoon and the little soaked cigar-box wagon.

The bush itself was almost battered to the ground, with many broken limbs. Annie tried to right it but it drooped when she stepped away. The arrowhead was mostly buried in the mud near the little pasque flower. Though it had been stripped of most of the blooms, the sturdy little stem still stood.

The wire cage, Annie found at the edge of the garden, bent and misshapen. Annie worked on it, pulling it back into shape. But she didn't like seeing the garden. The bright rows of lettuce and turnips were darkly blotched and splattered. As she hurried back to the house, the bulky cage banged against her hip. Now she realized why the cage was pliable. So she could do it.

Annie placed each item lovingly on the kitchen table. For a moment she stood looking at them, her eyes downcast, her palms pressed together. Then she remembered the knife. The thin bladed knife with the blue porcelain handle that folded open and locked into place. Grandfather's knife. It was supposed to go to Danny.

Annie opened the little curtain to the lower shelves. In the box of clutter towards the back she found the knife. Just as she knew she would. She placed it carefully between the spoon and the wagon. Yes, that would be all she needed. The bat was all right where it was. She didn't need to bring it here. It would be there in the dark corner of the smokehouse, ready when she needed it.

Annie drew a deep breath and slowly let it out.

When the time came, Mashed Potatoes came right to her. She had no trouble at all opening the little wire cage from the top and slipping him in. Solemnly Annie started down the path swinging the caged rabbit with one hand, aware of the unforgiving lump in her pocket made by the knife. The day sparkled with light and water. Birds flitted through the air and sung in the trees.

When it was over, Annie found herself standing gripping the wooden handle of the bat. Her vision had adjusted to the darkness of the smokehouse. She could see quite clearly that the rabbit's eyes, glazed with death, remained on her.

She laid down the bat. There hadn't been much blood. A little where the rabbit's flesh was broken around the neck and embedded with the jagged wire from when it struggled briefly. A little on the bat. But stronger than the spices and smoke, she could smell it, the blood. Or was it something else? Terror? Or maybe death?

Annie pulled loose the wire from the matted flesh and fur. Still the rabbit watched with pink, open eyes. She worked him loose and let the dead weight slide onto the ground.

Annie withdrew the blue handled folding knife from her pocket and locked the blade into place.

Suddenly, she wondered if this all was something evil. She had the same feeling she had in church sometimes....or when she saw the magic things at Katie's. That the magic might be evil. What if the rabbit was just a rabbit and the colored light coming in the church window was just colored light, and that the dragon wasn't in the bedroom at all? What if it was just the stump and fallen tree by the outhouse that had only looked like a dragon? But if none of that were true, what was there?

Pulling the head to one side, Annie expertly slit the rabbit's throat. Blood pooled, darkening the dirt floor. Annie scooted to one side avoiding the hot liquid. She let it drain for some time. Watching the rabbit watch her.

Annie didn't cry out. She didn't weep. She breathed deeply, biting her quivering lip. She sat in a tight knot watching the rabbit's pink, unblinking, all-seeing eyes.

In a few moments the bleeding slowed. She lifted the rabbit by the back feet encouraging the last of it. Annie knew to start the cut at the little hole between the back legs like with any other animal. She turned him onto his back and spread his legs. She knew not to cut too deeply, to avoid puncturing the guts. The cavity in the belly opened under the knife. She had gutted fish before, and of course watched both her mother and father many times butcher chickens and pigs, so she knew generally what to do.

She found a bucket on the shelf by the butchering table. Annie cut the intestines at both ends before removing the entrails. The slick sensation on her hands told her she was doing it right.

Then, beginning at the edge of the open cavity she began skinning. Annie peeled back the fur with one hand slicing the knife blade between the flesh and the hide with the other. The exposed muscles twitched. When she finished Annie lifted the rabbit by its front feet, and turned it slowly. The cavity gaped open. Fur clung only to the four feet and the head. Even now the rabbit watched.

When Annie found she couldn't cut off the feet with the knife, she brought the nude, little corpse to the butchering table at the side of the door. Above the heavily scarred plank, her father kept the massive meat cleaver, hung in a bracket on the wall.

With two hands Annie swung it over head bringing the blade down, breaking clean the bones just above the foot. When she had all four, she slipped the furry rabbits feet into the pocket of her dress, and hung the mutilated corpse on the meat hook.

When Annie stepped from the cool dark of the smokehouse, the light nearly blinded her. She stood a moment while her eyes adjusted. There was blood smudged here and there; on the front of her dress, her hands, beneath her fingernails. She pulled one of the rabbit's feet from her splotched pocket.

It was wet at one end. She touched it with a finger. There was a little pink flesh and ragged skin, around the pure white bone.

In the kitchen, the only sound was the light breathing that rose from the sleeping monster behind the bedroom door. Annie went to the door and looked in. There they were, all sleeping in the same bed. Her mother, her father and Humpy Chris. Very quietly Annie entered. She moved about the room, pressing a rabbit's foot into the right hand of each of them.

In the kitchen, Annie pulled out a chair and sat at the table waiting. Maybe it wouldn't work. Maybe everything was for nothing.

There was the spoon. She lifted the cool metal, warming the cup in the hollow of her hand. Very carefully she put the spoon back on the table. And there was the little wagon. She got up from her chair and began rolling the soggy and deformed shape round and round the table's edge.

When she finished, for a moment Annie sat staring. Then, she moved the spoon to one end of the table and the little wagon to the other. Between the spoon and the wagon and the arrow head, Annie laid the last disfigured rabbit's foot.

Annie stared at the bedroom door. They didn't come out. There was no sound what-so-ever. It had been a long time since any of them had eaten. Or even had much of anything to drink. Annie wondered if inside that room time was captured like something soft and white in a wire cage. If nothing would ever change. Maybe, none of them would ever leave. Maybe they would simply go on sharing the same body, each pulling in a different direction. Never really able to either come together or to separate. And she would never be able to do anything about it.

A wave of sadness flooded through her. Annie laid her head down on her arm, wailing out a song of sadness. When she lifted her eyes, the bedroom doorway framed her mother looking tired and drawn, but her blue, blue eyes were clear and true. "What is it, Annie? What's wrong, honey?" To Annie, it seemed like the first human voice she had heard in a long, long time.

Margaret came nearer, reaching out. "It's all right, Annie. Every thing's going to be all right." Margaret held her close. Annie felt the familiar rapid pat. "I know, Annie. I know."

In a few moments, Margaret was wiping the wetness from Annie's face with her hands. "Let's go sit on the porch."

In a while, they began walking the farmyard. With the sun directly overhead, there were no shadows.

"It's not so bad, Annie. There's nothing here we can't fix. Why, look there, the lilac bush is springing back! And the night crawlers! All over the place! That's a good sign! We should collect them and go fishing! Let's talk Urs into taking us fishing!" Joy surged through Annie with her mother's happy talk.

Margaret gave Annie a long look. "Look at us two, Annie." She put her hands to her face, laughing.

There were blotches of blood here and there--at the pocket and all over the front of Annie's plaid dress. Her mother's dress was a mass of wrinkles, slept in for days. Her hair stuck out in matted straggles. Annie laughed. They both laughed.

Annie carried pitchers full of water to the reservoir while Margaret pumped. When the reservoir was full Margaret rummaged through the kindling box. She had just managed to start a little fire when Annie held out the scraps of a cigar box and laid them on the little nest of flames. The fragrant cedar box had dried some, and caught almost at once.

Margaret opened the windows letting in the afternoon. When the water was hot, Mother and daughter washed their legs, faces, hair, savoring the clean soapy water. They rubbed their hair with soft clean cotton cloth, fluffing it out full, enjoying the fresh breeze, from the open window. It had a sweet, newborn smell.

Margaret put on a kettle of water for coffee. Surely she could find enough in the house to make a soup.

She rummaged through the cupboards. Nothing. There should be a few onions and maybe some potatoes in the root cellar. Nothing left looked fit to eat. There might be a few carrots in the garden, most certainly small, but big enough.... Margaret searched the cupboards as if preparing this meal was the most important thing she had ever done. She was down on her hands and knees looking, through her little cache of store-bought canned goods when she heard the kitchen door close.

In a few moments, there stood Annie, back again, flushed with running. She offered in her extended hand a skinned rabbit, its four feet crudely hacked away.

Accepting this offering, Margaret bit her quivering lip as a flood sprang to her eyes.

*

Annie and Margaret sat in silence on the steps to the porch. The slanting light of late afternoon illuminated the grass, the fields, the trees. The countryside glowed in greenness.

Chickens roosting in the tree by the gate began clucking. Settling in for the night. From the kitchen came the aroma of a rich, bubbly stew.

Margaret bent, kissed Annie's head, and started for the chicken coop. When she came out, a row of noisy chickens followed. Tied around her waist was Urs's old Sunday shirt.

Annie's face burst into smiles as Margaret began her ritual dance, flinging out the golden grain as the chickens scurried to her feet. Annie raced to find a long broken branch and began nudging the chickens out of the trees. Birds fluttered from everywhere to join Margaret in her dance.

Margaret ladled a steaming portion into each ironstone bowl. A wonderful smell rose. Annie carefully placed before each of them a bowl containing his own quivering reflection.

Margaret's hand flickered before her eyes, her heart. *"Komm Herr Jesus sei unser Gast und segne was Du uns bescherest hast."* Her voice, richer and stronger than before, flooded the quiet room.

Urs gazed from face to face as if he didn't recognize anyone. At the prayer's end, instead of crossing himself, he let his head fall forward and forced thick fingers through the matted, black hair.

Annie had helped Chris straighten his clothes and limp to the table. Now, two small, miss-buttoned mother of pearl eyes wavered socket-less just under his chin.

Drawn by the aroma, Humpy Chris leaned into the stew. There he saw small sweet carrots, onions, fresh greens, chunks of hard boiled eggs, meat, spices, and his own sad brown eyes.

Suddenly he erupted into a spell of coughing. Though Annie had tucked a pillow behind his lower back, his jerking sent an electric pain shooting down his leg. Chris struggled to quiet himself.

Urs picked up his spoon. A look of recognition eased the confusion between his brows. Then, there was the familiar rhythm as Urs swayed forward and back, forward and back, his mouth reaching for the spoon. His lids fell shut with the pleasure of the delicately meaty broth.

The only sounds were the clicking of metal against stoneware, Urs's lips opening and closing, and the sucking and swallowing. Once in a while there rose a gentle mmmmm as Urs's eyes flickered and fell shut. He smiled his thanks to Margaret.

Annie was nearly half finished when she noticed Chris sitting quietly staring. The last of twilight filtered through the kitchen window behind. From the counter, the special spoon glinted. Annie brought it to the table, polishing it on the bottom of her shirt. There was a slight scuffing of the wooden chair legs as she drew close to Chris. Side by side their faces wavered on the liquid surface.

Annie lowered the spoon, breaking the fragile scene and raised it brimming full. Over and over. The same rhythm as before. The hot broth soothed Chris's throat. Colors in the room were fading.

When Annie finished, she rested the spoon with a light click in the empty bowl.

"Thanks." Humpy's voice was soft, seeping in with the darkness. Then there were just the quiet sounds of the evening. Frogs singing down at the pond, crickets, evening birds. It was almost night. They sat quietly, reaching for each other in the dark--thankful for each other in the dark.

After sitting a few moments in the dusky twilight of the kitchen, Margaret rose, breaking the spell. She went to the lamp hung above the list of state capitals, and with ease of habit, lifted the glass chimney, trimmed the wick, and struck the match.

"Tomorrow morning, you men get those cows in for milking." Margaret's words were quiet. Matter-of-fact. They drew credibility from the light. "This has gone on long enough. Urs, "*wer rastet, der rostet,*" if you rest, you rust, you know that." She replaced the glowing glass.

"Chris, you'll sleep on the davenport. Annie, go ahead now and bring down some blankets from the boys' room, and help Chris make up his bed."

In the bedroom, Margaret stripped the bed. First, she threw off the blanket where Humpy Chris had lain and next, the sheets where Urs had tossed his story in the storm. Under the bedclothes was the thin gauze mattress cover. A shiny lilac color winked through here and there where the gauze was torn or threadbare.

Margaret went to the living room where Annie made up the davenport. Margaret pulled open the sewing machine drawer and retrieved her sewing scissors.

In the bedroom again, she cut through the gauzy mattress cover exposing the faded lilac satin sheet. How worn and thin it was. How stained. The silky fabric tore easily. Slowly and thoughtfully, Margaret wadded it up. Satin doesn't belong here. Never had.

Margaret worked easily in the lantern's glow. The clean smell of cotton mingled with the breeze, billowing the curtain sheers.

When the bed was made, Margaret helped Urs out of his chair. His arm rested heavy on hers, dry as last year's silage. She guided him to the freshly made bed.

In the kitchen, Margaret dipped hot water into the two enamel basins.

"Does it feel better with Lizzie's pillow under your back?" Annie's voice filtered in. "Tell me when it's in the right place. How about another one for your head? I really don't need mine." and then seeing Chris for the first time as a real human being, "Mr. Chris, do you have a Mom and dad? Do you have any little ones? Any babies?"

"Just you, you be my little one, Annie." Chris petted her arm.

Margaret laid out the towel and the washcloth on her arm. She placed the bar of soap in one basin and carried them to the bedroom. Annie's voice faded. "Are you sure one blanket is enough?"

Margaret closed the bedroom door.

She began by removing Urs's socks, bathing and rinsing his feet and carefully drying them with the soft towel. "Margaret, Urs said softly, did you know? Did you know all the time the baby was a girl?" Urs lay placidly as a doll as Margaret washed him.

"Not for sure, of course, sometimes the Hebamme is wrong, but yes she did say a girl." Margaret too spoke softly, a catch in her throat.

Next she unfastened his pants and pulled them down, slipping them off his feet. Then his underwear.

"Why, why then did you get my hopes up so? Why Margaret?" Urs spoke in a whisper. Tears were in his voice. Tears let loose as Margaret finished washing each part and patted it dry. She covered Urs with a light blanket.

Annie's voice from the living room was hardly audible.

Margaret went to the kitchen and drew fresh water. As she shaved and cleaned Urs's face, tears tapped, wetting the sheet. "I'm sorry Urs, I'm so sorry, I don't know now why I did it." Urs lay very still, looking up placidly.

Annie was saying her prayers and the bed squeaked as the child settled in.

In the living room, Chris lay as placidly as Urs. He didn't know what time it was or what day. He didn't even wonder. The small bag of gems, the files of notarized papers, Juanita.... It was as if none of that existed. Had it ever? The only thing he knew for sure was how good the soup had tasted. And how strong and soothing Annie's hands were on his back. Chris slept almost immediately.

Margaret knelt before Urs's bed. Feeling such deep tenderness for her husband, she wondered how she could have done it. She knew what she told herself at the time, but now none of that rang true. Margaret quickly undressed. Why had she lied? Every answer she exposed seemed false. She slipped in next to Urs. Silently, she had questioned herself to bedrock as she lay naked at her husband's side. Urs was clean and manly. Only the light blanket covered him.

She began by kissing Urs lightly on the forehead. The cheeks. The lips. Her glossy hair hung in curtains framing her face and his. In that intimate space they shared each other's breath, each other's secrets. "I think I know now why I lied, Urs…." Margaret's body trembled as she sobbed the truth. "I wanted you to love me." Her voice broke. "To respect and admire me if only for a little while, if only for a few months. I wanted your love." She was quaking. Looking deeply into Urs's eyes, she saw that was what he needed too.

Urs reached out with his good hand, opening the silky enclosure, letting her hair slide through his fingers. When had there ever been anything so soft so smooth. Tears swam in his eyes, wet his checks. Both held the other weeping.

Margaret moved slowly, kissing him lightly. Lightly, she stroked the coarse hair on his shoulders, his chest, his belly. With patient touching, she rekindled the dying spark.

A wedge of light from the lantern struck the blue of her eye. Her skull a fragile shell between his strong rough hands. She smelled of woman. This time Urs did not turn away. Down and down around him slow and strong she came.

Just before he lost himself, Urs saw her--as if for the first time. Then, he was lost, not sure if he were falling weightless or surging high. After a lifetime of struggle how could surrender be so sweet.

Margaret moaned, quivering.

~33~

Annie brought out a kitchen chair to the edge of the field so Chris could watch the family as they went about their chores and field work. Chris looked out across the monotonous landscape.

Now, if the bugs would just leave him alone. Little itchy things crawled up Chris's pant-legs and dug in around the elastic of his boxer shorts and the tops of his socks. Flies buzzed his nostrils. Mosquitoes attacked his scalp and ears. Chris thought about his Panama hat rolled up in the glove compartment of his car. If he just had the energy to go get it. Instead, Chris waved the insects away and slapped at his trousers. He was tired, and his back and leg hurt.

Every morning Margaret made him get up. He didn't always want to. And get dressed. And make up the davenport. Even today, when his back hurt. That first day already, she'd started them in on the housecleaning. Then the baking and the laundry. Next came the farmyard. Cleaning up after the storm. Righting the garden.

Margaret even taught him to milk. Two of the milk cows had gone dry, and needed to be stimulated every three hours or so. It was a job he could do sitting down. Annie had brought a chair out in the barn for him and helped position the cows in their stanchions. The first day, she even put on the kickers, though both these cows proved to be quite docile.

Chris guessed his back was getting better. Each day the routine of the farm made him do a little more. He surprised himself. He could do it. After an few hour's work, sometimes Annie would rub the stiffness away.

But this morning, the nerve in his leg was rigid with pain.

Chris repositioned himself in the chair. Mercifully, a light breeze started up and the insects disappeared.

Chris had never been one to really take a good look at this country...though he was born and raised nearby, and owned his share of land. It always seemed boring to him and gritty with dirt. What made people want to live out here anyway, he wondered?

When the wind blew, dirt and tumbleweeds choked the ditches, sometimes building up in giant drifts behind the snow fences. And in the winter--the bitter cold--farm families stranded sometimes for weeks with drifts blown hard as cement up to the rafters--animals freezing to death in the barn. Horrible. What did they see in it?

Chris surveyed the farm yard. The homely fence posts, the silo, the leaning barns, as ugly as they were, at least gave some relief from the monotony. As for the rest of it--flat. Flat, and monotonous, more or less as far as the eye could see.

Relaxing in the chair, he found that the morning was beginning nicely. They had all insisted (even Urs) that Chris wear one of Urs's blue work shirts while his own white one was drying on the line. Had he ever worn a work shirt before? Chris wasn't sure. It was soft and just right for the weather....a bit large perhaps but forgiving of his shape.

Then, in that comfortable morning, he had begun to see how each rectangular field or pasture had its own subtle shade of color-- light green, dark green, shades of green in rows marching, or in shaggy clumps where a field was left fallow. And there were rectangles and squares where nothing had come up yet: dark brown, light brown, shades of brown moist or dry, encircled by a shaggy boundary of fence and ditch.

On one hand was the pond, a relic from the time of glaciers. "Knob and kettle country," the phrase suddenly popped into Chris's head. Wasn't that what they called it in the geology class he took at the agricultural college in Minot so many years ago?

Remembering that time, Chris recalled how President Roosevelt had been crazy about this country. The Rough Riders and all that. Then, during the Depression, hadn't the other President Roosevelt, Franklin, approved of two wildlife refuges not far from here? Chris examined the landscape more closely. Other shallow ponds had dotted the land. He saw where retreating glaciers had buried chunks of themselves and as the buried ice melted, formed these little hollows. Most of the resulting ponds had been drained by now. Homesteaders and farmers did it, he guessed, to make more cropland. Now he could see where the ponds had been. The earth was darker there.

Almost at his feet, there was a flurry of quick slinky movements. Was it some kind of weasel, or a king snake? Too quick to tell. Chris was repulsed and then curious. He concentrated on the fence lines and the ditches. There must be all kinds of silent, hidden creatures still hanging on in the little patches between the fields. Creatures he had read about so long ago in the required classes he hadn't been interested in then.

Chris trained his eye on these shaggy places. He was rewarded with a furious fluttering near where Urs was cultivating. A short horned owl? Yes, it must be! And that jumping there, what was that? In a rapid flurry the owl pounced and then returned to its ground nest with a jumping meadow mouse. Chris concentrated in earnest.

As he focused his attention this world took on new life. A thirteen-lined ground squirrel scurried across a corner of the pasture. The state mascot! Chris had never seen one before. And here it was, right in front of him!

Mink, badgers, porcupines--they must all be here. How much he had never noticed! This dull, monotonous land was teaming with life! Insects, mice, toads, snakes, salamanders, and birds of every description. They were all right here!

Annie struggled from the barn with a bucket of fresh milk. Setting the bucket down to change hands, she waved. "I missed you milking this morning," she hollered. After resting a moment she added, "Maybe you could help me fix lunch. Dad's having trouble with the cultivator so we're going to break now, while he comes in for repairs. Maybe you could give me a hand with the sandwiches."

Chris sat dumbly in the chair. The cultivator and tractor had come to a dead stop. Urs's silhouette was bent studying the problem. Why hadn't Chris noticed the situation himself? Why was there so much going on right in front of him that he didn't see?

Chris rose slowly from his chair. He felt disoriented. Heat was rising, trembling up from the earth. The fields, the barns, the pond; all quivered in the rising heat. Was nothing solid? Was this farm and maybe life itself a quivering mirage? Or was this what was real, what he had overlooked all along?

The great, flat, quivering prairie curving to the edge of the world absorbed him. Before he took a dizzy step, the earth turned beneath his feet.

*

Chris sat at the kitchen table with the whole loaf of dark Russian rye laid out on the cutting board. He picked up the knife. Might just as well slice it, he guessed. He knew how to make chicken salad, at least. His Aunt had taught him that much.

Chicken salad, Annie had said, when she brought out the leftovers, and asked him to get started on the sandwiches. Annie was distressed about the cultivator. Chris had never known a child of her years could feel that connected to an enterprise, that responsible.

Slicing the bread made Chris feel more solid. He set his mind on holding the loaf firmly, of carefully handling the knife. All that about discovering the wild animals and the earth turning....all those funny feelings--what purpose did that serve?

So that old cultivator was on the blink, now, was it. That was something real, something he could get a handle on. He'd seen it. Wired together and falling apart. Must be twenty-five years old. At least. Probably made to use with horses. Urs probably rigged it up to use with the tractor.

Chris knew about a cultivator, almost brand new, that he could pick up at auction. At a place that was selling out. Could pick it up for a song. That would help around here a lot. A few pieces of good machinery could put this place in the black real quick.

With just a little inside information this family could buy this farm outright. If they watched the pennies close. But they seemed to do that ok. Why, if they knew what he did about how to get a hold of equipment cheap and where the government planned to poke through roads and electric lines, they could be doing just fine in no time. They could exercise that option in the lease.

Suddenly Chris's knife stopped mid slice. But what was he thinking? He could make a handsome profit off this farm himself. Let Urs pay him half the crop this fall, and then send them packing. He had every right to. And besides, all the kids and all the work in the world couldn't make this place produce without any real equipment. Why, just feeding those two old work horses must eat up half the profit.

But, something in Chris made him uncomfortable with this line of reasoning. Chris shook the new uneasy feeling away. Hadn't he been planning on getting out of here? Just as soon as he could? It was him against them, wasn't it? Just like it had always been.

After all, didn't they usually keep Chris right with them all the time. Or at least in their sight. So he wouldn't get away, he guessed.

Chris sawed away at the loaf.

They were right in not letting him go off by himself. In taking precautions. As soon as he could get around a little better, he would sneak away. Get the hell out of here. Maybe tomorrow. Maybe tomorrow he'd start up the car and drive away. As each slice of bread fell from the knife, Chris caught it and laid it in a stack. There really wasn't that much pain in his leg right now, was there? This morning's rest had done him good. But he wasn't so sure about working the foot feed for gas.

Chris used the knife to brush the cutting board clean of crumbs. He raised his right foot. It hurt. And the thought of pushing hard on the brake, that was worse yet. He wasn't really sure he could do it. Maybe tomorrow. Maybe tomorrow he'd give it a try.

And as far as that cultivator and the electric lines went, why should he be doing anything to help them? Sure, he knew the REA'd be bringing electricity through here in a year or so. He'd seen the plans. But why should he tell them? Place'd be worth a lot more then. Why, now was a good time to be thinking about evicting them. After all business was business.

After all, wasn't he really being held prisoner, right here on his own farm, against his will? The blade stopped its rhythm about half way through the slice. There, to the side of the cutting board was a neatly stacked pile of bread.

Chris began peeling the cold chicken from the bone. This was the first time he'd been alone in the house. Strange they left him alone so long. And all by himself.

Annie must be about finished with the separator. He listened for the outside pump. She must be taking it back out to the barn. Chris had never really known a little kid before. She wasn't so bad. That first day when he hurt so much he hardly got up off the davenport, she'd brought him one of the three cigars he kept locked in the glove compartment in case of emergencies. Chris leaned back letting out his breath, remembering. He'd die for just one more, now.

Maybe none of them were really so bad. Margaret made him help out it was true and get up even when he didn't feel good, but she had a gentleness, a kindness, he'd seldom experienced.

No, maybe they really weren't so bad, he conceded. Last night before bedtime, they'd popped corn. Annie'd brought in a few ears from the granary where a full gunny sack hung just inside the door. He and Urs shelled the corn by lantern light, looking across the table at each other with the dry cobs between their knees, loosening the sharp, pointed kernels 'til their thumbs grew red. Margaret had popped it up in a kettle, and turned the snowy blossoms yellow with generous dribbles of melted butter. What had ever tasted so good? They all crunched it by the handfuls, sharing a huge bowl as they took turns playing checkers. No, maybe they weren't just a nest of lazy crazies, like he'd thought.

Over the days, gradually he had figured out at least some of what had happened....About the baby....Maybe the craziness had just been a temporary thing. Maybe it was all just a dream. After all, he'd been so worn out. What really had happened, anyway? What really was real? And didn't he have his own interests to look out for?

It was as if Chris had come to a Y in a road. Back and forth. Back and forth he chased his mind down one line of reasoning and then the other. Back and forth.

Chris got out Margaret's mayonnaise. He guessed he could go ahead and make the sandwiches. After all he did have to eat. And he liked chicken salad.

"This sure does look good," Margaret said, greeting her sandwich with a nod.

Annie felt the color rush to her face. She couldn't have been prouder if she had made it herself. She felt responsible. She'd been spending a lot of time with Chris. It was paying off. When she came in from putting away the separator, she'd almost stopped in her tracks. Chris was fussing with the silverware, putting a fork to one side and a knife on the other of each plate. One chicken salad sandwich rested on each plate with a large glass of milk above it.

Annie stared from Chris to Margaret to Urs. They were so different. Her dad's big, strong, even teeth and curling black hair. Chris's thin forearms and froglike face. Her mother's graceful hands and blue, blue eyes. But there was something about them all that was growing alike, too. They were changing. Her dad had developed a softness somehow...towards her mom mostly. And, her mom, she was looking stronger and more slender every day. And she had started wearing her own shoes for the first time in months.

In fact, they all looked stronger, and browner. Even Chris glowed pink where his head was balding and on his fore head and cheeks. His hands were growing rough and darker...beginning to look like a man's hands.

And he had made the sandwiches. Annie felt a kind of pride. Like Chris was a baby she was raising up. Beaming, Annie picked up her sandwich and took a big bite. "It sure does taste good, too."

Urs leaned over his plate and began wolfing down the food. If that damn cultivator just hadn't gone on the blink.

Now, what was all this chit-chat about the sandwiches? Recently Urs had noticed something changing too. He was leery of it and unsure...not quite able to pin point what it was. To his ears, even the sound of Margaret's voice in prayer was different.

At first he had liked the sound. And the subtle unacknowledged understanding that something was different. The farm didn't weigh so heavily. He had even thought about asking Margaret's opinion of things. Things to do with the crops and the market.

But now he wasn't sure. He was weak then, too weak to think straight...and the feeling of change hadn't stopped just with the sound of her voice. As the days wore on, he began to realize maybe too much was changing. Little things, growing unpredictable, somehow getting out of hand.

Urs wolfed down half a sandwich and tipped back the glass of milk. Now he was feeling better. Stronger. He didn't need any changes....Weakness. That's all it was. Just weakness.

"Urs, I was just thinking." Chris interrupted Urs's thoughts. "Sometimes the bank has to foreclose on a piece of farm equipment."

Urs took the final swig of his milk. What was Chris babbling about? Of course he knew the bank sometimes foreclosed. Why, did he think Urs never bought anything on time? Urs took another bite and laid the corner of sandwich back on the plate. He reached for the empty glass. "What's this? No milk? Where's the milk jar, anyway? What's wrong with everyone today?"

Annie rose and got the milk. She set the jar down hard between Margaret and Urs. Without getting up, Margaret easily reached over and poured.

Urs moved the glass to its position above his plate. That wasn't really the kind of satisfaction he sought.... Chris, now he'd be the one who maybe needed another lesson in who was boss. Maybe he hadn't learned his lesson yet.

"What was that you were saying about foreclosure?" Margaret asked.

"Oh, nothing." Chris felt foolish. What had ever made him bring up the subject in the first place. What did these people ever do for him other than break up his marriage and hurt his back?

"What I'd really like to ask you about, Chris, is the flax." Urs settled back. Hadn't he always dreamed of making Chris squirm? Urs didn't touch the milk.

"You know that measly 40 acres I got in flax? That was your idea. Some of the best flax land in the state and you say 40 acres." Urs sat back satisfied, savoring his position.

Chris cleared his throat. With a hesitant finger tip, Chris idly pressed. "Well there's a reason for that, Urs."

Annie kept her head down. She felt the shadow of the old bear creeping into the room.

Chris artificially raised his voice. He picked at his sandwich. "I got a pretty good idea who all's got flax in and how much. If you flood the market, nobody'd get any price at all."

"You stupid son of a bitch!" Urs exaggerated his anger. "You got Ed Rhinert up by Ambrose putting half his crop in flax." Urs was feeling his old self. Better than his old self, in fact. He'd never before had the courage to confront the landlord with what he really thought. "That country's good for nothing but wheat. Any idiot knows that. Forty acres in flax here is worth eighty over there. We could both be making money this year if you had the sense of a frog."

Chris pressed a few crumbs into his plate. All he needed to do now was to get that maniac throwing right hand punches again.

Annie piped up, doing her best to divert the conversation. "Dad, guess what? I never made the lunch today. Guess who did?"

Urs looked Annie directly in the eye. "Well, it hadn't better've been you." He was feeling strong. He'd show them all now, who was boss. "Using half a chicken on sandwiches! At lunchtime! And not puttin' 'em on a plate in middle. So's a kid ends up getting the same amount as a grown man.... That cripple'd better do better'n that if he wants to earn his keep around here! No Annie, I didn't think it was you who made'em!" Urs let out his excess air. Now that he'd made his point, nobody'd better dare to speak.

But Margaret didn't give Urs's words much space. "Well, I been doing a little thinking lately myself." Her voice hit Urs like a slap. "I think it's about time we started getting back to church on Sunday. We missed way too much now already."

"Stop trying to change the subject, woman! We'll be going to church when I'm good and ready. What the hell did going to church ever do for me anyway?" Urs was flustered. Then, oddly, the old German saying popped into his mind. "At a time like this, Margaret, *Beten hilft nichts, was wir brauchen ist Mist!"* Praying is of no use, what we need is manure!

Hearing the old German proverb, Margaret burst into laughter, surprising everyone, including herself. It was funny, she thought, for Urs to say such a thing. The laughter came easily, puncturing the tension for everyone but Urs.

Urs felt confused, betrayed. What was happening here? Why was Margaret laughing?

Margaret touched Urs lightly on the shoulder, smiling at him directly. "Urs, I'm going to church, one way or the other. If you don't want to take me, maybe Mr. Nielson will," and then seeing Urs's distress, added. "I couldn't have gone to church myself last week, Urs, but now it's time and I'm going."

Urs stiffened. "Of all the ungrateful…. You think you can just go traipsing off wherever you want, whenever you want? Never mind me! Never mind this farm!" He stopped for a moment, catching his breath. "Can't you see I'm not up to it yet!" Urs's voice was fading. His mouth fell open. How could this be happening? How could Margaret join up with Humpy Chris against her own husband?

"No one's trying to force you to go to church, Urs." Margaret felt nothing against Urs. "You can go or stay as you like. Just let me know by tomorrow so we can get Chris's car ready before confession, if we need to." Margaret rose and started clearing the table as if that were the end of that.

Urs was more confused than ever. She hadn't reacted to what Urs said at all. Instead, matter-of-factly, Margaret leaned over his shoulder to get his plate. When Urs looked up, Margaret appeared as she had the night she made love to him. Strong. And separate. Was she really so different, or was it just his way of seeing that had changed? Urs wasn't sure.

He jumped immediately to his feet. "Here, Margaret, let me help you clear. You've been busy in the field all morning, too." The words came out, almost by themselves. And as he began picking up the plates, he didn't feel defeat. He couldn't explain the feeling, but it didn't have the too familiar taste of defeat.

~34~

Chris pulled back the curtain and reached down, to the back of the bottom shelf, ignoring the pain. About time he started earning his keep! Of all the gall things to say. Who did that idiot hick think he was talking to anyway? He'd be letting Urs know a thing or two about earning, and owing, and who'd be eating chicken sandwiches next year at this time.

Chris had seen the bottle earlier. Dusty and towards the back. He opened the curtain. As he reached for the bottle there was a postcard with a blond haired cowgirl and a rearing bay-colored stallion. What was this? The cowgirl smiled in a playful seductive sort of way, her pistol held before her face pointing to the sky. The stiff card was bent where it had been folded on one corner. Dear Mom and Dad, Wayne and me are working hard. Allen wants us to stay on for another week. He'll bring us home on Friday, June 15. He's paying us more too. The country is so pretty out here. Wish you were here. BCNU soon Love, Liz. Chris placed the card back inside the curtain. He had forgotten all about those other kids. Liz, that must be the older girl's name. And Wayne that must be the other boy.

Chris set the bottle down on the table hard. "Christian Brothers Whiskey." Definitely not what he would ordinarily drink. He poured himself about two fingers in a clean glass.

How about that little girl, Annie. Chris traced his finger around and around the rim. Who asked her to try to make such a big deal out of fixing chicken salad sandwiches? He brought the glass to his lips. Horrible! He broke into uncontrollable coughing. He scowled, shivering.

Quieting himself, Chris eased back into the chair. Scotch, now that was his drink. He liked it straight up and neat.

Chris rolled the golden liquid round in the glass. How that idiot had ranted. Of course he knew Annie didn't fix the lunch. Chris repeated the words in a sing-song voice like a sneaky child might speak, behind a teacher's back. "She has more sense than to use up the meat of half a chicken for sandwiches."

Chris took another drink from the glass, twisting his expression with his words. "Annie knows enough to stack the sandwiches on a plate in the middle so a hard working man wouldn't get the same amount as a little kid."

Again, Chris lifted the glass to his lips. The bright, hot fire in his belly fueled the anger. Next year at this time that fool'd be lucky to be eating anything. Once Chris got back into town, he'd send out the sheriff with eviction papers so fast it would make Urs's head spin.

And to think he was starting to trust them. What had ever made him want to do anything that would help Urs Wagnor? Now, he'd see to it that that clod never farmed again. All it took was a flourish of the pen. Just a flourish of his pen and Urs Wagnor would be nowhere.

Chris took another sip before testing his leg. It didn't hurt so much. He'd do it today. He'd drive right in to the bank and leave this bunch of paupers.

Chris managed to change into his suit and make his way to his car. Before inserting the key in the ignition, he fumbled his watch from the breast pocket. Somewhere along the line, it had stopped working. He had forgotten to wind it. Not like him. Not like him at all. Chris thought of all the meetings he must have missed, of all the appointments. People must be wondering where he is, looking for him. But when he tried to think of who that might be, no one came to mind.

Sunlight highlighted the texture of his suit coat, the wrinkles in his shirt. It must be after three clock, Chris thought, gauging from the light. He set and wound the watch, before returning it to his breast pocket. He straightened the suit coat as best he could. It was one of his favorites. A smart pin stripe. Navy and light gray. Now it was wrinkled and stained. And it didn't seem to fit right through the upper arms.

Chris scratched at a crusty spot on the lapel. It turned whitish where he'd raised the nap. He spit on his fingers and smoothed the area down. Would the dry cleaners ever be able to get it out?. Maybe he should just throw it away. Have a new one made that fit right.

Chris didn't think anyone had noticed as he made his way to the car. He tested his leg. It was now or never, he guessed, inserting the key. Chris pumped the foot feed a bit and turned the switch. The engine caught on the first try.

Bumping along the dirt lane, Chris began getting into the old swing of things. Almost as if this whole strange business had been a bad dream. But he hadn't made it out to the county road before the engine started to cough. The car jerked a few times and came to an absolute stand-still. What was wrong? He turned the switch, pumping on the accelerator. Pain jutted down his leg, across his chest. He pumped again, hot tears sprang to his eyes.

The engine let loose a sickening whine, getting weaker by the minute. Chris let it rest before trying again. Weaker yet. He scanned the gauges. Empty! The damn gas tank was empty!

"That bastard must have siphoned out the gas to keep me here," Chris fumed. "A prisoner on the farm I own!" The car ticked in the afternoon heat. Chris rolled down the window.

"Out of here. If I can just get out of here. If I can just get back to my store." Chris turned the ignition, listening to the whine of the motor, the whine of his whispered words. But no, everything was different now, wasn't it. The jewels were gone. Everything there was gone. And the gas tank was empty. A mosquito from the open window buzzed his forehead. Chris gripped the steering wheel. He banged on the dash board. The glove compartment sprung open. There was the blond balsa wood box that held his neatly rolled Panama hat.

Then, there arose in his core, the realization that all of this was his own fault. Chris grew more angry yet. He was the one who had neglected to stop for gas the night he went looking for Juanita! From his breast pocket rose a constant, faint, ticking. The annoying repetition reminded him over and over that all of this was his own fault....all his of own making. Chris batted the mosquito away. Out of here. He had to get out of here.

It couldn't be that far to the county road. The Wagnors' lane stretched away lumpy and raw looking. Up ahead, a swarm of gnats hung unmoving, in the air. Chris grew uncomfortably hot. He removed his suit coat and retrieved his Panama hat from the glove compartment. It would help protect his sun-burned scalp.

Chris started out on foot. If he could just make it to the county road. The county road. That was the one thought that kept him going. If he could just get out to the gravel, surely he could catch a ride. Swinging his Panama, he waved away the swarming gnats.

Chris took to the edge of the lane where it was smoother...dryer...avoiding the ruts. His limping pace took on a repetition of its own. The county road. The county road. The repetition of his steps seemed to beat out the words.

In a while his feet began to feel the natural lay of the land, his mind for once in silence. How long had it been since he had walked a country road?

Each time his shoe struck the dry smooth dirt, a light dusty puff rose in the afternoon light. It was as if he walked on something ethereal. Chris walked more easily than he had in days.

Then suddenly, he was there. Standing in the middle of the Y-intersection.

Chris looked in both directions. Nothing. Not a car in sight. In fact, it looked like the gravel petered out, to the West. What had he been thinking? There wasn't going to be any car coming out this way. Chris lurched in one direction and then the other. Now what?

He stopped, defeated where he stood.

Out of the blue, Chris was overwhelmingly homesick. But not for Juanita. And not for Mrs. Jensen's modern meals. He was thinking about the davenport--in the living room. And how it molded to fit his twisted form. And how nice Annie's welcoming hands felt when they rubbed away the stiffness. And when Margaret made hot chocolate with cinnamon that time in the morning. How sweet it was and smooth. Even Urs's unending stamina he missed, admired even maybe. When had Chris ever felt so accepted, so at home....not in a calculated way, but just the way he was?

Chris began his shuffling walk back in the direction of the car--the house. He came to the place where his Pontiac waited stranded, and walked on by.

A flock of yellow headed blackbirds rose chattering from the road side. After a few more steps Chris heard locusts buzzing in the ditch. Soon he found himself listening for the prairie sounds.

Frogs croaked and grasses rustled in the light wind. Humming bees worked the wild stands of chokecherries and wild plum. The constant, vast variety of vibrating sounds followed Chris as he went.

Sometimes new sounds joined the chorus of thronging life while others faded as he continued toward the farmhouse. Then a space opened. Chris became aware that one low steady vibration had abruptly shut down. He stopped in the lane, listening. Urs's tractor, maybe.

Chris again started his halting pace....thinking. Daydreaming. Maybe when he got to the house, the family would just be coming in from the field. He would lend a hand with the milking. Chris was getting pretty good at it, better maybe, than Urs, because of his hand. It occurred to Chris then for the first time that Urs, as large and terrifying as he could be, was crippled too.

A new sound interrupted his day-dream. Up ahead, coming down the road was the Ford Town car, with Urs and Annie joggling along in the front seat side by side.

Annie pointed up ahead, "That's him, Dad. There he is right there, walking down the lane. You were right I bet."

The day her dad hit Chris and he lay crumpled under the table, Humpy Chris had wanted a cigar in the same desperate way Annie wanted out of the house. He entrusted her with the key and sent her to get the three cigars he kept locked in the glove compartment of his car. All the way there, Annie held the car key tightly in her palm.

Inside the car that day, Annie had breathed a sigh of relief. So glad to be out of the house, but in the car, the air didn't smell right. She rolled down the window. There wasn't much of a breeze. She sat for a while on the driver's side noticing the luxurious leather, the polished wood. Timidly, she placed her hands on the steering wheel. Making a low sound in her throat, she pretended to drive.

The key was right there, pressing into her palm. She saw where it went, in the little slot on the dash. What would happen if she slipped it in? Would the car just turn on without any other effort maybe drive, too, with just a little guiding? She could steer all right if she could see the ground. Her dad and Danny, too, sometimes held her in their laps to steer down the lane towards home. This car must be easy to drive. After all, Humpy Chris couldn't run back and forth, adjusting the choke and turning the crank.

Annie observed the dials and gauges. Why not just put the key in the little slot and see what happened? Instead she had placed the key in her mouth, testing it's metallic taste, feeling it's slickness, poking her tongue in the little hole where Chris had taken it off the ring. In a while she extended her tongue so the key lay flat. Making a soft throaty sound she removed it and still wet, inserted and turned the key. There was a slight click. One of the dials lit up red. Had she broken the car? Annie had quickly removed the key and used it to open the glove compartment and get the cigars.

Now with Chris gone, along with the car, Annie told her father about the red light. "Chris never did smoke the cigars," Annie added. He was asleep by the time I came back in. I put them in his coat pocket."

Seeing Chris walking up ahead, their suspicions were confirmed. All afternoon, Urs had been feeling bad about himself. At lunch time, it had felt good getting the best of Chris, but the good feeling only lasted a little while. After all, Urs had beaten the man twice at checkers. Wasn't that enough? As far as hitting Chris, knocking him down and hurting him, Urs didn't like to think of that at all.

And what had Chris meant when he talked about the cultivator coming up for auction? And about the electric wires coming through? He hinted that the government might pay for the right of way, or hook the farm up to electricity for nothing if the right-of-way was ceded. Would Chris be telling Urs all this if he was just going to use it to his own advantage? Had Chris been trying to encourage Urs, trying to help? It seemed unlikely. But, what really had Chris been trying to say?

And hadn't the man been helping out as best he could? Those two milk cows. Chris helped re-freshen them both. They were giving milk better than ever. And now here he was out walking the lane, trying to escape Urs's meanness.

Urs pulled the car alongside of Chris and brought it to a stop. "Chris, what's going on? Where's your car? Annie said you were out of gas. When we couldn't find you anywhere and the car was gone we were worried. You all right?"

I'm all right. The car's up the way." Chris looked over Urs's elbow, into his eyes. All he saw was concern.

Of all the acquaintances Chris had, of all the boards he served on and meetings he attended; it was Urs who came for him, to see if he was all right. Heat and color deepened Chris's cheeks, with shame, embarrassment. He removed his hat and fanned himself.

"I don't have the gas can with me, but I can pump some. If you're ready to go back to town, why don't we get your things straightened out so you can go at a decent time tomorrow. If you're ready to go back to town that is." Urs leaned over Annie and opened the door.

Chris climbed in.

~35~

Annie scooted over some and placed her hand in his as Urs started through the gears. Instead of crimping the wheel and turning towards home though, he continued straight ahead. On impulse he asked: "Chris, I was wondering, there's a little piece of land, where the creek runs, down from the high plateau, where it looks like it's never been farmed. What do you know about it? Is it a part of this place?"

"I never walked the boundaries, if that's what you're asking. Never had any reason to.

Where is it, anyway?"

As the car bumped along the rutted lane, Annie linked the two by placing her other hand lightly on her dad's as it rested on the gearshift. When they came to the stalled Pontiac, Urs carefully maneuvered around it. At the end of the lane he made a right turn to where the county road dribbled out and there was only the grassy, patchy path for farm equipment that followed the creek.

Where the patchy road ran out, they started on foot. "Come on, Chris; Annie and I will help you. It's a little wild place. I want you to see it. I didn't even know it was there 'til I was out trying to find the boundaries." The three started down the fence line where the creek followed the edge of the field. With Chris in the middle, Annie and Urs steadied him along.

Briefly, Chris's thoughts began racing again, out of control. Where were they taking him? Had Urs said something about a gully? By himself, would he be able to walk out of here if they just left him? Was Urs going to leave Chris in a gully where he wouldn't be able to get out and no one would ever know the difference? Chris, looked around frantically for something to mark the way on this vast prairie.

Then, as though Urs had sensed Chris's anxiety and wished to reassure him, the farmer noticed the ten-foot-tall, dried up sunflower stem. "Look there! A compass plant!" Urs lit up when he saw it. The giant sunflower immediately took him back to his boyhood. Back to before all the death and trouble, to the time when his dad was still alive.

Urs touched a dry curled leaf on the towering stem. At the base, fresh green youngsters poked through the sandy earth, one waist high already. "Look here, how they grow," he said, showing the young plant to Chris. With the palm of one hand underneath, Urs used the strong single finger of the other to smooth out one of the new oak shaped leaves. "My dad told me how these leaves always align north-south. When I was a kid, people tied the tall stems with strips of cloth so, if a person got lost, they could find their way home.

"Yes, yes," Chris nodded vaguely. He thought he remembered it too....strips of colored cloth flapping in the wind dotting the way across the prairie.

Urs kicked at the dirt around the old plant. "The roots of these sunflowers are so deep, even a flood or bad hail can't tear them down."

At the fence, Urs stepped hard on the bottom wire and nodded for Chris to pass through.

Chris bent and removed his hat, hesitating. Was it wise to continue following? Chris bent, briefly glancing Urs's face. It was honest and open and smiling with the memory of the compass sunflowers. With Annie's steadying hand, Chris crossed through the fence.

The prairie grasses immediately gave way to elderberry, bur oak, creeping juniper and curling vines. The little wild place lay before them in a cupped hollow below the surrounding fields. At the steep embankment, the three stumbled downward, and into another world.

The little hidden patch of wild land had changed considerably since Urs was here last. It was green almost beyond belief, and the spring wild flowers were in full bloom. There rang out the many voices of gleeful bobolinks, and the piping of meadow-larks flitting through the trees and bushes.

"Is this part of our farm, Dad? Is it?" Annie was enchanted. Sunlight splashed on the shiny new leaves and, here and there, fell in slanting rays to the mossy floor. The falling light, the cool bank, the warming air--the combination brought to Annie's mind an earthenware bowl being filled with fresh cream. Then she noticed the tinkling sound, and a gurgling as they made their way to the bottom. There, the creek flashed and glimmered where the sunlight pierced.

Urs bent and, hiking up his overalls, sat on a fallen cottonwood that spanned the creek. "This is the place, Chris, I mean, Mr. Nielson," he said, motioning for Chris to take a seat next to him on the rough bark of the fallen tree.

Mr. Nielson, Urs had called him. Somehow, the title made Chris uncomfortable, even though it was how everyone addressed him. Chris had been in such confusion all day, he hardly knew who he was, or what he wanted to be called.

You can call me Chris, if you want to, Urs."

Then, that other name popped into his mind, from so long ago. "But you know what, Urs, my real name is David. David Christopher Nielson. My real name never stuck." What had made him want to tell Urs that?

In spite of the thick, rough texture, Chris found the height of the fallen tree just right and strangely comfortable. Under his feet grew a velvety mat of green moss, and the ground was littered with green fringed acorns. Where the old cottonwood was broken, new shoots were leafing.

As for Urs, he wasn't even sure why he'd brought Chris here. Who, in fact, in all the world, could have predicted that on this day these two men would sit side by side on a fallen tree with the creek dancing at their feet? White tissue-paper blossoms of prairie evening-primrose were scattered across the bank on the other side and floated like butterflies on the moving water.

Annie saw the blossoms, too. "Can I pick wild flowers, Dad? I won't go far. Can I take off my shoes and cross the creek?"

"All right," Urs nodded. "But stay close by, Annie." Annie quickly removed her shoes and socks, rolled up her pant-legs and splashed across the shallows.

The water had receded from the recent storm and now sang among the rocks and over the sandy bottom. The two men sat, side by side, each lost in thought, staring into the water. Sunlight through the trees dappled the bubbling eddies, the floating tissue-paper blossoms, and the smooth round mutely colored rocks. The water itself was so clear as to be invisible.

Gradually, it dawned on Chris how his cottony mouth still held the after-taste of Urs's Christian Brothers'. The water in the little stream looked so refreshing. Chris removed his hat and knelt at water's edge. Then, becoming acutely aware of Urs, he caught a hat full of water and offered Urs the first drink.

"Well, what an idea! What an idea!" Urs came forward accepting the hatful of water, helping Chris up. How the hatful of water so perfectly held shining liquid. Urs took a long drink. It tickled him, that the pliable brim could be neatly cupped so he could drink without spilling. "What kind of hat is this?"

"It's a Panama, Urs," Chris smiled. "Made in Ecuador, South America. ...got its name from the Panama Canal." Chris warmed to the subject. "They were all the rage for a while, in Minneapolis and Chicago. The best ones come in a balsa wood box and can be rolled so tight they'll pass through a ring." Urs seemed genuinely interested. Chris went on. "When the men who dug the canal didn't want to wear them or drink out of them, the workers would fold them up and keep them in their pockets!"

Urs flapped the hat dry on his pant leg and put it on his head. "How do I look?"

"Good, good," Chris answered.

Urs was enjoying himself...enjoying the green place, and the water, and the company of another man...and the hat! He looked it over slowly. Seeing the permanent crease, he folded it and carefully rolled it into a tight cigar shape. "What an idea! Ha! Here, Chris, it's your turn to drink." Urs unrolled the hat with a snap, knelt, and scooped up the clear singing water.

On the other side of the stream, Annie was picking a bouquet of wild flowers; colorful wild peas, prairie violets, shooting stars. She heard the men talking as she moved along the creek bed. A flock of chickadees sang out to her. "Hi Sweetie. Hi Sweetie."

Higher on the bank, furry bees hummed the radiant blooms of wild strawberries. Annie studied the bees as they crawled in and out of the pinkish bells of snow-berry blossoms. How could they manage to fly? They looked so fat, and their hairy legs heavy with pollen. Perhaps in this generous, joyful place anything was possible. Annie began humming as well...humming out her happiness.

Then, remembering not to wander off too far, Annie started back toward the men.

Through the twisting vines of morning glory, Annie saw they were facing each other, standing toe to toe. They were talking loudly. Shouting even. She heard the word "cheat!" and "stupid hick!". She stood watching. With the sunlight constantly moving in the trees, dappling the scene, she couldn't see Chris's humped back or her father's hand. Even the colors distinguishing their clothing were muted to sameness. It occurred to Annie how alike they were. Both men. Standing their ground. Trying to make their place, trying to find their place.

Clutching her bouquet, Annie moved up the opposite bank. As she broke above the brow of the hollow, the wild land behind disappeared, plunged in shadow.

She was staring into the giant yellow setting sun. Momentarily blinded, her only sensation was of the raw earth under her bare feet. As her eyes adjusted, she found herself in a patch of big bluestem that bordered a wheat field. Light swept the land, emblazing the springtime wild grass a bright aqua-green.

Annie could hardly believe how one step of her foot had changed everything. She stepped backwards. Again she was plunged into darkness, this time deeper than before. Annie played with the sensations. Dark. Light. Dark. Light, as she stepped from darkness to light, .from light to darkness.

When she stepped into darkness, a negative of the light appeared. The sun became a huge black hole. The bright field had turned itself inside out.

*

Margaret stood before the western window, holding the pierced ivory box before her eye. Back and forth, back and forth, every so slightly she moved the lace like openings, playing with the sunlight as it pierced her eye.

She'd been arranging flowers in a fruit jar, when a red and black lady-bug humped along the green leaf of a Zallia. Juanita's little humped coop, Margaret thought. As her hands went about the work, she noticed, sunlight lit up a creamy corner of the ivory box sticking out from the folded cloth in her sewing basket. She had avoided the box since Danny's graduation. When Juanita placed it in her hands, it had been heavy. Since then, Margaret kept it out of sight. But, she was always aware of it there, just under the cloth.

Back and forth, playing with the light. Light and dark. Light and dark. As the negative piercings filled with light, sunlight struck deep into her blue blue eye. Deeper and deeper into light and darkness. In and out of the light and dark. Margaret felt the salt wind of an unknown seascape; mountains and green, green valleys, an ocean stretching. Light and dark. Light and dark. Her mouth watered with the taste of salt. She felt for certain then, Danny was ok.

Dark and light. Dark and light. An blast of insight shook her almost to her knees. She rose again in the light. Dark and light. Dark and light, 'til she came to that core where dark and light were one, where her mind no longer understood; where all was pierced with joy.

In a little while, Margaret stepped away from the window, her precious box so smooth in her hand.

*

Annie stepped into the light. This time, the flash and glimmer of the emerging wheat field claimed her attention. It eddied and rippled, looking right at home with the native bluestem and the switch grass. They were grasses all, weren't they. They belonged here. All.

Further down the way a short grass meadow. The short grass was spotted with purple coneflowers and wild indigo--splashes of color blazing in the green. Beyond the meadow, the high plateau, was touched by the light and shadow of the prairie evening. It loomed hugely, magnified by the bending light.

Memories crept in, sliding into the gully, the ice, the wet cardboard, the eyes of the dead dog. A dragon's lair she had thought, a dragon's treasure.

Had this lovely little wild place been transformed from the ice and trash, the dead dog and the cardboard? Ugliness transformed to beauty?

Annie started down the shaded bank. In the darkness at her feet was a little patch of pasque flowers. She stooped and added a few to her bouquet.

"Annie?" she heard her father questioning.

"I've only got a few years left," Chris said. "There's no way left to stop the infections. It's what I want to do."

"What would she do with a farm?" Urs was stunned.

Further down in the darkness Annie saw two glowing red points, and tasted the smoky odor of cigars.

Acknowledgements

Thanks to the National Endowment for the Arts who decades ago gave me the courage to try. Without their help this novel never would have been written. I am grateful to my teachers at Western State College in Colorado and University of Alaska Anchorage and UAA Homer. They taught me how to really read. Thanks also to Christopher Kleckner who translated my ancient Osborne disks to a computer program that would work today. Isolde Gibson, Rita Wettach, Dagmar Haney earned my appreciation for their help with the German. Anne Chandonnet, Dawn Marano and Yolanda Butler were great readers and caught many problems before the novel went to print. The encouragement of Trish Caron, Adrielle Porter, Judy Arko, Leslie Cates, Sally Lincoln, Annalee Beck and Mary Bonogofisky, kept me at it when I wanted to quit.

My most sincere appreciation goes to my husband and his family for sharing their stories. Thanks also to the Germans from Russia Heritage Society headquartered in Bismarck, North Dakota for their ongoing work documenting the history and traditions of these people. Finally, this novel would never have been completed without the understanding and support of my children Sonja and Benjamin and of course my husband Robert.

❖ Questions for careful readers and book groups.

CONSIDER THESE INSIGHTS FOUND IN THE PROLOGUE
- What is the meaning of the name Sophia?
- What sounds does Annie make outside the curtained room that find their way into what the women read in each other's eyes?
- What sounds outside the porch make their way into the women's visions?
- What physical characteristics of Margaret's eye make their way into her vision?
- Margaret sees the Hebamme's past. What hint does she see that could explain the dark eyed, dark haired children such as Urs, born to this fair race?
- In Margaret's eye the Hebamme sees her future. What knowledge does she hint at regarding Margaret's pregnancy and childbirth?
- As the novel develops, seven year old Annie imagines Margaret, Urs and Chris as mythical archetypal beasts on the vast prairie. What animal do we begin to see associated with Margaret?
- How does the meaning of the German name Urs suggest what beast he will become in Annie's eyes?

❖ **CONSIDER THE FOLLOWING AS THE NOVEL UNFOLDS**
- As the story reveals itself, how does Danny's puzzle of the three nails locked together in conflict, take on greater meaning?
- How does Danny act out the part of St. George from the stained glass church window?
- Who is the golden boy?

- In what ways does the landscape reveal that the farm Annie loves and knows might not belong to her family?
- In the end Annie's archetypal creations become human. How does this young child help bring this about?
- The novel is filled with mirroring, reflection and symbolism. What other examples can you find? How does this prepare the reader for the storm?